What the Heart Wants

What the Heart Wants

Tiana Laveen

TULE
PUBLISHING

Dedication

This book is dedicated to Ruth Bader Ginsburg, RBG, and Elijah Cummings. These two individuals changed the fabric of our country and society through their political, professional, and social endeavors, with their bravery and desire for all people to be treated equally. These role models stood strong on the belief that people should be judged by their characters, not their gender, socio-economic status, race, ethnicity or creed. This book is henceforth dedicated to love, and to the belief that even through less radical heartfelt procedures, we can grow and become better today than the day before. It is dedicated to the belief that we're all in this together, and when it's all said and done, we may look back and say, "I tried my best," and know, deep in our heart, that this is the truth.

Letter To My Readers

Greetings to each and every person who has decided to pick up, download, and/or read this book. You are about to embark on a journey about love. This story is a voyage to redemption and all this entails. I've written over fifty novels, and this is by far one of those that has required much research, the need to speak to people from all walks of life, and even be honest with myself regarding various beliefs and outlooks on life. That withstanding, it is a romance that delves deep into who we are as a people and as a society, and how that ties into love of oneself and others.

We have here a tale about honesty, transformational love, and the realization that no metamorphosis of emotion occurs in a bubble. It takes a village to help each and every one of us reach our true potential. Whether this helps comes from supportive friends, educators, medical professionals, self-help books, inspirational videos, or articles on self-improvement, we are tasked to grow and find the sunlight and replenishment required to ensure that we manifest all that we can become. Growth is different for each individual. So it is that the characters in this book are forced to evolve and endure some painful truths, and then, make a hefty call to action. This is not a cuddly romance novel.

You won't feel warm and fuzzy feelings all throughout this book. This story is not politically correct, nor was it meant to be. It's an unapologetic look at actual beliefs woven inside fictitious individuals who very well could be your neighbor, close friend, or relative. Perhaps you. The goal is not to assign blame but to admit truth and trigger forgiveness. This includes forgiving ourselves so we may attract a love like we've never known.

What the Heart Wants is a book from the heart, about a heart, given in the most selfless act of love. Now, this book is in your hands.

Thank you in advance for reading and going along this trip with me, Cameron, and Emily.

Now, our journey together begins.

Chapter One

A Song and Dance for the Ancestors

"HE'S GOTTA GUN!" someone yelled. Pure pandemonium broke out as the crowd screamed and ran in all directions. Someone shot their weapon.

Brooke Coleman froze mid-song, clutching the mic, and looked frantically in all directions. The mood had definitely changed. She sang another line, but her voice broke as angry voices got louder. From her vantage point on the stage, all she saw was chaos. Her heart threatened to beat out of her chest. The music stopped as bright white flashlights lit up the area, showing a few police officers moving toward the scene of a fight.

"Hey, let's not do this!" she screamed out into the microphone, her voice drowned out by the yelling, curses, and screams all around her. Opium, her trusty black and tan Rottweiler, stood at the edge of the stage, his fur raised, growling. Not normal behavior for the dog. Just moments earlier, he'd been resting peacefully out back. Something was wrong...very wrong. "We're all here for a good time."

More gunfire rang out and her heart practically jumped out of her chest. She took several steps back. People started to run all over the place, as fast as their legs could carry them.

Panic rose inside her and formed a lump in her throat as the fear of someone being hurt, trampled, or worse yet, killed, hit her. Opium barked, snarled, and growled some more, going berserk. He now stood by her side while the gunshots amplified, all over the place, turning everything into a living nightmare—a horror movie being played out right before her eyes. Some terrible, rotten seed had been planted, buried into the soil, and was growing some hideous monstrosity in a matter of seconds. Bloodcurdling screams rang out.

"Brooke," Viktor, her close friend and right hand, yelled as he crawled across the stage toward her, his dark wash baggy jeans and black leather jacket gathering dust. She'd known Viktor for years, and his sharp skills at talent promoting had proved instrumental in launching her career as a jazz artist. His platinum-blond hair was the only thing in place, combed in an old-fashioned pompadour and gelled from roots to tips. The look of terror in his eyes broke her heart. "Brooke...get down."

She dropped down onto her stomach and placed her hands over her head. Police car sirens blared as more of the vehicles approached, then she felt a tug around her waist as Minx grabbed her and helped her down the side steps of the stage.

"Opium? Where's Opium?" she yelled out as they raced ahead, people swishing past them like streamers.

"He's in back. We've got him," James yelled, standing off to her side.

In the near distance she could see Viktor's car, a white Ford Explorer. The back opened and two of her band members got Opium inside while they all began to pile in the SUV. A police officer was chasing someone on foot. They drew closer and closer. Suddenly, more gunfire rang out, and then once again, this time closer, *much* closer. Opium barked louder than she'd ever heard him do. He was going crazy, scratching and pacing in the back of the vehicle.

"I busted yo ass. I'll die for this shit, mothafucka!" some man yelled, panting as he raced past.

The officer kept after him and yelled, "Stop running, you Black motherfucker," while the sound of sirens burst through her eardrums. She got into the car, her chest heaving up and down—and then pain, a terrible ache flowed from her neck, then her chest.

Something's not right…

How fast the world could change. One minute she was singing her heart out, swaying to the beat of the beautiful music played by her band. And the next…here she was. Running for her life. Terrified—for herself and her loved ones.

As she sat in the back of the car while it pulled away from the curb, she looked down at her sheer white peasant blouse. It was soaked in blood, all along the right side. James wrapped his arm around her, then his expression changed. His eyes grew big and he yelled in horror.

"Viktor, go to the hospital. NOW. Brooke's been shot. Her neck. Shit."

She began to shake, her temple going from hot to cold, over and over again. She fought the urge to vomit. Her head throbbed and she wasn't certain she recalled how to breathe.

Everything became glassy, as though she was seeing

through the windows of an old church. No, a Catholic cathedral. The kind with the gorgeous stained glass in vibrant colors depicting the Virgin Mary holding baby Jesus. Pretty colors filled her mind, spreading out like stretched cotton candy in combinations she'd never seen before. She could taste them, hear them, smell them. Opium's barking faded, like footprints in melting snow. Streetlights blended. The colors blurred...the red, yellow, and green transformed to cherry Astro Pop lollipops.

She placed her hand on the car window, then rested her forehead against it, smiling as she looked out. She could feel and hear her own heartbeat, practically touch it as it slowed down. So slow...like African drums. She saw the ancestors dancing around a fire, the flames wild. Their rich, dark skin glowed under the vibrant setting sun.

I want that warmth. Let me stand by that fire. Let me dance under the sun, too.

"Brooke. Stay with me," Viktor yelled, but his voice sounded as if he were underwater, swimming beside her. Was she drowning?

"Make sure she doesn't fall asleep," someone shouted out.

More barking. Opium's voice rang out like an alarm. Then came the whimpers.

I'm so sleepy...

"Brooke. Fuck. Brooke. Wake up."

I'm so...so...tired...

Someone grabbed her chin and shook it. Her eyes flickered, but then the ancestors' flames competed with that pull and sparkled brighter, faster, hotter...Such a pretty white light.

Song lyrics sounded as if they were in 3-D, the musical notes forming into humans made of beautiful yellow flames. *You told me, it was forever, but forever never came...*

"Come to me, forever, forever, forever. Here's your heart, here's my soul, they'll be together, forever." The sweet song played in her own voice, but it sounded so foreign, like someone else was singing the melody she'd written. So lovely—angelic, really. The music was smooth and inviting, like nothing she'd ever heard.

She could feel moisture around her eyes, but she smiled as she gripped the limb of someone holding her. A masculine grasp. Strong. In need. Whoever it was held her tight; they didn't want to let go. She could no longer hear the people around her, but she could feel their spirits...

They're so sad, so angry, so hurt.

She began to slip out of herself, bit by bit, as if freeing herself from an all-familiar cocoon, a costume she'd worn for years.

The ancestors grabbed onto her light limbs, and she undressed from a gown made of bloodied and weak flesh, now completely free from the physical confines and pain. She floated away, but as she looked back down, she felt terrible sorrow. Something had happened that should not have, but she could not quite figure out what.

There, on that seat in the car, sat a young woman with smooth, milky-brown skin, her head of soft black curls looking like a halo of half-moons spun from the blackest love lyrics against the whitest of sheet music she'd ever seen. Her soul looked down at her core. Her spirit was coiled against the flames of Heaven and the dusky clouds of Hell.

What is she doing? What am I doing?

The woman's face rested against a cold glass window. A man yelled at her, tears streaming down his face, his arm wrapped around her. He pressed his head against her shoulder and rocked against her. The driver of the car gripped the steering wheel so tightly, it might break in two any minute.

The woman with the halo of ebony curls didn't move, didn't speak. She was a mere shell, and as each second passed, her body grew colder and colder. They looked at one another one final time, and she watched as that shell released its very last tear. The bead of liquid spilled from her eye like overturned coffee and ran down her face like rain, staining the entire world around her as if her existence were nothing more than white fibers. That tear was leaving an imprint upon the canvas of life that would never dry. The pain would remain forever and a day...

As "GIRLS LIKE YOU" by Maroon 5 played through Emily's earbuds, she bobbed her head to the music, drowning out the loud car honking and boisterous curses that burst from the bumper-to-bumper traffic in Manhattan's morning rush hour. She gripped her iPhone in her right hand and her Starbucks vanilla latte in the other, keeping a keen eye on her surroundings.

"No. What are you doing? I told you not to get in this lane. Don't you understand English? We've already been over this."

"I was just—"

"I said, go over *there*." She forcefully pointed across the street, her body jeering forward so her long blonde hair, which she'd just had cut in stylish long layers, fell out of place. Tucking it behind her ear, she continued to yell as her angst took over. "You people don't listen." She sneered at the deeply tanned man with a jet-black, wooly beard who smelled of turmeric and curry, a taupe turban piled atop his head.

Looks like a damn beehive. I hope he's not another fucking terrorist.

The man stared at her through his rearview mirror, from under bushy brows set over black eyes so glossy, she could practically make herself out in them. His pockmarked cheeks seemed to have turned a shade darker as she snapped at him. She sighed in frustration. This was her third foreign Uber driver in one week.

"'You people don't listen'?" He repeated her words with a thick Indian accent. "I'm Sikh. You have a problem with me?" He pointed to himself as his forehead wrinkled in irritation, yet his tone remained calm. "I don't understand what you—"

"Yeah, yeah. Look, listen up. Word to the wise. I was born and raised here, unlike some." She sucked her teeth. "I know my way around. Never, and I mean *never*, get in this lane this time of morning trying to get to Fifth Avenue, okay? We'll be stuck here forever and I can't afford to be late today. Too late now, huh? What was the point of even telling you?"

Not expecting any answer except the loud huff he emitted, she flopped back down into the seat, happy to have made her point, and swiped a perfectly manicured thumbnail across her phone screen. Her anger melted like butter when she scrolled over an incredible table setting from one of her favorite designers posted on Instagram.

Nice. Chic. I think I'll order it.

Next she read a hilarious joke posted by one of her favorite local comedians, which featured an illustration of a little Black boy wearing a kippa, speaking with a White man who looked like a rabbi: *A Black Jewish boy runs home from school one day and asks his father, "Daddy, am I more Jewish or more Black?"*

The dad replies, "Why do you want to know, son?"

"Because a kid at school is selling a bike for $50 and I want to know if I should talk him down to $40 or just steal it!"

Emily burst out laughing, slapping her knee as she fell back onto the seat. Damn, it felt good to chuckle after such a shitty morning. She kept scrolling, checking out political posts from her favorite channels and media outlets.

There's no fucking collusion with the Russians. How pathetic. The snowflake liberals lost the election and still, after all of this time, they can't deal with it. Trump has done more for Black people than Obama ever did, and he had two terms. Brainless sheep.

Several minutes later, before the vehicle had even come to a complete stop, she opened the back door, grabbed her computer bag and purse, and leapt out, her red Louboutin heels beating the pavement among a sea of people walking with purpose, a good number with their faces in their phones, or frantically hailing a taxi. Racing into Rockefeller

Center, she made her way past several storefronts to Windsor Financial Group, a company started by her grandfather that she'd worked at for years.

"Hi, Danielle," Emily called out.

"Hello, Ms. Windsor. Cathy wants you to—"

"Cathy's issues can wait. Do you have my papers from Marconian International and Mr. Smith?" She snapped her fingers at the receptionist, who shoved a manila folder in her direction.

"Here it is."

Emily snatched it off the front desk. "Thank you," she muttered before disappearing down the short hall to her office. She walked inside, closing the door with a bump of her hip. Making her way to her desk, she navigated around a plant, then sat down in her chair at an angle that afforded her a wondrous city view of Fifth Avenue. It was eerily quiet that morning, just as she liked it.

She opened the folder and began to read through it to prepare for her appointment. Mr. Andrew Smith was an important client. She'd been wooing the wealthy YouTube influencer for weeks. He'd made millions creating gaming and exploration videos; a young twenty-four-year-old who'd moved from Iowa to New York in desperate need of someone to take his wet-behind-the-ears ass by the hand and lead him to money-green pastures. Finally, she was getting her chance to impress the young man.

Emily prided herself on the courting process she used to get clients, the way she made them feel special and wowed them with her expertise and charm. Her father, now CEO of the company since the death of her grandfather, had encouraged her to use her natural-born gifts to garner more business, and that's what she excelled at. She was more than capable; after all, it was in her blood. She followed a perfect plan, and it worked like a charm.

Looking good was the first order of each and every day. Her personal stylist helped ensure she wore the most flattering and expensive suits paired with simple yet elegant jewelry. Her nails and hair were always professionally done, and she used red lipstick as a color enhancement on her porcelain face, framed by blonde tresses. The perfect pop of platinum highlights had taken her six months to fully achieve to her satisfaction.

Not only was she in control of her appearance, she had a steel grip on her own destiny and wouldn't allow *any*thing to stand in her way. She'd graduated at the top of her class from Fordham University, proving she could hold her own in a male-dominated field. She'd then worked her butt off in the family business, earning her way to becoming a top financial analyst. The Windsor Financial Group happened to be one of the best firms in the entire state of New York, and she had a high standard to attain to deserve her role in the company. She took great pride in her work, and she'd even appeared on NBC several times to discuss stock market news, investment advice, and the like.

Flipping to another page, she read for a while, then suddenly paused, wrinkling her nose.

Smells like an old, rotten banana in here. Where's that coming from?

She grimaced as she looked about the place, left to right, ahead and behind herself, then took a peek below her desk to ensure the trash had been dumped from the day prior. It wouldn't have been out of the question for the presumably Asian-run cleaning service to purposefully skip her office— trying to save time, get paid for nothing, and game the system. The plastic liner within the small, Pottery Barn can was intact and empty, clean as a whistle. After one more cursory look as she reached for her coffee and took a sip, she shrugged it off.

Must've been something stale in the air that has come and went. It looks good in here. Good thing I removed that white-board. Far more tasteful now.

Emily's office was spotless, a minimalist haven much like her apartment in the coveted area of Gramercy Park.

"Great investments," she whispered as she set her coffee down and flipped to another page.

Just then, her desk phone rang. She smiled when she looked at the number and recognized it immediately.

"Laura," she squealed. "How was Prague?"

"Beautiful as always." She could hear her best friend practically grinning through the phone. Just as Laura began to get into the small, at times less interesting, details of her two-week vacation with her latest fuck buddy, a throbbing pain began from Emily's head and seemed to spread within seconds to her chest. She blinked several times, feeling a bit dizzy. Perhaps she'd moved too quickly, throwing off her equilibrium. "And then we visited St. Vitus Cathedral," the woman continued.

"Mmm hmmm…that's nice…" Emily ran her hand along her face. Her body felt loose, as if all the bones were melting, leaving behind only a pile of flesh. She attempted to rise from her seat, but her limbs failed her. Intense pain radiated in the core of her chest now. She grimaced and clutched her white silk blouse beneath her blazer. Blinking more times, she flailed her arms in a fit of panic, soon knocking the coffee onto the floor. She watched in a daze as the light-brown liquid seeped into the plush white carpeting.

Ruining it.

"We always see Charles Bridge, but this time, we noticed far less people. Isn't that wild?"

Emily's vision began to blur and she could barely speak. Her tongue felt heavy, her mind a blur, like the watercolors of her best friend's daughter's picture depicting a sunset rising along the beach in Cancun.

"Luh…Laura…He…help."

"And then we—Huh? What did you say?"

"H…Help…me…"

"Emily? Help you *what*?"

She let the phone drop to the desk, and the sound seemed to echo through her entire body as she slid out of her chair, hitting her head on the way to the floor. Things soon grew fuzzy around the edges and darkness fell all around her. She pressed her fingers into the soft carpet, her eyes once again fixating on the brown coffee in the white fibers, soaking into it, merging…

She could now hear her friend screaming her name at the top of her lungs through the phone that rested on the desk above her.

"Emily? Are you there? EMILY?"

"NO, MS. WINDSOR, I don't think you understand me." Dr. Giannopoulos leaned forward as he sat on the side of her hospital bed. His salt-and-pepper hair caught the light from the window quite attractively.

"I've told you a dozen times or more. Please call me Emily." She smiled.

He's so handsome. I wonder if he's ready to date again. He should be. That divorce happened at least two years ago.

"Fine. Emily, this isn't one of your little episodes, as you call it. We're not going to look at your medications and change things up. This was different, it's beyond all of that. We're at the point of no return. Your congenital heart disease was manageable up to a while ago, but now the oxygen is not flowing properly and twenty-five percent of the valves of your heart are barely functioning at all. You need that heart transplant."

"Well." She rolled her eyes. "I know that. I've been on the list for several years now, but I've always been able to make do. The other doctor said before that it was controllable and—"

"It doesn't matter what was previously said. That diagnosis was made when you were a teenager. Right now you're thirty-one, and your heart is failing. It is giving out. No amount of treatment, medications, or wishful thinking will change this prognosis. Look at this."

He opened a folder, the same damn one he'd shown her before, which featured a heart that looked more like a shriveled piece of sausage—only it was no butcher cut. The thing resided within her.

"Look at it, Emily," he said sternly. She turned and

glanced at it, then fought tears. "Do you see the progression of deterioration from even three years ago?" He snatched out an old X-ray, placing them side by side.

"Yes." She barely coughed the word out.

"This is it." He slowly closed the folder and stood to his feet. "We have to proceed with the transplant. I will look at the list and ask the board to expedite your situation. It's dire. Now, will you please allow your father to come inside? He should know about this, too. You need a good support system, and it must be made clear that you cannot return to work right now."

"No. I mean—" She clasped her hands together and looked down at her lap. "No. I, uh, I'll talk to him myself. Thank you."

He nodded and offered a sad smile before patting her hands and walking to the door.

"It's not like I'm going to die tomorrow." She laughed nervously. "I can—I'll still be able to do a lot. I mean, this will take years. I'm healthy. I do yoga three times a week. I have a few glasses of wine on the weekends." She shrugged. "I eat right, I exercise. I'm fine. We'll handle this."

"Emily, listen to me." He shook his head. "Don't do this to yourself. It's not productive. You were born with this. You've *always* had it, you've always known about it. None of what you mentioned matters right now regarding the yoga, exercise, and all the rest. This isn't your fault."

"I know it's not my fault, and between myself and my father, we can afford any specialist I need. Let's get on the phone and get a second opinion. I demand it." Her voice rattled as she struggled to not fall apart. "Any doctor worth their salt wouldn't just give up. They'd—"

"I haven't given up. That's the whole point. You can't tell me how to do my job, Emily, just as I can't tell you how to do yours. Now look, I need you to be realistic about this. You can't escape or talk your way out of it. Tossing money at the issue won't make you any less sick. Feel free to get a second opinion. They'll tell you the same thing. Time is not on your side. Right now, your character and approach to life will do wonders. This attitude of yours is hurting you, in more ways than one. Purchasing a new Chanel bag won't make this problem go away, either, Emily."

"How dare you. So much for bedside manner."

"I've been your doctor for three years, and you are one of the most difficult patients I have ever had. When you come in here, I've had nurses tell me they refuse to work with you. You can be abrasive, condescending, and rude."

She crossed her arms, vexed.

"Regardless," he continued, "you've always thanked me for my honesty. You never wanted anything sugar coated, so that's what I'm presenting to you. The pure, unadulterated truth. These are the facts: You have an extremely stressful job. Your family's reputation and pedigree are of the utmost importance to you, and you're highly competitive. You've admitted this many times. Hell, the first thing you said once you became conscious today was, 'I am missing my appointment.' Not 'How am I doing?' This has to stop, Emily. This is your life, and it's hanging in the balance."

She hung her head, shame filling her, though she'd never admit it.

"You will not live another six months if you don't have

this heart transplant."

Her breath hitched as her world crumbled right before her eyes. Running her hand along her arm, she squeezed, needing to feel alive, to feel pain, to remember what it felt like to live before it was far too late.

"What if, what if no viable candidate shows up? I know it's not done by who is first on the list, but by priority."

"Well, your situation is critical now, so all we can do is be proactive and hope for the best. It may be a long shot, but I hope we can get a viable candidate in the next few days if not sooner."

She nodded and looked at the clouds passing by outside the window.

"How does this happen? I haven't cried about this in years, ya know?" She shifted her attention to one of the many monitors she was hooked up to and shook her head. "Why is it that people that piss their lives away by taking a bunch of harmful drugs, complaining, and making excuses about their lives get to live until a hundred years old and here I am, working hard, living my life, loving it, and my existence is threatened? I'm not on crack. I am not out here living some wild, crazy life. I'm not a thief or murderer. It's not right. It's not fair."

Tears streamed down her face, born from unadulterated rage. Dr. Giannopoulos remained silent, his gaze on her. Then, he crossed his arms and took a deep breath.

"Emily, not everyone's definition of quality of life is the same. What you may consider squandered, they may feel is decent, perhaps even happiness. Answer this question, and be truly honest with yourself: If your health were fine and with this removed as a problem in your life, would you consider yourself *really* happy?" She stared blankly a long spell, then turned away. "What I want you to focus on is not what everyone else is doing, okay? Don't worry about the choices that someone else made...Instead, I want you to focus on what *you* need to be doing."

"And what's that? Waiting to die?" She picked up a flower vase from the table next to her and tossed it across the room. Glass shattered everywhere when the damn thing hit the wall. Her tears flowed faster and her heart pumped violently in her chest, the pain excruciating, but she didn't care. She didn't care about any of it at all. Dr. Giannopoulos casually looked at the broken vase, the fragments of glass scattered about the floor like the broken pieces of her life. Everything was dark against white fibers. Everything ugly and horrid was soaking into the last shred of dignity she had, soiling her hopes and dreams with the sooty, dark filth she didn't deserve. The doctor glared at her, and then at her heart monitor, before reaching for the door and opening it. Before he stepped out, he threw her one last look from over his shoulder.

"No Emily, you need not focus on waiting to die. Rather, how about racing to live?"

Chapter Two
A Cry for Help

"THE UNITED NETWORK for Organ Sharing called." Those were the last words Emily heard before she began to frantically sign papers from her seat on the hospital bed. She went through the motions, barely reading what was written. A viable candidate had fallen out the sky, materialized from thin air like some answered prayer—the kind she seldom believed in.

According to her doctor, the donor lived in the area, had a similar body type, shared the same blood type, and had just passed away two hours earlier. She asked few questions as her anxiety rose to a level she'd not felt since her college days, particularly the week of final exams. Taking a sip of water, she glanced down at her wrist, reading her hospital bracelet. She itched to be out of there, living her life. The staff, the smell of the place had begun to drive her crazy.

Her father stood in a corner of the room, shrouded in darkness, but his smile could be seen as he crossed his arms along his broad chest and nodded a time or two. Dad remained strong, encouraging her to move forward with what needed to be done. When she was all finished with the paperwork, she answered a few questions and was once again alone with her father.

He took a seat next to her bed. Pulling up close, he grasped her hands and held them. She closed her eyes, her body suddenly feeling cold, clammy. She shook as the tears fell down her cheeks.

"There's no need to be afraid, Emily." She breathed in slowly, then exhaled. The scent of his rich cologne subdued her. He'd worn Armani Eau Pour Homme for as long as she could remember. "We've been waiting for this moment." She nodded in agreement, but her sick, racing heart refused to hear anything of it. "I have full confidence in the staff here. They'll take good care of you." He patted her fingers. "They've been properly vetted. Top-notch."

She opened her eyes and peered into his kind, blue eyes, framed with crow's feet. He looked so majestic, so wise.

Dad's skin was a light beige color, as if he got just a touch of sun all year-round. His silver hair was brushed away from his broad forehead, and his mane was still thick, a sea of light in the illustrious platinum waves. He was clean shaven, sporting a deep cleft chin and a small scar along his lower lip that he'd gotten while wrestling with his brother as a child.

"You'll be up and running in no time." He leaned forward and kissed her forehead. Many of her friends had stopped by until staff informed them that visitation, with the exception of her father, had to cease. It had been nice to see everyone's faces, but her mother's hadn't numbered among them. How could she be? Mom had been dead for over ten years.

Emily took deep breaths, only to fly into one of her

many coughing spells. Minutes later, a balled-up tissue in her hand and chest pain burning through her ribs, she lay back in her bed, glaring at the ceiling. Nurses and doctors entered the room, speaking to her. She heard them, but didn't care. Nothing seemed real or important at that moment. Nothing felt organic; it was just individuals going through the motions, including her.

She could feel herself being lifted and moved to a gurney, but she barely made eye contact with anyone. Her lips remained sealed. She had no words, nothing to say. She shook inside the white sheets when one was pulled over her, up to her waist. Her body grew increasingly cold, as if she were going into shock, but she knew it was all in her head. What games a brain could play; the cruelty was surreal. Her father spoke a few last words of encouragement.

"Emily, you'll be fine and back to work in no time."

Her eyes darted in his direction and she blinked back tears. He smiled as she was whisked out of the room and into the hall with blinding light shining down upon her. She kept her eyes on him until all she could see were the faces of the people rolling her down the hall, into the operating theater. On a dare with herself to keep her damn composure, she closed her eyes and took several deep breaths.

You're being silly. This doctor has done hundreds of these surgeries. You'll be fine. Get through this operation and you can reclaim your life, go back to business as usual, only in much better shape.

Minutes later, the surgeon was explaining the process while they prepared her for anesthesia. In no time flat, the room began to get fuzzy and frosty around the edges until all she saw was light. A beautiful feeling came over her—warm, like a tight, loving hug. She blinked several times, then slipped away into a stark white dream.

"SHE WAS AN organ donor," Mrs. Coleman explained as she gripped her white foamy cup of coffee with trembling hands, her head bowed. Spirals of thick, salt-and-pepper curls fell forward, hiding mahogany skin. "My daughter was always giving somethin' away. This was no different."

The middle-aged woman smiled sadly, her dark brown eyes like pools of maple syrup as she blinked away another wave of tears. Cameron could hear muted voices all around them in the hospital. At one point, someone in the distance broke into laughter. It unnerved him, shook his resolve.

"Cameron, we've got to take this day by day."

They met eyes once again. Cameron could see Brooke in Mrs. Coleman's face and the sight halted his breathing. He sat across from the woman that was supposed to become his mother-in-law in the not-so-distant future…but now they were sitting inside Lennox Hill Hospital, in mourning. He wasn't certain what to do with his body, his mind, his heart. They were all breaking at the same time, falling apart, dropping to the floor and shattering like fragile pieces of glass.

This can't be happening, he kept telling himself. But it was happening all right, every agonizing second of it. Here he was in this cold, sterile place, not the type his girlfriend would wish to be in while taking her final breath.

Just a few hours prior, he'd been at work setting up at the club for a few acts, missing her performance due to prior obligations. And then, all hell had broken loose. He'd lost his love. Just like that.

He looked down at his hands as the recent memories played back over and over, like a recurring nightmare. The images took over, crushing him. Would he ever be able to sleep again?

"Cameron!" Eli yelled for him to come to the phone in the club.

Several of Brooke's bandmates had attempted to reach him earlier, but he hadn't heard his cell phone going off. When he answered the club phone and heard, "Brooke is at the hospital...On a ventilator...Brain-dead..." everything inside of him poured out. He became weak at the knees and vomited the contents of his stomach, then banged on the car door all the way to the hospital, his boy driving him, trying to keep him relaxed. It didn't matter what Eli said as he raced him to the hospital. Nothing mattered at all and the only words he wanted to hear were: "You've been misinformed. Brooke is fine."

When he walked in those doors, he rushed to the front desk only to have security try and calm him down. Nothing was making sense.

Soon thereafter, Brooke's mother approached him, along with her aunt and cousin, all of them looking frantic, gripping cups of coffee, tears in their eyes. The doctor came and explained the situation. Once again he was told that this wasn't a dream. Brooke was really gone.

"The doctor and her friends that were with her said it happened rather quickly." Mrs. Coleman placed her coffee down and blew her nose. "The bullet went into her neck and by the time she arrived at the hospital, she barely had a pulse. They said she was brain-dead, no activity, but her heart was so strong, Cameron, that it kept trying to hold on. Kept on beating, pounding, demanding a second chance at life."

She closed her eyes tight, shook her head and took a deep breath. Clutching the edge of the chair, she tapped her feet, just like the women in church before they caught the Holy Spirit. Then, just like that, Mrs. Coleman opened her eyes and smiled at him.

"She was one of the strongest women I knew, but she came across as so gentle." He could barely utter the words.

"She was like a robust flower, wasn't she? Then the alarming second wave of news arrived, right? We all were told at the same time. Brooke had signed up to be not only an organ donor, but a heart donor specifically." She lifted her finger and waved it about. "Cameron, see? That's what I am talking about—grace of God. My baby was always thinking about other people. A good soul. She was always a good soul."

He turned away, not wanting to hear any more. In retrospect, he shouldn't have been shocked. Brooke's father had passed away when she was only thirteen from heart failure. He'd never received the surgery he so desperately needed.

"Cameron?" Mrs. Coleman shook him out of his thoughts.

"Huh? Oh."

"Baby." The woman got to her feet and came to sit beside him. Wrapping her arm around him, she placed a kiss on his earlobe. "It's going to be all right. I promise you that

Brooke, though young and so full of life, would be happy that at least her heart will keep on beatin'."

Mrs. Coleman was so strong; he was in awe. He just couldn't muster that feeling, think positive in any manner. The woman sat with her chin high, her grace and class apparent as tears streamed down her cheeks. She was keeping it together for everyone else in there. Didn't matter that it was her daughter who lay there, deceased. The woman had lost her husband, her son in a car accident over ten years ago, and now, her only daughter, too.

Who upstairs is punishing Mrs. Coleman? What kind of God took a woman like Brooke away, struck her down in her prime?

His body shook as waves of uncontrollable, unsurmountable grief overcame him. He rocked in his seat and wailed, the pain finally breaking free with no barriers. She held him tighter.

It was just the two of them now. The waiting area had cleared out quite a bit. Loads of Brooke's friends and family had paraded inside, but Mrs. Coleman urged them to say their goodbyes quickly, right before the surgery. Time was of the essence in these cases. Once it had been made clear that Brooke was never coming back, Mrs. Coleman had signed the necessary paperwork to have her daughter give what she gave to everyone she met—her whole heart.

He took Mrs. Coleman's hand, squeezed it and leaned forward, doubling over. Blood rushed to his head. She ran her hand along his back as the tears fell.

"We were going to get married."

"I know. I know, Cameron." She kept on soothing him.

"I think everyone knew that. You loved each other so much."

"She was so happy to be performing in the park tonight. It was my idea. I had been beggin' her to do it. I harassed her manager, went online to see about it. I knew that if she got in that park, her fanbase would explode. I was promoting it, flyers everywhere. I even bought some ads. And now look? She's dead. This is all my damn fault."

"Nuh uh," the woman stated calmly. "We're not doing that today, Cameron. All right? We're not doing that at all, ever. We're not chasing something or someone to blame—definitely not ourselves."

"But it's true."

"It's *not* true. Brooke was doing what she loved best—singing. People perform in parks all spring and summer in the city. That's what artists do. They sing. Perform. My daughter was an entertainer. You can't keep a songbird cooped up in a cage all day. Brooke loved being with her fans. She loved performing, you know that."

He could feel the woman's gaze on him, but he kept his eyes on the glossy white hospital floor, his hands clasped, his rage and distress flowing freely, dripping everywhere.

"She wanted it as badly as you wanted it for her," she continued. "The people to blame are the ones who chose to take out a gun and shoot at one another in a space full of innocent people. I won't have you sitting here doing this to yourself."

He looked at the woman for a brief spell, then turned away, the pain too much. Mrs. Coleman was pretty much an older version of Brooke. He couldn't handle it.

"I want them to find who killed her. I need justice." He

gritted his teeth.

"I want him found too, especially before he hurts someone else. I believe they will; too many people saw him. Right now, I want you to think about the good times you two shared together. Your love for my daughter knew no bounds."

She placed a kiss against his cheek. He smiled, but the anger and resentment kept growing. She got to her feet, grabbed her purse, and made her way over to the nurses' station. He couldn't hear what she was saying, but within moments, a doctor approached and they began to talk. She looked over her shoulder at him and waved him over.

"The surgery went well," the doctor explained, his dark brows slightly furrowed. "Your daughter was in excellent health and—I'm sorry about this, I really am. I know it's difficult. I've been performing heart surgeries for over sixteen years, including heart transplants, and it never gets any easier when I have to speak to the donor's family. What your daughter did was incredibly selfless and allowed another young woman to live, one who would've been dead in a matter of months if she hadn't received Brooke's gift of love."

"Gift of love?" Cameron questioned.

"Yes, that's what some of us call it since the heart represents love," the doctor explained.

"It's the gift of life, man. My girlfriend is dead because some bastard shot her dead, and now, her *life* is saving someone else's. Love doesn't have shit to do with this."

"Cameron." Mrs. Coleman's eyes widened as she stared at him.

"It's okay," the doctor stated calmly. "Anger is part of the grieving process. Brooke's death was not natural. I understand. Only time seems to make these things a little easier."

"Time doesn't do shit, either. Time didn't care that she was only thirty years old. Who is she?" Cameron barked.

"Who is who?"

"Who is the woman who has my girlfriend's heart now?"

"We're not at liberty to discuss that unless the patient has signed consent forms to allow disclosure to the donor's family. I will check her paperwork and follow up with you about that, okay?"

Cameron hesitated for a spell, then nodded before turning away.

"Cameron, honey, where are you going?"

"Just to step outside for a second. I need some fresh air."

Mrs. Coleman smiled sadly at him, then turned back toward the doctor. In a few minutes, he was standing outside the hospital, looking up into the night sky. He slid out his phone and looked at his missed call log—it was well over fifty. On a sigh, he sat down on a nearby bench and began to compose a generic mass text message:

Thank you to everyone for reaching out to me. I can't really talk right now and don't want to chat at this time. Please understand that I need some space, but no, it's not a rumor. My Brookie, as I often called her, passed away. She's gone. To those asking who did this, the police are searching for her killer. Wrong place, wrong time. Bullet not meant for her—he was shooting at someone else. The police have several street camera photos of the guy and there were witnesses, so they hope to find him soon. Please just keep Brooke's family in your prayers. When I

27

*have final details about the funeral service, I'll let you
know. Thanks. Cameron*

He slipped his phone back into his pants pocket and huffed. Just then, his phone rang. He had no intentions of answering it until he noticed it was his mother.

"Yeah, Mom."

"What's going on?" the woman cried. "Cameron, your father and I have been trying to reach you for hours."

"Mama, please. Not right now. I already told you that I was going to the hospital."

His mom was silent for a spell.

"She's really dead, isn't she?" she whimpered, sounding somewhat like a child.

"Yes." He cleared his throat and blinked back tears. The next few moments felt like an eternity. Mama sobbed on the other end of the phone. He could hear his father in the background, saying, "Oh, no."

"Cameron, your father is trying to find us a flight back home." They were in Puerto Rico on vacation.

Pops was taking control, as usual.

A tall, dark-complexioned Black man, his dad played the saxophone for pleasure, but worked as a journalist for a small paper and blog that dealt with the healthcare needs of the elderly. Mama was a pharmacist and active in her church. They'd both taken a liking to Brooke, undoubtedly believing that somehow, she'd tame him, make him a bit less wild.

"Mama…"

"Yes?" she said between gasps for air.

"I never loved anyone like I loved Brooke. That connection…I can't even explain it. Mama, I'm dyin'. I can't breathe, Mama." His heart began to pound painfully. He gripped his chest and swallowed his voice, a scream trying to force itself from between his lips. He looked around, wanting to beat something to death, and wanting to die, too.

"Dad and I will be home as soon as possible. He's looking into airlines right now," Mom repeated, as if that somehow would help. He knew she was trying her best. "Oh, God." Mom's voice faded and suddenly, he heard his father speaking.

"Cameron." Pops must've taken the phone from his mother. "Cameron, I'm sorry, son. I know you're upset right now. We'll be back home as soon as possible." *Stop telling me that. Both of you stop saying that to me.* "Where are you right now?"

"The hospital. With Brooke's mother." He sucked his teeth and kicked a pebble across the way.

"Can I speak with her? Is Mrs. Coleman close to you?"

"I'm outside. She's talkin' to the doctor who did the surgery."

"Surgery? I take it they tried to do surgery and it failed."

"No, that's not what happened. She was dead on arrival, brain-dead that is. Brooke was a heart donor, Pops. I never knew that." He shrugged. "Anyway, they just did the transplant operation. Some woman got Brooke's heart now."

He swallowed his resentment as he looked around, watching people and cars go by. He felt as if he wasn't supposed to be indignant, to feel so ugly inside, but he couldn't help it.

"Okay," his father said after a brief silence. "We'll see you soon. When we get to the airport, I'll text you."

"All right, but Pops, there's nothin' you or Mama can do." Cameron shook his head. "You can't bring her back. I keep thinkin' every few minutes that I'm going to wake up. But then, I look at my phone and see messages I missed. People asking me, 'Is Brooke dead?' Or I look behind and see the hospital, smell that place all over me. I went to her social media pages and uh…" He hung his head. "Hundreds upon hundreds of people are posting on her page, Dad. I imagine it will be thousands within the next twenty-four hours. She touched so many people, so many people."

"She did. She was a wonderful young lady, son, and I'm so, so, so sorry about this. We're hurting with you. She was like a daughter to us."

"I was gonna ask her to marry me next month, Dad." A tear streamed down his face. "I had the ring and everything. I mean, we've been together almost four years, ya know?" He shrugged. "I settled down because of her. No more messin' around. I wanted her just that bad. She made me a one-woman man. I don't know what I'm going to do without her. I can't breathe, Pops, I can't fuckin' breathe."

"Cameron, you're still in shock. Look, go back inside with Mrs. Coleman. You shouldn't be alone right now. I bet—"

"Did you hear me, Dad? You don't understand." He jumped to his feet. "I DON'T WANT TO GO BACK INSIDE. She's in there, dead." He pointed to the hospital. "I want to stay out here, where she's free. Where she's still alive. I can't do this." He spun around, the tears falling faster and harder. "Everybody expects me to be strong, but I'm anything but that right now. I am nothin' like my real self, or maybe this is the real me after all."

"What do you think is the real you, Cameron? You have got—"

"I'm nothin' without Brooke. I ain't shit without her." He sobbed, coming undone. He didn't care about the people now staring at him as they walked past. "She was with me when I didn't have anything, nothin' to give her. I ain't have any money, could barely pay my damn bills when we first met. She encouraged me, taught me shit I didn't even know. I ended up opening my own club with her help and support. She was my ride or die. It was *her* that was the backbone. Nobody ever had my back like Brooke, Pops. NOBODY. Now my baby is gone, I'm dead inside. You hear me? They may as well have shot me, too, 'cause I'm good as gone."

Chapter Three
I Lost Myself and My Best Friend

T HE STARK WHITE hospital walls seemed blurry, then returned to normal. Emily hissed as the distortions kept coming and going like some cruel joke on repeat. She rested her eyes on a partition to her right. This wall was adorned with a cheap-looking discount-store-type painting, the rustic frame worn and weathered. It drew her eye still, hoping she could soon make it out and her vision would come back, allowing her to see crisp, defined lines once more. The painting only got worse though, seeming to melt like a stick of butter.

Shit.

She ran her fingers through her hair, blinked several times, and strained her eyes, opening them as wide as possible, as if that would somehow make the indistinct world around her typical once again. Suddenly, she felt a dull pain in her chest and aches in several joints. The medicine made her brain spin like a record. Like a bad case of vertigo. She gripped a fistful of her sheets, lulled her head back and sighed.

How many hours have passed? Days? Weeks?

She leaned forward, pushing through it all, refusing to

not try again and again. She'd already been briefed on what recovery would feel like, although she hadn't expected the pain would be this damn debilitating. Her body throbbed all over and now the chest pain was getting worse by the minute.

"Shit." Falling back onto the flattened pillows, she searched for a call button, a bell, hell, a wooden spoon to lop the metal frames of the bed with—anything to get someone's attention, to make that horrible feeling stop. After taking a deep breath and getting her bearings, she found the little red help button and pushed it frantically while screaming, "Nurse. Nurse. Somebody, please."

She waited a few moments. Nothing.

"Jesus Christ. Doesn't anyone work here, or does everyone keep bankers' hours?"

After what seemed like an eternity, a slender Black woman donning nurse scrubs approached. Her knotted, long black hair in skinny braids was pulled back with a bright pink scrunchie, and she sported a pleasant smile.

"Hi, Ms. Windsor. What seems to be the problem?" The woman rocked back on her thick-soled taupe shoes. Her scrubs had little rainbow-colored hearts and blue stars printed on the fabric.

"I'm in pain, that's the problem." Emily rolled her eyes. "I just had surgery."

"Yes, I know. I hope you've been taking it easy."

"Taking it easy? What else would I be doing? Running a marathon? I'm stuck in this awful hospital, for God's sake. It's not exactly the Hamptons. Look." She took a deep breath. "My fucking heart was ripped out and replaced with a new one and now my chest feels like it is on fire. Like this is Hell. And of course it is. I fucking need something. Give me something for the pain." Just then, her vision seemed to improve to near perfection. However, the chest pain remained, refusing to let up.

The nurse kept standing there with that goofy, sweet smile, then turned her attention to a board in the room. She made her way over to it and took her sweet time studying it. When she was done, she shook her head.

"I'm sorry, Ms. Windsor. You aren't due for another dose quite yet, and due to the infection you had, the doctors are being careful not to—"

"Infection? What infection?"

"Don't worry, it's common, Ms. Windsor. You developed an infection after the surgery, but you're recovering well."

"When did—when did I have an infection?" Emily asked, confused.

"That was last week, about five or six days ago, I believe."

"Last week?" She ran her hand along her arm, feeling the hairs rising all along. She'd lost complete track of space and time. So unlike her.

"So, how did everything go? I can leave real soon, right?"

"So far, your body is not rejecting the transplant and your graft is healing well. No problems with your kidneys, either, but that isn't out of the question yet, so the doctor wants to keep monitoring you for a while. You're being watched closely, no worries. You did really well. Despite that, you are looking at another week at least."

"Another week? Are you crazy? I have a big client coming

and I'm behind on work. We could be losing millions of dollars if I don't get out of here soon. At the very least, I need to be able to work from home. I can't get anything done here with all of this noise and constant invasion of privacy. This is unacceptable. And what about my pain? I need something for this. I feel like someone stabbed me in the chest. I can't believe this. I can*not* freaking believe this shit."

After a brief hesitation, the nurse took a step toward her and placed her hands into the pockets of her scrub jacket. She tilted her head to the side, looking a bit condescending, sarcastic—with that plastic grin and those doe-like eyes.

"I tell you what, Ms. Windsor, let me call the doctor and he can—"

"No, screw that. I need out of here and I need some medicine and I need it *now*. This is fucking ridiculous. You should be fired. You are completely inept. Hell, you didn't even offer me a damn aspirin." The nurse's eyes practically doubled in size. "Why can't you do your job, and what's with the bad attitude and crazy facial expressions?"

"Attitude?" The nurse raised a brow and shifted her weight from one foot to the other. "The only person with a bad attitude right now, Ms. Windsor, is you. Offering you an aspirin would not help, and considering how you've been behaving, you would have had something to say about that, too. All I am trying to do is explain to you that—"

"For fuck's sake." Emily rolled her eyes and sucked her dry tongue that felt thick and swollen like layers of sandpaper. The flavor along her palate was abominable, as if she'd not had a drop of water in days. "Why do you need help to do your job? You people are so damn worthless. Jesus. You're lazy. You *never* want to help anyone if it interrupts you watching the latest Oprah or Real Housewives show, playing games on your phone, or maybe chatting it up with your third baby daddy."

"Uh, you know what?" The nurse laughed dismally. "I am going to have to leave before I say something I regret. They don't pay me enough for this shit." Shaking her head, she headed to the door to exit.

"Come back here. I am a paying patient. I have—" Suddenly, a pain like she'd never known seized her. She jeered forward and grabbed the hospital railing, shaking from head to toe. Liquid pooled in her mouth, then poured out, as if she were spitting up all over herself. One of the machines she was hooked up to began to show strange graphs, lines moving frantically up and down, as her body tremored in the most violent of ways. A loud bell began to ring, echoing through the room, making her ears hurt. Seconds later, all she could hear was scrambling, feet pounding the floor, and voices all around her.

Lie back. Can you hear us? Emily...Emily...Emily...

She gasped for air as she looked into a sky of earth-toned faces, all of them various shades of the human rainbow. Their eyes were much the same, ranging from inky black to icy blue.

Her heart beat hard, fast, and heavy within her. She'd never felt anything like that in her life. It was a foreign spirit, a rocking spirit. A beat that was forceful and commanding, one that demanded she not whisper another word.

Something had grabbed her from within and snapped

her into submission.

Flashes of light came before her, as if someone was taking a photo, one after another.

Am I being taken back into surgery? She screamed when she looked to her right and saw a white casket with a spread of deep, red roses paired with a silky silver sash.

"IT'S FOR ME, ISNT IT? OH GOD. I'M DEAD. I'M DEAD."

"She's hallucinating," someone yelled out.

Blackness surrounded her…

But the beating heart kept thumping so loudly, she could hear it in her eardrums like percussion. It sounded like music, a well-tuned band with the best acoustics in town. She could hear singing, the most beautiful voice, deep yet feminine and haunting, foreign and familiar at the same time. She couldn't understand the words but somehow, she knew the lyrics well.

What is happening to me? I'm scared. I'm so scared.

Two weeks later

CAMERON SAT IN the hazy apartment filled with sage smoke and incense smolder. He rested his bloodshot eyes on the box filled with Brooke's coveted song lyric books and photo albums. It was a mere two feet away from him, sitting there like an unwanted child, shy and hated, withdrawn, drawing cold. He shuddered then wrapped the thick, black towel he was sitting on around his waist. Sniffing the air, he let it take him back to a space and place in time where life made sense.

I remember how you'd do it, baby.

It had been Brooke's ritual. Each and every morning, she'd light sage, incense, and candles. She'd pray, meditate, whisper salutations, then return to the bed where he was undoubtedly either still asleep or playing on his phone. They'd lie down next to each other for a spell, perhaps make love, then shower together while beautiful soul music played, drifting through the open floorplan of their shared space. She'd usually finish last, towel off, wrap her gorgeous thick curls in an old towel or T-shirt to soak up water, slip on the Kimono-style robe he'd gifted to her, and head to their kitchen to prepare their first meal of the day. Some days it was fruit salad—thin-sliced kiwi, big chunks of sweet and juicy strawberries, diced pineapples, wedges of papaya and a handful of green grapes—just as he liked it. Other times it was toast or bagels with a side of quinoa, seasoned slices of ripe avocados, and huge servings of red potatoes and sautéed onions. That was one of his favorites.

He gripped the sheets impossibly tighter and lowered his head. His brain seemed to be throbbing as the torrid memories marched through his skull like ants, carting the images of her around, parading her in his mind's eye, making him die a little bit more inside.

He blinked back the pain, fought hard and sighed with relief when he realized he'd won the battle. The recollections were tossed aside, the ants flat on their backs, out of the way. Gone.

I can't keep going through this. I gotta get out of this funk. I can't function. I still feel like I am trapped inside a nightmare with no way out. I'm in prison. It's a place I can't escape.

Running his hand over his wavy black hair he liked to keep short and needed cutting, he thought about how he'd been drinking too much as of late. One night he believed he'd blacked out, something that had never occurred before. He'd been awakened by Opium licking his face and whimpering.

More minutes passed when he sat on that bed, not moving a muscle. His gaze landed on five empty bottles of imported beer and a wineglass lying on its side as if it had fallen but thankfully didn't break. Had he put it there? His face itched from lack of shaving, snatching him out of his deliberations.

I gotta do something about this beard that's growing out of control.

He hadn't had a trim since right before the funeral. He'd been doing the bare minimum—washing his ass, brushing his hair and teeth. He reached across the unmade bed, naked with the exception of a wooden beaded necklace with the colors of the African flag—black, red, and green—and glanced at a small framed picture of him and Brooke that he kept on his nightstand. He played with his hair, twirling several strands between his fingers. It felt good, just like how Brooke used to do it. He looked at the alarm clock and sighed. Her mother, Mrs. Coleman, would be over in an hour, but he couldn't move from his position, sitting on the edge of the bed they'd shared, frozen in time and space.

He scanned the bedroom and tucked his toes into the rumpled teal and black rug on the floor. The original exposed brick walls, which had been the main selling point of the apartment they'd selected after finally agreeing on a place they both liked, no longer looked the same. Something about it all seemed different, as if invisible, crude graffiti were covering the walls from top to bottom. The furniture looked different, too. The whole place had changed, and yet, everything was just as it had been. The air in the apartment wasn't nearly as sweet, no longer scented with her essential oils and heavenly perfumes. Things were no longer beautiful, kind, nifty, smart, and soulful. They were ugly, cruel, ordinary, simple-minded, and evil.

He threw a glance over his shoulder and stared at her side of the bed. He hadn't moved her pillow except to brush his face against it and inhale her scent. Her natural aroma was beginning to fade. Another one of life's betrayals he'd yet to fully accept. On the side of the bed sat her old black slippers, exactly where'd she left them, and her satin magenta sleeping bonnet, the almond oil stain still prominent right in the center of it like some bullseye.

Cameron blinked back tears, balled up a fistful of burgundy silk sheets in his left palm, and closed his eyes, daring himself to fight another round—a war that was going on within himself twenty-four seven, never letting up. He swallowed. Hard.

I can't keep this up. I don't want anything to change, but it's changing without me anyway. I never gave the world permission to move on without her. Don't you people know Brooke died? Don't you know my baby is gone? Or is it me? Am I the one that doesn't know it? Yeah, maybe it's just me, 'cause I still half expect her to bring her ass through that door, her jean jacket on, beanie on her head, purse on her shoulder. She'd complain about the train being late and tell stories about her microphone shorting out or someone asking to touch her hair.

Opium barked, shaking him out of his thoughts.

He smiled when the big Rottweiler made his way over to him and sat before him, looking dutiful and sad about the eyes. Cameron rubbed on his head.

"I guess I need to get dressed, huh? Can't just sit here for hours. I showered almost an hour ago. You need to go outside, don't you?"

The dog barked and leapt up and down. Cameron got to his feet and within ten minutes, he was dressed in a plain white, long-sleeved shirt, loose jeans, and his favorite Nike Air shoes. Opium followed him toward the front door, where he grabbed his black jacket and slid it on, then the leash from the small hanger on the wall. He hooked it onto his furry friend's collar, then made his way out the door and down the five flights of steps, bypassing the elevator.

"All right, we gotta make this quick. Brooke's mama is coming over to get some of her things."

Opium pulled on his leash, eager to reach the treelined sidewalk in Brooklyn's trendy Dumbo district. A light breeze blew the smells of the world around him, forcing them to blend and merge into something new. Some of the aromas smelled sweet like donuts and candy apples, some were stale and pungent, like a dump truck passing by.

Opium paused by a pole, sniffing it with all of his might before lifting his leg to christen it. Cameron shoved his hand in his pocket and bounced about, trying to dispel the nervous energy that was filling him like a goblet. The sounds around him seemed to amplify, voices carrying in various languages and dialects. Across the street, a bright red Corvette moved around the bend, the driver—a middle-aged White man—focused on the road.

Cameron pulled at Opium's collar, urging him on up the block.

Nobody understood me like Brooke. We would finish each other's sentences. She got my sense of humor, understood how my brain worked. She'd listen to me recite my poetry and let me bounce club ideas off her for hours. I trusted this woman with my secrets. She's taken them to the grave.

He'd taken it for granted. He'd taken their card games for granted, the times they'd played Uno in the middle of their bed with a big bowl of popcorn between them, the TV on mute, the music blasting before the neighbors routinely complained.

He'd taken for granted the arguments they had. How passionate and beautiful she'd look during those heated quarrels. Even when she'd been pissed at him, she still loved him through the hurt and pain, reserving her anger only for the ones that truly had her heart.

He'd taken for granted giving her foot massages after a long day, how he'd always hoped they'd lead to sex, and she'd somehow convince him she never suspected his ulterior motives.

He'd taken for granted the way her long, floral wrap skirts hugged her gorgeous, feminine hips. He'd taken for granted the dip and arch of her neck and the specks of light in her eyes. His own filled with tears at that moment, and his chest felt like a vise around his fast pumping heart. Vision blurred from sudden moisture born of pure anguish, he stopped walking. Pressing his back against a building, he

WHAT THE HEART WANTS

took several deep breaths as his anxiety climbed brand new, frightening heights and threatened to jump.

"What the hell is wrong with me?" he whispered to himself. "I've lost people I've loved before. Plenty of them. Shit, I'm Black in America. How could I have not? Brooke, you gotta help me, baby. I'm losin' it. I can't tell if I'm coming or going. I've smoked enough weed this week to paralyze a fuckin' horse. I've drunk enough, since your death, to pickle a million men's livers. I'm seriously losing my fuckin' mind." He ran his hand against his face as Opium sniffed along the cracks of the sidewalk, trying to find something of interest while he waited for his human father to get his shit together. "I can't do this shit. Everywhere I look, I see you. I hear you. I smell you."

You haunt me like a ghost. You kiss me good night; then when I wake up I realize our life was all a dream...

I never knew that the last time we made love would be the last time.

I never knew that the last time we danced would be the last time.

I never knew that the last time I heard you sing in our apartment would be the last time I'd hear your voice.

He took another deep breath and heard music in his head. A bomb ass tempo. He began to rock his head back and forth, beat his foot against the pavement.

And yet, that last time was the worst time, and the

worst time was poorly designed.

    It was like a doorway to Hell being ripped open and me being cast inside.

    I can't dance with flames. It was ocean, I wanted to ride.

    I miss the dip of your love and the curve of your kiss.

    I miss granting your desires and seducing your greatest wish.

    I want a jet-black
blue-black
pitch-black snack.
I want my fuckin' woman back.

    I want to feel the silky universe between your thighs.

    I want to see the explosion of colors in your inky eyes.

    I want to swallow that day, make it all go away.

    I want a blind man to see your heart and your spirit.

    I want a deaf man to say, 'Hush! Her soul? Yeah, I can hear it.'

    I want the whole damn world to pause for the cause and take a look.

    If you read my first and last chapter, they both are the book of Brooke.

Tears streamed down his face as he recited his impromptu spoken word piece in his mind. Starting the trek back to his apartment, he went over the verses again and again until a sad smile creased his face. Opium stopped in his tracks and launched another investigation. This one led to a russet donation of sorts. After the dog was finished, Cameron removed a plastic bag from his pocket, cleaned up the pungent deposit, and discarded it in a bin. Soon, they reached his building. As he stood outside, he noticed a cab pull up and Brooke's mother step out. He grinned and waved when she walked, placing one foot in front of the other, as she always reminded him to do while traveling this bullshit he called life. She was a bit early, but that was okay. He figured he could use the company.

"How are you doin', baby?" she said, her colorful poncho swaying back and forth as she approached.

"It depends on when you ask me, Mama." He chuckled sadly. "Right now? I'm in a daze. Yeah, just reading the chapters of my life, ya know? So far, I'm not really diggin' this one. Basically, I gotta believe in something right now that I can't see. I have to believe in an imperfect God, 'cause a perfect God would never do somethin' like this to me. Definitely not to *you*. Nah, that's just not possible. They say God is love, right? Well I'm not really feelin' the love right now. I am feelin' the loss, though. I only feel it when I inhale and then again when I exhale. In other words, I still can't breathe, and with the way things are going, I'll need to be on life support."

Chapter Four

A Change is Going to Come

WRAPPING THE PLUSH white blanket around her hunched shoulders, Emily rested her feet atop a sage-green pillow. She crossed her ankles and wiggled her dark pink painted toenails. She'd only been home a few days, and yet, things felt odd. Her home looked as if it belonged to someone else, as if it wasn't her place anymore. Something was off, though she couldn't quite put her finger on what it could be. She'd attributed it to her medications giving her foggy brain, but her typical OCD behaviors trumped that, so she kept second-guessing herself.

Had her taste in décor changed so quickly? The high-ceilinged dwelling boasted a breathtaking view, clean lines, and a selection of fine art she'd coveted. Now, however, everything seemed meaningless and cold. She wouldn't dare admit it, but she had to sleep with the light on, fearing at times that some invisible being was watching her from the shadows, feasting on evil, waiting patiently to attack. No. That wasn't it. In fact, on second thought, this was no boogeyman theory at all. It was a familiar stranger, if that made one damn bit of sense. Yes. She felt split in two, as if *she* were watching herself from afar.

I'm losing my mind. I'm losing my damn mind. This can't be good.

Beyond her closed bedroom door, she could hear footsteps. The sound snapped her out of her panicked thoughts. She hissed and sucked her teeth, hating having a stranger romping about inside her home. She couldn't wait to get the woman out of her house.

It had all begun with fatherly interference, as usual.

Dad had insisted she have a nurse on call since she'd decided to check out of the hospital a few days before her scheduled release. The staff and general environment were driving her mad, which she believed hampered her recovery, making things impossible. Who could argue with that? After all, if her well-being was everyone's priority, then they had to take her sentiments into consideration, be they exaggerated, outright fabricated or not.

Taking a deep breath, she reached for her cup of hot green and blackberry tea that rested on the handcrafted Bubinga wood nightstand and took a delicate sip. The brew had a drop of cream in it, just how she liked it. Due to her situation, the doctor had urged her not to drink anything that could cause heart palpitations, and he'd provided a lengthy list. She now despised him, too.

No energy drinks.

No sugary juices or sodas.

Coffee, her favorite of all, was off the damn table, in the trash can, placed on the curb, collected and sent away to the landfill of her deepest desires.

The doctor suggested decaf. What a joke.

Emily scoffed at the memory. Talking about adding insult to injury. She explained to the physician that she'd rather drink expired dog food blitzed in a bullet blender than allow a single drop of horrid decaf coffee—the ugly stepsister to the *real* cup of joe—to touch her tongue.

She set the teacup back down and lost herself in her thoughts.

Being back at work made her smile. Just the thought of sitting behind her desk gave her goose bumps.

Dreams, the good kind. I miss those.

The night before she'd left the hospital, she'd had a horrible dream—the same one she'd had each night since the operation. That night, though, had been the final, crooked straw; she needed out of that damn place. Those terrible nightly hallucinations, for that's what they'd felt like, had caused her to wake up in a cold sweat feeling completely disoriented. It always began the same way.

A white shiny coffin sat on one side in a dark room, illuminated by a single light that hung from the ceiling on a cord. Dark red dying roses were arranged atop it while a haunting melody played very low, so low one could barely hear it. Faceless people moved about the room, drifting close to the casket, the men dressed in dark suits and the women in long boring dresses, mostly in shades of gray. She could always hear heavy breathing throughout the dream, then the breathing would slow down and finally stop abruptly right before the end.

The funeral scene would eventually fade away, the room replaced with rows and rows of evenly cut, vibrant green grass going on for miles, as far as the eye could see.

Flashes of light sparked in the distant sky, like lightning

bolts booming to a heavy drumbeat, followed by screaming and what sounded like a stampede. State of panic. She could never figure out why these invisible people were screaming, running about, and why she could only hear them, not see them. The grayish-blue sky held evidence of a looming storm and the clouds kept rolling, threatening to do damage. The nightmare was discombobulated, but always left her feeling terror, sadness, and sorrow, as if something wicked was on its way. And then, it would happen.

Someone always spoke at the end, just before the breathing stopped. A female voice. Emily could never make out what the woman was saying, but a part of her was fearful of understanding the words. The lady talking sounded as if she were drowning, underwater, speaking with a mouthful of sea salt and reef. Her voice grew louder and louder with each dream, but it was always muffled. The final dream was pretty much the same, only it was pouring rain in this latest version and there was chanting and an African drumbeat that was hard to miss.

That was it. Emily had had enough. She blamed the hospital and the terrible workforce for pushing her into the cruel arms of madness. Everyone was driving her crazy. She believed she'd proven her theory correct, for on the first night when she got home, there was no dream.

But that didn't last long. On the second night, the fucking nightmare returned, and then on the third night, too.

"Shit." She jumped when she heard her cell phone ringing. With a body full of medicine and a mind that now wandered endlessly like a lost child looking for its mother, she felt so out of sorts. Grabbing the phone, she answered quickly, almost dropping it in the process. "Hi, Dad." She threw on a faux cheery voice. Might as well make those six weeks of acting school pay off.

"How's my favorite daughter?" he chortled.

"I'm your *only* daughter." She grinned and rolled her eyes at his favorite joke of all time, then glanced down at her laptop. "I'm doing well, actually, just looking at these reports. Looks like Greg did a pretty good job while I was away." She tried to sound sincere.

"He did. I looked over his work as much as time would permit. He handled everything in an expert fashion."

"Yes, well, I did find a *few* items that I feel need to be addressed. I'll make a few adjustments and then you and he can meet with the client in a few days, give the suggestions that I add, no fee to the client of course, and then move forward."

Silence ensued. Dad was taking far too long to respond. Perhaps he was distracted.

"Emily, you are going too hard, too fast, and too soon." She sighed loudly and fell back against her mauve quilted headboard. "The doctor said you needed to take it easy."

"But I am. I am in bed."

"In bed working, that's not the same. You assured me you would do as asked." *As asked? I'm not some five-year-old.* "I thought you were just going to read the reports, not try to pick them apart." She could hear the disappointment and worry in his tone, yet her irritation grew nevertheless.

"Well, I mean," she shrugged, trying to form her sentences just so, "I'm not actually picking the reports apart, per se. I'm merely reviewing them." She was met with steely silence, this time worse than the first. "I just uh, you know, thought of a few suggestions regarding changes Greg should make to them is all." She heard him take a deep breath on the other end. "We'd do them a disservice to not follow up, Dad. It's not a big deal, nothing earth shattering, but definitely matters that need to be taken care of."

"I know I'm going to regret asking this." He huffed. "Like what?"

"Like, they're being far too aggressive with some of these stock options, for example. I've highlighted them in yellow. Secondly, their expenses could be reduced by a minimum of eighteen percent if the company would change healthcare providers, and the services offered would be relatively the same. Another issue is the profit and loss margin is forecasted to be significantly smaller this fiscal year due to these elaborate functions they are having. Gas cards, shopping trip vouchers, frivolous employee appreciation dinners, and the—"

"Emily. Emily…"

"I mean, seriously." She scoffed. "Taylor and Fete is a small upscale clothing company, not Saks Fifth Avenue, for Pete's sake. It's fantastic in theory to be a kitten and liken yourself to a tiger, but you have to actually take a trip to the jungle to get the full gist of the wildlife, not just play make-believe. Now, don't get me wrong, they're certainly impressive, Dad. They've accomplished a lot in a short amount of time in a cutthroat industry such as retail, and I'm not second-guessing Greg's assessment, but in the grand scheme of things, Taylor and Fete have no business sending twenty-three employees, first class I might add, to Rio de Janeiro for five days and four nights."

"Emily."

"And have you seen the depreciation of their spring collection? They might as well have taken a big industrial-sized lighter to their money and set it on fire. Who in the hell is handling their quality control? The entire rollout was a disaster, two years in a row. It appears to be happening during production, but of course, that's not my expertise—the point is, it used to be their main bread and butter and was featured countless times during Fashion Week. Now? They'd be lucky to get it presented in a back alley. I'm afraid they've put all their eggs in one basket, but this one had a hole in it. This is what happens when you depend on only a one-trick pony for all of your continued success. What happened to the backup plan having a backup plan notion? As fickle as the market is, you'd think they'd know this. It's going to be at least—"

"EMILY." Her father's voice boomed through the phone, ringing in stereo in her ear. "This is *exactly* what I did not want to happen. You're doing it again. You have embedded yourself in your work within mere days, like a damn tick on a dog, all over again. Have you learned nothing? I bet you were not home for more than two hours before you were combing over inquiries, answering email queries, and sending out correspondence."

He's right about that, but that's not the point.

"Why are you yelling at me? I can't believe this. Dad, don't you want me to be involved anymore? You told me I'd be back to work in no time. Now that I am, you're finding fault in it. I'm in the bed, not there at the office. That's a compromise. I thought you'd be happy with me bringing this information to you. I did it for you and the company." She sulked. It seldom happened that her father screamed at her in such a manner. A mixture of sadness and anger brewed within her, and she hated every second of it. "Do you not want me to do my job anymore?"

"No. I mean, yes," he said in exasperation. "I want you to be back at work. You're not just my daughter, you're a valuable asset to the company, irreplaceable, but not at the expense of your health, Emily. You just don't get it. You must stop this at once. What good are you to anyone, including yourself, if you're dead?"

"You're being overly dramatic." She took another sip of her tea.

"I don't believe that I am, Emily, and drama is not exactly a part of my personality. The facts remain the same. You just had major heart surgery, or did you forget that? The slightest bit of stress, irritation, the smallest of annoyances at this time could send you right back to the hospital. Is that what you want?"

After a moment of hesitation and blinking back tears, she worked up the strength to answer.

"Of course not."

"You're still healing. Your body is still trying to get used to this new organ inside it and here you are, talking to me about a spring clothing collection and how it is the downfall of a multimillion-dollar company that can make thousands of dollars in ten seconds with the snap of their fingers."

She blinked back more tears. Angry tears. "But Dad—"

"I do not want to hear one more word about this report,

do you hear me?" She swallowed, shocked by his tone. "DO. YOU. HEAR. ME?"

"Yes."

"Good. I'm glad I've made myself perfectly clear." *You old jerk. How dare you speak to me like this?* She shook as he socked it to her. "Your nurse is there at your apartment to ensure that you receive proper pain management and care."

"Oh goody."

He ignored her words and continued. "I have hired you a personal chef to take care of your breakfast, lunch, and dinner starting tomorrow, and as you know, you begin physical therapy in two days. Please take this time to do things you never do."

"Like what? What do you suggest?" She yawned, not giving a damn. *Researching the rate of hair growth on assholes of a lost but not forgotten Norwegian tribe? Perhaps skinny-dipping in a large pool filled with lime Jell-O and a drop of flesh-eating acid?*

"How about reading a book for pleasure? Watch a good comedy program? There are other things too, like playing solitaire. Listen to your favorite music. Now that seems right up your alley. You used to love listening to music in your room when you were a teenager." *I was also stabbing your picture repeatedly with my furry pink unicorn pen after you'd confiscated my Stone Temple Pilots CD.* "You'd be in there for hours. If that's not to your liking, you could take a long, luxurious bubble bath, maybe with some of those nice bath bombs I've seen." *Certainly, and get a raging vaginal infection that has me scratching an unstoppable itch that dwells in my nether regions. In front of mixed company. Thanks, but no thanks.* "Honey, all in all, I just want you to enjoy yourself, not allow work to define you. I already made that mistake." He paused for a moment, then said, "Live your life, your *new* life."

My new life. This is a new life, isn't it?

Something struck her then. Dad's words were painfully accurate, and for some odd reason, he'd said the right thing at the right time. Her world revolved around her job. There was no denying that. Practically everything she did, every place she went, she had business on her brain. Who could she run into to shoot her shot? Who could she meet and rub elbows with? What conversations could she strike up to weave herself into the perfect position to offer her card to a millionaire or two? Even her dating life had suffered.

Some men had outright admitted that she was so career-focused, it made them feel, well, lesser than. She was a barracuda and she knew it. Emily always figured that if a man couldn't handle the fact she was driven, then he simply wasn't the one for her. But perhaps she did shoulder some of the blame? Her ex-boyfriend, Brian, an attorney and avid golf player who wished to turn pro, had stated that one of his biggest issues with her was that she put work above all else. She figured he'd just been blowing smoke up her ass to explain away his infidelity and how he'd make regular penile deposits in other women's accounts. As she'd tossed all his shit into a duffel bag and told him to get the hell out of the apartment they'd shared back then, she hadn't once considered that what he'd told her might have been true. But what if it had been? What if it still was the case?

"My new life," she said, repeating her father's words like

a mantra.

"Yes. Your new life. This is a brand-new start, a first chapter all over again. You're one of the privileged, a select few. You are so fortunate, Emily. You don't understand how worried I was." His voice cracked and her new heart broke for him. Yes, it was clear now. Something had been wrong, *terribly* wrong. "I couldn't tell you, I had to be strong for you, but after losing your mother, Em, I could not lose my daughter, too. I'd go insane. I know you already think I'm crazy." He chuckled. "But imagine that ten times worse." She hung her head and smiled as tears streaked her cheeks.

"I don't think you're crazy, Dad. Maybe *I* am, though." She sighed. "Hey, speaking of crazy, I need to confess something." She placed the phone down and put it on speaker as she leaned back to catch her breath. The tightness in her chest had returned.

"What is it?"

"I feel like, I feel different. Not like, in a bad way, but in the sense that I'm thinking things I've never thought about before, in a whole new way. It's kind of hard to explain."

"For instance?"

She took a moment to mull things over, second-guessing herself. Perhaps she should've never brought this up. The last thing she wanted was to sound kooky, out of her mind.

"Just strange dreams. Look, uh, I have a question." She'd decided to go down another path and change the topic. No need to open that can of worms. He'd call a shrink that did house calls for certain, and if that didn't work, he'd try to have her committed. That would be the last thing she needed.

"What's your question?"

"When I was a child, I didn't have many friends."

"That doesn't sound like a question."

"It's not." She chuckled. "That's just a fact. You and Mom kept me so sheltered, I barely had time to get to know anyone. But I don't think that was the main reason for my issue. I can't blame anyone, actually."

"That's absurd. What about summer camp? The horseback riding group? What about the acting classes and all the friends you made during high school and college?"

"Those weren't friends...just associates. I am talking about someone that I could pick up the phone and call at three in the morning to come pick me up from a bar because I was too sloshed to drive, no questions asked."

"What a lovely thought." They both laughed at that.

"I'm serious, Dad...a real friend. Someone who'd be there for me through thick and thin. I've heard people describe these borderline romantic friendships. Women who've been friends since they were babies or maybe met in college and are now in their sixties and still tight, close as butt cheeks. I don't have any friends like that."

"Am I not your friend?"

She smirked at his words. "You know what I mean. And besides, you tell me things I don't want to hear sometimes. Not exactly the comrade I had in mind." She poked fun at herself, and it felt good.

"Oh," he stated dully. "An enabler."

"Dad, basically, a friend that would do anything for me, and vice versa, regardless of my background. They would think I was fantastic even if I only had five dollars to my name. So, back to the subject at hand. I wanted to know if you remember that one girl I used to hang with in ninth grade? I can't recall her name." It was driving her crazy; the memory had popped into her head that morning, but for the life of her, she couldn't recall the girl's name. "She was really sweet and we used to have a lot of fun together. I even invited her over to the house several times."

"Hmmm, I'm sorry, Emily, I don't remember. There were so many young ladies in and out of here due to your popularity and associations you were involved with. You may feel that you didn't have a lot of friends, but it certainly seemed like you did. I'm certain your mother would beg to differ, too."

"Those were just people I was trying to impress, get them to like me. They never really liked me, Dad. No one really did…well, maybe a couple. Most of them were just using me or came to the house out of sheer curiosity. I bet they hated my guts. What a bitch I was, right?!" She gasped, shocked at the words coming out of her mouth. Where in the hell had they come from? Never had she said such things. Never had she thought of those visits that way until right then. Right *now.*

What is going on?

A wave of emotion flooded her and her eyes filled with angry, hurt tears. Rejection was a slow-plunging knife in the heart. It twisted back and forth, ever so gradually, dragging out death one woeful whimper at a time. She gripped her silky black nightgown, the material covering right over her heart, and squeezed.

"Emily," Dad said softly. "Why would you say something like that?"

"Because it's true! I realized it just now, Dad. It's like I never understood it before. I'd fooled myself into believing some lie, something I convinced myself was true, but it never was. I tried to…" She patted her wet face with the back of her hand. "I tried to have friends, but it didn't work out too well. Yeah, I had associates, Dad, plenty of them, but I always wanted a *real* friend. The kind you paint your nails with, gossip about boys you liked with. I never had that, not really. Well, I did for a brief time, but she wasn't popular so I got rid of her and now I can't even remember her name. I did all of those things, but I always knew the girls I hung out with didn't really care for me, didn't care if I was around. I bet they forgot my name, too."

"Don't say things like that."

"Why not? It's true." She sniffed as more tears rolled down her cheeks. "I was ostentatious, pushy. On the bright side, I enjoyed math. I wasn't boy crazy; I mean, I had my share of crushes and lost my virginity at seventeen, but it didn't rule my mind."

"I could have done without those details, but continue."

She could hear the smile in her father's tone. He was such a good man, a damn good man.

"Sorry, I guess I coulda kept that to myself. Anyway, I liked nice things but I understood the value of money and how it worked. You and Mom taught me that. I didn't want to grow up and be a model, actress, or plastic surgeon. I wanted to be a mathematical whiz! I only took acting classes because Mom believed it would help me with expressing myself better; she was right. My true passion was with numbers. I used to fantasize about teaching calculus at some elite college in Europe. I couldn't admit that to anyone or they'd hate me even more. That wouldn't be considered cool. I'd get the title of 'nerd,' on top of everything else. I was weird. So I struggled, ya know?"

"From the outside looking in, Emily, you appeared quite popular."

"Yes, it did look that way, but not everything is always as it seems. You know, Dad, if I would have vanished into thin air, no one would've missed me. In fact, they may have celebrated. The bottom line is that they were only there at the house because you and Mom were friends with their parents. Period. That's a friend by default, not by real connection. There's a difference, Dad."

"Emily, I don't know where all of this is coming from, but—"

"Nobody liked Emily Windsor...not a single person." She dropped her head and sobbed, not certain what had gotten into her. But it was pouring out like lava, burning her pretty, pretentious past all along the edges until it was reduced to a melted mess.

"Okay, that's it. Emily, you stop this pity party right now. None of what you're saying is true. You had a boatload of friends and they adored you. Besides, you're incredible. You've cheated death multiple times. I think the pain medication is making your brain loopy. Now look, I want you to get some rest. You'll feel better in the morning. I'll call you, okay?"

She nodded. Though he couldn't see her, she did it all the same.

"Maybe it's the pain medication and just the terrible ordeal I've had, like you said. Yeah, okay. I'm sure you're right." But deep down, she knew it wasn't the medication. Her mind was lucid, and she wasn't trapped inside a nightmare. This was a harsh reality. Something had blown the sheets off her life, her very existence, and exposed it to the elements. Something within her had split open and exposed a glowing certainty. It shined like a pearl from within a dull shell, daring her to come closer and check it out. And she did. She saw it for what it was.

The cold, beautiful, yet hideous truth. Now, it was time to take an even closer look, if she dared.

Three weeks later

"THE PSYCHOLOGIST SAYS I'm fine and the physical therapist said I've been cleared to walk, get a bit of exercise, as long as I don't do any long distance marathons. They don't want you sitting still for too long, but they also don't want you hanging from chandeliers quite yet, either. You surely don't have to worry about that."

Emily chuckled as she stood at the light amongst a crowd at the crosswalk, waiting to cross the street and get to the other side. She held the phone to her ear while her friend, Laura, berated her for being out of bed. She knew the woman meant well nevertheless.

"I just…well…I suppose if you feel up to it." Laura sighed.

Emily jogged in place a bit, her blue and black Lycra leggings hugging her calves just so and her matching jacket fitting a bit tighter than usual. She'd been bloated as of late and was certain she'd put on about ten pounds from being so sedentary. She was determined to get it off; after all, in two months, she had an important business affair to attend and she planned to wear the hell out of her dress that was being tailor made. The air felt great blowing against her face as she bounced about. The crowd around her grew as cars crawled past the green light, stuck in a bit of a jam. The light turned red at last.

Finally.

As she made her way amongst the migrating crowd, her legs moving quickly while the "Don't Walk" sign flashed, she heard music pouring out of a nearby car. She slowed, the tune calling to her as if the lyrics had been written with her in mind.

"Ah, Laura, let me call you back."

"Well, I was just going to—"

"I'll call ya back." She disconnected the call and approached the car that was now stuck in traffic. Several drivers honked at her as she made her way over to the black Toyota Corolla, not giving a single fuck that she was in the damn way. The driver, a White woman with red, wavy hair and thick dark-rimmed glasses, looked at her suspiciously, her bright blue eyes twinkling. Emily waved and smiled as authentically as she could muster. She was in a city known for lunatics and eccentrics, so she couldn't fault anyone for being too cautious. Yet, she was one of the lunatics now, too. "Sorry to bother you. Can I ask you something?"

"If it's money, no."

"Money? No, no, no." Emily chortled. "What uh, what song is that you're playing? I like it." After a brief hesitation, the woman turned it down a bit.

"It's 'Wait A Minute' by Willow Smith." The woman studied her hard, as if trying to decide whether to relax or whip out the Taser or switchblade she kept in her glove compartment.

"Willow Smith, you say?"

"Yeah, Will Smith's daughter. She's a singer. My friend told me about her. I don't usually go for the teenage music stuff." They smiled at one another. "But I like it. It's nice, right?"

"It's perfect. Really good, actually. I need to get a copy of that. I guess I'll download it from iTunes." She wanted to ask the woman for other recommendations, possibly ask what type of music she enjoyed, too. She wanted to talk to the lady about things like that. About places she might go to listen to a good groove, but Emily figured that would be far too bizarre. The woman might even think she was coming onto her. The traffic began to move again.

"Gotta go," the woman blurted, tucking her hair behind one ear.

"Yeah, thanks." Emily waved as the car inched ahead. She watched for a few seconds then jogged back to the sidewalk, her mind whirling. Never had she done such a thing in her life—walk up to a stranger and engage in conversation. The song kept playing inside her head, over and over, haunting her. It was beautiful. Simple. Joyous. It made her want to move, sing, stretch her arms out and spin about.

I want to hear it again. Willow Smith. Remember that name.

She stood on the sidewalk, the smell of the city wrapping around her like a comfortable shawl. The smells she took for granted, like baking pretzels, stale sweat, rotting trash, grilled meats, fresh citrus fruit, and beautiful roses all wafted in the air and woke her ass up.

"Do you smell that? I'm not dead. I'm alive." She cracked up laughing. She began to sway her hips from side to side and snap her fingers. She'd never considered herself a good dancer, but right then she was feeling the rhythm, and when she caught her reflection in a storefront window, she thought her movements were on point. Most of all, it all felt *normal*. No one paid her any attention, which made it all the better, all the richer, all the more incredible. Mouthing the lyrics to the song she'd just heard, she began to walk again, her new heart beating hard but not painfully. Minutes later, she realized she'd walked much farther than she'd anticipated. She was caught up in a daydream, her world full of strange, enchanting colors, emotions, and the like.

"I better turn around and go back," she muttered begrudgingly to herself, wishing she could stay out and people watch all night long. As she turned to go back to her digs, she spotted a couple, a woman and a man, with a large white dog in the near distance. The dog's thick, pink tongue flopped out the side of its mouth. She hated dogs.

Emily stiffened up as the couple approached, distracted, talking amongst each other, while their four-legged companion bounced happily on a leash. Rather than going on about her business as she'd normally do, she simply stood there, her fresh heart beating like a drum.

BEAT...BEAT...BEAT...

Her lips curled in a grin when they reached her, and her excitement shot through the roof.

"What's her name? Can I pet her?" she said eagerly.

The couple paused abruptly, then all three of them smiled at the same time.

"Uh, yeah. Her name is Abby. How'd you know she's a she? Everyone says he right off the bat." The woman laughed.

"You know what?" Emily reached down and ran her hand across the dog's head. She was so soft. "I don't even know. She just seemed like a she to me. She's gorgeous. Labrador retriever, right?" The dog appeared to truly be enjoying her touch.

"Yup," the guy said proudly, like a new dad.

"I won't keep you. Lovely dog, though."

"Thanks."

She slid her hand away and stood up straight. "Bye, Abby." She waved as the couple and their fur baby trotted off.

Emily stood there, fighting back emotions—prickly, unfamiliar feelings that made her want to burst into an explosion of tears. Where had these sentiments come from? How the hell did she even know what a damn Labrador retriever looked like? Her hands shook, her eyes filled with moisture. She sniffed her hand, and instead of being repulsed by the odor, wincing and bursting into the nearest restaurant to wash her hands, she found it in some way comforting, as if it were something she missed.

She began to walk back in the direction of her apartment, her feet pounding the pavement as she navigated through the crowd. Breathless, losing her mind, she pulled out her phone.

"Hi, yes. I'm a patient of Dr. Giannopoulos. I need to speak to him, please."

"Oh, I'm sorry. He's in surgery right now. Can I take a message?"

She hesitated for a spell.

"Uh, yes. Please tell him to call Emily Windsor back as soon as possible. My number is 212-555-0102."

"I have it now. I will pass this along."

"Thank you, and please, if you don't mind, tell him it's urgent."

"Well, in that case, ma'am, you may want to call 911."

"No, not urgent as in I am dying. I can't really explain it. Just uh, please…" She sighed, closed her eyes, and rested against the wall of a random building. "Just tell him to call me."

After disconnecting the call, she made her way back home. She showered, put on her thick, plum-colored robe, then sat at her small circular dining room table with Willow Smith's "Wait A Minute" playing off YouTube from her laptop and a bowl of vegetable soup cooling off to the side. She pulled up another tab on the browser and typed in:

Heart Transplant Patients – Change of Personality

Chapter Five
Mountaintops with Sunrays

RED LIGHTS GLIMMERED throughout the 6th Dimension Club while music played and thick cigar, hookah, and cigarette smoke filled up the place. It was almost one in the morning. Cameron fist-bumped, high-fived, and slapped hands with so many people who'd come to party at the club that night, some regular patrons and some newbies, that his wrist began to feel sore. It had been a while since he'd stepped foot inside the place for more than ten minutes. At times, it had been too painful to endure. He'd tried, but would find himself becoming overwhelmed. To avoid making a scene or drawing negative attention, he'd simply disappear, slink away before anyone caught him with a tear in his eye.

I haven't been taking this shit well at all. I gotta do this. I gotta find a way to put a stop to this.

He'd had no idea how much the spirit of the love of his life had been infused within the place until after her death. That was a huge issue, because he couldn't bring himself to go to work in that environment, not when it caused him so much pain. He'd created this business, followed his dream doing what he loved, and Brooke had been right by his side, helping him build his empire.

The deep purple color of the walls, for instance, had been Brooke's idea. He hadn't been on board at first, believing it too ladylike, but after it was finished, he had to admit that it was dope. It was the right shade of purple, dark with a slight reddish undertone, a color he hadn't imagined he'd like and would work so well. That had been just one of many of her ideas he'd rejected at the outset, but soon discovered she'd been onto something. The woman not only had the voice of a goddess, she had a damn good eye, too.

It had also been Brooke's idea to place gold-framed photos of many rap, jazz, and R&B greats as well as African-American and Latino poets on the walls. Not only world-famous ones, but local musicians, too. She wanted New Yorkers to be celebrated, and indie artists to get their just desserts and accolades. It had even been his baby's idea to have his Afro-Puerto Rican heritage on his mother's side celebrated, along with his paternal Black side, through displaying and promoting the artwork of Black and Afro-Latino local artists.

She'd helped him with the layout of the club, the featured drinks menu, the stage setup. One day, she'd shown up wearing paint-splattered jeans and an old ratty crop-top shirt that somehow made her look even sexier and had proceeded to help him and the crew take care of some handyman-type work. She hadn't seemed to know much of what she was doing, but he'd appreciated her efforts all the same.

On nights when her schedule was more open, before she'd blown up and became so well-known that she could no longer walk the streets without being recognized, she would even sing on his slower nights to help entertain the crowd, keep people in their seats and the drink orders coming. Brooke had been a bartender at a restaurant many years back, so she wasn't beyond getting behind the counter and pouring drinks when they were swamped with patrons. Cameron had never needed to ask her to do a thing. He'd just look over, and his baby would be gone, doing what needed to be done.

"Hey, man." His boy, Alfonso, placed his hand on his shoulder, shaking him out of his thoughts. "Good to see you tonight."

"Yeah, good to be here. I missed being here. It's good to be back. Nice seeing you, man. Thanks for coming out."

"Yeah, man. This is the place to be for some good drinks, neo-soul, and spoken word! The 6th Dimension is in the top three spots I check out for that sorta thing. No doubt, man."

"I appreciate that, man. I really do."

"Cameron, I uh, I don't know what to say. Ain't seen you since Brooke's passing, man. It's strange, for real. I knew her for so long, sometimes I forget she's gone, man. It just doesn't make sense."

Cameron hung his head briefly and nodded. "Yup. That pretty much sums it up. I'll check you out though, man. Have a good time tonight, all right? Your drink is on me. Just tell Bri that I said so."

"Thanks, man."

"No problem. Anyway, gotta go talk to the DJ for a second." They fist-bumped and Cameron made his way toward the Saturday night deejay, DJ Fly, and placed the bottle of beer he was holding down on the platform next to the guy's computer. Leaning close to him, he spoke loud into his ear.

"Yo, man, I'm gonna do a little somethin' tonight. A piece I wrote."

"Word?" DJ Fly grinned at him.

"Yeah. In a few minutes, put on the instrumental to "Crown Royal on Ice" by Jill Scott. Then, when I'm ready to start up, transition to "Alone Together" by Daley with Marsha Ambrosius, the instrumental version. Have it on repeat until I finish. This is gonna take a while. It's a long piece, but I've been holding a lot inside. Gotta detox, get it all out. I might lose my nerve, not drunk enough for this shit. Wanna clear my mind, though. It's long overdue."

"You got it, man."

Cameron bobbed his head to the beat of the music that was already playing as he stood high on the platform watching people dance, couples embrace, people sit and drink, all dressed and looking beautiful in their tapestry of soul and desire.

Smoke eddied toward the sky like the last syllable of a dying prayer. Cameron took the final drop of his liquid courage, tossed his empty bottle in a nearby trash can, and headed toward the main stage. He heard his musical request begin, grabbed the mic from the stand, and the club erupted into thunderous applause. Everyone seemed to know what was up.

He began to walk the stage, falling into the groove and gathering his thoughts.

"Hey, everybody. Hope everyone is having a good ass time tonight." Whistling and clapping ensued. "It's been a minute since I stood on this stage, but...it's time to re-emerge, come out from hiding. My baby made me come out.

She actually made me get my ass out of the bed, put my damn clothes on, and speak my mind." He smiled sadly and looked down at his shoes as people cheered him on. "She's not here anymore. She, uh, she got into my subconscious and did it, as crazy as it sounds. It's true. I know it's true."

His voice trailed at the end, and he wondered if he should stop before it was too late. "If any of you have ever lost someone you were in love with, then you know how I feel tonight." The room became so quiet, he could almost hear his own pounding heartbeat. "For those of you that don't know, this might be your first time here, or uh, you just don't know the details. Something terrible happened, all right?" He swallowed hard, mustering the courage to go on. "My girlfriend, my soul mate, my soon-to-be-wife, my queen, my better half, my *every*thing. She uh, she was accidentally shot and killed not too long ago."

He could hear people murmuring while others were yelling out words of encouragement. "Some days, I get up and think, 'Today, I'm okay.' Other days, I stay in bed all day. I just lie there, looking at the ceiling. It's just how it is." He shrugged. "So, I'm not going to delay this any longer. I just want to vibe with you all for a minute. I wanna say something to you all, and to my baby, my Brooke. Can I do that with you tonight?" The room erupted in applause. "That's what's up."

The music grew louder as he stood in the middle of the stage. The lights dimmed all around the club, but a red spotlight now beamed down upon his head.

"I was that rough Black kid from Brooklyn who grew into a

man. Had two hardworking parents with pensions and a plan. But I saw the world differently, couldn't sit still, would bend God's will, amen…

You know, the hood had my heart, smart kid that hung out in the streets. Beautiful, lovin' mother, strong Black father who refused to ever show weakness,

But I confess, I was a mess…Damn. So much strife and stress. One autumn day,

I was hearing a song…a voice that had wings.

I grew up in a matter of seconds, put away childish things to hear this Nubian queen sing…

She stood at the crosswalk wearing a tight pair of jeans…

And I tapped her on her shoulder, but she ignored me and kept doin' her thing…

No ring…Cool, she's single, at least no king…

But she must've smelled my doggish ways and wasn't impressed by the little bling.

I didn't have much back then, but I fronted, tried to play the role, you know,

To get the baddest chicks you had to pretend you ran the show.

She saw through that; she was not a new jack. She was in control…

And she left me standing there as she went on her little stroll. Alone.

I could still smell her perfume. It was like love libations, beehives and honeycombs. I was sticky from her soul, suddenly feeling forlorn…So I stepped out and chased her, like some dog on the roam, and she paused…

She paused…

She paused…

She turned to see me, said, 'Don't follow me. Why don't you go home? I don't want the shit you're selling; there is nothing you could say. Even if you were invisible, you would still be in my way…'

DAMN!

She said, 'I don't like your energy, your vibe. I don't like the way you sway. Your vibration is low like valleys, and I'm a mountain with sunrays.'

She didn't hurt me with her words, but she cut me with her eyes. I knew she was different from the rest. This was authentic, no disguise.

And still I rise…in every sense of the word, because this woman turned me on, so I ignored what I heard. Undeterred.

I asked her out on a date. She laughed and said, 'Boy, be gone…'

'I'm no boy, I'm a man—now I gave you time to talk. I followed you from a distance, because I like the way you walk. If you are willing, ready and able to try something new out for size, you'll see that I'm great, a prize…I'm more than meets the eye.'

She said, 'Oh really? I've heard that all before…This is the part that I choose to ignore.'

I told her, 'I am not infatuated with gold diggers, bimbos, and whores. You caught my eye, 'cause you're classy, show a little skin, not a lot…just enough, to feed femininity, make me respect you and make me hot.'

She said, 'It's summer, what did you expect?'

I told her, 'A date and a kiss on the neck…'

I come correct.

I come prepared—

'Try me out, if you dare…'

One week later we were fine, at a restaurant, sipping wine. She told me she sang, I told her I worked. She said that's good, paychecks are perks...

Now I'm not gonna lie, Brooke was fly. She caught the eye of most any guy...

But the sexiest part was her lack of care. Her confidence made me declare...that this was it.

If she was with another, I'd have a damn fit...

All other women aside, I had to have her. I could not hide...my true intentions, but did I mention...her kiss? Her kiss...her kiss...I died, and came back alive. It was her touch that became my biggest wish..."

He took a deep breath, his heart skipping beats, challenging the rhythm of the music, then continued...

"Weeks turned into months then years, she was healing my soul like a shaman...

I couldn't believe there was someone like me; we had so much in common. And she fixed vegetarian meals while I was still eating pork chops and ramen..."

Rustles of laughter radiated throughout the room.

"My temper isn't the best. She was the only person who could calm me down. People knew not to fuck with me, if my girl wasn't around. Incredible Hulk—I was sore, she was my Band-Aid, and so much more. I was cancer, she was chemo...I was lost, she was finding Nemo..." He smiled sadly.

"She found my ass, dusted me off. With her I could be vulnerable and soft...

Out in this world, the injustice of it all. I wore Timberlands to feel tall when sometimes I felt small. Marchin' with my Latino, African, and Black brothas down the street, wavin' our flags, demanding justice and peace…

There was a time when I was in the thick of it all.

Fightin', heavily strapped, ready to go to bat for the wrong damn thing…

Her voice became my elixir, I'd heard heaven sing.

Love changed me, made me realize I had to get this lady a ring…

Make this shit official, make her Mrs. Davis, ASAP, but some dude that I marched for, fought for, got put in jail for, came in and changed all of that…

The same mothafuckas that I begged the cops to stop killin' were ready and willin' to steal my joy. Stole the mother of my unborn baby girl and boy, from the vessel I'd planned to plant my seed…

But now the only seed I see is in a bad batch of weed…so I need a reason to get the fuck up in the morning, because the nights are covered in liquor and the days are a hazy blur…

I found myself fuckin' the sheets, dreaming she was beneath me, thinking my damn pillow was her…

I just wanted to touch her again…you know, to feel her hair and get a private taste…I just wanted to touch her heart and feel her sweet, warm breath against my face.

I just wanted to hear her complain about the rain, or some dude she almost had to mace…I just wanna hear her laugh about when we first met – how a dog named Cameron gave chase…

I just wanna wake up tomorrow and someone tell me that this entire time has been a dream…And then I look over to the other side of the bed, and there's that mountain with the sunrays…and there lying beside me is my Queen…

They say the good die young, but that's bullshit.

We all know fucked up people that died way after age thirty…

We know babies that die as soon as they take their first breath, and for life, surely they are more than worthy.

People have told me it gets better with time, but the wine is telling me that's bullshit, too…

Time don't do shit but draw out the pain. It stops tickin', and then what can you do?

Some say I'll meet someone else, as if that's what this is even about. I don't do shit for clicks and views, like on YouTube. I am not one to chase clout.

I don't give a shit about someone else to screw, someone to date, or the belief that things will get better. I'm not a glutton for abuse, and that's the truth – but how can you accept storms when you lived in a place always blessed with sunny weather?

I loved her from her thorny crown to her polished toes, and yeah, I know she'd want me to move on, to heal, not live this life, allowing time to stand still and impose. That's not how this goes. That's not how she rolled…

She saw everyone as fluid. We're energy, just sharing space and time and walking the path we chose…

The flesh is just an illusion, and in her conclusion,

life never ends, time is always prime. It just fast forwards and rewinds…

She told me no one ever truly dies; there is no such thing as death…

Well, if that's true, Brooke…then, uh, why doesn't my heart know that yet?

'Cause the damn dog was wailin' for a week, and for days, I could not speak...and your mother told friends that pain is sometimes bittersweet.

So, that's what we do — we cope, we tell ourselves these things, so we don't commit suicide...but deep down, we know that shit is all lies.

We've always known that it hurts, and it never goes away, but there are pieces of you, leftover clues, that are destined to stay...

I still find your hair sometimes. I used to complain about you clogging the drain...

Now I spend hours, just whispering your name. I know you're gone though, baby, but I'm so damn glad that into my life you came...

I don't own you — you had to go, so on your soul, I have no claim...

I'm so sorry for bein' selfish, and questioning God's plan for my life. It's just hard when he showed me my rib, and I knew you were going to be my wife.

So through this strife, I'm coming through, the lessons you taught me I won't forget...

But this love I have for you...what am I now supposed to do with it?

It's just...here, you know? It's big, taking up all this space.

I guess you'd say, give it to myself, or to the next woman...

But you can't be erased or replaced...

Everybody loved you, Brooke. You didn't have a single foe. To know you was to love you, completely...heart and soul...

So, I'm standing here tonight, cryin' my eyes out, but celebrating your life. I'm going to try to do what's best, I know, I know...tryna do what feels right.

'Cause I can feel you standin' around me. You can't even cross over right.

Because I haven't let go! You make me wake up in the mornings, you send Opium, or the alarm is real fucking loud. You're a familiar smell in the kitchen, you're a strange whisper in the crowd.

I've been drinkin', I've been sleepin', I've been getting high as a kite.

The other day, you shoved me and said, 'We're not doin' this same shit tonight!'

I swear to God I felt you push me, and I don't even believe in ghosts like that, but you made me a believer, telling me, 'Stop it, that's not how to act.'

I realized I had to get this out, say my piece, and at least try...but you got my ass up here, makin' me fall apart and cry. Got me lookin' like a pussy, when I'm a boss...but then you died...

You died...
You left me, baby, I tried,
then I lied to myself,
said, 'That's all right!'

Your mother told me the other day, 'Cameron, God is in control.'

I said, 'If He is, and he's the Wiz, then tell Him to restore my Heart and my Soul...'

Your mother said to me, 'He did! Her heart beats still to this day.'

Her soul is part of the human tapestry of the world. That always stays.

I want to tell you that I'm sorry, for anything I said to you in a hurtful way,

And I want to tell you that I'll always love you, Brooke, until my final day…

I know we'll be together again, but for right now, I am setting you free!

The next time you see me, I won't be sloppy drunk. I won't be all up in my feelings…This is it. The last of it…It's a good time to call it quits. But baby, you were a real one…Beautiful. Authentic. Legit.

I can't wait to look into your eyes again, and it'll happen, one of these days.

It took me years to be on your same soul vibration, but now, I'm at the top of the mountain with the sunrays…

Bye, baby…I gotta do right by you.

Because you're my heart and soul—you're the best part of me.

So with these final words, I'm lettin' go…

You're finally free…

to just…

be…"

His voice trembled and his knees buckled as hot tears streamed down his face. People jumped to their feet; the applause was deafening. In seconds, a small crowd rushed to the stage, each person wrapping their arms around him, pulling him in a tight embrace. He dove within himself, going to a quiet place. A safe place. A place where he could breathe…

Inhale. Exhale.

One solitary, labored, celebratory, healing breath at a time.

Chapter Six
On Repeat, Like a Broken Record

F *ACE THE MUSIC* sat wedged between a coffee shop with a tin roof and a little store with a red door that, according to the signage, sold vintage dirty movies, dildos, and obscene practical jokes. Emily entered the music store and immersed herself in an entirely new world for her. Some musical artist by the name of Marsha Ambrosius was featured on a glossy poster plastered in a lopsided fashion on one of the store walls. Emily paused and inhaled. The strong scent of sweet incense perfumed the air. People milled about, eyes focused on the shelves and racks, many of them sporting dreads, twisted braids, or long, stringy platinum-blond strands. *So odd looking. So bizarre.* Their bodies were clad in unusual attire, from weathered, fringed hippie vests to worn sneakers. Emily rubbed a palm nervously over her dark jeans, feeling out of place.

I shouldn't have come here. Why did I come here? Oh yeah.

But then, she remembered. She'd awakened that morning, desperate for a bean fix. After preparing some vile decaffeinated coffee, she went to her computer and turned on her new playlists at high volume and danced about her apartment, without a single care in the world. Moments later, she'd gotten a wild hair up her bottom to find some place to purchase physical albums, the kind she could hold in her hand. She didn't want the new stuff but older, classic tunes from legendary artists, but it shouldn't have come as a surprise; she'd been on a music binge for the past two weeks. It had gotten so bad, the desire to hear the music now interrupted her sleep. But there was a welcome payoff: the nightmares had ceased.

She'd get up at three in the morning like clockwork, turn on her computer, and search for songs she dug, music that reached inside of her and danced with her soul. She'd sway and groove all over her house, sometimes butt naked, becoming intoxicated from the sounds. Musicians she'd never heard of before, she suddenly fell deeply in love with, and proceeded to purchase their music from iTunes and Soundcloud. But it was never enough; it didn't stop there. She needed more. This was when the research began.

She was soon reading articles about the life of a musical duo called "Outkast." She abhorred rap and hip-hop music as a rule of thumb, and yet, she liked this group. Something about their style of rap music was different; it felt futuristic in some way, and the lyrics, though at times belted out at a fast pace, she could understand. On occasion, she could even relate to them.

Emily's digging didn't stop there, though. That was only the beginning of the madness. Some strange musical genre called neo-soul, one she'd never heard of that sounded like poetry married to seductive, slow guitar riffs and deep drums, became her ear-gasmic lover.

She'd stumbled across an eccentric and outrageously brilliant woman named Erykah Badu via her research on Outkast. Apparently, one of the men had dated the woman for some time, eons ago, and they shared a son. Emily was done once she heard Ms. Badu's voice. That was the moment the dark purple rabbit hole got deeper...*much* deeper. She'd watched enough YouTube videos of the singer's concerts and interviews to practically know the lyrics of several of her hit songs.

And then there was her entirely different journey to the land of rhythm and blues and classic jazz. The final piano stroke, denoting her fall from grace, was when she admitted that this was her new addiction, and it felt amazing to float on cloud nine, so high. Classic jazz and southern blues were now an obsession in the truest sense of the word. She simply couldn't let it go. This was completely out of the ordinary. In the past, her preferences were stuck to a few pop and contemporary country tunes, not quite minding Celine Dion's masterpieces, Charlie Puth, Adam Levine, Meghan Trainor, and Ed Sheeran's newest selections. Now, the possibilities were endless. The gates had been blown wide open.

"Hey, how ya doin'? You look like you might need some help. Can I help you with anything?" a tall Black man asked, rocking and rolling her out of her deliberations of how she'd ended up there in the first place. His skin was so opaque, it reminded her of rich dark velvet one may find on the lapel of a 1974 suit jacket collar. His thick black hair was dreadlocked, pulled back in a ponytail, and draped down his back like ropes. She couldn't help but wonder if it was clean. Did it smell?

"Uh, no, thanks though. I'm just uh...just browsing."

The man nodded as his smooth, purplish lips curled in a smile, showcasing almost perfect snow-white teeth, one on the bottom row a tad bit crooked. For some reason, that fit him, made him all the more beautiful. Beautiful? Yes. The whites of his eyes were practically sparkling like crushed stars blended with the brilliance of the Milky Way, and though she tried to not stare, it was damn near impossible. Emily looked into those eyes and a strange sense of peace came over her. She wasn't looking through him, she was looking *at* him, and he was mesmerizing. He wore a poncho-type shirt in vibrant stripes of lemon yellow and lime green, and his slightly wrinkled tan cargo pants had large pockets, one of them clearly holding something heavy. She wondered for some odd reason what was in it. Perhaps a phone or wallet.

"Well, let me know if you change your mind." She nodded in appreciation. "I'm the manager. My name is Kem. We've got a twenty percent off sale today too, on all posters. All of this month we've got a program where if you donate any of your old CDs or cassettes, you can—"

"CDs or cassettes?" She laughed. "Really? Those are still around?"

Kem shrugged and tossed her a friendly smirk.

"Yeah, I know, but there's a buyer's market for them again. You'd be surprised. Anyway, as long as they're in good working order, you will receive a ten percent voucher for each off your next purchase, up to five, so you could get fifty percent off one item just like that." He snapped his fingers.

"Well, I don't have any CDs or cassettes, but I'll pass that information on. Thanks for letting me know."

"Yeah, no problem."

He walked off, not gone for a few seconds before someone waved him down for assistance. Forty minutes later, she found herself heading to the cash register with a heavy red basket chock full of secondhand albums featuring the likes of Duke Ellington, Frank Sinatra, Charles Mingus, Mongo Santamaría, Donna Summer, Prince, The Police, and Eurythmics, just to name a few. When it was her time to be rung up and pay for her finds, the cashier, a White woman with light-brown dreadlocks, dramatic black cat-eye winged liner, and a matte red lip that truly was to die for tossed her a sly grin.

"Wow...You did good, girl. You have excellent taste."

"Thanks." Emily's cheeks flushed. "You had some pretty good bargains. I'll have to come back in a few weeks to see what other gems I can find."

"Yeah, we get new stuff in all the time."

Emily realized she'd not told the entire truth. She didn't give a damn about a bargain. If she wanted something badly enough, she had the means and resources. She rarely went to such stores, especially ones like this in a strange area of Harlem to boot, but ordering the items online or hiring a middleman to fetch them on her behalf wasn't an attractive option, either.

She'd been driven to place her body within those walls, to stand there and inhale the scent of the dusty, dank aromas of old shit people had tossed aside from their basements and attics. Shit they'd once held dear. And it felt so natural to walk among music enthusiasts and aficionados of their genre of choice, to hear sounds through speakers that somehow pacified her soul. She surmised this place was much like some people's church. They entered, they prayed, they paid.

"You seriously lucked out. We just got this Eurythmics one here this morning. You snagged it before I could get my hands on it." The woman grinned as she placed it inside a plastic bag, a mixture of adoration and 'woe is me' on her face. "Sweet dreams—"

Emily belted out the words of the song, the lyrics rolling off her tongue, line after line, like waves from an ocean. Her voice boomed over the soft, tranquil jazz music playing in the store, sounding out of place, yet, fitting in some odd way. She could feel eyes on her from all around, but she kept right on, compelled to keep on crooning the lyrics until she'd finished half the damn song. Pockets of applause burst throughout the establishment once she forced herself to shut her damn mouth, and the effort was immense. The cashier's sparkling blue eyes grew wide and then she cackled and slapped the counter, a shocked expression on her face.

"Lady. You can *really* sing. Wow. See? Looks are deceiving."

"What do you mean?"

"You look like someone that would be on Wall Street, maybe even an elite lawyer. But you've got soul."

Emily's heart was beating a mile a minute. Where had the dynamic, robust voice come from? It was hers, that much was certain, not a disembodied sound or an echo from some shy songstress. It was definitely coming from within, spilling out for all to hear, but it was oddly surprising—foreign, an invader. It was finely tuned, yet cracked a bit initially, as if it were a baby bird trying to fly from the nest for the first time.

By the time she'd reached the second verse, she was in full swing, had complete control, not one note out of sync. She sounded melodic, laden with raw talent, blessed with ability she'd never possessed a day in her life. Her voice held each note like a lifeline and didn't dare let go.

If anyone was shocked, it was *her*.

"Uh." She laughed nervously as the employee shoved the receipt in one of the plastic red and black bags with the store emblem that resembled a genie bottle and handed it to her. "Thank you."

"You're welcome. You have a great day and enjoy your music."

When she exited the store, she decided to board a bus, something she'd last done as a child with her mother when they'd gone into town for a special Christmas play.

Emily changed modes of transportation and caught a cab ride into Lower Manhattan. After that, she decided to get out of the cab near Grand Central Station. She found herself bypassing several illegally parked taxi cabs and not reaching for her phone to call an Uber or Lyft, either. Instead, she made her way to the subway.

She hadn't ridden the subway in years. She hated the horrid heat of the place in the summers, and the bone-chilling bite of it during the winters. She detested the begging street performers who'd do odd things, like contorting their bodies to flute music in order to render a guilt-tripped coin tossed in their hat. She loathed the strange people who wandered about, drugged out of their damn minds or just plain insane—yelling at themselves in a foreign language or perhaps one they'd made up all on their own.

The subway smelled like rotten piss and dejection, and she typically wanted no part of it. Besides, she had money to do otherwise, and often drove when she didn't mind fighting traffic. Today, though, she was climbing down rows of concrete steps, going deep into an underworld filled with tunnels she had practically forgotten even existed.

Several minutes later, she was trying to recall how to use the damn MetroCard. With a little help from some androgynous Hispanic teenager sporting a long, dark brown river of waves and a heavy emerald-green backpack, she managed and soon was on the train. She knew she was going the wrong way as she sat there taking in the sights of people wearing earbuds or chatting with a friend, but didn't really care. She took a deep breath, then another, before pulling out her phone and checking her call log.

She'd contacted her doctor several times, but had yet to receive a call back. She swallowed hard and lowered her gaze, focusing on a crumpled silver gum wrapper on the ground. Her eyes watered as worry, excitement, and fear of the unknown consumed her. Cradling her bag of albums to her chest, she drifted away in senseless daydreams as she perused the streets. When she'd had enough, she got off the train and exited the subway. She stood outside for a spell, breathing slow and easy, taking in the sights, the smells, her surroundings. She spun in several directions, trying to get her bearings. She didn't feel lost, but she certainly didn't feel found, either. Making her way up the street, she clung to her sack of songs, then paused and leaned against a bodega window. The smells of fresh salads and fruits drifted out of the place. Pulling out her phone from her pocket once again, she sighed and dialed her doctor.

Maybe this time I can reach him.

"Hi, this is Emily Windsor. I have called several times for Dr. Giannopoulos. I—"

"I'm sorry, he's gone for the day. You can call back tomorrow or—"

"I know he's gone. I don't mean to interrupt, but this is really important. I'm a patient of his. He had his assistant or whatever she was contact me a few days ago, but she wasn't really any help and I asked her to have him call me directly. She said that she would, but he didn't. I need to speak to him. Tonight. Please." Tears wet her cheeks as her emotions overflowed. "I had a heart transplant. I came in for my follow-up and couldn't speak to him because he was out of town then. It's always been something, ya know? Someone else examined me, and they did a fine job I suppose, but this situation is one that I wish to speak to him and him alone about. I don't mean to sound desperate, but I am. Please, I am begging you. Have Dr. Giannopoulos call me as soon as possible. I just can't talk to anyone else." There was a long silence on the other end. "I'm just so frustrated. My life...my life is falling apart."

"I'm sorry that you're havin' such a hard time. I tell you what. Hold on a second, okay?"

"Okay."

Several minutes later, the evening receptionist returned to the phone. "He's not the doctor on call tonight, but I did leave a message for him on his private emergency line, all right?"

Emily smiled as the tears continued to fall. She was grateful for the woman's compassion in her time of need, regardless of the possible outcome.

"Thank you so much."

"You're welcome. He's pretty good about checking messages on there because they're usually critical in nature. Call back later if he doesn't call you in the next two hours or so, okay?"

"I will. Thank you again." Emily disconnected the call then requested an Uber.

It wasn't until forty-five minutes later that she realized how far away from home she'd traveled. Once she entered her apartment, she was relieved to find the nurse gone for the day. The nurse was now only working part-time hours, much to Emily's father's chagrin. She pulled out the record player she'd ordered from Amazon.com, removed the Duke Ellington album from its sleeve, and placed it on the turntable. Then, she prepared some microwave popcorn—sadly for her, without butter. She wasn't supposed to consume fatty foods until further notice. While the snack popped, she poured herself a glass of ice-cold diet cola, turned off the album, then made her way to her living room. Folding one leg under herself on the couch, she reached for the remote and turned on the television.

Let's see what's on Cinemax. Hmmm, maybe HBO or hell, even Lifetime. Someone's life has got to be more bizarre than mine right about now.

Her phone suddenly rang. She snatched it up once she saw a telephone number she didn't recognize.

"Dr. Giannopoulos?" she blurted out.

"Yes, hi Emily." She took a deep sigh of relief upon hearing his voice. "I understand you needed to speak to me directly. Everything okay? I was told you were quite upset."

She ignored the microwave signaling her, letting her know her snack was piping hot and ready to go.

"Dr. Giannopoulos, there's no easy way to put this, but uh, first I'll just ask for what I need and go from there."

"What is it you need?"

"I would like to know who my donor was. It's been on my mind a lot lately and it would really help me from an emotional standpoint at the very least. I understand that the donor left voluntary personal information about herself for the recipient of her heart. I'd like to know what that information is."

"Well, I'm not at the office right now and don't recall her name off the top of my head. I do remember, however, that she had given consent for such information to be given to you should the recipient of her heart request it. Let me see, uh..." He seemed a bit distracted, then she heard papers shuffling about. "Let me make a couple of calls and get back to you in a few minutes, okay?" Anxiety filled her like a vessel. "I promise I won't take too long."

"Okay, thanks." She disconnected the call, retrieved her popcorn from the kitchen, and returned to the comfortable couch, this time pulling a sage-green blanket over her body as she lay on her side, gazing at the television. As soon as she took a bite of her food, her phone rang again. This was a different number altogether. She snatched it up. "Hello?"

"It's me calling from my landline. Okay." She could hear what sounded like him typing. "I got the password from a colleague to look in the database. Here it says, for you, that your donor's name is Brooke Coleman."

"Brooke Coleman," Emily repeated, saying it over and over in a whisper. "Anything else?" She sat up and put the television on mute.

"She was African American, age thirty."

Emily swallowed and played with the collar of her cream night shirt.

She was Black?

"What uh, what was her profession? Does it say what she did for a living?"

"Hmmm, let's see…Says here listed for occupation, she was a singer."

The phone tumbled from her hand. She could hear the doctor calling out to her as she fell to the ground, groveling about trying to retrieve the damn thing.

"Yes, yes, I'm here. Sorry." She laughed nervously. "I dropped it by accident. Anything else?" She sat back down on the couch, breathing hard and heavy. Sweat broke out all over her body, making her gown stick to her flesh.

"Well, she was in great health, that's for sure. Says here under hobbies that she enjoyed walking around a lot. She also did yoga, just like you. She was a vegetarian, worked out sometimes, too. Of course, beauty is in the eye of the beholder, but according to this photo, she was a very attractive woman, too. Quite pretty."

"Was she married? Any children?"

"I see she wasn't married, no children either, but she was in a long-term relationship with a boyfriend, whom she lived with."

"Any other hobbies listed? Interests?"

"Let's see. Okay, here's something. She listed singing, naturally, poetry, fashion, the vegetarian lifestyle, and cooking, dog parks and—"

"Dog parks? She had pets?"

"Yes, a dog, but I don't know what breed or anything. Emily, what is this all about? Or are you just genuinely curious?"

She sat there twisting that collar tighter and tighter, not certain if she should be truthful and risk being ridiculed or worse, called crazy.

"I'm curious. I was just…Oh, the hell with it. Can I ask you something?"

"Yes."

"Have you ever had any of your heart transplant patients, like, have a change of personality after an operation?" She was met with a wall of silence.

The doctor cleared his throat.

"I have not personally heard of any of my patients stating that, but I…Never mind."

"No. Tell me, please."

"Well, I have heard of a few rare cases where some patients believed that their personalities had somehow transformed, if you will. That they weren't completely themselves anymore after the surgery."

"Did they say they took on the personality traits of the person who'd donated their heart?"

"Not in all cases. Some just stated that they felt different, as if their thoughts, passions, and desires were different than they used to be. I attribute that to people valuing their lives more, quite honestly. The surgery you had makes some people reflect on life differently, cherish it more, if you will. Do you…Do you feel out of sorts, Emily? If so, I have a list of wonderful counselors I can refer you to who can help."

"Thank you. I may take a look at your list after all. Yeah, a bit out of sorts you could say—that's a good way to put it. Thank you for calling me back, Dr. Giannopoulos."

"Emily?"

"Yes?"

"You sound different. Are you okay? Do you need to come to the hospital?"

"I'm fine." She squeaked the words out as she ran her hand through her hair and pressed her eyes shut. "I guess it's an adjustment period is all. I wanted to know who'd been my donor, too. I'm quite surprised."

"Some people want to know, some don't. It's a completely private choice and understandable either way. I'll be in the office tomorrow, okay? Call me if you need anything. I can have that list of counselors emailed to you, as well."

"That sounds good, and thanks again. I know you weren't scheduled tonight, so I appreciate you making an exception for a non-urgent call. I know you're quite busy, so yeah. Thanks."

"Emily, please don't take this the wrong way, but you seem subdued in a way, not as high strung. You also are showing gratitude."

"Yeah, so?"

"Well, how do I put this? Look, I am so proud of you for making efforts to slow down your life and smell the roses, as they say. Even the nurse that left me the voicemail said, 'A nice but unhappy woman called and needs you right away.'

When she said your name, I thought she had the wrong person." He chuckled. "Emily, nice? What a joke." He guffawed.

She rolled her eyes and sucked her teeth. "Thank you, Dr. Giannopoulos. That helps a bunch."

"That was terrible of me. I'm sorry." She could still hear him chuckling. "I truly apologize if I sound uncaring, but this is just such a pleasant surprise and it seems to me that you've taken the advice that has been given to you. I can already hear the improvement in your mood. If I don't hear from you soon, I'll see you in a couple weeks, just as scheduled for your next follow-up regarding your lesion that's formed where we made the incision."

"What about getting it looked at by a surgeon?"

"Yes, I remember. You'd stated you'd be interested in plastic surgery for the wound if it didn't look the way you wished. We can discuss that, however, six months from now when it's had time to fully heal. I want to be able to make a good assessment of the situation, and it's just too soon right now to determine that."

"Okay, I understand. Thank you again for calling me back. I'll see you soon."

"Good night, Emily."

"Good night, Dr. Giannopoulos." Emily ended the call, stood from the couch, and made her way to her bedroom to retrieve her MacBook, then headed back into the living room. After turning the music back on, she got situated on the couch and turned the muted television off. She took a sip of her cola, then placed the computer across her lap and typed: *Brooke Coleman New York City singer.*

She began to scroll the various Google links, looking at pictures and reading countless headlines.

Okay, that's not her. That woman is in her fifties. That's not her, either, or at least, I don't think so. Wait a minute, this might be her.

Up-and-coming singer shot and killed. What? Hang on, that date coincides with when I had my surgery. Oh my God.

Fifteen minutes later, Emily's face was soaked with tears. She'd read of the untimely death of a woman who, according to the articles she'd dug up, was already a local legend, even at the tender age of thirty. She kept reading through the tears, the blurred sight. Two more diet sodas and a decaf coffee later, well into the wee hours of the morning, she was still scrolling through photos of the gorgeous lady, played a YouTube video of her singing, and sobbed uncontrollably throughout the entire performance. Not an emotional person by nature, Emily was certain she was now losing her mind.

She hadn't even noticed that the record had been skipping. Getting to her feet, she made her way over and cut the album off. She leaned against her wall, ankles crossed and eyes closed.

Her curiosity was piqued. This was it. There was no going back.

I want to know everything about you, Brooke, and I mean everything. I know you are within me. I can feel you. I'm so confused, this sounds so crazy, but I feel like if I look into your life, everything will be all right.

Emily blinked back tears as she reflected on her conversation with Dr. Giannopoulos. For one, she'd been startled that her donor was Black. She had assumed the woman had been White—perhaps the wife of some baseball player or an attorney who'd perished after a car crash. None of what she'd envisioned about her donor was true. The lady who had literally given her her heart embodied so many traits that Emily didn't care for or struggled with.

Art, creativity, nonconformity.

She made her way back over to her computer and after a bit of intrusive digging, found out her last known address. She had no idea what she'd do with the information, but she knew she wished to see it, walk past the building, take a step where Brooke had moved her feet, lived her life. Emily quickly sent herself a text message with the details of the address then fell fast asleep on the couch.

There were no dreams of white caskets and drums—only white noise that played within her brain, and the throb of her beating heart.

Chapter Seven
White Privilege

CAMERON AND OPIUM passed Peas 'N Pickles restaurant as they enjoyed an afternoon walk.

"Opium, I'm hungry as hell. I skipped lunch, was too busy working on the computer today. Damn. Let's go back home. Maybe I'll stop and pick up some spaghetti or something like that along the way." Opium barked and began to walk a bit faster, too. "Don't go getting all excited." Cameron chortled. "I bet you want a little something too, but I'm not sharing my food with you, Opium. You've got your own and it costs a lick."

He put his earbuds in and played Ella Mai's, "Shot Clock." The sound of the music vibrated through him as he paused every now and again, allowing Opium to do his business or sniff a pole that was of great interest.

"Opium, we got food at home. I just remembered that leftover pizza. Guess I'll smash that tonight, along with that piece of carrot cake I picked up a couple days ago from Hannah's birthday party. Who the hell has a carrot birthday cake? Hannah, that's who." He grinned at that.

As he drew within seeing distance of his apartment, he noticed a woman standing in front of his building, her hands in her black swing coat pockets. The hem of the garment blew in the draught, as did her long, straight, blonde hair that was parted down the middle. Her feet were encased in red high heels below matching, form-fitting pants. The shit looked mad expensive.

She crossed her arms, but kept her eyes on the windows, as if waiting for someone important to poke their head out and wave her inside.

"'Sup," he said, startling her as he removed his earbuds and jammed them in his pocket. He laughed when she jumped, hand on chest, then smiled. "Didn't mean to scare you. You need some help or something?"

The woman studied him for a while, never answering his question. Perhaps she was surprised he didn't say anything out of place, off-putting. "You okay?" he asked.

Opium begun to sniff the woman's shoes and jerk on the leash, trying to get at her. "What are you doing? Opium, stop it." The dog pulled hard, straining to break free, whining and jumping at her, flipping the hell out. He didn't seem agitated but more amused...excited. She took a few steps back, confusion on her face. At least she wasn't afraid. Opium let out a series of deep barks. "Sorry. He never does this."

"It's okay," she said softly. "Beautiful dog, by the way. That was a nice greeting." She smiled big and wide.

Cameron swallowed as he took notice of her lips, the bottom one a tad fuller, painted red, then her eyes, and her mouth once again. Something about the sound of her voice was soothing, like a lullaby.

"Yeah, so uh, everything okay? You know someone who

lives here?"

The woman kept staring. After long moments, she lifted her chin and smiled—but a smile marinated in sadness.

"No. Well, perhaps. You know what? The architecture of these apartments and the condos in this area are amazing. Truly lovely."

"Yeah, they're nice, right? I stay here. The rent is high as hell, but worth it." He offered a half smile.

"You're right. It's definitely worth it. If you can swing it, it's a great investment, too. You're in walking distance from practically everything you need, and the neighborhood is safe, too. Great places to eat, parks, you name it. Amazing schools from what I hear." She crossed her arms over her chest.

"Are you a real estate agent or somethin'? Is the owner selling the building?"

"Me?" She pointed to herself. "Oh, no, no. I was just uh...taking a walk is all and stopped to admire the place."

"Oh, all right, well...I'll let you get back to admiring." He cracked a smile before making his way around her and up the steps. He paused, turned around, and the lady was still standing there, staring up into the windows as if they held the answers to all of her life's questions. "There's probably a spot comin' up for rent soon. Maybe you can sublet it."

She arched an eyebrow. "Really? I thought there were no vacancies."

"There aren't, but I'm thinking about moving. I imagine probably in the next few months."

"Moving? Someone will snap this spot up in a flash."

"Yeah, probably." He wrapped the leash around his wrist

and led Opium back down a few steps, toward the White woman with the long, blonde hair that blew in the wind.

"This place is nice. If nothing else, I could see renting it out," she said.

"Hey, you got a card or something? If I decide to let it go, I could give you a call." The woman pulled out a card from her red leather purse and handed it to him. He looked down at it and read it aloud.

"Emily Windsor—Chief Financial Analyst for the Windsor Financial Group, Rockefeller Center. Damn. Nice. You're a financial analyst, huh?"

She smiled and nodded. "Yeah."

They were quiet for a spell, just looking at one another.

"Shit, I could use some tips, Emily. I mean, I have a financial advisor, but I don't know if I am getting the proper bang for my buck, if you know what I mean. I have investments too, things I want protected."

"What do you do for a living?"

"I own a specialized club. The 6th Dimension."

"A nightclub?"

"Not quite. We cater more toward the art scene. I try to transcend and educate while entertaining, not a shake your ass type of place. I bring in poets, we have wine and art nights and we have some serious slam talent." She nodded in understanding. "We serve tapas, too. I've got some amazing staff. We're known for our great drinks and singers, for the aesthetics. Local and national artists come to perform. Had Saul Williams just last week. He's the GOAT. Ever heard of Saul Williams?"

"No. Sorry."

WHAT THE HEART WANTS

"Well, he's dope."

"He's a goat?"

He couldn't help but crack up. "It's just a figure of speech, means he's incredible. Anyway, we have a lot of interpretive dancing, performing. It's chill, you know?"

"Chill?" Her lips curled upward. "I like how you say that. Well, good for you. Sounds like a really interesting place. Is business going well?"

"Extremely." He pointed to the building behind him. "It's the only way that I could ever afford to stay in a place like this. Bills aren't my worry right now. But uh, I have a lot of memories here. Some I may need to let go of…most of them are good memories, but not even good memories are always good, if you know what I mean. I have to do it for my own sanity."

For some reason, he was enjoying the banter with this broad. It wasn't amounting to much, just typical chitchat with a little zing, but he enjoyed the twinkle in her eye, her energy, her vibe. Cameron could talk to all sorts of people and find a commonality, a thread, though he had to admit, talking to glamorous, swanky White women wasn't his typical thing. Nevertheless, he liked the way she spoke, the way her voice wrapped around the words, regardless of how proper she spoke and how stiff she appeared, as if her muscles were locked up. She was well put together. He could tell she put a lot of thought, time, and energy into her appearance. She looked rich without being bitchy. It was nice. He dug it.

"I hope I'm not imposing, but what memories do you want to run from? I mean, it seems like things are going well for you." She cocked her head to the side and appeared to look right through him. As he faltered, trying to find the best way to respond, Opium broke free from his grip and made a mad dash in her direction.

"Shit. Opium, cut it out." He raced toward the dog and got him back under control, but by that time, it was too late. Opium had jumped high and licked her face. Emily was laughing so loud, it was practically unnerving. She stooped low and ran her hands all over the dog's fur, hugging and squeezing him like they were the best of friends. Opium was fairly friendly, but not that way with strangers. In fact, he was a growler whenever someone even rang the doorbell, rather protective by nature. His behavior right then was just plain weird.

"Sorry again. I don't know what's gotten into him to-night."

"He's fine." She finally got to her feet, but Opium stayed put by her side. "You don't have to apologize."

"I take it you're a dog lover."

"Not really."

A long pause stretched between them.

"That's too bad. You're missing out. My uh, my girl-friend loved dogs. This is her dog, actually. We both lived here. Those are the memories I was talking about earlier. She passed away not too long ago, so I'm just takin' care of him now all by my lonesome. Single dad," he joked, forcing the words out, trying to break away from the beginning stages of another funk.

Her smile disappeared within a snap of a finger. Her brows bunched and she pressed her hand against her chest.

She took a few steps back, stumbling. "Hey lady, are you okay?"

He grabbed her arm, stopping her from falling and busting her ass, or worse yet, her head on the concrete. He caught her around the waist and they stared deeply into each other's eyes. His heart began to beat a mile a minute. In those blue eyes was that sparkle again, that twinkle that made him feel warm all over.

"I'm fine. Thank you so much." She took a few deep breaths and snuck a brief glance at the building, then opened her mouth, hesitating, as if she had so much more to say but had no clue how to start. "You know my name, but I don't know yours."

"Oh, my bad. Yeah, it's Cameron." He extended his hand to shake hers. The act felt so formal, when he had the odd sense it shouldn't have been. "You got some sorta health problem? You seemed to get dizzy all of a sudden. Should I call 911?"

Suddenly, tears began to well up in her eyes.

Okay, this is ridiculous. First Opium is acting a fool, now this. This White lady is fucking crazy. She goes from laughing to crying, almost passes out. Probably schizophrenic or something. Why do I always attract people like this? Oh well, at least it'll make the night interesting. He chuckled to himself.

"Cameron, I was sick. Actually, I was sick for a very long time, on and off most of my life. I was born with congenital heart disease. I uh..." The tears fell as she looked down at the sidewalk for a moment, then back into his eyes. "I had surgery though, a couple of months ago. And since then, some really, really wild stuff has been going on in my life."

She shifted her gaze to the cars going past as if needing a moment, then faced him again.

"Damn. I'm sorry about that. Are you doing better now though? Did the surgery fix the problems?"

"So far, so good, but I have other issues to deal with now."

"Like what?"

"I don't know how to quite tell you this, but, I think…I think your girlfriend was my heart donor. I was given her name, found her address, and came out here. I took a walk around the block and came right back to this spot. I just needed to be here, even if only for five minutes."

Everything got heavy at that moment—his shoes, his shirt, the sky, the sun, and the moon and the stars, too.

The world sat on his shoulders like bricks stacked one on top of another. Before he could speak, before he could turn and run away, before he could even breathe, Emily tugged at her blouse, pulled it down a smidgen and exposed the top part of an angry red scar.

"This is where they cut me."

He looked at the incision, his chest now heaving up and down. His fist balled up, his hand rose to reach out, to touch, then he stopped short.

"I think you better go." He grabbed Opium and turned to walk away, his heart beating so damn fast, it hurt.

"I didn't expect to run into you. I didn't even know anyone was still here."

"Well, now you do. Bye."

"I just wanted to see where she lived. I had to see it, because, I don't know, I can't explain it, but I needed to lay my eyes on where she slept, ate, and laughed."

He paused and turned back toward her. His shoulders slumped and stayed that way, no matter how hard he tried to tough the shit out. Too much was happening too soon, too fast.

"See, this is that White entitlement bullshit I can't fucking stand. You think you can find out about my woman's death and sacrifice, come over here, and think it'll be okay? She had a name, damn it. Brooke was amazing. How damn disrespectful. This isn't a game, something to play with. We're real, this is my life. I'm not some freak show for you to gawk at. You can't just pop up like this, you can't do shit like that. I'm a real fucking person, not a puppet." He pointed at himself. "It's all about what *you* wanted. You didn't even think about what would happen after you got here, did you? You've got what you wanted, now go home. I hope you're happy."

"Far from it." She blinked away tears.

"I just had the first week, since Brooke passed, when I didn't wake up screaming," he said through gritted teeth, pointing a finger at her. "This is my first week of not drinking until I can get myself back under control. This is the first week I felt kinda like myself again. The first week I could stand on my own two feet without fallin' apart. I wouldn't wish this kinda pain and grief on my worst fucking enemy. And then, here you come, busting outta nowhere, stalking my fuckin' home. Go away, please. Like, for real. NOW."

"I'm sorry. I didn't mean to upset you." Emily clasped her hands together, her pale skin now donning a peachy glow about the forehead and cheeks.

What did I expect her to do? She more than likely didn't even know she was talking to Brooke's boyfriend, didn't know who I was. I still can't do this shit though, I just can't. He climbed to the building entrance, away from her, and shoved his key in the front door, ushering Opium inside the shared foyer area.

Before he could get up the steps to his crib, he heard her yell out, "I am so sorry, Cameron. She makes me sing. She makes me remember. She makes me cry. She makes me dance. It wasn't my choice. She made me come here. She must've known I'd see you. She must've known." And then, she turned and walked away.

Chapter Eight
Eat Your Heart Out

"MY DONOR WAS Black." Emily leisurely crossed her legs, forcing her slate-gray, knee-length skirt to slide ever so slightly up her knee. She flipped through the pages of a *Vogue* magazine, then set her gaze upon her father, who was lounging in his office chair at his home. The room smelled of rich vanilla and tobacco. Dad took a sip of his gin, then set it down, his eyes on her the entire time. Fingers steepled, he began to pivot back and forth in his seat.

Emily looked away, focusing on a model wearing a jade-green swing jacket in the magazine, then turned the page.

"That's surprising to you, I suppose."

"Right. But why?" She shrugged before tossing the magazine onto his desk and clasping her hands across her lap. "When Dr. Giannopoulos told me that the woman was Black, I'm going to be honest, Dad, I was disappointed." Dad cocked his head to the side. "Don't you find that to be an inappropriate reaction, Dad?"

She squinted and sucked her teeth. Her father glared at her with hooded eyes then nonchalantly shrugged.

"I suppose."

"What do you mean, 'I suppose'? She's dead, gunned

down like some animal in the park, and I am still alive because she was a perfect match. I get a death sentence with a soft RIP date and she gets a toe tag, and that's what I think about?" She tossed up her hands and shook her head. "I'm confused by this. My gut reaction was to be sickened that the organ inside me didn't belong to a White woman, like me, as if that meant I'm somehow now poisoned."

"That's extreme."

"It's more than that, it's horrible; and yet, I still feel that way, and then again, I don't. Something is going on within me that doesn't make sense. I have been fighting with myself ever since the surgery, Dad. Literally, on a daily basis, I feel as if I am being pulled into directions I don't want to go. My life before the surgery was different. I was happy." She huffed.

"Happy in your ignorance?"

Several seconds passed before she was able to fall back into her line of thought, get back on board.

"I guess, but is it really ignorance? Why would I want the heart of someone who could've been a bad person? I never even thought about that before. I just made assumptions, bad ones."

"So her being Black automatically makes her a bad person?"

"Yes. I mean, no." She pressed her eyes shut so hard it hurt, running her hand across her forehead. Slowly opening her lids, she focused on her father, though she couldn't ignore how incredibly hot she was becoming. The anxiety was climbing and climbing. "Not too long ago, I was at the record store and spoke to the manager there. He let me know about some deals they were offering." Her father listened intently, his blue eyes sharp yet kind. "I found him interesting to look at, but at the same time, I was disgusted with his hair. Strangely enough, I didn't feel the same way about the White cashier who also had dreadlocks. For the first time in my life," she said, waving her hand, "I began to think about my responses to these people. I mean, really think about it. Why? I can't seem to break free from it. And then I met…" Images of Cameron flooded her mind, taking her asunder.

When she'd laid eyes on him, she'd been shocked at her response. The man was striking. Right off the bat, she was physically attracted to him. Emily couldn't recall ever finding a Black man attractive, seeing one that actually made her do a double take. They just were not her speed. She much preferred the European guys—fair skin, dark hair, and gorgeous light eyes. Black men embodied the worst in humanity. Overly aggressive. She didn't like the loose way they walked, their pants sagging down, and definitely not the way they spoke in that urban, silly vernacular and calling each other, "nigga" every chance they got.

She hated how so many of them would stare at her or whistle, as though she was a piece of meat. Ogling. When White men did it, it didn't seem as assertive, but of course, she never fancied herself attracted to Black men in the first place. It disgusted her, caused her to hate them on a level that perhaps was unreasonable. What made Cameron different? She had no clue as of yet. He was definitely Black. Cameron stood about six foot two, had a deep caramel complexion and wavy, jet-black hair trimmed short in a Caesar-type cut, tapered at the sides and back. His eyebrows were equally dark and thick, but well groomed. He kept a low-cut beard—typically not her thing, but it looked good on this guy. Real good.

Her stomach had flipped with instant attraction when they'd begun a conversation. A lustful volcano erupted from her core each time he uttered a syllable. His voice was so fucking deep, it rippled through her soul. He spoke as if he were singing, and yet, he wasn't. Cameron's eyes were slightly upturned at the ends, and one side of his mouth was tilted, which made him look like he was smirking at times. He smelled amazing—fresh, with a healthy dose of bravado and rich cologne. He had such a handsome smile and adorable laugh, and yet, there was sadness in his warm, brown eyes. She knew that expression, the look one was saddled with when they'd lost someone they loved with all of their heart and didn't know how they'd carry on.

"You met who? You were in mid-sentence but now you're not speaking. Are you okay?" Her father jerked her out of her thoughts.

"Yeah, I'm okay." She forced a smile as she resituated herself in the chair then stroked her chin. "It doesn't matter what I was talking about before." She waved him off. "But I do want to get back to work and—"

"Now hold on, this is important, Emily. You said you found out who your donor was and it surprised you because she was Black. I can understand that surprise, but you being upset about it is, well, strange. I'll try to help you understand it, if I can. Did something happen that I'm not aware of? Did you have some bad interactions with African Americans that kind of, what's the word…spoiled it for you?"

She looked into her father's blue eyes, seeing bits and pieces of her fractured reflection in them.

"I want to say no, but honestly..." She shrugged. "I don't know how to answer that question. It's like one part of me is upset about it, wishing it would have been someone else, and another part of me is grateful." She lowered her gaze. "I spent the better part of the morning asking myself tough questions, Dad. Questions I don't have answers to but I'm sure of one thing. I'm a racist."

"No way." The older man grinned and chuckled in disbelief. "You're not a racist, honey. You're just—"

"No, it's true. I honestly believe so." She stretched her legs and briefly shut her eyes. "I looked up the definition." She reached for her purse, pulled out her phone and looked at it again. "Says here, a racist is a person who believes in racism, the doctrine that one's own racial group is superior or that a particular racial group is inferior to the others." She flippantly tossed her phone back in her purse and scowled at her father. "I *do* think we're superior. I have always believed that White people are intellectually better than Blacks, Hispanics, most other races.

"I deemed the articles I've read regarding brain size that cosign this theory as factual. Asians, particularly the Chinese, are pretty comparable to us as far as acumen goes, but I have always believed that as a whole, we have a firmer grasp on discernment and judgment. There are exceptions of course, some brilliant Black people sprinkled in society here and there, but they aren't the rule of thumb. I look at the news and more times than not, you see a Black person yelling and cursing on the screen, robbing someone, then going off about police brutality and injustice. It just became so annoying. Because in my heart, I felt…I feel, hell, I don't know anymore, past tense or present, who knows?" She swallowed. "I believe these things to be true. That makes me a racist."

She spoke without emotion, yet deep inside, she was bleeding badly. Her father cleared his throat, his cheeks flushed now.

"Well, let's look at this closely, okay? There's *some* truth in some of your beliefs. For instance, the lack of accountability you described with your example of robbing someone and then blaming the authorities once they are confronted and apprehended. I wish African Americans as a whole would spend *less* time blaming others for their downfalls and more time finding solutions that would benefit them. Legal ones, of course. I don't think that's such a crazy idea." He smiled ever so slightly. "I don't think it's a matter of intelligence. I think it may be ingrained in their culture and the ones who break free from that are successful. They seem to have a mob, all-or-nothing mentality at times. I have a few Black associates who are quite intelligent and definitely a prize to their community. In fact, I—"

"First of all, much of what you just said is based in ignorance or debatable, the rest is completely inaccurate. Regardless, from what I've been discovering, there are plenty of Black Americans who share your views, right or wrong, but I've discovered it's not being shared in the media as much as polarizing views. You can make of that what you will. Secondly, if that's the case, then why have you never hired any for the company?" She cocked her head to the side and glared at her father.

"What do you mean?"

"I mean exactly what I said. Why have you never hired a Black person to work for you?"

Dad's complexion deepened and he began to stutter, stumble over his words as he tossed his hands up.

"Well, hell, Emily, it wasn't a conscious choice, if that's what you're implying. I don't believe any have ever applied for a job posting or if they had, they obviously weren't qualified or someone else was a bit more qualified who was competing for the same position."

"That's not true. I saw many of them come in and hand in their resumes from everything to cleaning the floors, working at the front desk, doorman, accountant positions, security, actuary, attorney, I.R. associate and credit analyst, you name it, and I don't recall seeing any of them return for an interview. You said it yourself, I'm a workaholic. Anyone who came through that door I at least got a glimpse of. And my memory is quite good, especially in regard to faces. The receptionist would take their information, hand it over to Maggie, our HR aficionado," she rolled her eyes, "and it would disappear into trash can heaven. If they emailed their resumes, the delete button was hit so much that I'm surprised it didn't burn up."

"You're being ridiculous and making outlandish assumptions. How would any of us know someone was Black by an emailed resume?"

"Simple. An ethnic name would be a dead giveaway. Or if they went to any historically Black colleges. If they mentioned any organizations that had liberal or left-wing views, we sometimes assumed from that, too, that it may be a person of color. Then of course, a simple search online sometimes rendered quick results for those still in question. God forbid they had any social media pages. They'd be busted like a balloon falling toward a field of razor blades."

"Are you accusing me of being a racist too, Emily?" Dad's voice boomed. "How dare you. Now if you're having an issue or are examining your *own* life, that's fine by me—in fact, I encourage it—but don't try to throw me in the middle of this shit. This mess you are concocting in your head. I have *never* not hired anyone because of their race." He pressed his finger into his desk, his expression blazing with anger. "Not one damn time. I believe that Black people are as capable as us when it comes to doing the same work. Yes, I am a conservative. I am a proud Republican, as was your mother, but that in no way is synonymous with racism, intolerance, and prejudice."

She looked at him long and hard before turning away, casting her gaze toward a window which gave a clear view of the city.

"Did you know that historically, the Democrats were the ones throwing Blacks under the bus?" he continued. "Welfare was the worst thing to ever happen to this country. It helped put them in a position of powerlessness and the Democrats have done so much damage to the Black community under the guise of assistance just to get a damn vote, that they may never recover." Dad continued to rant and rave, but her thoughts became watery as she faded away within herself, then snapped out of it when he hurled another curse word. So unlike him.

The guilty yell the loudest. This is an intelligent man sitting before me, and yet, he is saying these foolish things. He has no idea how foolish he sounds. These statements are prevalent, rampant inaccuracies. Worst of all, my father thinks these are rational thoughts. Accurate. The truth. It's skewed logic that has been passed down for decades.

She scanned the room, studying his trappings.

Her father's estate, a beautiful condo in Tribeca, New York, on Barclay Street, boasted twenty-five-hundred square feet of sumptuousness. Crystal chandeliers and custom-made furniture adorned the place, screaming money. She'd grown up there, though it had received extensive remodeling over the years and barely looked the same. This was where she normally was most comfortable, under that roof, but right then, she felt out of place, as if she didn't fit, didn't belong there.

"I don't regret what I said," she stated, then pursed her lips, interrupting his rant regarding his political views.

"About me being racist?"

"About *me* being racist. I am just trying to find out, Dad, how I got these thoughts. That's it." She raised her hands as if in surrender. "You became highly defensive, and all I did was ask a question."

"Bull. You know what you were doing, Emily. You've always struggled with the same thing you've accused Blacks of—accountability. I've known you your entire life. I am fully aware of the slick verbal games you play. I will not tolerate you twisting and turning this, being manipulative. It's absurd." He scowled as his brows dipped.

"I'm not trying to blame you, though I fully understand

that it may sound that way." After a few brief moments of silence, she got to her feet and grabbed her purse. "I better be going. Anyway, again, I'd like to come back to work next week, please."

"I'd rather you wait a bit longer. Let's see in about a month." Her father abruptly ended the conversation by snatching up his landline phone and calling a colleague, his expression colored with raw resentment. Emily hesitated, but he avoided eye contact. She'd ignited rage within him. Fact of the matter was, she wasn't actually certain that her father was racist at all, but she knew that he was prejudice. He simply hadn't faced it yet. He was like most people in the world, believing they were somehow better, more evolved and knowledgeable than they actually were.

She left his office then, pausing when she heard him burst out laughing at something the person he'd called must have said. She was soon outside the condo waiting for her father's driver to come around the block with the black Lincoln town car. She tried to bury her resentment that he would not let her return to her office just yet, but she detested him for being so damn stubborn. She needed that distraction. She needed to work like she needed air. The car pulled up and she got inside, then went over the tapes within her mind.

As she sat in the back seat battling with herself, her thoughts a tangled mess, her cell phone rang. Not recognizing the number, she allowed it to go to voicemail.

Not in the mood to hear an automated message from some robo-caller. You get on the DO NOT CALL list, and they still fucking call.

Once home, she slipped out of her clothing, took a cool shower, and slid on an ivory silk robe. After that, she proceeded to fix a nice salad for an early dinner. As she washed a cucumber in the sink, debating on peeling the skin, she peeked at her television, taking in bits and pieces of the news. Just then, her cell phone chimed, notifying her of a voicemail she hadn't checked. Cutting off the running faucet water, she dried her hands on a towel and played it back.

"Hey, this is Cameron Davis." She swallowed. Hard. "You might remember me. I'm Brooke Coleman's boyfriend. Well, your donor's boyfriend, I should say. I uh, I still had the business card you gave me and I'm glad, because I've decided to call you about something. Look, it's been a few weeks and I've had some time to calm down, some time to think. I wanna first apologize to you for biting your head off. You popping up at my house just threw me off guard. There was no warnin', no call, or anything. You were just there, ya know? Anyway, regardless, I imagine this hasn't been easy for you, either, so if I had been thinking straight, I would've responded differently.

"Secondly, when you were leavin', you said that uh, you said she makes you sing, dance, made you come there to see me, some shit like that." She smiled at his words. "I wanted to talk to you about that. So, if you can, let's meet up for dinner in the next day or two and sit down and talk. My treat. You're curious about Brooke, and honestly, I'm curious about what you said—*all* of it, as wacky as it sounded. Call me when you can, aight? Thanks."

And that was that. She played the message back once more, then set her phone down. Her chest tightened, her heart beating so fast, she needed to lean against the counter to catch her breath. Excitement filled her, and she warmed up like dark, hot coffee, the kind spilled on a soft white rug.

CAMERON TAPPED HIS foot nervously on the barstool footrest as he sipped on some Sprite with a wedge of lemon. He wished it were something stronger, that was for damn sure. He sat hunched over, half listening to the loud conversations around him, his black leather jacket feeling hot as hell. Still, he refused to take it off; it felt like a cape of sorts, some type of protection or shield from any danger that may come. Checking the time, he hissed.

Where the hell is she? I didn't think White people were on Colored People time, he joked to himself as he recalled all the times he would wait for Brooke to get ready for their outings, sometimes causing them to be late.

Emily had called him back less than an hour after his request and they'd agreed to meet up at the Ocean Prime restaurant on 52nd Street.

When he was starting to think it had been a bad idea to set this meeting up, he saw the tall blonde coming his way, wearing a black parka and a black V-neck satiny shirt beneath it, paired with a white skirt and black stilettos. Emily walked like a model, as if she were commanding a runway. She drew closer and smiled at him with ruby-red lips, and before he knew it, he was on his feet, wrapping his arm loosely around her tiny waist and giving her a friendly hug.

"It's raining," she said as she sat down next to him, her purse speckled with raindrops.

"Yeah, it was sprinklin' a bit when I came, too. You get here all right, though?"

"Yes, everything was fine." She turned toward the bar and he caught her reflection in the mirror.

"All right, so uh, they should be clearing a table for us. I made a reservation." He snuck a quick glance at his watch.

"Good thinking. I haven't been here in a while. It's nice. I'd almost forgotten about this place." Her pronounced cheekbones developed an instant ruddy hue as she grinned. "Have you ever been here before?" She seemed a bit nervous, more so than when they'd first met.

"Yeah, many times. Come on, they are calling us over." He helped her down from her seat and before long, they were sitting at a table perusing the menu.

"This is a nice place. I already said that. Damn it." Emily placed her menu down on the table and ran her fingers through the light wheat-colored strands of her hair, briefly closing her eyes. "You think I'm crazy, don't you?" She smiled sadly as she peered at him through a curtain of blonde tresses.

"Nah." He set his menu down, too. Honestly, he wasn't quite sure. That's what he was there to find out. "I think this whole thing is strange, you know? But that's out of our control. Brooke made this decision to be a donor. You're just going through some things it seems. God knows I am, too."

More awkward silence stretched between them. The waiter came for their drink order and they both ordered a glass of wine.

"I need this." She laughed lightly as she took a sip and set her glass down. He looked at the red lipstick stain around the rim she'd deposited from her kiss.

"I'm just having this one." He chuckled. "No more self-medicating, stuffing down my feelings with booze. I sound like someone from an AA meeting. I'm not an alcoholic, but these past couple of months, it seemed as if I was auditioning for the role of the town drunk." He kept his voice light, though he was serious. Emily nodded, a pretty smile on her face. She didn't come across as judgmental at his statement; in fact, she seemed understanding. He studied her as she discussed her job. She was using big words and appeared to truly enjoy what she did for a living. As he continued to observe her, he realized that though he couldn't take his eyes off her, she looked nothing like his Brookie. In fact, she was almost the complete opposite, though their body types were almost identical in height and shape, and their smiles bore similarities, too.

I mean, I'm not checking her out or anything. She's definitely not my type, even if I were. But, to keep it all the way one hundred, she's kinda cute. Nice looking lady if somebody is into that whole Barbie doll look. I mean, White women aren't my thing, especially a blonde, but she's okay. Not bad. She's got some nice legs, nice smile. She has a decent ass for a White woman. Smart obviously, with the type of job she has.

An overwhelming sense of guilt crept within him. He lowered his head, feeling lower than low.

I'm sorry, Brooke. I'm so fucking shitty. I swear I haven't even looked at another woman in that way since you've been gone. I promise. I don't know why my mind even went there.

"I'm allowed to have an occasional glass of wine," Emily stated, breaking into his thoughts. She lifted the glass. "Come on, this is cause for celebration."

"Oh, yeah. Let's toast." He grabbed his glass, thankful to be free from the remorse-driven deliberations, and clinked his glass against hers. "To life. To a *new* lease on life that is, second chances, new blessings, a new chapter, all right?"

Emily's smile faded.

"What? Did I say something wrong?"

"No." She shook her head. "Just familiar. You said something familiar. Anyway." She composed herself fast. "Cheers."

After they ordered their entrees, they engaged in small talk—nothing earth-shattering, nothing that gave him pause. In fact, it felt rather normal, as if he were just meeting up with an old friend. Regardless, there was a serious matter on the table, and someone had to address it.

"I need to tell you that—"

"Look." He tossed down his napkin on the table, cutting her off. "We've been dancing around the elephant in the room. We have to discuss the real reason we're here."

"I was going to say pretty much the same thing. It's not every day you get a heart transplant and have dinner with your donor's lover." She burst out laughing, placed her glass down, and covered her mouth with her hand as her eyes twinkled with mirth.

"Can't argue with that. Ladies first." He leaned back in his seat, giving her the floor.

"Um, okay." She cleared her throat. "On a scale of one to ten, how sensitive are you?"

He twisted his lips and crossed his arms. "I uh…I'm not sure where you're going with this."

"Can I be honest with you? That's what I'm asking."

"Oh, hell yeah." He shrugged and smirked. "No need to lie about shit. Seriously. Please do."

"Okay, well, I feel like I'm losing my mind and I feel like it's being taken over by your deceased girlfriend." She chuckled, but he could see she was far from amused. "She wanted to see you. I've figured that part out, so here I am." She tossed up her hands. He simply sat there, looking at her, working out his thoughts. "I knew it. You think I'm crazy." She crossed her arms, mirroring his stance.

"You might be." He shrugged. "You might not be. I have no idea how this works. I mean, it wasn't like a brain transplant or anything. It was your heart. A heart shouldn't be able to control a person that way. But something…Never mind."

"No, no, no. Come on, we've got to be honest with one another. Tell me." She leaned forward, clearly interested.

"You said when you were in front of my building that she makes you sing and dance. See, as you now know, Brooke was a singer. She also was a really good dancer, though she didn't do it professionally or anything like that. Now uh…" He scratched his chin. "She told me one time that she always wanted to be able to sing and dance, no matter where she went, like, after life was over. She and I used to have real deep conversations like that.

"We'd talk about souls, God, ghosts, life after death theories, religion, all types of stuff like that. We'd just lie in bed sometimes and discuss the universe, energy, this experience we call life. She told me that if reincarnation truly existed, then she prayed that she'd be able to sing and dance in her next lifetime, even if not professionally; she just wanted to be able to do it, couldn't imagine that skill ever being gone forever. So, see, when you said that, you know, that she makes you sing and dance, it kinda messed me up." He averted his gaze, needing a minute. Seconds passed in silence, but it felt like hours.

"I have a confession. I don't just sing, I sing well. This is a new development. I could not sing to save my life before the operation, Cameron. I can call any of my friends and ask them, let you hear them answer and explain that I sounded like a crow being choked when I'd attempt to do that. But now I can. It came out of nowhere." He slowly met her gaze. "I also went and bought a shitload of albums from an old music store, music I'd never entertained before, and I hadn't been to this record store, ever. It was a place out in Harlem. I rarely go to Harlem. It was like I was in some dream, only I was fully awake."

"Harlem? What was the store called, out of curiosity?"

"Face the Music."

"Are you fuckin' with me right now?"

"I'm not. I promise you, this isn't a joke." His chest began to heave up and down. "Take a deep breath. Sip some of your water there before you hyperventilate," she stated calmly. He did as she instructed and blinked back the emotions.

"That used to be her favorite spot to get her albums. She even had a lifelong discount because she bought so much music from there. Our home was filled with albums from that place." He reached for his wine and took a taste. "Let me hear you sing."

Emily's eyes bucked. "No. Not right here in front of all these people. Besides, it's too loud in here for you to hear me."

"Yeah, I want you to sing right here. Come on. Lean forward, across the table, and let me hear you sing."

"You don't believe me, do you?" Her perfectly shaped brown brows dipped.

"No, I don't. Prove to me that this is true, that this all really happened. You might be some psycho."

The thought hit him like a ton of bricks right then. Brooke knew a lot of damn people. She was a celebrity, after all. She'd just gotten invited to the BET Awards and was given accolades in several magazines. There were people who practically worshiped her, and he imagined, some wished they could've been in her shoes while she was rising to the top. For all he knew, this lady knew full well who Brooke was, regardless of her being the recipient of her heart. Maybe this was some sort of gimmick, a way to get money, chase a bag. She could have already called a bunch of tabloids trying to sell her story, saying a famous dead woman was now speaking through her. Some crazy shit like that.

"What is going on here, Cameron? Do you even believe I have her heart? That I'm the recipient of her donation?" she asked, as if reading his mind.

He sucked his teeth and took a swig of his water.

"Yeah. I checked into it a few days after we met. I called her mother and asked her to contact the hospital and find out who'd received her heart since my request was denied because I wasn't her husband or next of kin. My mother-in-law got back in touch with me. The name on your card matched and so did some other information they gave."

She nodded, though she seemed unnerved.

"It looks like you're upset about something. Did I cause this?" Her brow arched.

"Yes and no. I'm upset about a lot of shit surrounding this, but most of it can't be changed. One minute I'm happy that her heart is still beating inside of someone else, the next I'm not, I'm resentful. Look, just sing for me. Any line, from any song, I don't care. Get up, lean into my ear, and sing. I need you to sing right now," he said through gritted teeth.

He had no idea what was driving him, but the desire to put this woman to the test, to find out if they were both out of their damn minds, needed to be figured out. She rose from her chair, coldness now in her blue eyes. She looked angry as hell as she tossed her napkin down onto the table, walked around it, and stood right before him, casting a shadow. She bent down and brought her mouth close to his ear.

She began to croon "Get Up" by Amel Larrieux. He bowed his head and his lips curled as his eyes watered with fresh tears. He began to lightly beat the table, making music to this lily-white woman's incredibly soulful voice. When she finished, she stood to her full height, a scowl on her face, and calmly returned to her seat. When their food was brought out, they began to eat, both taking sneak peeks at one another, but neither willing to speak for quite some time. He couldn't help but notice that her plate was much like Brooke's would've been—devoid of meat.

"You a vegetarian?" he asked as he cut into his steak.

"As of a month ago I am. The sight of red meat now sickens me. I tried to eat filet mignon, which was my absolute favorite, and threw up." Her tone was terse, borderline hateful as she stabbed the sautéed carrots on her plate, the pretty things sprinkled with parsley. "Let me guess. She was a vegetarian or vegan." She jammed the carrots into her mouth and glared at him.

"A vegetarian. She ate eggs, butter, cheese. No chicken, beef, pork, or turkey though. I could count on one hand how many times I saw her eat fish."

"How did she feel about you eating steak?" Emily's brow rose as she eyed his plate.

"She didn't care for it, but she let me be me, accepted me as such. I did eat much less of it though when I was with her. So uh, look, Emily." He slammed his utensils down onto his plate and clasped his hands together, elbows on the table. "There are far too many coincidences going on here. Crazy shit. Out of all the record stores in Harlem, you found that one. You said something to me that Brooke told me when we were confiding in one another. Even the way you pronounce certain words sounds like her. Now, you're a vegetarian and you can sing, and sing very well, too.

"The cherry on top is that it's the same damn song she would sing to me to make me wake up in the mornings to go take Opium out for a walk, when all I wanted to do was sleep in. I never told anyone she did that. I never repeated that song or sung it, either. That was something *she* did, something between the two of us. You're killing me here, Emily."

He smiled as tears now streamed down his face. "Either you're the best damn con artist in all of New York, or some really wild supernatural shit is going down. Some deep, spiritual, frighteningly beautiful shit. I was just getting to the point where I was healing, getting better, but now here she comes. Through you." Emily's eyes misted over and a tear streaked her face, too. "How do you feel about this, Emily? I mean really?"

She reached across the table and grasped his hand, then held and squeezed it.

"I'm scared and excited. I wish it wasn't happening but at the same time, I accept that it is."

"You seemed like you were successful, had it not been for your heart condition, anyway. How was life for you before you had to have the surgery?"

"I enjoyed my life before the surgery, but uh, things are not quite clear cut anymore. I still can't believe any of this is happening. I'm a logical person and if it weren't happening to me, I would never believe it in a million years. People who talked about out-of-body experiences, reincarnation, and seeing God seemed crazy to me. It, hmmm…it sounds kinda outrageous. I feel kinda foolish. Everything's changing." Her shoulders slumped. "That person I was, the one I used to be, the woman named Emily, is changing. The jury is still out if it is for better or worse. I can't even describe it, Cameron. I can't put it into words. I just have to get up each morning and live and find out what the day brings. I want to believe what my mother used to say, that things like this happen for a reason. I just don't know what that reason is quite yet."

"I believe that, too. There's really no such thing as coincidences."

"Well, in order to prevent my head from exploding, I just have to go for the ride." She chuckled as she picked up her fork once again and worked it through thinly sliced zucchini. "Thank you for sharing more with me about Brooke." He nodded. "Did this meeting tonight, so to speak, help you? Was it therapeutic in some way?"

He rolled that thought about inside his mind.

"That's a good question. I think it actually just made me more curious about *you*."

"Are you certain that you're more curious about me, Cameron? Or are you just hoping to connect with Brooke again, *through* me?"

After taking a final sip of his wine, he set it aside.

"It's probably the latter, but I can't be certain either way. Let me ask you something. Would you be willing to continue talking to me? Getting to know one another?"

"You mean get to know Brooke again. Just admit it. I don't mind. You are morbidly curious about this." She smiled, and he did the same. "I haven't told a soul about this by the way, and I hadn't planned on telling you, either. But I just kinda blurted it out when I saw you walking away from me that day."

"All right, yeah. I am extremely curious. It's not that I think you're Brooke—you're obviously not, you're your own woman—but it does seem at least a little bit of her has uh, I don't know, bloomed again, through you, I suppose you could say. And trust me, I don't plan on discussing this with anyone. It sounds insane and that's not the type of attention I need. But Brooke believed in stuff like this." He shrugged.

"So, she may have been on to something. She was one of the most spiritually, emotionally, and mentally mature women I'd ever known."

"You really loved her, didn't you? I can tell."

"How can you tell for sure?" He laughed. "I've always had a way with words, so you can't trust that. I have the gift of gab, and I'm a poet. You can't trust poets, Emily. We're slick." He winked at her and was met with a seductive smile.

"Oh Cameron, believe me, in my line of work, I am fully aware of the art of words and mind fucking. It's not just what you're saying that I'm paying attention to—it's how you look at me. You look at me as if you're looking at *her*. And that, my friend, is a look of love."

Chapter Nine
A Bunch of Hot Air

S HE CHEATED.
  Emily took a sip of her reheated coffee from Starbucks and savored the rich, warm flavor as it filled her mouth and went down nice and easy. She'd purchased it earlier that evening and placed it in the refrigerator after a wave of guilt washed over her, albeit fleeting. She was still on the 'Do Not Drink Caffeinated Coffee' watch list.

The brew wasn't fresh now, but she didn't care. It had been so long since she'd savored a good cup of joe. The taste was amazing.

This'll be the only one, then back to decaf until further notice. Hell, I wasn't supposed to have that glass of wine, either, but the doctor said occasionally was fine.

She sat in her bedroom at her small desk, polishing off her list of excuses for living her semi-best life, flavored in forbidden beverages. The laptop before her was on, the glare from the screen the only light in the space. It was about two in the morning and her bones ached from some half-assed stretching and low impact walking on the treadmill. Her mind was full of worries, new thoughts and ideas, many of which made her truly uncomfortable. Added with that was a dash of paranoia.

What would people think if they knew she was having this experience? She knew the answer to that; thus, it was still her little secret.

There was one thought train, however, she couldn't seem to free herself from. Her newfound attraction to Cameron Davis.

They'd not spoken since they had dinner the previous week. He'd told her he was quite busy, so when her call wasn't promptly returned, she surmised that was the issue. He did eventually follow up with a single line of, "Hope you're doing good," but that was it. Though fairly confident and not one to lose much sleep over the likes of a man, a small part of her took his generic, late reply as a possible rejection.

How bizarre of me. We're not dating, he barely knows me, and under the circumstances, what did I expect?

Even with past lovers, if they hadn't responded in a timely fashion, she rarely felt any particular way about it. In fact, she'd been accused of being cold and rigid like an icicle—elusive, detached.

Yet that evening with Cameron had felt different. The fine wine, the candlelight. Perhaps it was the strange circumstances in which they'd met? No, her gut told her it was more than that. Their conversation had been awkward, flirty, and fun at the same time, transparent yet somewhat guarded. Definitely mentally and emotionally draining, as well as enlightening, when they offered confessions and revealed bits and pieces of their selves.

She'd discovered Cameron considered himself Black, and

he looked that way in her eyes too, but his mother was Puerto Rican with African roots, Afro-Latina to be exact. He went into great detail about the African ancestry of many Puerto Ricans, something that she wasn't aware of but was too prideful to admit. His parents were middle class, well established, college educated. She was impressed.

Cameron wasn't the type of man she'd imagined, and though he didn't know it, waves of shame for her prejudices washed over her mind as she realized she'd stereotyped him. He was supposed to come from a broken home, product of a single mother raising a slew of children with different fathers. Cameron was an only child and his parents were married before he was conceived. He went to a high school that catered to gifted children—another surprise to her. She wished to know more about him, so much more, but it seemed as if some invisible door had been closed by him, and he sealed himself off without so much as a warning. It didn't deter her; rather, it made her wish to find ways to discover more.

He's a gentleman.

She smiled as she recalled what he'd done when they'd left the restaurant—more because the place was going to close than a desire to go back to their individual lives.

After a goodbye hug, they'd parted ways. Then, Cameron had sent her a text, asking her to promise that she'd let him know when she got home safely.

We connected that night. There's no denying it. Maybe he's changed his mind, though? Maybe he got what he needed and just wants to move on with his life? Certainly I'd have to respect that.

But he held me in his arms for such a long time, much longer than what was needed.

Life went on, though, and that dinner wasn't the only thing on her mind.

She sighed as she closed her eyes and grimaced.

Dad. Shit.

The true heart of a woman was her intent. But which woman? Brooke or Emily?

I can't tell him about what's going on, even though I'd like to. I definitely can't tell my friends, either. They'd have the same reaction as Dad...actually, much worse. I've been avoiding everyone. People have been asking too many questions. But what could I possibly tell them? "Oh, guess what? I think that heart I got is controlling my thinking and desires, now I do the same crap that the donor did when she was still alive." I even like dogs now and eggplant and here's the cherry on top: I'm a bigot. Yeah, that's not new, but I just realized this about myself, so that means I must have racist friends, too. Cool, huh? YIIPP-PEEEE.

She rolled her eyes at her thoughts, then lowered her head, trying to figure out how in the hell this had happened, and why her? Why not? She picked up her phone and clicked on the number she wanted.

I'm going to call my father and just try my best to explain what's going on.

But then she hung up.

She winced each and every time she thought about that tense conversation with him.

It was ugly and raw.

She'd bumped heads with her father at times, but never

to that degree. Never had she sunk her fangs into him that way. She worshiped her father, but she'd gone at him like some ravenous lion galloping after an antelope. More importantly, the topic of conversation was one that stained her mind like a bottle of spilled red wine, and she was intoxicated with the aftermath, never becoming fully sober. She sometimes lay in bed thinking about her feelings regarding such matters.

Why do I automatically vote the way I do? I never even review the Democratic ticket. I don't even do any research for it at all. I just assume that each and every one of them is a bleeding liberal out to destroy the foundation of this country. Does conservatism equal racism, or is it like Dad said, they are independent of each other? Is there no correlation between the two and I'm now relying on stereotypes to find my way? Why was I so upset about some of the NFL players' national anthem protests but didn't feel as outraged about the alleged ruthlessness from police officers against people of color that fueled those actions in the first place? Why did I not read the article about police brutality in the newspaper that time? It was right there on the front page. Instead, I flipped past it and read about a new art exhibit at the Metropolitan Museum of Art.

Why do I cross the street if I see a bunch of Black guys, or wait for the next elevator if one of them is on there, alone? Why is it that when I see a Hispanic or Black young woman with children, I automatically think she is on public assistance, taking my tax dollars while she pumps out more kids she can't take care of because the system is rigged to reward her being a baby factory? I do in fact believe the system is flawed, but that doesn't mean every young woman fitting that description is actually on welfare. Why do I do that? How does that benefit me? What does that say about me as a person?

There were so many damn questions, ones that bothered and haunted her now, like the matter of her heart.

She couldn't explain why it didn't feel right anymore being in the skin she was in, and she wasn't even certain what exactly was wrong with her thought patterns in all instances, either. Perhaps taking them on a case-by-case, individual basis would be best, but they suddenly felt wrong now, as if they needed to be examined to the fullest.

I'm driving myself crazy with this. It's an obsession. None of this is helping.

She took a sip of her coffee and ran her fingers through her hair.

I can't stop, though. I have to figure this out. I have to make it make sense. Who am I kidding? It'll never make sense.

Fact was, examining them would be tantamount to admitting she'd been wrong. A fall from grace.

I should probably call my father back and this time not hang up. Apologize to him. I hate apologizing, but if I want my job back anytime soon, it's probably the smart thing to do.

Since their verbal altercation, every time she'd spoken to him he seemed friendly enough, but there was definitely tension between them that she wasn't certain would be bridged anytime soon. After taking another sip of her coffee, she placed it down on the clear desk next to her computer and googled more photos of Brooke.

Her lips curled in appreciation as she studied her features.

She liked looking at her, studying her qualities.

Her wild, curly, dark brown hair was like a mass of soft

coils, or at least she imagined they were soft. Her skin looked extremely smooth, practically blemish free, and her full lips were often covered in sheer or neutral lipsticks. The singer's sense of style was rather unique, though she'd seemed partial to shades of green, accented with gold. She favored draped clothing that only allowed a shoulder or a sliver of her taut stomach to be exposed. She wore wooden jewelry, large earrings—often hoops—and an interesting collection of rings and sandals, and wedge or bedazzled high heels. She was a beautiful woman, there was simply no denying that. Her smile belied both kindness and wisdom. She looked younger than her years, but her eyes held the secrets of a million lives, decades upon decades of civilizations.

Emily turned on some soothing classical violin music as she continued to look at the pictures on the screen.

After a few minutes, she let out a blood-curdling scream, almost falling back in her chair. Scrambling to stand, she looked down at her computer, but the problem was no longer there, or had it been there at all? The picture she was looking at was Brooke in a park, leaning against a large stone. Her hair was flowing, and she wore a dark brown crop top and baggy dark brown and gold printed pants, paired with a taupe pair of sandals. Fashion aside, Emily could've sworn that Brooke had just winked at her and smiled. It wasn't a video but a photo, one of her favorites that she'd saved.

I'm just tired. It's been a long day.

She shut the computer down, climbed into bed, and plumped her pillow. She prayed for plummy thoughts and visions, pleasant dreams. Perhaps some much-needed sleep would be the magic cure to her sudden bout of hallucinations. Yet somehow, some way, she knew that Brooke was tapping on her shoulder, trying to get her attention once again, and closing her eyes would not be the means to tune her out.

CAMERON STOOD FACING the stage in his navy-blue blazer, a trail of sweat meandering down the side of his neck. After swiping the sweat away with a cocktail napkin, he tossed it in the trash and cursed under his breath, taking note of the time on his watch. The air-conditioning was on the fritz in the club, and Cameron had grabbed every industrial fan he could find and placed each one in a strategic position about the place before patrons started to flood the doors with their dancing shoes and snapping fingers. The DJ was just then setting up.

"What tha fuck? It's hot as hell up in here, man. You gotta do somethin', Cameron," one of his employees called out before disappearing into a back room, a scowl on his face.

"Really, Lamar? Thank you for telling me that. I would've never known had it not been for your extensive knowledge and infinite wisdom. You think I've been standing here doin' a two-step, huh? Out here whistlin' love songs and slicing up pickles for tiny picnic sandwiches or some shit, having a good ol' time?" He watched the guy walk farther and farther away, ignoring him.

"I can't work in this heat," someone else called out.

He felt ganged up on, and his temper flared.

"You think I'm standing here living my best life? What the hell is wrong with you people? I've been trying to get it fixed." Cameron muttered a few more curses before he snatched his phone out of his pocket and dialed the heating and cooling company again, but only got the voicemail.

"Yo, this is Cameron Davis at the 6th Dimension Club, man. Someone was supposed to be here two hours ago. I have a full house coming tonight and it's hotter than the crack of the Devil's ass, so if you don't mind, I need someone here like you said you'd be. This is my last call, and if someone isn't here in thirty minutes to fix this shit, then I am calling an emergency number that's going to cost me an arm and a leg and then I am going to leave a bad review for y'all on Yelp, Angie's List, all that shit. This is completely unprofessional. If someone is running literally hours late, then they need to call. Period. You're playin' with my time and money, and I don't take that lightly."

He angrily hit the END button, snatched his blazer off, and cast it on the stage before making his way to the empty bar. Sade's music played in the background, mocking his uncool, uncalm, and uncollected mood.

I need to change the name of the club to SAD—Sweaty Ass Draws.

"Hi."

He spun around and met eyes with Emily. She sported a white button-down shirt and form-fitting black slacks. White-and-black polka-dot heels with ankle straps were adorned with a small silver buckle. They looked fun and sexy at the same time.

"Oh…hi." He gave a slight smile as confusion reigned. "It's uh, it's nice to see you. What are you doing here?"

She made herself comfortable at a nearby table.

"Just thought I'd check out this place." She began to rummage through her purse. "I read about it. Great reviews." She then pulled out a small, electric handheld fan and he couldn't help but snicker. She turned it on, and he could hear the little buzzing sound. Drawing closer, he looked down at her. "But no one mentioned that it was hotter than a cat on a tin roof in their review."

He chuckled and clasped his forehead.

"It's not usually like this. I thought you told me that you were born and raised in New York?" He pulled out a chair and sat across from her, elbows on the table.

"I was."

"Then how would you know about that saying, 'hotter than a cat on a tin roof'? That's a Southern saying."

"Must've heard it from somewhere." She smiled and shrugged.

"Let me get you an ice cold glass of water." He returned moments later and placed the glass before her, garnished with a thin slice of lemon.

"Thank you, Cameron." She quickly placed her fan down and took a big gulp.

"You're more than welcome."

"Anyway, so what do you have planned tonight?" She looked around the place, then back at him. "Being Saturday, I am stunned that your establishment feels like this. Going for a Texas theme?" He snickered. "Today is unseasonably hot. We're in the fall after all, but hey, maybe you miss the summer. I recommend some blow-up beach balls and a sand pit," she teased.

"Nah, this definitely wasn't planned. I've actually been waiting for a repair guy to come out, but he stood me up. This sucks. I know people are going to be complaining, and rightfully so." He shrugged. "I might have to run downtown and get some more air conditioners, box fans, as many as I can and put them all over the place."

"You'll just be blowing hot air." She whipped out her phone.

"Funny, I've been accused of that before."

They both had a good laugh at that. She leaned back in her seat and crossed her long legs.

"Hi James, it's Emily Windsor. Yes. I'd love that." She laughed gayly as she looked up at the ceiling, exaggerated mirth in her eyes. "Look, I have a bit of an issue. I have a friend whose bar had the central air-conditioning go out. I know it's late notice and you've closed at noon, that's why I've called you at home, but he's got a big show tonight and it would be a true shame to have his patrons sweltering in this ungodly heat. Umm, hmm, of course. It's called the 6th Dimension. Yeah, mmm hmmm. I don't think it's more than twenty-five minutes from your apartment, actually, if memory serves me correctly…Oh yes, that makes sense."

Emily began to swing her leg back and forth as she toyed with the thin silver chain around her long neck. "Can you swing by in the next, I don't know, thirty to forty minutes, tops? He's really short on time and this is an emergency." She glanced down at her watch. "I understand. I'll pass that on to the owner. Okay, beautiful. Yes. I owe you one. Kisses to Pam and the little ones."

She disconnected the call and gave him a pleased as pudding grin. "In thirty minutes, either James himself or one of his technicians will be here to take a look. If it's simple, he'll get you up and running. If it's complicated to the point that parts need to be ordered, then he may be able to do a patch job if possible, but they'll need to see what the problem is before they can say either way."

"Look at you working magic. You are amazing. Thank you so very much." He smiled wide and adjusted himself in his seat. Finally, he just may get some results.

"Am I the GOAT?" Cameron cackled at her question. "See? I remembered."

She laughed as she turned her handheld fan off.

"Yes, you did, and yeah, that's a goat move for sure. So uh, you just happen to know AC repair people who will drop whatever it is for you like that, huh?" He steepled his fingers and crossed his ankles.

"Don't give me more credit than I deserve." She smiled coyly as she placed her fan back inside her purse. "I used to date his brother many years ago." She rolled her eyes as if the mere memory made her nauseated. "So, after Chase and I were done and over, his brother and I remained friends. In fact, I remained friends with his entire family. James needed a loan for his company a few years back, but no one would help out. So, I sat him down and gave him some free advice, a consultation if you will. I told him *exactly* what to say to the bank he had an appointment with the following week and what papers to take so he'd get approved right then and there."

"If you don't mind me asking, and it doesn't have shit to do with the story, obviously, but why did you and Chase break up?"

"My tryst with the two-timing slime ball sibling was ridiculous. I can handle a lot of things, Cameron, and I'm not unreasonable. Relationships have ups and downs, they ebb and flow, I get it, but cheating? No." She shook her head. "That's totally disrespectful and I will never tolerate it. In fact, any woman who does is weak. There are too many fish in the sea to keep chasing the one that's swimming after all the shit-eating, bottom-feeder catfish. I tell my single but looking friends to find themselves a shark and live happily ever after. At least a shark will eat you right."

"Ouch." He grinned, enjoying the banter. Emily was no softie, that was for sure.

She shrugged. "I call it as I see it. Anyway, James is a great man and thanks me for helping him in his time of need, so, as they say, he's just paying it forward, I suppose. Well, I know you're busy. I won't keep you." She got to her feet and placed her purse across her shoulder.

"Oh." He stood slowly and pushed his chair in. "You're leaving so soon? I was hoping you'd stay and hear some of the talent tonight. You could even call a few of your friends to come through. Drinks on the house for them. Hey." He eagerly snapped his fingers. "I know. Maybe you'd like to sing tonight."

She shook her head, her face pale as if she'd seen a ghost and began to make her way to the door.

"No way, Cameron. In front of all of these people? Anyway, I got what I needed. I just wanted to see your business and you too. It's really nice, and so are you." Her blue eyes twinkled. "You have a great night, okay? James is very reliable, so I trust you won't have any problems. If you do, give me a call. I always have a plan B."

"Wait, Emily."

She threw him a glance from over her shoulder.

"Yes?"

"Did Brooke wanna come down here to see me, or *you*?"

Emily looked at him long and hard for a while. "It was me I suppose this time." Her feet turned a bit inward, as if a case of nerves was overcoming her. "It was maybe my intuition that you needed help, who knows? I don't feel she had anything to do with it, or it could be wishful thinking on my part. I'm not sure any of that matters anymore." She turned to leave once again.

"Emily, hold up. What's your schedule like next weekend, on Saturday?"

"My father fired me. Well…" She smirked. "He told me I can't come back yet until he believes my heart can take it, so, in other words, I'm a free agent." She crossed her arms. "What did you have in mind?"

"Let's get together Saturday around two. I've got a speaking engagement at the Weeksville Heritage Center. I'd love for you to come. Maybe we can do something afterward. A play? Movie? We can figure that out later."

"I've never heard of the Weeksville Heritage Center before. Sure, I'll come." Her cheeks bloomed with color.

"Good." He waved to her as he took several steps backward, motioning toward the exit. "Thanks for comin' down, good looking out." He smiled wider than he wanted to, but he couldn't help it. "I'll call you."

She nodded and departed the place, leaving him there with only the lingering scent of her intoxicating perfume.

What an interesting woman.

The truth of the matter was, he'd had a hard time getting her out of his mind. In fact, he was worried about possibly becoming attached to her, because of her link with Brooke. So much so, he'd forced himself not to call her so he could move forward, release the pain and memories once and for all. That morning, he'd said a little prayer...

"If I'm not supposed to see or talk to Emily ever again, somebody up there give me a sign. If I am supposed to see or talk to her again, though, let me know that, too."

And then, she'd walked through his damn door.

Chapter Ten
Making HIStory

"YEAH, THEY WERE in danger of closing, but with the help of the community and some great sponsors, the doors stayed open," Cameron explained as they walked about in Brooklyn's Weeksville Heritage Center.

Emily wrapped her white button-down cardigan snugly around her shoulders, aware of how overdressed she was. Everyone seemed to be in jeans and T-shirts while she had on a black and burgundy pinstriped swing dress paired with pointy-toed black heels.

"This place is so inspiring to me, Emily." His dark eyes gleamed with hope. "This is one of those places that teaches so much about the contributions of Black people, *my* people, in this country."

She forced a smile as they moved along. Cameron was rather animated when in his element—so different from her. She'd have found it entertaining, were it not that she felt so much like a fish out of water.

She'd spent so much time preparing for their date that she hadn't even looked into what the Weeksville Heritage Center actually was.

Now she knew.

Anxiety filled her to the point she felt an annoying earlobe tickle every now and again when her nerves were worked.

This center was a tribute to the contributions and struggles of African Americans in the United States. A place of upliftment, and the energy was palpable. She was surprised to see people of all colors and ethnicities visiting the establishment. Some of the exhibits were painful to observe.

Lynchings.

Beatings.

Civil Rights Riots.

Sure, she'd come across similar images before in history books, but somehow, they hadn't resonated like this. Maybe she'd never truly seen them.

"So, what do you think?"

"Oh, huh?" She clutched her cardigan, her palms sweaty. "I'm sorry, I was so enthralled by some of the displays, I missed what you were saying. What do I think of what?"

Cameron crossed his arms, looking remarkably handsome and smelling like a dream come true. The muted autumn sunrays filtered in from a large window, settling on his features.

"I asked, what do you think of this place? It's amazing, isn't it?" He smiled. "It means a lot to me. I worked hard on a fundraiser to raise money for it last year, too."

"I can tell it's important to you. It's enlightening." She searched her mind for other words, something that would sound sincere.

He stopped and frowned at her, dwarfing her with his sheer size. He slipped his hands into his pockets.

"Did you know even this location has meaning? Crown Point has so much history for Black people, Emily. Right here is where they could move about and work freely post-slavery."

He reached for her hand and placed it over his chest. She felt the strong, hard pecs through his long-sleeved black shirt.

"You have a strong heartbeat."

"That's my soul dancing," he said with a wink. He released her hand and they continued to walk. "You can admit it to me."

"Admit what?" The space had cleared out a bit, and now she could hear her own heels clicking against the floor with each step she took.

"When I gave my speech earlier today about cultural appreciation and historical legacy, I watched you a few times. Right now, none of this is really hitting home for you. Am I right?"

"Well, I mean, it's all amazing but since I'm White, I can't really—"

"Nah, see, that has nothing to do with it. You being White doesn't disqualify you from having at least some curiosity. White people are part of our history, too. Like the White abolitionists, for example, and those who marched with Dr. King. See," he said, "I know people can change, Emily. I've studied it. I *am* the change. We are all in this together."

He smiled. "Now there is still a way to go, and allies are needed, so saying you're White is no excuse." Her face flushed with heat. "In fact," he looked about the place,

"White people come here all the time. Some leave crying or full of appreciation. We have a shared history, we're Americans, but my history is so different from yours, and many of the chapters are not pretty. Right now, I see something in your eyes, kinda like that look a child gives her mother when she's trying to explain why taking out the trash or treating people kindly is so important."

She briefly lowered her gaze. "I've struggled with these issues." Her heart exploded. Cameron had such an enormous presence. Not only was he good-looking, sexy, fun, and intelligent, but he had an aura about him she couldn't ignore.

No wonder Brooke fell in love with him.

"What issues?"

"Race issues." As they stared at one another, her heart beat so hard, she feared she may need to sit somewhere and rest. Cameron was incredibly hard to read.

He tapped his finger against his chin, his eyes narrowed.

"Emily, I am going to ask you a series of questions."

"Okay."

I don't like the sound of this.

"I'm going to first ask you one that is the basis for many jokes. Do you have any Black friends besides me?"

"Currently?"

He nodded.

"No."

"Have you ever?"

"One."

"Don't make excuses for these next questions I am about to ask you. A yes or no will do."

148

"Okay."

"Do you empathize with the struggle of Black Americans in this country?"

Sweat broke out on her forehead and her chest felt tight.

"I…I can't really answer that with a yes or no."

"Yes, you can. This is a black and white question, pun intended. Again, do you empathize with the struggle of Black Americans in this country?"

"No."

"As a whole, do you believe we're problematic?"

Her eyes began to water. "Yes." She caught a wayward tear before it slipped down her face.

"Do you think most Black registered voters supported Barack Obama because he's Black?"

"Yes." Another tear fell. Then another.

"Do you want affirmative action done away with?"

"Yes."

"Even though it helps White woman more than any other minority group in this country? That's something many don't know."

Shame started to rear its head.

"Next question. Would you be afraid of me if I were a stranger passing you by at three a.m. in slouchy jeans that exposed my boxers, a snapback, a gold chain, hoodie, and my Timberland boots?"

"I don't know."

"Answer, please."

"Yes. YES. YES." She buried her forehead in her palms and sobbed her eyes out.

He continued on, never raising his voice, never pausing.

"Do you think that housing discrimination against people of color exists, and if so, are there ever valid reasons to discriminate against someone based on their race or ethnic makeup?"

"Yes to both questions." She started to shake and kept her gaze averted.

"As someone who works in finance, have you ever discriminated against a non-White client?"

"No." She slowly lifted her face, certain her mascara was smeared and her complexion splotchy. Cameron's brow rose. "I'm serious, I'm telling the truth. I never have. Money is green." He nodded and smiled. "Wait? You're not pissed at me for my responses?"

Taking her hand, he tugged gently and they resumed walking.

"Emily, I'm almost thirty-five damn years old. Now, to many, that's still considered fairly young, but I've seen and heard a lot, okay? It takes a hell of a lot more than what you said to get me all riled up." He shrugged. "I'd only have been pissed if you lied to me. So, my next question is simple. Do you want to change?"

He stopped walking. She swallowed, hesitating.

"Yes," she said with a nod. "I do."

"Why?"

"Because I don't like who I am anymore." More tears fell as her face warmed with embarrassment. "I'm so ashamed." She sobbed, attracting some attention. This was so unlike her. "Ever since the transplant, I feel so much humiliation and I look at things a lot more closely. I mean *every*thing. I dissect my life now. Everything I do, I think about the why, you know? I'm constantly looking at myself in the mirror and it's wearing me down. Everything is changing, Cameron. Some of it is out of my control. I have to keep digging, searching, or I'll never be satisfied. I have to keep up with my heart."

She placed her hand over her chest and smiled sadly.

"Feeling fearful is a good acknowledgement because that's what racism is somewhat about, Emily. Fear of not being the top dog. Fear of not being in charge, not the majority. You think the powers that be want a bunch of niggers, wetbacks, chinks, and spics thinkin' we are on the same level as them?" Her eyes widened at his word usage. "That's right, I said those words I've heard so many times. That's how they see us."

"So, how do you believe this is being controlled and implemented?" She crossed her arms, fully intrigued.

"Religion." He began to count off his fingers. "Authority figures, the prison system, and destruction of our culture through our music and other artistic expression. They know Black people are real religious folks. You'd be hard pressed to find a Black person raised in a majority Black community who doesn't believe in God, including myself, and yet, our crime rates are through the roof. Now, our crime is a multi-tiered issue but again, that's too complex to get into now. We can discuss it later."

"I'd like that."

He smiled. "Here's the problem, Emily." His deep voice vibrated through her soul. Taking her hand in his, he sat her down on a nearby bench.

"We've got a church every half mile, a liquor store on

every corner, a drug dealer runnin' every block, a sex trade business in every damn hotel, and a Black ass preacher that looks like the father who wasn't in our home, the husband we never had. We want him tellin' us prayer is gonna make it all right, and to put our hard-earned cash in that collection plate while he ignores our plights and drives off in his new Benz. That's not a coincidence. That's by design. The true men of God who try to help the community get ignored and devalued because they're not flashy enough. They don't have a big following online, aren't as slick with the vernacular. It's an uphill battle. You just can't win for losing. Faith without works is dead, but somehow, that scripture got buried. When God is used as a political and manipulative tool, you sully the beauty of God. When it's not God that's the problem, it's the greedy hearts of mankind."

"You also mentioned authority. How does that play into it?"

"Why in the hell do you think we've still got cops beatin' our asses and getting off scot free? It's not because the government loves police officers so damn much and wants us all to be law-abiding citizens. It's because as long as you have a symbol of influence still terrorizing you, giving you PTSD, then you will *always* remain on that plantation, at least, mentally." He pointed to his temple. "Slave masters didn't die or relinquish their power. They just traded in their whips for a badge."

"Can I ask you something about that?"

"Of course. You can ask me whatever you want."

He squeezed her hand.

"I understand what you're saying, but what about Black-on-Black crime, Cameron? That's a horrible reality, too, but it seems that whenever a White person brings up this topic, we're silenced, told we cannot understand."

"Well, you're right, and it's not just White people. Some Black people, including celebrities, have also complained about perceived hypocrisy. Look, here's the difference, Emily. Yes, Black-on-Black crime is a huge problem and it's not being addressed the way it should be. But as a society, we are supposed to be able to trust the police. When you have a demographic of people who've been alienated, profiled, subjugated, and abused, who are afraid to even call the police for a breaking and entering crime in progress in their own damn home, or a rape, mugging, whatever, you've created a cocktail for disaster. You know you can get beaten or killed because you had the audacity to question why you're being stopped. Being shot in the back when there's no reason to. This is not the Black person's or White person's problem; it becomes a problem for all of us. A societal setback."

"Are you speaking from experience regarding the police?"

"What do *you* think?" He grimaced.

"I don't know. That's why I'm asking."

"I have been followed by the police numerous times. I have never mugged anyone, Emily. I have never sold drugs, either. I've never pimped a woman out, did nothing that society says I, as a Black man, would likely do twenty-four seven. I have never physically attacked anybody unless it was in self-defense, either. And yet, I've been pulled over for no damn legit reason. When it happens, I've been asked a bunch of personal questions that had nothing to do with the reason I was pulled over in the first place and I've been asked how I could afford my car. When they look at my address, they question how I can afford to live there.

"Also, when I'm dressed in a manner that you may think is intimidating, like a ball cap or baggy clothes, I get it ten times worse. Hell, I may have just gotten back from the gym. I've seen White people cross the street to put distance between us when I and my friends are not even paying any damn attention to them, just minding our own business. I've waited for what felt like an eternity for a cab to pull over and get me. Meanwhile, people who look like *you* would barely be standing there for one minute and they're lining up to get that fare. There are small aggravations in life," he said, animated, "and things that make your life a living hell when you're Black in America. I've said a lot, probably too much for you to ingest in one sitting."

"But I'm enjoying this."

His eyes hooded as he took his sweet time studying her.

"We can talk about the rest later." He released her hand and cleared his throat.

They got up from the bench and continued on. He slowed as they approached a display showcasing an old newspaper that read, "The Freedman's Torchlight."

"Check that out," he instructed.

Emily read every word on the page, Cameron standing quietly beside her. Then, he intertwined their fingers and brought her hand up to his lips, kissing it. Shivers ran down her spine.

"If you have any questions, let me know." She nodded. "Education is the key to unlock hope, as my father says. It cures ignorance. Remaining willfully hateful, steeped in racism after being given opportunities to learn and do better, is not ignorance; it's mental and emotional suicide."

She slowly turned in his direction.

"I didn't know what this place was before I got here. Can you believe that?"

"You knew. On some level, you knew what it was from the name of the establishment and uh, maybe even from Brooke. You came here because you needed this. Don't kid yourself. The best gift you can give yourself, besides a new heart, is a new heart, if you catch my drift."

He slowly released her hand and walked off, leaving her there. She watched him for a bit, then turned back toward the display. After that, she walked to the next, and the next, and the next.

Her mind filled up with information—fascinating facts, interesting tidbits, and the like. Cameron was no longer two-dimensional in her eyes; he was flesh and bone. He was real.

He laughed. He learned. He loved.

She reached for her cardigan once again and bunched the material in her grip.

I like him too much. I could get hurt. He's so passionate about his culture, there's no way he'd entertain being with me. I can't even believe I am still thinking about him like this, but I am. I want him.

I want his knowledge.
I want his company.
I want his kiss.

Chapter Eleven
Making Amends

"I WASN'T PLANNING on staying long. These are for you." Cameron handed her the beautiful, high-end bouquet he was holding. "I was in the area and thought of you."

Emily sniffed the flowers, smiling. "Thank you, Cameron. These are beautiful."

"You're welcome. Glad you like them."

Placing them down upon her desk, she gestured for him to sit in the leather chair in front of her.

"But I don't want to hold you up or—"

"Sit down, Cameron. I can spare at least fifteen minutes for an amazing man who, I might add, is allowing me to handle his portfolio for the next twelve months. That's an honor."

She looked deep into his rich cocoa eyes. Cameron pulled out the chair and sat down. She noticed a striking diamond ring in a platinum setting.

He definitely seems to enjoy his jewelry. I mean, it's not over the top or anything, but he's borderline flashy.

"Nice ring."

"Thank you. You look great, too, by the way. That outfit

suits you." He pointed at her white blazer and matching knee-length skirt, which felt a little tighter than usual. She'd certainly been enjoying herself too much these days, going on dinner dates and such with Cameron.

"Oh, thank you. I hadn't worn this in a while. Saw it in the back of my closet this morning. I was going to actually—" She was cut off by the sudden ringing of his phone.

"Oh, sorry, Emily. Hold that thought." Cameron held up his finger. "This is business related."

She turned to her computer as he answered the call.

"Hey, man…Mmm hmmm…Yeah, probably around three or so." Cameron glanced at his Rolex watch. After placing the phone on the desk, he put it on speaker and stood from the chair to fix a sock that kept rolling down.

"So, Cam, there's about a fifth or so of that left and then around four today, Andre will be here to set up. I'll ask him to bring more if he has any."

"He doesn't. Don't bother. I will handle it when I get there. I told Andre he couldn't set up that early, though. Call him and tell him to wait."

"Why?"

"He causes too much of a distraction by engaging everyone in conversation when they're supposed to be working and then he goofs off instead of making the most of his time. So, when it's showtime, he is behind schedule. He can't come before six o'clock p.m. Period. I already told him this and I mean it."

"Maaaan, this nigga like already on the way. I can't call him and tell him to turn around."

"I don't care if he's inside the damn building saving

souls. He doesn't do what I ask him to do, and then, while customers are coming in, he has his damn boxes, Bubble Wrap and shit all over the place and the backdrop is still not finished. I am tired of jumping in and helping. That's not my job anymore. What the hell am I even payin' him for? Look, he's your friend, not mine. I hired him as a favor to you. Now correct this shit."

"Awww, Cam! Nigga, you bein' too hard on him. He been going through some shit."

Cameron stood to his full height, looking vexed. He plopped back down onto the seat, took the phone off speaker, and resumed his conversation. When it was all over, he slid his phone in his pocket. She was responding to an email, but could feel his glare upon her.

"Sorry about that. It's always something." He sighed.

"Not a problem. I understand. You're a businessman, after all." She hit send, closed her laptop, and clasped her hands over her desk. "Cameron?"

"Yes?"

"Do you mind if I ask you a question? A touchy one?"

"You always do, and I always answer. What is it?"

Leaning back in her seat, she crossed her arms over her breasts and pivoted back and forth in her seat. "Why do you and your friends refer to each other with the 'N' word? I've seen many Black people do it, but White people are not allowed to."

Cameron mulled her question for a bit. "A better question would be, why do you *want* to use it?"

Wow. I'd never thought about it that way.

"Well, see, that's just it. It's not that I actually want to use it, but if you find it so offensive, why are *you* using it?"

"Okay, first of all," he held up one finger, his tone remaining even, "you've never heard me use it except for that one time at the museum, and that was in the context of the discussion. I wasn't calling anyone that. I've never been around you and let that slip from my mouth. You heard my employees use it. You've probably heard my friends use it when I've been on the phone with them, but never me. Now, have I said it? Yes. Often. I would be lying to you if I said I haven't. I am trying to strip it from my vocabulary though. This has been an ongoing challenge, but I've gotten much better."

"And what's your personal reasoning for trying to eradicate it from your vocabulary?"

"Because of who I am as a person now. Like you, I've changed. We're always evolving, or should be. If I'm the same person I was five or ten years ago, that would be a problem. Every day, we should be learning something new."

"Why do I suspect that's something Brooke taught you?" she said with a grin.

"You'd be right." He smiled back. "And speaking of Brooke, she never used that word, Emily. Not all Black people use it. My mother doesn't. My father uses it rarely. See, that's another misconception some White people have. You want to use a word that not even everyone in that demographic is using, it's crazy to me. Some women call each other bitches, but does that give me the right to a call a woman that just because I suspect she calls her friends the same? Can I walk up to some lady and be like, 'Hey, bitch, can you tell me what time it is, please?'" She snickered at his words. "I'm serious. Most women would probably be insulted by that. I'm not her female friend; she doesn't know me. Do you see the difference?" She simply stared at him. "Okay, maybe you're still confused. Let me break this down in layman's terms. There's a difference between 'nigga' and 'nigger.' All right?"

"What's the difference?"

"Intent plays a big factor, as well as who is saying it. Nigga is often used as a term of endearment such as a Black woman calling her boyfriend or husband her nigga. Example, 'That's my nigga. I love him.' You don't hear us using the 'er' version. A nigger, by definition, is an ignorant person, right?"

"Correct."

"So that means, Asian, White, Indian people, etcetera, can all be niggers but that doesn't exclude contextual meaning and definition. The actual meaning of the word bitch is a female dog, but the contextual meaning has altered that, so we have to be careful, see? The word nigger was used to cause harm, not to uplift. The word nigga was used to unite. I feel though, in today's society, it is no longer uniting us at all. Again, it took me getting a little older to see this. In my youth, I didn't find anything wrong with it. Most of my friends said it, the music I listened to had it in the lyrics. It was just how things were. The word 'nigga' was created to also take the power out of the word 'nigger,' so it could no longer be used against us as a people."

"Okay. To take ownership away, basically."

"Exactly. Now you're getting it, but that's backfired, too. What I don't understand, though, is non-Black people's desire to use it. This brings us back to my original question: Why do so many White people ask that question? Why do you want to use the word, huh? You need to ask yourself that, because to me, it is far more important than any vernacular that someone is using among their own people. Like me callin' a gay man a fag is not okay, but they can call themselves that, as it should be. There are probably hundreds of examples of this. Cultural lines that can't be crossed, and yet, White people like to focus on the word *nigga* so damn much. It's like an obsession. So tell me, why?"

"But I just told you I don't want to use it. That's not what my question was about."

"I don't believe that. I think many White people want to do everything we're doing, and then some. You want to be able to dress up in blackface or wear Indian costumes for Halloween, and think that's okay. That's someone's heritage you're using for a holiday. You want to call sports teams the Redskins and all this other bullshit, but if someone called a baseball team the White-skins, Saltine Crackers, or Pink-skins, you mothafuckas would have a fit."

"Oh, come on, Cameron." She chuckled. "You're really stretching it here. Being Indian was seen as being strong, a warrior. Now don't get me wrong, I understand why you're saying that and, in this day and time, I'd say no, it's not an appropriate name for a baseball team. But it's not the same."

"Sure it is. Let me ask you something. Have you ever called someone a nigger before, Emily?"

She swallowed.

"Not to their face, but yes." He shook his head, looking disgusted, then laughed dismally. "I thought I could be honest with you, Cameron?" she snapped.

"You can, but that doesn't mean I am not allowed to *feel* something in regard to your answer. I *like* you. That would be like me admitting that I slapped some White person upside the head all because they were White. You wouldn't appreciate that, either, especially since you consider yourself fond of me now. And let's get something straight. I've noticed that when we have these discussions, if I don't keep my voice real low and quiet like some church mouse, you get all beside yourself."

"Now you're just lying."

"No, I'm not. I'm serious. I'm not a robot. I'm a human being. You are someone I'm interested in, regardless of how we met, and you say you're interested in me, too, but we have a lot of mental unpacking still to do."

"What do you mean by mental unpacking? Oh, did you want something to drink? I have some—"

"No, I'm straight. By mental unpacking I mean that I need to know who the hell you are. Who is the *real* you, not the big-time financial analyst, not the part occupied by Brooke, but the true-blue Emily? The part of you that you never let anyone see because you're too busy showin' off, tryna look pretty, bust some balls to prove you can hack it in a male-dominated field. And prove to your rich, White daddy that you can do this shit and then some—be the son he never had. That's who the hell I'm tryna deal with, okay?"

His words had bite. They hurt.

"You're angry." She shook her head.

"I'm passionate, Emily. I'm in complete control of myself right now. That's another issue I have with you."

"And what's that?" she asked dryly as she tossed an empty cardboard cup in the trash can.

"No person of color can have a serious discussion with you, particularly a Black person, without you thinking they are angry. And by you, I mean many White people I've dealt with in business, friendships, whatever." His face twisted into a frustrated expression. "I am sick and tired of voicing a grievance to a White person, and they stare at me like they want to call security, like I'm King Kong climbing up some building out to get them. It doesn't matter what I am wearing, how articulate I am, if I even raise my voice one damn octave." He held up one finger. "They are clutchin' their pearls."

"I believe you, I do…but I do have another question that might piss you off."

He laughed and tossed up his hands. "You do that all the time, anyway. That's part of the reason why I like you, Emily. I know I am getting the real deal. You're just lost, and I'm here to find you."

"Okay, so don't be mad, but I'd like to know why the race card, the victim mentality, is played so often even in areas where it doesn't apply."

"What do you mean? Explain to me what you're saying exactly so I can respond accordingly."

"Past pain can cause future paranoia. That's a fact."

"You're speaking like all this pain and all this racism comes from the past alone. No, baby. Black people live this shit daily and to think otherwise is utter bullshit."

"You're using emotion and not logic, Cameron."

"I can use both at the same time because I'm a juggler

and I'm smart and I'm a Black man in America. I have to use both in order to survive. Do you see how easily I can speak articulately then go back to urban slang with my buddies and family? Black people in this country have to be damn near persona magicians just to survive and get along with you, and you bastards still aren't happy. I know who I am, though, and I know how I'm viewed and where I stand. You better know who you are, and get in where you fit in."

"What does that last bit have to do with this conversation?"

"Entitled White dudes have talked down to my father, in front of me, Emily. Called him a boy. A grown ass Black man with a degree who had no kids out of wedlock, is married to my mother, and was just trying to live his life in peace, raise his kids. And those same dudes have no respect for women like you, either."

"The world's not fair, Cameron. That doesn't mean I have to go around acting bitter."

"Lying down and taking it never solved a problem. I'm a problem-solver. White men don't like a guy like me making moves on a woman like you. To them, you're the crème de la crème, and you know it. You're tall, blonde, thick, and you have your own money and a rich daddy. That's a damn dream come true. Yet, they will not think twice about hurting you, cheating on you, though they will scream at the top of their lungs about how Black men are corrupting their women. There are bad men and good men of every color, but these guys will never see that." His voice boomed throughout her office.

"Please don't be angry with me, Cameron. I am just trying to understand. You've encouraged me to ask questions."

"Emily, baby, I'm not mad at you. I'm mad at the system. I couldn't even be with you if I believed you were holding onto a certain mentality. You're different." He pointed at her. "You inspire me because you are trying to understand. I can see in your eyes that you care, that you are trying to deconstruct years of beliefs that lie inside your head."

"Well, that's something we both can agree on."

"Good. We both can learn from one another. Oh, I almost forgot. You brought up the victim mentality and the race card. Yeah, it happens, and I have no problem talking to you about that—but see, we can't even get into a full discussion about the race card being played, Emily, until the *real* race issues are acknowledged and addressed. I can't walk around debating fake grievances when real grievances are on the table that you and others turn a blind eye to. That's like when someone gets robbed down the street and no one cares, then, an hour later, someone else says they got robbed in the exact location, but they lied. So all people do is focus on the lie, talk about it all morning, noon and night, rather than discuss the true incident that actually occurred earlier in the day—because this first case didn't fit their narrative. See, that's how Black people feel when you all say we use the race card. The point is, there shouldn't be any cards on the table in the first place because my life isn't a game."

She nodded and sniffed. He was right. She couldn't deny that.

"When I'm loud, that doesn't necessarily mean I'm angry, okay?" he continued, his voice calmer.

She nodded again, her emotions welling within her, leaving her practically speechless. "I'm glad you asked me these things. Everyone has that button though, you know? And this is mine. Sometimes I just offer tough love is all."

"I'm glad you understand. I feared our friendship would be ruined if I asked certain questions." She hung her head, feeling so bleak.

"I would *never* end what we've got because of something like this. You are so thirsty for this information, and I'm proud of you. I know it's not easy." She smiled sadly. "That doesn't mean it's easy to talk about, either."

"I wish we could all talk peacefully, everyone in this country. We can't get overly emotional about things."

Cameron placed his hands on her desk and leaned forward. He offered a cocky smile, the kind that said, "I know something you don't."

"Hurt people hurt people. That's what Brooke used to say. Who hurt you, Emily?"

She frowned.

"I never tried to hurt anyone." She scoffed. "What are you talking about?"

"You have tried to hurt people. You know what you're doing, and you'd have hurt me, too, if I let you. This is why you ask the tricky questions. The ones that could possibly get a rise out of someone like me."

"You said I could ask anything. I cannot believe you—"

"Your problem with me is that I intimidate you and you don't like it." She scoffed and rolled her eyes. "Nah, I'm serious. No man has had the balls to talk to you how I talk to you. Why? Because you're typically the one doing the intimidating. Not me. I'm an alpha man. A true alpha doesn't have to tell anyone they're an alpha. Their actions show it. I've never said this to you before, or any woman I've been involved with. It was unnecessary. I get it, though. You're an alpha woman. So was Brooke, but she knew how to keep her femininity and be a listening ear, as well as show emotion. She's working on you real good and she's going to *break* you. She's going to break you the fuck down from the inside out until you submit."

Emily's nostrils flared. "You don't intimidate me, Cameron. You intrigue me."

"If that's what you need to tell yourself, that's fine." He shrugged. "But I'm not your father. I'm not going to coddle your ass. You want to be able to tell me your truth, but not always hear mine. It doesn't work that way. By the way…"

"Yes?"

"Speaking of parents, you never talk about your mother. Where is she?"

"She's dead."

"Okay." He didn't offer an, "I'm sorry to hear that." Nothing. "Were you young when she died?"

"What does any of that matter?"

"Oh, it matters because you're hurt and this pain isn't recent. This is old and festering. She had a major impact on you. Let me guess. You were fifteen?"

"I was sixteen, almost seventeen when she died."

"See, people who hate cling to their warped beliefs because they are hurting. No one just wakes up and decides they hate someone. Children aren't born racists, Emily. Children don't daydream of strapping themselves with bombs and blowing up buildings in the name of Allah, or killing somebody because of the color of their skin. No, a hurt adult taught them that, poisoned them."

"Are you trying to tell me that my mother poisoned my mind?"

"Nope. You said that. I didn't." He stared at her coldly. "Did your mother like Black people?"

"Oh, for God's sake."

"No, come on. Answer."

"I don't know." She tossed up her hands. "We never discussed it."

"Oh, you know. You loved your mother; she was good to you, so you don't want to say anything bad about her. But let's come full circle with this conversation. Your mother, probably beautiful like you if not even more so, used the 'N' word freely, didn't she?" He smirked. "You heard her call someone a nigger more than once. Your mother was a racist, just like you. You walked right in her high-heeled footsteps."

"Shut up."

"Say it. Say your mother called someone a nigger."

"Cameron."

"Come on, baby. This is your chance to use the 'N' word again. You want to say it, right? Say it. Call me a nigger."

"What the hell is wrong with you?"

"Nothing is wrong with me." He laughed mirthlessly, showing his snow-white pretty teeth. "You wanna dig, right? You wanna push my buttons, get off on the show, see the Black man dance and hop around. Or do you want to get to the truth?"

"I want the truth. You actually teach others about this

very thing, so I thought we could discuss it, but it seems that you are—"

"You wanted to find out why you can't call me a nigga but my friend can, right? I told you. I want you now to look me in the eye and tell me why your mother was also racist? That's where you got it from, right? You felt comfortable doing it too until your old, hollow, rotten, diseased, broken and fucked up heart got snatched out of you and replaced with one worth having."

"Because she didn't know any better!" Tears welled up in Emily's eyes as she shook like a leaf. "Because my mother was raised hearing it, too."

Cameron stood straighter and plunged his hands into his black blazer pocket.

"Feeling emotional? Perhaps angry? It happens. Welcome to the real world. You found my button today, and now, I've found yours. We're even."

He walked around the desk and pressed his lips into her forehead. She kept her eyes averted while her emotions went all over the place. He pulled back and jiggled his car keys in his pocket. "We don't have to hate someone we loved just because they'd taught us the wrong thing. You just have to toss out the bad shit they gave you, but first, you have to acknowledge that it's bullshit in the first place. That's your new assignment. See you tomorrow, beautiful." He kissed her cheek, then headed out the door.

EMILY SAT CROSS-LEGGED on her messy bed with the

overhead light on, clutching her phone in silence. The roar of traffic could be heard through the closed windows. The curtains were drawn but a sliver of afternoon light made it through. There had been sleepless nights. Too many to count.

The nightmares had begun again, though now, they no longer involved a funeral; it was all about her, standing naked in a white room, decked in blackface, laughing. Her reflection showed a stark white face, crying. Blood poured from her mouth as she giggled in the nightmare, and every word she said made the bleeding worse. With every thought she had—the ugly, prickly, nasty things—worms crawled out of her ears and collected around her bare feet.

She sniffed, blew her nose, and put her phone back to her ear.

"Yes, I understand that. I don't want his number, though. I provided you the date of the ride in question. I don't have to have his number, but he was my Uber driver that morning."

"Yes, I see that here. This number is for urgent matters only, Ms. Windsor. This was quite some time ago."

"It was, but I just realized it, you see? I fully respect Mr. Chhugani's privacy. I hope I'm pronouncing his name correctly. This *is* an urgent matter. I have something of his that I accidentally picked up from his car during the ride." She cleared her throat. "According to my Uber records and the beautiful one-star review that he left," she smiled faintly as a wave of embarrassment washed over her, "I see he's still an active driver. Is there some way that you can leave him my number and he can contact me?"

"Yes, Ms. Windsor. Since you want to return something of his, I will contact the driver and then he may contact you at his discretion. Can you tell me what it is, please? I'm certain he'll ask."

"Something expensive. Thank you." Emily left her callback number and disconnected the call.

She hummed to the tune of "Human" by Daughter as she had a shower. After drying off her body and hair, she slipped into a pair of fitted jeans, a white button-down shirt, and black slides, then picked up some of the paperwork she'd been sorting the night before. Her phone rang then. She hurried to pick up the call, figuring it was her father or perhaps one of her friends, only to see an unusual number.

Her heart skipped a few million beats. Her eyes watered, and her brain felt as if it were swelling. She cleared her throat and answered.

"Hello?"

"Hello, I wish to speak to Ms. Emily Windsor, please." The thick accent clung to the words like a shawl; only this time, instead of feeling annoyance at the sound of his voice, she felt relief. Or dare she say it, peace.

"Mr. Chhugani, you may not remember me, but I was one of your riders a while back, in your car for Uber."

"I remember you," he stated curtly. "I have had hundreds of riders since then. But I remember you. I'm busy right now. What do you have of mine?"

"I have your peace of mind. I tried to steal your dignity."

He was quiet for a few moments.

"I do not understand what you are talking about, Ms. Windsor. I am very busy, so—"

"Please, let me explain. I first want to apologize to you, not only for how I spoke to you, but for my arrogance, ugliness, cruelty toward you, simply because of your race and the way you dress." Her voice trembled as she leaned against her coffee table, feeling sick to her stomach. Sick because she'd hurled her hurt, prejudices, and dysfunction in his direction. "I don't deserve your forgiveness, I deserve nothing from you at all, but before you hang up the phone, I want to tell you...I know how wrong I was that day. How hateful I was. How there was no excuse on this planet that would justify me barking at you as if you were some disobedient child. Worse yet, not even human. I have played that conversation over and over in my head, and instead of it getting easier, it gets worse. I become more and more mortified. More devastated. I went through life shitting on people."

She took a deep breath. "Please excuse my language but I was a person who surely didn't deserve any compassion or forgiveness from anyone I intentionally hurt. My actions were intentional, and that makes them even more horrible. It is one thing to be ignorant, and there was a bit of that, too, but I wanted to crush you. I wanted you to feel badly, simply because somewhere deep inside of me, I did, too. I still struggle with getting to know myself, but I'm trying. Again, Mr. Chhugani, I am very sorry for how I spoke to you and treated you that day, and if there is anything I can do to make up for it, please let me know."

She was met with a few moments of silence, though it felt like an eternity.

"Are you pulling my leg?" He chuckled, causing her to

smile and shake her head.

"No. I am serious. The only joke is the fact I had convinced myself I was a great person, when I was far from it. The joke was clearly on me. Now, is there a charity you're partial to? Perhaps I can make a donation to it on your behalf or maybe—"

"I don't want your money. Money doesn't solve everything, Ms. Windsor."

Her cheeks felt hot.

"I know. I know it doesn't. You're right. I just wanted to, uh, make this right."

"Perhaps. Perhaps not. I think you just want to make yourself feel better, too. Cross me off some checklist? Maybe you had a wake-up call of some sort and now want a pat on the back." His harsh words were somehow coated in a kindness, and the contrast was unnerving. Unexpected.

"Perhaps you're right."

"Like, eh, what do they call it? Like for alcoholics, yes? They make amends first? Confess?"

"Yes, like the twelve-step program." She let out a breath. "The difference, though, is that this is more than twelve steps for me and I am not following a program. Maybe I should. Maybe I became addicted to my own entitlement, my own sense of self? It's getting worse, this feeling in my stomach, as I speak to you. That's probably a good thing. It means I'm not off the hook. Look," she plopped down onto the couch and rubbed her forehead, "I have been through Hell these past few months. Without getting into all of the mundane details and to spare you the pity party, trust me, the cake isn't all that good. It may not make sense to you, but I had to do this, Mr. Chhugani. This is not just to make me feel better because I actually feel worse as I speak to you, much worse, but in grief, we sometimes do, right? I am grieving the image I had of myself. The lie. I really don't understand how anyone was able to tolerate me. I will spend my life, in one way or another, trying to correct my wrongs."

"Ms. Windsor, in my beliefs, Sikhism, we believe in no hatred, and definitely not seeking revenge. I probably should not have given you a one-star review."

"Of course you should have." She chuckled. "If negative stars existed, I should've received that instead. The punishment should fit the crime."

"Yes, but we all have committed wrongs. I did it, the one star, because I was angry with your behavior while I tried to take you to your destination. Naturally, that would make sense, but it did not help you in your journey. It did not help me in mine, either. It only confirmed what you were—full of anger and hatred. I became a mirror, instead of a beacon. I should have left you three stars, Ms. Windsor."

"Why three?"

"Three would mean I do not hate you. It would mean I feel sorry for you, and that, perhaps, you have room to grow." She swallowed hard as tears filled her eyes. "And though your offer regarding a charitable donation was generous, I suspect from your appearance that day that you are well-to-do. This emphasizes the have and have-nots in not only this country, but the world. Somehow, the rich are seen as more favored by the Creator. That maybe the Creator punishes others with hunger and poverty. That is absurd. In my faith, we do not believe in such things. Caste systems exist in India, though America has its own version. We're all humans, Ms. Windsor. We were all created by the same supreme Creator. There is no greater love for the wealthy than for the poor, for the dark-skinned versus the light. We are one. We are the same. You've made mistakes. It doesn't mean you cannot make good choices now, too."

"Thank you for that." She sniffed. "I don't deserve how nice you're being to me. It shocks me, actually."

"Kindness is how we change the world. Ugliness changes nothing. It's human to make mistakes. It's extraordinary to own them and make changes. It's not my position in life to try to own the gift of forgiveness. It's not mine exclusively. It is to be shared. If I cannot forgive, then I am no better than you. I'm no perfect man. No one is. I get angry, I get tired, but I believe you're truly sorry."

"I am." She pressed a tissue to her nose. "Thank goodness you see that. You are such a wonderful person. I don't think many would respond like this, but I do mean what I've said to you. I am genuine."

"Your words feel true in my heart. I have to go now, so—"

"Yes, yes, of course. I won't waste any more of your time."

"You didn't. You've simply stopped wasting your own."

Chapter Twelve
Love is Blind

SITTING ON HIS couch, Cameron rolled the smooth red and white dice between his palms. They clinked together like ice cubes as they warmed to his touch. While he enjoyed the smooth texture of the game pieces, feeling soothed, he let his mind travel. The scent of sky and linen candles filled the place, stoking his senses.

Brooke had purchased them a few weeks before her death. She had a thing for candles, essential oils, incense, and the like. He'd decided to light them that afternoon. It was an overcast day, so he sought some good vibes, flickering light and warmth. Besides, he'd been curious to see what they smelled like. He loved their smell.

Brownstone's "Grapevine" played on his old CD player, making him bob his head to the music. What a classic.

Setting the dice down, he reached for the old beat-up CD cover featuring the all-female band from the glass coffee table before him and ran his fingers down the front of it, smiling sadly as memories flooded his mind.

A childhood gone by, a young Black boy growing up in Brooklyn.

I remember when I first heard this song. I was so young. A kid. My mother used to play this on repeat in her car. She loved it. I guess I should give her a call soon or she might report me missing to the police.

He smiled at the thought of that. His mother had been complaining that he didn't call enough lately. It had been difficult. She claimed to understand he needed time and space. Yet, it was deeper than that. He didn't want to discuss Brooke and she often brought her up, or other times, he did want to discuss her but his mother would try to encourage him to move forward with his life. He knew she was only trying to help, but it didn't. In fact, it made things worse. He *was* moving on, that was the problem. That was why he was on edge.

And at the same time, he was standing still, hanging on to anything and everything to have the memories stay alive and in living color. He didn't believe anyone would ever come close to Brooke, no matter what. His mother was a great person to speak to usually about affairs of the heart, but this was different. Too many layers, too much sorrow, too much pain. There was a time or two he wanted to tell her about Emily, but changed his mind. Mama wouldn't understand.

He placed the CD back down and flopped back on the black leather couch, crushing the blood-red pillow beneath his weight. Closing his eyes and leaning his forehead into his hand, he drifted away to somewhere safe. He could hear Opium's snappy footsteps approaching and he grinned when the big dog placed his heavy head against his knee. In no time, the big fur ball was whining and begging for a savory morsel.

"I know…I know," Cameron said with a slight smile but kept his eyes closed. "You want something else to eat. My grocery bill is high because of you. I might as well have a couple of kids to feed."

Getting on his feet, he refilled the dog's large steel bowl with a few treats he'd picked up from Trader Joe's. Cameron stood in the kitchen, not quite motivated to get on with his day just yet. Things had been rather strained and crazy lately, to say the least.

Work was a madhouse. New acts were coming in and needed to be coordinated. He'd hired two new bartenders to help out with the high demand of the weekend crowd and he needed to interview another MC. His beer distributor had a slowdown in production; it was one of his top sellers at the bar, so in the interim he'd had to scramble to secure a new supplier that wouldn't cost him an arm and a leg. He'd almost listed his property for sale, had met with an agent and everything, but then decided against it, feeling wishy washy, going back and forth.

He'd even begun to pack his stuff, then put it on pause. He'd gotten the rest of Brooke's belongings boxed and placed in a closet, with the exception of a few treasures of hers he was keeping for himself. The place still felt like Brooke's though. Theirs. Shared space where souls had once combined. There was a big hole inside him, and he was concerned because initially, he'd been filling it with booze and anger like he'd never known.

Now he was filling it with something else…or *someone* else would be a far better description.

That someone else had sky-blue eyes—eyes that looked

both foreign and familiar.

He'd been spending more time with Emily, to the point that it was certainly causing heads to turn. She'd been at the club a few times, and he didn't miss how people looked his way, their glances questioning. They'd gone for walks together, met at Central Park. They'd been to movies, plays, dinner.

He thought about Emily quite often. He loved her voice, the way she dressed, despite it being so vastly different from Brooke's style. Her fashion sense was timeless, and she could hold her own. They seemed drawn to one another like moths to a flame. In fact, they were on the phone practically every night for at least an hour or two, chatting so much that it was becoming his routine—a welcomed one. It felt comfortable. It felt right, but it felt wrong, too.

I don't wanna let this go, though. I just feel like I might be usin' her. Am I?

He was fighting the attraction, the curiosity, the confusion.

It bothered him that Emily was White, though he was ashamed he didn't have the guts to just tell her. He never figured himself to be racist, but he simply preferred Black women for dating and romance. In fact, he could count on one hand how many times he'd dated a non-Black woman, and all that had happened in his younger years, before he became "enlightened."

I don't want to hurt her, and I don't want to hurt her feelings. She doesn't deserve that. It's obvious she's interested in me, that's a no-brainer. This bothers me though. This whole thing is just bizarre. It bothers me because now I'm attracted to her as more than a friend. If she were just a friend, I would happily spend time with her, not even think about it like this, but I know it's more than that. I really, really dig this woman. This is a mess.

He sighed, lowering his head for a spell, taking a moment to hear the traffic going by.

She's been working so hard to be open-minded and even when we don't agree, I don't feel like she's being, uh, dismissive, I guess I could say.

He opened the refrigerator, pulled out a gallon of distilled water, and poured it into Opium's water bowl. Brooke had the dog so spoiled that she rarely fed him from the tap.

Tap. Emily told me she used to take ballet and tap dance for years. She was good at ballet, showed me some old pictures she had on her social media. But then she said she liked bread and pie too much to continue. He laughed at that memory. *She listens to my reading suggestions on topics of culture and race and she's been a wealth of information to me regarding investing—all free of charge, on the house. This is her bread and butter, and she didn't even think of sending me an invoice. This is bullshit. Who the hell am I kidding? It wouldn't matter what she was doing for me. I just like her. Why do I keep going through this? I like the parts of her that aren't like Brooke, too. So that's not it. I thought that was just it, but I am seeing we're beyond that now. Yeah, Brooke is deep inside of this woman. That was our connection, the pull, the lure; I can feel it, smell it, hear it when she sings, but there are still components of her that aren't like my woman at all.*

She's snarky, funny sometimes. She thinks fast on her feet. She's kinda sneaky, too, but not in an unnerving way. She's calculating, and I can't knock her hustle. She's smart as hell too, and though I keep telling myself she isn't my type, any White guy out here would love to get their hands on her. She is like the epitome of White beauty. Why do I have to say "White" beauty? Isn't beauty just beauty? Nah, not really. Well, because there are White beauty standards in this country, ones that I don't agree with. The whole tall, slender, blonde and blue-eyed thing.

Emily has a nice little ass though. I mean, it's not big, but it sits high and it's just enough to hold onto. She's got curves, probably 'bout a C cup in the breasts. I mean, the woman's body is bangin'. Am I trying to put my own Black beauty standards on her now? What the hell is goin' on with me lately?

And now here I am arguing with myself in my own head. Silly and stupid.

He chuckled to himself as he leaned against a wall and stared out the window, people watching.

We've been out quite a few times now, and there's a shitload of sexual tension. This is gettin' crazy. I have had to restrain myself so many times from making a move. I can feel it, and I know she can, too. It's like, neither one of us wants to be the first one to admit it, then do something about it. I mean, I have no idea what to do. There's a lot of moving parts. I'm going to have to bite the bullet and just talk to her about this. We can't stay in limbo as we are. This ain't even my style. Something is going on between us. Something has to give.

He shrugged as he took note of a crowd gathering at the crosswalk.

He yawned and headed back to the living room when he heard his phone ring. He quickly answered it.

"Hey, I was just thinking about you, Emily." He slumped down on the couch and cleared his throat. "We need to talk."

EMILY SAT AT her desk at work, much to her father's dismay. He'd finally agreed to allow her to return full time, and thus far things were going fine. In fact, it was just the distraction she needed to stop obsessing about Cameron. Things had come to a head. They'd gone to a local actor's play together the other night, and their lips brushed against one another as they hugged and stared into each other's eyes. She wasn't certain if it had been intentional or not, but the look in his eyes as it happened definitely made her think it had been. The world around them had slowed down, and then, as if snapping out of a trance, he'd pulled away. He'd looked so confused, she didn't know quite what to make of it.

His gorgeous, dark eyes glossed over with what appeared to be resentment, yet his body pressed hard against hers as he enveloped her in one of the best hugs she'd ever had the pleasure of receiving. Cameron was strong and passionate at the same damn time. She'd never encountered a man like him: one who was intelligent, proud, and had what a friend of hers called "swag." Now, she understood it. She wasn't certain if this was a "Black man" thing, but Cameron had it in spades.

It wasn't over the top. It was there in layers, like in a huge tiered wedding cake peeking out from between the light, airy frosting, spilling forward in appetizing doses. She'd finally gotten the balls to show a friend of hers his picture, to test the waters a bit, dip her toe in the lake of public response. Yet, she'd been careful not to divulge who he was and how she knew him. She'd simply stated it was a new client. In some ways, that was true. She had in fact taken a look at his financial portfolio, noting so many matters that needed addressing, and wrote him up a report with suggestions that would undoubtedly save him six figures over the next two years, as well as grow his earnings by at least twenty-four percent.

So, when she'd showed Erin his picture from a local publication, her friend had said, "This is your new client? He's hot. If he's one of your clients, he must have money, too. Wow. Is he single? I don't usually go for Black guys, but I think I'd make an exception here. He's gorgeous. He looks tall, too. Is he tall?"

And so the conversation went. Emily had never revealed to Erin, Laura, or any of her friends that she was falling for this man. That she thought about him each and every night and the start and middle of every day. That they'd been spending time together—quality time, the kind where they shared more and more of each other and she attended events with this man that she'd never believed she'd be caught dead at.

But she'd ended up there, happily.

Emily wouldn't dare share that she'd invited him over one evening in hopes of having drinks and possibly more, but he'd turned her down, saying, "Maybe another time." She'd been heartbroken by his refusal and prayed that he wasn't pulling away, that they weren't drifting apart when they'd just begun.

I can't stop thinking about you, Cameron. You're amazing.

She swiveled back and forth in her chair, slid her foot out of her left shoe, and let it hit the floor. Rubbing the ball of her foot against her other leg, she fell into a silly daydream and couldn't wipe the smile off her face. He'd brought her joy, he'd brought her lessons, he'd brought her new understandings.

Every time he'd call or text, her heart would go pitter patter. And while she looked around her office, seriously considering a revamp to a warmer, cozier style, she held the phone, about to dial him up. How could she concentrate on work this way?

"So much for distractions to help me stop this crap," she mumbled with a smirk as she phoned him. Cameron soon answered and told her they needed to talk. Her heart beat faster, fearful he was going to pull the plug.

"Okay. What's on your mind?" She reached for an ink pen and twirled it about in her hand, trying to steady her nerves.

He took a loud, heavy breath.

"Emily, I like you."

"I like you, too."

"I like you as more than a friend, though I doubt you find that surprising." She swallowed, but remained quiet. "I find this, uh…difficult, I guess you could say. It's almost like a conflict of interest, ya know? On one hand, it's kind of understandable; on the other, it's totally unacceptable. I am a pretty decisive man. When I want something, or someone, I go for it. I put my all into it. I don't back down from a challenge, especially if it's on my bucket list or someone I could see myself with.

"In fact, Brooke used to complain that I was too assertive with my business maneuvers. You even accused my financial advisor of being too aggressive with some of my stocks, but I explained to you that was all my idea, not his. That's just how I am. Now, as far as how I go about relationships, I mean, it's been a minute, right? I've been outta the game. I was with Brooke a long time, but I remember how I would roll. When I was pursuing her and anyone else I wanted before she came into my life, I would keep going, full steam ahead until I had them. With you, Emily, it's different. I'm trying to be careful, move slow."

"I know." She grabbed a glass that resembled a science class beaker, and took a sip of the cool water flavored with fresh mint. "I also know why."

"Well, I was gonna tell you, but now I'm curious. Why do you think it is?"

"Because you probably feel guilty about being attracted to the lady who is alive because your girlfriend is dead. Because the circumstances in which we met are heartbreaking and a little weird. Because...because I'm White."

"Shit," he said in a whisper. "Well, yeah. That's it in a nutshell. That's it pretty much. I've been struggling with this for months now, okay? Since the moment I met you until this very second, this has been a roller coaster for me. At first, it was like, 'Okay, she's cool. No problem. She's got Brooke's heart and she acts like Brooke somewhat, too. Actually, she acts like Brooke a lot and maybe I can have a little more time with Brooke through her. Maybe this is God's way of lettin' me get some closure.' Then, weeks later, it was like, 'She's good-lookin' and I like her personality. She can sing, too.' That specific talent in females has always been a huge turn-on for me. That's when the guilt set in, because I felt like I was thinkin' about you too much, wondering what you were doing, wanting to ask you a bunch of questions. Quiz you, basically.

"A part of me hoped you were crazy or full of shit. You weren't. So, I had to accept that yeah, as crazy as this is, it's really happening. The heart transplant caused you to take on certain characteristics of my baby. Then, weeks after that, it's like, 'I'm really diggin' this lady. I like her, for real.' And then now, here we are, and it's like, 'Under any other circumstances, I would be pursuing this woman to the utmost. I like her style. I would be rolling out all the stops, extending myself. But how can I do that?'"

She nodded in understanding, though her eyes glossed over with worry. His tone sounded as if he'd come to a decision—one that wouldn't bode well for her.

"I know this is confusing. It's over the top for both of us. I really like you too, Cameron. I'm repeating myself, but it bears repeating, you know? I just wish we'd met under different circumstances, but then that doesn't make sense because we would have never met had it not been for my poor health, and then I wouldn't have experienced this transformation I am having had it not been for Brooke. It all lines up. Everything happened for a reason. Let me ask you something, Cameron."

"Yeah, go ahead. What's up?"

"Do you think you'd be dating at this time—like, if I wasn't in the picture, do you think by now you would have started to entertain the idea of socializing with other women?"

"Emily, I wasn't ready to date and no, I wouldn't have

been dating now. That's highly unlikely. I know it's been several months, but that's still too soon for me, at least I believed it was. I wasn't looking to get involved with anyone for a long ass time. It was the furthest thing from my mind and, not to sound crude, but fucking and dating are two different things to me. I am not going to sit here and say that I may not have had some booty calls eventually, but it definitely wouldn't have been any more than that. But then you came along."

She smiled at his words. "We crossed paths. Our discussions have changed my life, Cameron. Brooke was so lucky to have you."

"I was lucky to have her, Emily. And that's just the thing. It's like she unlocked this gate. You said initially she made you come and see me. It was like she was using your body to get a second lifetime. I can't believe I'm even sayin' this shit, buying into this." He chuckled nervously. "We went from talking to dating in what felt like a matter of seconds, only we hadn't defined it that way. I was intrigued by you, Emily. I resented you. You represented everything I was having a problem with, fighting against—a sense of entitlement; closed-mindedness; lack of passion, art, and vision; racist; stuck-up. But I'd judged you too harshly."

"And I deserved the judgment because I was, and still am to some degree, all of those things." She smiled through the pain as her chest radiated with warmth.

"I can't throw stones at you when I have my own shit to address. I'm far from perfect. Anyway." He sighed heavily. "I felt something for you, and that feeling grew. When you looked at me and told me basically that you had some problems, that you were messed up, and that you wanted to change, your admission did something to me, Emily. It solidified the fact that you were climbing to a higher level, and I loved it. Then when we had that big blow-up in your office the other day, I saw in your eyes and could hear your ambition in that conversation to learn, to self-correct and heal. Growth hurts. I love watching people grow, period. I don't even know what to call this, what we have. We both know this isn't platonic or just to do with Brooke anymore. It's *more* than that now. I think I felt like I was using you because my initial attraction to you was because you were becoming so much like her, and I selfishly wanted to get a second chance with her, too. I was just gonna use you to do it, like you were some pretty packaging that I didn't give a shit about. I just wanted the prize that was inside. You're not a Cracker Jack box."

"It wasn't selfish," she whispered.

"Huh?"

"It wasn't selfish, Cameron. I knew what you wanted, and you knew what I wanted. A permanent part of me, my heart, wants you. My heart is not mine; it's Brooke's. It will never be *fully* mine. I'm just a host. You'll never have me without Brooke, or Brooke without me. I had to spend so many waking hours pondering this." Tears filled her eyes as she lowered her gaze to her lap. "Cameron, I have read articles about this sort of thing until I went cross-eyed. This has happened to other people. It's met with a lot of skepticism, but it happens. So, unless I kill myself, which I have no intention of doing, this is my fate. This is where life has brought me. I am a White woman with the heart of a Black woman. Not just physically, but her very embodiment.

"Everything she loved I love now, too. That's what a heart does. It loves. She loved music, she loved her dog, she loved to sing, she loved people, *all* people from all walks of life. She loved. She *loves* you." Silence stretched between them for a few moments. "Cameron, I care for you deeply. You don't have to do anything about that. You aren't obligated. My love for you, however, came through Brooke, but it is growing to be mine, too. One day, if this continues, I will be in love with you as well. There's no other way this could end up. There's no other conclusion."

She could hear him inhale and exhale, as if attempting to stay in control of his emotions.

"You know, as we've spent more time together, Emily, I feel things for you. If I didn't, we wouldn't even be having this conversation. Yeah, we both know what's happened. There's no way that you could know the things you knew about me and Brooke not be a part of you. You knew things about me, our life together that you shouldn't have. You know me, the *real* me. I don't let people get that close to me, Emily, not like *that* anyway, but you knew some of my secrets. Things only Brooke knew."

She smiled sadly. "So, Cameron, it looks like the day of reckoning has come." She swiped a tear away from her eye as she laughed. "What's the verdict? Obviously, you've been thinking about this for a while, and that's understandable. I think we both have. I don't want to cause you any pain."

Her heart broke as she waited for the inevitable, for him to let her down easy.

"I think that, uh, we need to do what Brooke did."

She slid her foot back into her shoe and stopped swiveling in her seat.

"What did Brooke do?"

"I think we need to follow our hearts. Our hearts are telling us that this could be something special. So, let's see." Feeling buoyed, she resumed swiveling in her chair. "Why don't you come by tonight?"

"What? You're finally inviting me over. Wow," she teased.

"Yeah." She could hear the smile in his tone. "I think that would be a good idea. So, uh, come over and what will happen will happen. This isn't a booty call." He chuckled. "I just figured we could have some delivery, watch some television, talk, whatever. Are you allowed to drink tonight? I can get some wine."

"I better not." She grinned. "I've limited myself to one glass of wine a week and I've already had it yesterday."

"Okay, cool. I understand. I'll make some Thai tea then. You like that? You know, the kind with the cream in it?"

"I love it, actually. That sounds delicious. Thai food tonight? Delivery to go with it?"

"Yeah, if you like that. I don't know what type of food you like besides vegetarian now."

"Yeah, I love Thai food."

"All right. I know a great place around here that delivers late into the night. Now look, we've been out many times and the conversations have sometimes been heavy, but tonight I just want it to be chill. Let's just talk. Again, no pressure."

"Why do you keep bringing that up?" She laughed.

"Cameron, you must've been out of the dating game far too long, just like you stated, because I can see what you're doing a mile away."

"Huh?"

"Don't huh me. You are trying too hard to convince me that this won't lead us to the bedroom. I think you *wish* for it to happen, and you're just trying to cover for it."

He burst out laughing.

"Maybe. Shit, I don't know, but I am serious about the chill part. Okay, do you want me to pick you up or do you want to—"

"No, that would be a waste of time, gas, and energy if you come to my home, pick me up, then drop me off. I will just drive over. What's the parking situation over there for visitors? I won't be just coming over for a few minutes like before to look at where Brooke lived. It'll be for at least a couple of hours I imagine."

"Oh, well, I have a designated parking spot but Brooke had one too. Even though she didn't drive, we still paid for the space for visitors. Come on through. It's right behind my car. Just call me when you're close and I'll come out and help you."

"Okay, great. What time?"

"What time is best for you? I won't be at the club long tonight. It's a Haitian art festival, so there isn't much I need to do when they have those types of functions since neither the bar nor DJ or anything are involved."

"I can be done here about four, so let's make it six. Is that good?"

"Yeah, that works. All right, see you later on tonight.

Oh, I almost forgot. I took over the entire conversation," he said. "What were you originally calling me about?"

She crossed her legs. "I was just calling you to tell you that I was thinking about you." They were quiet for a spell. "We'll talk more about what we discussed in this conversation later."

"Definitely."

"Cameron?"

"Yeah?"

"I don't think this'll be easy, but I think it may well be worth it."

Chapter Thirteen
Home is Where the Heart Is

"HIGH CEILINGS, EXPOSED brick, hardwood floors throughout. You said it's got two bedrooms and two and a half baths, right?"

"Yeah, and an office, too. The master suite has its own bathroom. There's a full one in the hall back here." He pointed to a door. "And then a half one for guests, but I also use the sink cabinet in there for extra storage."

"Nice. And you keep it so clean. Impressive. Who is your maid service through?"

Cameron hung Emily's camel leather jacket inside the small closet by the front door.

"Maid service?" He chuckled. "You've seen my portfolio and all of my financial investments, my expenses, all of that. I clean my own shit up. My parents were clean freaks, so they kinda passed that on to me." He shrugged. "I used to drive Brooke crazy. She was kinda messy and I'd get on her about it."

He smirked when he realized Emily had finally dressed down. He hadn't known what to expect, though it was always fun to see whatever she'd chosen to wear. It was the first time he'd ever seen her in just a plain pair of jeans, but she'd paired it with an expensive-looking, simple black long-sleeved shirt with a small satin bow detail at the center of the collar, three-inch black stilettos with pointy toes, and a white and black checkered necklace that he'd describe as a statement piece. Her longish nails were painted clear, and her lips were a neutral muted pink, much different from her signature bold red.

"You look nice," she said, her eyes bright and glossy. He led her by the hand into the living room. "Smell good, too."

"Thank you. So do you." Opium burst through the room like some wild beast, awakening from his slumber once he'd realized someone had entered his domain. The dog sped right past him and practically tackled Emily to the floor as if she had the last steak in town. Emily fell back hard against the couch, her long blonde hair swaying in a million directions as she cackled loudly, almost drowning out the music. Estelle's "Thank You" played on Alexa.

"Here he goes again." Cameron sighed, shaking his head. "Opium, get off her."

"Awww, leave him alone. He's fine. He just missed me is all," she said with a big grin as she showered the dog with affection. Cameron paused. The words she uttered made him feel a bit strange, yet comforted, too. He was certain it had a double meaning.

Emily rubbed behind the dog's ears, making Opium's eyes practically roll with elation and pleasure. He stood there for a second, taking it all in, loving the scene.

Is this supposed to be happening? Yeah, it is. Brooke, I know that's you.

While Emily was preoccupied with playing with his fur-pal, Cameron glanced around the room making sure everything was exactly how he wished it to be. Nag Champa incense burned from the bedroom and poured out, discernible but not overpowering. The long, black glossy dining room table had two white plate settings on it, along with white linen napkins, silverware sets from his mother, a pitcher of freshly brewed Thai iced tea he'd made for his date, and a red rose lying across one of the plates, just for her.

"All right, Opium, that's enough. Bring your ass over here and leave her alone." Cameron whistled, and the dog immediately sprinted over.

"He was fine," Emily said with a big smile. "He's such a gorgeous dog. Nice. What a sweetheart."

"Do you know how strange he's acting? I don't know how much you know about this breed, Emily."

"I don't know much about dogs at all, period." She shrugged. "I never liked them. I mean, it wasn't a dislike, per se, but I just never was inclined to want one. They've just recently been on my radar. I even looked into adopting one, but I don't think now is the time. Eventually I will, though."

"Well, let me tell you about this guy right here. Opium here is a Rottweiler. This breed is known for being physically strong. They're muscular and powerful. They're protective and Opium personally has been hostile if he feels I am in trouble, for example if a stranger walks real fast toward me. They kinda get a bad rap as being vicious when they're really not. That only happens when provoked or they've been abused or neglected. Maybe this isn't the time for me to get all into dogs." He chuckled. "If I bored you, sorry. We can talk more about it later."

"No, no, no. I know you love him, and I like him, too. I know how important he was to you and Brooke. That means, in some way, he's important to me, too." He smiled at her thoughtfulness. "Tell me more about Rottweilers. I really like how that breed looks, by the way."

"Yeah, they're great. Well, they make great family pets, actually, and they're good with children, too. They just need to be trained, which he is. Brooke had him in an obedience school for six weeks, every other day. It was expensive, but it did wonders. Anyway, he's devoted, loyal, a great friend. Brooke loved him almost more than me." He laughed sadly, and her lips curled in a smile as she nodded. "Yeah, he is a total baby when it comes to me and people he knows—very affectionate and sweet. But he doesn't really know you, and has only seen you twice. I told you a while back that he doesn't act this way with people he doesn't know. You're the exception." He lowered his head for a spell. "When he sees you, he jumps on you, wants you to play with him, acts like he knows you. He treats you like you're—"

"Like I'm Brooke."

He pursed his lips and mulled over what she said as he petted the dog's head. He then led Opium into the kitchen.

"Opium, stay in here, all right?" The dog whined as he slumped down on the floor, looking dejected. "Don't give me that face. I mean it. You stay put. You've got food, water, toys. I'm not locking you in here. I just need you to stay out of the way for a little while, okay?" Cameron smiled before rubbing the dog's head one last time. Heading to the hall bath, he washed his hands and checked out his face in the mirror, making sure his short beard was well trimmed and his fade and the waves of his hair were on point. He then returned to sit by Emily on the couch. He handed her a paper menu he'd laid out on the coffee table earlier. "Look it over and tell me what you want, then I'll call our order in."

"Okay." She opened the red, white, and black decorated paper menu with a small tear in the bottom and a grease mark on the back, and began to read through the options.

"So." He sat back on the couch and she perused the offerings, her expression a bit intense. "I wanna tell you that it's real nice to have you over here, Emily. Thanks for coming."

"Cameron, you knew I wanted to come by. I've asked you to come to my place, and I've asked to come by yours. I think you knew I'd say yes and I'm happy to finally be here. A person's home tells a lot about them." She snuck him a brief glance.

"Well, pace is everything, princess. I gotta keep some kind of mystery about myself. Can't let you see all of this fantastic-ness in one sitting. That might make your head explode."

She burst out laughing at his joke, shaking her head.

"Your home is really nice." She looked about the place. "I know I said that, but seriously, it's very clean but feels homey and well put together. Like I told you a long time ago, the architecture of this place is amazing, too. Still thinking of putting it on the market?"

"I don't know." He leaned forward and clasped his hands together. "I love it here, but again, it's a little uncomfortable now because of what happened. I've become so indecisive lately, Emily, it's crazy. That's not like me at all."

"I believe you. You lost the love of your life. Of course you'd act different." She rested her hand on his leg. He looked down at her long, manicured fingers.

"Anyway, the jury is still out on that whole moving thing. Do you want some tea?" He pointed to the table. She slowly slipped her hand away when he leaned back from her, creating some distance while his heart beat a mile a minute. Emily's energy was doing something to him. It was like Brooke was in there with them, but not in a strange way. It was like his dearly departed was a wisp of perfumed smoke floating about the room, encouraging him, urging him on. Was this what she wanted? "I've got water, of course. I've got a couple different juices, too."

"Water is fine, thank you." He got up and returned with a chilled bottle of water, which he handed to her. "Thank you. Cameron, you always smell so good. I said that already, too, but it's true. You really know how to wear cologne. It's never too strong, always just right." She leaned in close—so close, her long, golden hair brushed against his neck. She inhaled hard then smiled, and their gazes locked.

"Thank you." Before he could form another thought, she leaned in and kissed his cheek, then kissed the side of his neck.

"What are you wearing?" she asked breathlessly.

"Nothin' special. Jimmy Choo Man Intense."

"It smells superb with your chemistry. You smell good enough to eat. Can I eat you? I've wanted to be with you like this for so long, it's been driving me crazy." Her warm breath was sweet and minty. Cocking his head to the side with a smirk, he cracked his knuckles and looked into her eyes.

"All right, enough of this shit. I'm not the beat around the bush kinda guy so, uh, let me ask you something."

"What?" She placed the menu down on the coffee table, a shit-eating grin on her face.

"First of all, is this Emily comin' on to me or Brooke?"

"Let me ask you something. Does it matter, Cameron?" She shrugged. "We're a package deal now." She smiled sadly.

"It *does* matter because I don't want to use you as some rebound. If this is what you want, that's fine, that's good. If this is only Brooke, then it feels like I'm invading something I'm not supposed to. You didn't like dogs, now you do. You didn't deal with Black men romantically, now you are. I'm not about to walk into this shit blindly. Tell me which one of you is trying to get into my bed tonight. I need to know."

Emily seemed to mull his words over, then finally said, "The truthful answer is *both*."

"All right, I can accept that. Now, here's another question before you get me all hot and bothered and revved up." She chuckled. "Have you been cleared for sex? I read that there's a waiting time after surgery. Is that true?"

"Yeah, there is, but I was cleared a long time ago. I only had to wait eight weeks after the surgery, after my breastbone had healed."

"Mmm hmm, I see." He crossed his arms as he looked down at her, his thoughts and questions whirling and growing. Her left sleeve inched lower as she shifted closer to him, exposing a creamy shoulder. "And, uh, have you had sex since your surgery?"

She grimaced. "What?"

"You heard me."

"Why would you ask me that?"

"It's a normal question, Emily. Have you fucked anyone since you've had the heart transplant?"

"Is that really any of your business?" She crossed her arms over her chest, mirroring his stance, and glared at him, though her lips twitched, fighting a smile.

"Yeah it's my business if we're tryna see what's up, trying to see where this can go, what we can get into."

"No," she finally said after a long pause. "I haven't fucked, as you so wonderfully put it, another man since the surgery."

"Don't try to be slick and pull some Bill Clinton word-play tournaments. I know how you are. You enjoy these semantics games. Have you made love? Had sex? Had your pussy ate? If yes to any of those questions, was it another woman? I gotta clear all bases here since I know you choose your words wisely when you're trying to be sly. You can't outplay a reformed player. I'm a wordsmith, too, so just answer the questions. All of them."

"No, no, no, and no." She giggled then rolled her eyes. After picking up the menu once more, she glanced at it, then set it back down. "You're paranoid. Anyway, I'm getting the Thai basil stir fry," she said casually.

"The one with the tofu?" She nodded as he checked out the menu himself.

"Let me guess. That's what she would order."

"Yup," he answered, keeping his eye on the menu.

"I could freak you out right now, Cameron. Want me to try?" A mischievous look danced in her eyes.

"Haven't you done enough of that already?" He smirked. "You sung me that song she used to sing, you know shit about her, about *us*. All right, the hell with it." He laughed. "Now I'm curious. Go ahead, do it."

"Okay, this just popped into my mind. You told Brooke about your fifth-grade teacher, Mrs. Mary, one time. It was one of your first times dealing with death. You were heartbroken when Mrs. Mary died of complications with AIDs." He swallowed and perused the chicken choices. "Am I right?"

"Half right. Something must've gotten messed up in translation, but yeah, her name was Mrs. Mary. She taught math. She was my fourth-grade teacher, actually, and she died of cancer."

"It was diagnosed as cancer, but the cancer was caused by AIDS."

He looked up at her. "That's not true."

"I think Brooke sees these people, the ones that have crossed over. I think she saw Mrs. Mary." He swallowed, a bit sorry he'd allowed Emily to walk down this creepy road. "It is true. She'd contracted HIV in the late 80s from her husband who didn't know he had it, either. She didn't find out until several months before her death, but it was ultimately her body's inability to fight cancer due to the AIDs virus that took her out." After some hesitation, Cameron snatched his phone off the table and called one of his best friends, Charles. He put him on speakerphone.

"Hey, Charles. What's up, man?"

"'Sup, Cam. I thought you was comin' to the club tonight? I'm down here with Tinesha. We decided to stop through and get some drinks. There's an art show. Pretty dope."

"Nah, man, didn't need to. Yeah, enjoy that, support those brothas and sistas. Hey, I'm here with a friend of mine discussing old times. Do you remember our old teacher in elementary school, Mrs. Mary?"

"Yeah, fourth-grade math, man. We all loved her, she was cool. Made the subject fun."

"Yeah, do you remember what she died from?"

"Cancer." He smiled and nodded, feeling a bit smug. "But a few years later somebody said she'd had AIDs. I don't know. Back then, she may have. You know people didn't really talk about it like they do now."

His smile slowly faded, and now, Emily was grinning ear to ear.

"Oh, okay. Well, uh, I won't hold you."

"That's what you called me about? Yo, Cameron, lately you've been acting weird as hell. Thomas said you've been hangin' with some White lady, too. Who is she?"

Much to his surprise, Emily covered her mouth and stifled a laugh, amusement in her expression.

"It's a friend of mine. She's good people, chick named Emily." He winked in her direction.

"All right, straight. Look though, you need to get down here and do somethin' about Rob and all these mothafuckas cloggin' up the damn toilets wit' shit, tampons, and wads of tissue, my nigga. I am sick of this. Because yo crew know I'm a plumber they always try to make me go in there and fix the shit when I stop in, like because you hook me up with free drinks, I gotta pay that shit forward. I'm here to have a good time. They act like I just walk around wantin' to do this, man. That's disrespectful, my nigga. I was just in there and—"

"Gotta go." Cameron quickly disconnected the call, only to hear Emily burst out laughing as she wagged her finger.

"Why did you cut him off? It was just getting good." She cackled, growing red in the face. "And you can't stand it."

"Stand what?"

"You can't stand being wrong, even in matters such as this. The male ego is fragile. How sad."

"You were still wrong," he muttered, trying to keep from smiling and giving in to the pile of truth she'd laid before him. "It wasn't fifth grade."

"Sore loser. I got the gist of the story right, and that's all that matters."

"How exactly do you do that, anyway? I mean like, how does that work? You know, you getting this information from her?"

"I don't know." She shook her head. "I just kind of know it."

He nodded. "I just want to let you know, if Brooke told you that, right here, right now, then yeah, I'm freaked out. See, I told her that story, opened up to her like that right before…Never mind."

"Cameron, no, tell me." She reached out and turned his head to face her.

"Okay, it happened like this. I'd known her a couple of months. She told me she didn't just have sex with anyone, that sex was important to her, so she was choosy and selective about who she gave her body to. She said I needed to open up more, tell her about things that affected me, mattered to me, that she would not accept my silence or my walls. So, for some reason, the story of Mrs. Mary popped into my mind that day." He stared at the floor. "I told her how it had affected me and my classmates real bad because she really cared about us kids, and she was a damn good teacher. We all went to her funeral. It was the first time I had cried after losing someone. I was messed up for a while after that. Later that night, Brooke gave herself to me for the first time."

Baby, is this your blessing? Are you tellin' me to not feel guilty about liking Emily and just give in to my attraction and desire for her? You must be. I can't believe this.

"You want any appetizers or anything to go with your rice?" he asked after a moment of silence, switching lanes, needing desperately to make his way out of the depressing conversation.

"No, that's enough, thanks."

Cameron called in their orders, grabbed the remote control, and turned on the television. He leaned back against the couch and she nestled against him, snuggling beneath his arm. He hesitated for a spell, then wrapped his arm around her, bringing her closer. She looked up at him, and he down at her.

One kiss on her forehead aroused his senses. He kissed her forehead once again, and a split second later, he turned her toward him, hand cupping the back of her neck, and drew her in for a kiss. The soft warmth of her lips stirred him, and his dick jumped and lengthened in his boxer briefs, soon straining against the fabric. His tongue danced with hers as he deepened the kiss, passion exploding between them. He reached for her breast, lightly thumbing and caressing it over her shirt. He loved how her nipple stiffened beneath his touch and her airy, feminine moans filled the room. He slowly drifted away from her mouth and navigated to her neck, delivering warm, slow pecks. Emily wrapped her arms around him, pulling him closer, embracing him.

She kisses like Brooke.
But she's not Brooke.
Accept her for who she is.
I can. I will.

He moved his lips back toward her mouth, needing a bit more of her flavor.

"I want you," he groaned before snatching himself away and tearing his shirt off his body, casting it aside.

"I want you, too." He didn't miss how her gaze roamed over his arms, his chest, his stomach. "I didn't know you had this many tattoos." She ran her fingertips against them. "When did you have the arm sleeve done? Are those hiero-glyphics?"

"'Bout eight years ago. Yeah. All of this is Egyptian—the pyramids, pharaohs. Got Osiris right here." He pointed to his shoulder. "Horus. This is Isis. On my chest is the ankh in the center. Bast right here, the sphinx. Over my abs I have written, 'Fight Until Your Last Breath' in hieroglyphics. On my back, I have Adinkra symbols." He twisted his body so she could see. Emily's eyes widened with wonder as she reached and touched him once again. "I traced some of my ancestry to Ghana, in West Africa."

He got to his feet. Looking down at her, he reached for his belt and undid the buckle. Before he could finish disrobing, the doorbell rang, bringing them both back into the folds of reality.

"Dinnertime." She cleared her throat, her cheeks a deep red.

"Coming," he hollered out to the delivery guy. As he made his way to the door, he tossed her a narrowed-eye glance. "Usually they have to be buzzed in. Someone must've been coming or going. Anyway, I was hopin' for a *different* kinda dinner." His eyes dropped down to her groin, then he licked his lips real slow. "A bit of a kiss to your vertical smile, a taste of that hot pocket." He rubbed his hands together as if famished, and Emily blushed deeper. "But I guess we can eat the carry-out food first," he joked, making her laugh and suck her teeth, averting his gaze shyly. He made his way to his front door.

She looks so cute when she does that. She's a little nervous. I can relax her. I can take care of that.

"Besides, you'll need your energy, Emily. But of course, a part of you may already know about me." He unlocked the door and opened it. "What's up, man? Thanks."

The delivery guy handed him the food. Cameron grabbed some cash from the table by the entrance and tipped him. After locking the door, he returned to her holding two large plastic bags of piping hot food.

"And what do you think I know about your sexual prowess?" she urged, a naughty grin on her face.

"That I'm a heavy hitter, all ten rounds, baby, then a TKO. I haven't had sex in like forever. So, uh, looks like we both have some pent-up energy to expel."

He placed the bags on the dining room table and motioned her over with a curl of his finger. Emily got to her feet and approached, moving like a cat, in stealth mode.

Damn, she is sexy.

His dick was happy at the sight of her. After pulling out her chair, she sat down, and he scooted her in. She picked up the rose and sniffed it, eyes closed.

"Thank you for the rose. Cameron, I'm not going to even try to pretend." She smiled. "You are going to be a handful, I can see that. I love your bravado. It's funny, but somehow I know you mean it. Raunchy wordsmith foreplay, how sweet of you, Mr. Poet." She winked at him and he smiled at her as he checked the bags, making sure everything they'd ordered was in there. "I can't believe the crazy chemistry we have. It's amazing." She picked up her glass of iced tea and took a sip. "Can you believe it?"

"I'm trying to not overthink this anymore, Emily." He took his seat. "We keep getting signs, the green light. I'm doing this. It is what it is." He shrugged. "We like each other, we want to spend time together, we want to see what potential this has, end of story. We don't have to tell everyone our business, at least not right now. As time goes on, I'll let people know what's up when the time is right. Right now, my focus is on you and getting to know you better, in *all* areas. Mentally, emotionally, sexually, spiritually."

He plopped down in his seat and placed his napkin over his lap. "I told you this was a night for chilling, and whatever happens, happens. I have to stop crawling on fear, ya know? Afraid I'm upsetting my girlfriend. My love for her caused that, but her love for me is telling me to follow my heart. She was my heart, and now that heart is inside of *you*." His eyes narrowed on her. "Gotta start running on faith in myself and the unseen, like I used to." He removed his food from the bag and opened it. "Time for the old me to return. He's been gone way too long."

"And I'm glad about that."

"You should be. You were instrumental in this, Emily, and I thank you from the bottom of my heart. You've changed my life forever. In so many ways, you reminded me of who I am, of my purpose. You're helping me heal. That means you're good for me."

"As are you for me. I guess my mother was right. There really are no coincidences, and everything does happen for a reason." She paused before adding, "I'm still surprised, though. This could've turned out a million different ways, and yet, I'm here."

"You're here because you're supposed to be, and now, you're *mine*. Eat your food." He waved his fork at the bag he set beside her plate, the delicious aromas of the spices filling the place. "I don't want it to get cold, but regardless, I plan to keep you warm all night long. You can take that to the bank and invest it. It's a done deal."

Chapter Fourteen

Sex, Drugs, and Rockin' Poetry

"BY THE POOL" by independent artist Lakey Inspired played through Cameron's speakers in his bedroom.

"This guy's a good musician. You should check him out," he told her.

Cameron had eclectic tastes in music, though neo-soul, hip-hop, and jazz appeared to be his favorites. As of late, she cosigned his musical leanings. With deep breaths, she watched the beautiful man as he pulled the stormy-gray bedroom curtains closed. The streetlights were immediately shut off like someone had flipped a switch, and they were shrouded in darkness. Then he lit the candles, turned on two modern silver metal sconce lights hanging on either side of the bed, and tossed some bits of paper in the trash, sprucing up a bit.

The muscles in his back contorted, stiffened, and relaxed as he casually went about his business. She sat on a clear scoop chair in that gorgeous bedroom decorated with pops of retro-1960s spring-green artwork and décor, a black and white fuzzy pillow against her back. In front of his bed was a long, clear table, and the bed's platform sported black shelving all around, room for books and the like to be stored.

"Play it again?" she asked once the song came to a stop. Without hesitation, he walked over to his laptop and did as she asked before continuing with his chores. He picked up a joint from an ashtray and lit it. After taking a hit, he offered her some. She shook her head.

"I don't smoke. Anymore." She chuckled. She'd indulged on occasion with one of her girlfriends from California who'd introduced her to some weed that had blown her mind. It had been her dirty little secret, until now. "I miss it, though."

"Brooke and I only smoked on occasion." He took another hit and snuffed it out, then lit a fresh incense stick. He picked up a cloth that lay on top of his headboard.

"All the other rooms in your home are so well kept and cleaned. I'm actually surprised you had receipts and gum wrappers on the floor here." She grinned.

He paused. "This is my thinking area. I create my poetry in here often. It's like my studio. See, I listen to music, zone out, and I almost become detached from my physical self when I'm writing, tweaking my words, and memorizing them. By the time it's over, I look around and see empty cups, scribbled-on notebooks, pens missing their caps, empty bags of kettle chips, shit everywhere, stuff I don't even recall tossing. So, at the end of the day, I pick it up. I don't question what and how the shit happened. I just accept that it did. Yeah, I keep my craziness in here. This way, too, I can keep myself contained to one room."

She burst out laughing.

"What's so funny about that?"

"You make it seem like you're Opium, like you're some

dog that needs to be caged."

"Definitely not a dog, at least not anymore." He winked. "Maybe, in some ways, I *do* need to be contained." She sat straighter, then crossed and uncrossed her legs. "When I'm writing, I feel split in half, like I'm two people vying for center stage. One part of me, the one I show the world on a daily basis, is organized and lowkey. The other part of me is creative, messy, violent, passionate, loud, but only when I'm working on a new piece or performing. I'm an artist of words. I think it just comes with the territory."

She swallowed hard when he reached into a dresser drawer and pulled out a bottle of lube and several gold-wrapped condoms, casually tossing them onto a black nightstand.

Magnums. He's a big boy. Thank God.

He cast her a sexy smile from over his shoulder, his thick black brows arched ever so slightly.

"You good? Everything okay, Em?"

"Yeah, I'm fine."

"Take your shoes off. Stay a while." Her entire body flushed with nervous heat. Wiggling out of her shoes, she pushed them to the side with a swipe of her foot.

"That's better."

"Hey, tell me something."

"Yeah?"

"Why did you or Brooke name your dog Opium?" she asked.

"One of my favorite poets was an opium addict."

She smiled. "A classic poet?"

"It was Samuel Taylor Coleridge. A white cat out of Great Britain. He was innovative. Brooke let me name the dog. I didn't want him at first. Too much mess and clean up, but I ended up going crazy over his ass. That's my boy." He chuckled.

He turned off the music then walked over to a closet, or so she thought. He opened the double doors and exposed a huge stereo system.

"What in the world? Looks like something off *Star Trek*."

With a light laugh, he pushed a few buttons and pulsing lights of various colors came on. "Cranes in the Sky" by Solange started to play, and Emily bobbed her head to the music. Crossing her ankles, she closed her eyes and began to sing the lyrics, falling in love with the song all over again. This new voice that came out of her, the one that sounded like her but didn't, poured out without hesitation. Before she knew it, he was standing before her, dripping with sensuality and pure power. She opened her eyes.

He mouthed the lines of the tune, then his deep voice burst free as he reached for her wrists and brought her to her feet.

"That's right, baby. Come on, let's sing and dance."

He wrapped his arms around her waist and they moved around, singing together like a rehearsed duet. His singing voice wasn't half bad. Their feet and bodies moved in sync and she fell into the groove, having a great time. She laughed, feeling light and airy, free and without a care, secure in his strong arms.

"This is too good to be true." She looked up into his eyes as they swayed back and forth.

"Why do you think that?" He landed a quick peck on her lips then waited for her answer.

"I'm too busy thinking about how I never want this night to end, and we haven't even started yet. I feel like I need a remote control so I can hit rewind and a pause button, too." She stood on her tippy-toes, ready to receive another kiss. He delivered, a lingering one from which he pulled away nice and slow.

"There's no rush tonight. Enjoy the race; the finish line never moves. We'll get there exactly when we're supposed to."

When he pressed his warm, full, soft lips against hers again, she instantly melted from his impassioned touch. Her stomach fluttered as she felt the erection in his pants against her stomach. She squelched a scream when he suddenly grabbed the back of her thighs and hoisted her legs around his waist, forcing her to hold on tight as he scooped her off the ground. With ankles locked around the small of his back, she secured herself, never wishing to let go. She wrapped her arms around his neck while he pulled her impossibly closer and slid his soft tongue within her mouth to tangle lazily with hers.

They slowly grinded and moved against one another, right in tempo with the music. Their kiss was hot, wet, juicy. She could taste traces of the marijuana, Thai food, and minty gum. He slowed and somehow, she could feel him looking at her, even with her eyes pressed shut. She opened her lids and shuddered at the intensity of his stare. Heavily hooded dark eyes framed with thick, black lashes amidst bright, stark whiteness zoned in on her.

"You're killing me, Cameron. Come on, baby. I want to feel you." Her voice cracked as she pressed her forehead against his and ran her fingertips along his short, soft black hair. The rippling waves and textured tresses were like nothing she'd felt before. She liked the curliness, so different from her own, the experience brand new.

"Slow and easy wins the race."

Every fiber of her being was on fire for him, alive and electric. Her heart throbbed.

Carrying her protectively in his arms to the bed, he placed her down on cool white and gray sheets that smelled like the incense smoke that floated about in the air. He stood over her, looking down at her as if she were prey, then unhooked his belt and slid it through the loops.

"Let me see those pretty titties. Take your shirt off."

She rose onto her knees and removed her shirt, sliding it over her head, then tossed it on the dark-stained wood floor. Her lacey lilac bra was practically see-through. Eyes fixated on her breasts, he licked then sucked his lower lip.

"They're real." She caressed them proudly. It was true; she loved her breasts, one of her finest assets. Now they were marred with a scar meandering down between them, and the realization of that took away her smile.

"I know, I can tell," he stated breathlessly as she cupped her right breast, lifted it to her mouth, and slid her tongue along her hardened nipple through the flimsy material of her bra. Letting go of her breast, she traced her scar with her hand. He grasped her fingers and shoved them away, his gaze never leaving hers.

"You're a beautiful woman, Em. That scar don't mean shit to me, 'cept it's a battle wound. Be proud of it." Her lips curled and her cheeks warmed. "Oh yeah, we're gonna have a

WHAT THE HEART WANTS

lot of fun tonight." He lowered his head and kissed her scar, making her shiver with emotions she wouldn't dare examine just yet.

She'd opened up a box that could never be closed.

He pulled his jeans down his bronzed, muscular thighs, got them off and discarded them. She followed suit, reaching for the button of her high-waisted jeans and releasing herself from their confines in no time flat. She was dying to see what lay beneath his boxer briefs. The bulge was impressive; in fact, it gave her pause. Her breathing accelerated in anticipation and her matching lilac lace panties became soaked with her creamy essence. She glared at the silky black path of hair that trailed down his taut stomach, disappearing behind the elastic band of his briefs.

He's absolutely beautiful.

Cameron reminded her of some Egyptian prince. He wore a thin gold chain around his neck, and his torso and arms were covered in black ink. Her pulse raced and she got dizzy for a spell. In the past, sex to her had been a means to an end—an at times enjoyable event during which she spent the majority of her time working toward an orgasm in anticipation of going to sleep soon afterward. With Cameron, it was different. Yes, she was eager, but her excitement felt more like she was getting something she'd missed, something perhaps even that she'd never experienced. She could sense in advance that this would be special. Though this was their first time, Cameron was familiar, as if he'd already been inside of her before.

She took a deep breath. Her heart was playing an out-of-tune song.

He suddenly swooped over her like an eagle, pressing her down onto the bed with the greatest of ease. The heat and warmth of his eager mouth titillated her senses and drew a sigh as he christened her neck with a kiss. Wrapping one arm around his shoulder, she writhed as he eased her thighs apart with a nudge of his knee. He worked his mouth all along her collarbone, then back up to her face, delivering slow pecks to her chin and cheeks.

"No rest for you tonight, baby. You wanted my dick? You're about to get it," he said with a wicked smile.

Reaching up to her hand, he intertwined their fingers and squeezed. Her mouth parted as she stared at the ceiling for a spell, trying to slow her breathing. She glanced at their hands, studying the contrasting colors—her light, peach flesh against his deep, roasted-caramel tone.

He wore a small gold ring on his index finger, the metal glimmering in the dull lights.

"Your kiss is everything," she whispered, then moaned when he drifted down to her bra, working his hands along the globes, gently squeezing them. He ran the tip of his tongue all along the reddened scar, moving his hips back and forth like the ocean between her thighs, grinding slow, then fast.

"You haven't felt *anything* yet."

Her breath hitched as he released her breasts from their lacey restraints then tossed her bra haphazardly across the room, exposing her scar completely. He looked hungrily from one breast to the other, then engulfed one into his hot, wet mouth, his face practically disappearing from sight. Palming the back of his head, she squealed when he sucked hard on her tender nipple, taking it slow then fast, switching his pace, alternating like an expert in the art of lovemaking. He toyed and played with the other, massaging it with his lithe fingertips, then administered the same treatment to it.

Her back arched uncontrollably from his touch and her pussy wept in anticipation as he bumped his hard cock against her zone. With one hand, he jerked his underwear down until he had them all the way off, refusing to release her nipple in the process. Soon, he rose onto his knees, and her eyes immediately landed on his slightly curved nature.

Her stomach fluttered at the sight of the massive organ. Slipping her finger into her mouth, she tried to squelch a pleased grin to no avail. He smirked at her response, then stroked himself while she removed her panties, inching them down her hips.

"Give me this shit."

He snatched them the rest of the way down her legs and threw them hard across the room, then thrust her thighs open. Without warning, Cameron slipped his tongue between her pussy lips, lapping at her juices, feverishly sipping her natural cognac. She must've screamed in ecstasy a thousand times as he consumed her essence.

"Baby, you taste so fuckin' good. Mmmm."

Wrapping his arms around her waist, he pressed his nose against her pelvic bone as he delivered slow, torturous licks.

"I could eat your pussy all night, baby," he slurred between tongue twirls and solid swallows.

"Oh, God."

He worked her like a machine, alternating his pace as he concentrated on her tender clit. Sucking then licking, the slurping sounds rivaled the music, and the sweet, smoky scent of the room blended in with their sex as he had his way with her, devouring her whole.

"Don't hold back, baby. Cum in my mouth. Feed me. Give me your life force."

He slid a slow finger inside of her pussy. She cooed and bucked against him, her eyes teeming with unspent, ecstasy-induced tears.

That tongue of his is good for more than spoken word. Shit.

She hissed as her eyes rolled back. Grabbing the sheets in her fists, she came undone. He groaned and moaned right along with her as she trembled, her entire world an enraptured mess. Seconds turned to minutes after her breathtaking orgasm ceased, but he kept slowly circling her labia and clit with the tip of his tongue, glancing up at her on occasion. She shuddered when another orgasm hit her and took her under. When she'd finally stopped screaming and bucking against his mouth, he crawled up her body, slow and easy, and ran his lips against her neck. She held onto him tight—possessively—with all of her might.

Mine.

He's mine. All mine.

He hugged her back, gently sucking on her earlobe and grinding softly between her legs. Moments later, they were both on their sides, looking at one another, smiling. In love? He reached for her hair and wound several strands around his fingers, tugging gently, releasing, then tugging again.

"What? What are you thinking about?" she asked with a smile.

"Women always ask stuff like that." He chuckled. "Usually we're not thinkin' about shit." She laughed at that. "Nah, actually, I was just looking at your hair, your body. You're beautiful, Emily, you know that?"

"Thank you."

"I'm just not used to feeling hair like this, seeing it, having a true blonde in my bed. It's different for me. You'll leave hair strands everywhere, Farrah Fawcett swoops."

She felt her cheeks heat from his perusal.

"The colors of your body are different from what I'm accustomed to, but you're just like any other woman I've taken to bed. It's amazing how much we focus on variances, ya know? Shit that doesn't even matter. There's so much that's *not* different at all. I wish everyone could see that, but until then, I have to keep doing what I do."

It was almost as if he were working out something in his mind, and she let him do it, uninterrupted. Her pussy pulsed with need as he wrapped his hand around her neck and brought her in for another kiss. When he pulled away, she glanced down at his veiny dick, the head grazing her stomach. She looked into his eyes, then glanced down again. It was simply magnificent. A work of art.

"Why do you keep staring at it?" He kissed her briefly. "I like when you look at it. You want to feel me inside you. Does the sight of my hard dick excite you, baby?"

She nodded. "Yeah. It's perfect. Long, dark, and thick. Impressive. I want to taste you, Cameron."

She bit into her lower lip as she slid down the bed, then came eye to eye with the beast. Taking it into both hands, she eagerly slid the bulbous head into her mouth, eliciting his earthy moan and tightened muscles. Folding one hand under his head against the pillow, he sighed and groaned. She held on to his bucking hip as she remained on her side servicing him, glancing up at him a time or two as she took more of him into her mouth, gauging his reaction.

The buttery smoothness of his nature felt wonderful against her working tongue. She flung her head back, forcing her mouth to make a popping sound as she released him. A trail of precum attached from her lower lip to the slit in the head of his huge cock before she went down on him once again, almost climaxing from the image and taste of him alone. His groans grew louder as he wrapped his hand around the back of her head, making her take more of him in while he thrust inside her mouth.

"Emily…Shit…Damn." He exhaled.

She stared up at him to see his eyes shut tight, the lines visible around them. His Adam's apple bobbed as he swallowed hard, his brows gathered, his face tense. He shuddered and cursed and tugged on her hair while he fucked her mouth faster, with due diligence. Abruptly, he slipped his cock out, leaving her breathless and confused.

Wrapping his arms around her waist, he pulled her up and turned her on her stomach, practically slamming her. She sighed when she felt the heavy weight of his body on hers, pinning her down beneath him. Before she could take another breath, he reached for one of the condoms. The golden wrapper fluttered in the air like a falling leaf after he opened it, floating to the glossy wooden floor. Finally, she'd get to feel him inside her. He didn't take long to sheath himself, and then he hoisted her ass up, flush with his groin.

She caught their reflection in a dresser mirror and her

breath hitched with disbelief. She was in the midst of something she never imagined possible, and yet, her mind, body, and soul wanted it—*needed* it. He followed her gaze and stared at their naked bodies while he caressed her. Then, reaching between her legs, he stroked her pussy, making her coo and beg.

"You like that, don't you, baby? The way I touch you."

"Yes!"

"This wet, juicy pussy is all mine, baby. Be careful what you ask for. You walked in here, but you might be limpin' out." He grinned as he finger fucked her. Hard.

She clawed at the bed as he gently bit the back of her neck, his hot breath filled with the aroma of the spices from their dinner, mixing with the salty essence of her nature.

"Do it. Do it. Fuck me," she screamed, needing him in the worst way. He tightly wound her hair around his hand and yanked.

With clenched teeth, she suppressed a shriek as he plunged ruthlessly inside her. She glared at their reflection in the mirror as he slammed against her, over and over, never slowing. Gripping her hips, he slid his dick in and out of her love, each blow faster than the last. Stretching her wide with each thunderous stroke, he rotated his hips, delivering the deliciously deep thrusts until he was balls deep. Her inner thighs moistened with her raining juices; her pussy cried in his honor, driving her nature to flow like a waterfall.

"Cameron. Oh God…"

She blinked back tears of ecstasy for he never stopped except to deliver sweet, soft kisses along her spine. Her breasts swung back and forth, the hard, dark pink nipples pointing downward as he worked her over. Brown skin against white flesh—dark coffee soaking into a white rug.

She shivered as she came. His fingers danced along her clit as he reached around her once more and brought her impossibly more pleasure.

"Feels so good," she whispered, her voice weak when aftershocks of her orgasm made her practically jump in her own skin.

When she settled, she suddenly realized he was murmuring, talking, saying things that were almost inaudible.

"Cravings, broken hearts, and healed minds. Funny how lovers meet as they travel life's timeline. I told her to cum again. The pussy is all mine." He bowed his head and rested his forehead against the middle of her back, yanking her ass into his groin with each quick, angry, hard thrust.

"I feel you so deep." With a trembling hand, she ran her fingers along her stomach, halfway expecting to feel him that deep inside her. Pressing her flat onto the bed, he took complete command of her body as he slammed into her, emitting loud, sexy moans with each plunge he effortlessly delivered, shaking the bed at each turn. With a guttural moan, he quivered against her form, followed by a warm rush of his final release filling the condom. They lay there panting, him still on top of her from behind, their fingers now intertwined and his dick motionless inside her.

She gasped for air, wanting to pinch herself to believe it was real, that she'd truly made love to this enigma of a man. Then, he rolled her over onto her back and resumed his position between her thighs. With a crooked smile on his face, he moved strands of her hair out of the way, then supplied a sweet peck to her awaiting lips.

"Gimme like ten minutes, and, uh, I'll be ready to go again," he said, sounding rather out of breath.

"Only ten minutes? Wow, remarkable." She laughed lightly, wrapping her arms around him.

"Well, shit, I'm not eighty." He chuckled. "I can still handle my business. When I was a teenager, it only took a couple of minutes. Name shoulda been jackrabbit."

She chortled at that.

He slid the condom off carefully with one hand and tossed it in a nearby trash can close to the bed. Before she knew it, he was slowly grinding against her nature, his tongue sliding inside her mouth as he kissed her with the passion of a million men. Several sensual songs played back to back, ones that made her feel in love. In Heaven. Happiness reigned supreme. He stretched over her, reaching for another condom, and tore it open. Rising on his knees, he slid it on and bumped the head of his erect cock against her pussy, as if knocking to come in.

He kissed her again while entering her, hand clasping the back of her neck, making her lose her breath. Slow, intense thrusts. She held onto him as they looked into each other's eyes, riding one another until she came once again. She couldn't recall when she'd orgasmed so much, unless she was including her battery-operated boyfriends. She laughed at the thought.

"What?" he asked with a big, gorgeous grin.

She wrapped her legs around his waist and crossed her ankles.

"Nothing, I'm just being silly. I love how you make me

feel. Not just physically, but *every*thing." She caressed his shoulder, then gave him another kiss. His stamina was incredible, his control admirable.

Taking a nipple into his mouth, he continued to thrust within her, faster and faster until his back muscles locked. The warm rush of his relief flooded her gate as sweat dripped from his body onto hers. Moments later, he reached for his phone and turned the ringer back on. She hadn't seen him turn it off to begin with, but perhaps she'd been caught up in the moment. They lay next to one another, their backs against the quilted black headboard, holding hands, listening to music.

"I guess I better get going soon." She leaned over and kissed his cheek before snapping the sheets back.

"Nah, why? Stay here tonight. You can leave in the morning."

She smiled.

"Are you sure? I don't want to impose."

"Yeah, I'm sure," he said, his eyebrows furrowed as if it were obvious. "How are you imposing? We're doing this, just like we discussed. I'm not going about this half-assed. We're dating, we're together—just me and you. It's official. Besides, I don't want you heading out this late by yourself either, so just chill, relax. Do you want something to drink, baby?" He motioned to get up.

"Yes, some water please."

He got to his feet but before he could get out of the room, his cell phone rang.

Emily noted the time—2:48 a.m.

It's awfully fucking late for someone to be calling. She was immediately filled with jealousy, and immediately hated herself for it, too. But she couldn't help it.

He looked at his phone curiously, then snatched it up.

"Hey, Mama. Everything all right?"

His mother? I hope nothing is wrong.

"Yeah, I had my phone off. Sorry. Uh huh. What? No, you have to be kidding me. How did they let this shit happen?" Emily grabbed the sheets and brought them over her breasts, feeling a sudden chill in the room. "I know…I know…" He closed his eyes for a moment and paced the room. "All right…yeah. I know…I know that but…yeah, okay. Thanks. Yeah, thanks for tellin' me. Okay. Love you, too."

He disconnected the call and sat on the bed. She stared at his back. He barely moved for several minutes, didn't offer a single word. Emily crawled over to him and hugged him from behind.

"What's wrong, Cameron? What's going on?" she asked, breaking the silence. He didn't answer. "Who was that on the phone?"

"That was, uh, that was Brooke's mother." He dropped his head and shook it. "Police called her tonight and told 'er the guy who shot and killed Brooke is still on the run. They finally identified him, and he fled. They almost had him, got a tip and went to get him but someone must've tipped him off. He could be anywhere now. Fuck."

He picked up a clear ink pen holder and threw it across the room. It hit the wall and shattered. Emily took a deep breath, then slowly ran her fingers along his back before wrapping her legs around him, pulling him close into her embrace from behind. He stiffened from her touch, then relaxed.

"Cameron, I know that this is not the best news, but you have to have faith that they will find him, okay? I believe that he will be caught eventually. He can run, but he can't hide forever."

After a few agonizing moments of silence, he cast her a glance from over his shoulder.

"How do you know?"

She smiled sadly at him then placed her hand against her heart.

"I don't know for sure. I just trust what I feel."

He nodded, swallowed, and turned away. Seconds later, he caressed along the back of her hand as she clasped him around the waist. He pulled her close like a comforting blanket, keeping her near. Resting her cheek on his back, she closed her eyes. They remained that way for quite some time, the soft music playing as rain started to fall outside.

Emily realized something at that moment regarding soulmate connections. For now, she was certain that he and Brooke were just that. As she sat there holding him, trying to comfort his broken soul, she recognized she could practically feel his sadness, predict his moods. Right before he answered the phone, she could sense something was wrong, just as she imagined Brooke would've been able to do. She smiled and kissed his shoulder.

"I know it's tough right now, Cameron. I'm here, we're here, together. I can't say that I know exactly how you feel, but I do know what it feels like to lose someone who means the world to me. I will stay like this for as long as you need, all right?"

"Good, because I need you so badly, Emily. I need you more than you'll ever know."

Chapter Fifteen
Poetry in Motion

I T WAS A crisp, autumn evening, not quite the dinner hour just yet. The doors of Cameron's club would be opening to the public in a couple of hours. Rush hour was in full effect as on any Friday night in New York City.

Cameron had been sitting at the bar, nursing a purposefully watered-down gin and juice for the past hour. He had the front doors propped open to let in the cool breeze and air the place out after the previous night.

He glanced up at the chalkboard menu that hung close to the front door and read the daily specials to ensure they were accurate:

DRINK SPECIALS:
Espresso Martini
Whiskey Sour
Negroni
Long Island Iced Tea
Buy one get one 50% off

FOOD SPECIALS:
Garlic Curry Wings – 6 piece

Vegetarian Nachos
Cuban Shredded Pork Eggrolls
50% off 8:00 P.M.-9:00 P.M.

He bobbed his head to the tune of "Nights over Egypt" by The Jones Girls, which played at a low volume through the speakers. He floated away in his mind, feeling that all-too-familiar wave of inspiration come over him. Shoving his beverage aside, he opened his black dog-eared notebook with a coffee stain on the first page and began to jot down some ideas.

I saw her scars.
Not the ones on the outside, no...but the wound that tried to hide behind a masquerade of lies.

Raised, velvety angry flesh
Soft kisses between her breastbone
She's a blended brew of the old and new
Her heartbeat tastes sweeter than a honeycomb.

A long, scarred journey from the hospital gurney to an early grave.
A slave made trade from the palest of the pale, once dwelling in caves.

They stole our land, now she stole our man?
Damn.

She's harboring a fugitive so that she can live
By the beat of a heart that isn't hers to own or give.
Somewhere between the black abyss and the white give and take

She sings and counts money alone, to protect her mental and emotional state.

When I touched her for the first time, I felt coolness and death
When I kissed her the last time, I was hard in the mental and my spirit was erect.

When I entered her body, I stole her heart like a crook
When I released inside of her, I accidentally called her Brooke.

I'm shook.

How can I protest this gift, when she's been nothing but a friend to me?
And yet many will say, I'm educating and fucking the enemy.

And yet, I can't let this go because this woman, the color of snow, makes me smile in the early morning dawn.
She's done a 180. What is the monster I've made?
What ivory deviousness have I spawned?

If it has to be a secret then maybe it's not something that should be held.
Yet I'm compelled to expel the crooked truth, like a dead tooth, rotting away from the root, in need of being extracted and justice officially upheld.
But I failed.

When she left, there were three long blonde hairs on my pillow.

They were the trinity—Isis, Osiris, and Horus, too.

A chorus in rhapsody, they are now strings on my heart's instrument.

She sings like she was birthed from a horn and torn from a piano's womb.

Her damn heart birthed me, but will be my tomb.
Her expensive perfume lingered in my room.
It's a spell, can't you tell? But please don't wake me up too soon.

Does she have the powers to make me rise from the dead?

Is she a witch and I'm just a heartbroken, lovesick son of a bitch…that's been misled in my own head?

No, not that one, the little one, not the one on my shoulders.

But when I look at her, I say, "Fuck it, let's do this shit. We've only got one life to live, and we're getting older."

There's so much to lose and so much to gain
Like when I grabbed her for the third time and heard her scream my name
I devoured her sweetness in the rain, ensuring that she came…and came…and came…

This morning, she woke me from snoring.
A gentle nudge…I didn't budge.

My eyes fluttered when I looked up and saw a blue-

eyed angel mounted on top of me.

Going up and down, around and around, an astounding fantasy.

For my entire heart and soul to see.

I gripped her around her waist, heat and sweat flushed my face as I made love…No. I fucked this woman with all that was in me.

Eyes wide shut, dreaming of eternity.

See, "making love" sounds so cliché and fake,

But it saves me from having to explain and try to force others to relate.

This is my story, my fate.

They can't understand it even if they tried.

Most wouldn't be able to cope.

Wouldn't matter if I beat their asses with the truth or wrote it on pink paper as a love note.

Here's just the way it is:

I'm in love with a White woman who used to cross the street if she saw me or my kind coming.

Now, as soon as I pick up the phone, she comes uh runnin'…

Ain't that somethin'?

A changed heart is one you can never part from while others choose to remain blind, deaf and dumb.

Numb.

If I expect her to grow, I must grow, too.

How can I question myself, when I have the answers

and know exactly what to do?

This woman is a mystery yet I can figure her out with the greatest of ease.

But just when I solve one of her puzzles, here comes trouble, and I'm back on my knees.

Praying to God in hopes of seeing the forest for the trees.

I've never met someone so afraid and yet so brave
I've never seen someone so masterful, yet still a slave.
I've never watched someone move so sexy and at the same time, be so skittish and reserved.
I've never seen someone sway so slow, then in an instant, be nothing but a fiery blur.

She's not Brooke. She's Emily.
Though, without Brooke, who would she really be?

Cameron straightened his navy-blue blazer, stood to his feet, and lit a cigar. His phone pinged twice. He looked down at the text message and smiled. It was Emily confirming he could come over the next day for dinner and discussion.

He couldn't imagine anywhere else he'd rather be.

EMILY STOOD IN the hospital lobby area with a bouquet of flowers and a long list of regrets. Her self-loathing practically seeped from her pores as flashes of the horrid memories consumed her.

*I told her she was lazy. I cursed at her. I said, "You people,"
and made a jab about a "third baby daddy." I hate myself for
this. I'm going through with it this time, though. Time to face
the music, and I better learn the lyrics, quick.*

Her nerves started to dwindle. She hated to admit it, but
she was scared out of her damn mind.

She hadn't been on that floor in the hospital since she'd
had her surgery. That had happened so long ago, it seemed
surreal to stand there now, taking in the sights, scents, and
sounds. After a prolonged hesitation and a battle of wills, her
heart thumping a mile a minute, she approached the visitors
counter.

"Hi, uh, my name is Emily Windsor. I called earlier this
morning and the day before that, and the day before that,
too. Anyway, I was told that a Mrs. Sapphire Daniels, a
nurse, was working her shift here right now."

"Yeah, Sapphire is here." The short, wide woman behind
the counter eyed the large bouquet from over her thick-
framed black glasses, then tossed another glance at her.

"Okay, great. If she's not too busy at the moment, I'd
like to hand deliver these flowers to her." Emily mustered a
silly, nervous grin, certain she looked like a damn fool.

Without another word, the woman at the front picked
up the phone and paged the nurse.

"You can have a seat if you want." She pointed to some
chairs in the distance, one of which she'd been hiding on in
the corner moments prior.

"Thank you. I'll just stand though."

The lady kept plugging away at the big desktop computer in front of her. Less than five minutes later, the tall, thin

Black woman approached, her hair in the braids she recalled, but this time, her scrunchie was blue, not pink. The nurse walked in measured steps down the hall, her yellow Croc shoes softly tapping on the glossy white floor. When her gaze settled on Emily, she paused, then continued her trek toward her. Once she was five or so feet away, her lips twisted and her complexion deepened. She crossed her arms over her chest.

"You?! Oh, hell naw!" The woman laughed, spun around, and waved her arm in the air.

"I know, well, I don't have to ask. You obviously remember me."

"Everyone remembers you," the lady snapped, eyes narrowed.

"Bet you didn't expect to see me again." Emily smiled ever so slightly, feeling like an idiot.

"Nah, I *hoped* to never see you again. You are, by far, in the top three of worst patients I have ever had, and I told people while you were here to *never* send me to you again, even if I was the last damn nurse in this hospital, the last nurse in New York or the entire free world, or I was quitting. And I meant that. Every damn word of it. You're lucky I have a sense of professionalism because let me tell you something." The woman pointed an accusing finger at her. "If we'd been out in the street and you said that same mess to me, I would've smacked the shit outta you. Now, what could you possibly want?"

"I actually came up here to—"

"To tell me about how I'm probably on welfare and defrauding the system? Or maybe you want to discuss with me how you think I got a bunch of scholarships because I'm Black, a free ride in school so I can work this obviously posh, high-payin' job I have?" The nurse rolled her eyes, her tone harsh, unyielding and deserving. The sarcasm was dripping off her words like sweat on a sinner in church.

"Everything you've said I deserve and then some." Emily braced herself, taking a moment to gather her wits. "I came up here to apologize. I can't blame how I spoke to you on anything or anyone but myself. It wasn't the medication. It wasn't my pain or the surgery. It was *me* and I own it."

The woman grunted and regarded her with suspicion.

"I've had some time to think, to reflect." Emily looked down at the floor, the flowers drooping in her grip. "And I don't expect your forgiveness. Forgiveness is expensive, or at least it should be. I came here just to tell you that you're an excellent nurse, and you had a horrible patient. Me. I hate to have been responsible for leaving that sort of imprint, for creating such a horrible memory in your mind." She closed her eyes and took a deep breath, her palms growing sweaty. "I have affected you, so much so, you are still quite angry about our last encounter, as is to be expected. These…these are for you." She offered her the flowers. Sapphire scowled at them, then wrapped her hand carefully over the ribbon around the stems and took them.

"I know you probably want to throw them at me."

"I thought about it."

Emily smiled, feeling impossibly worse, but she was determined to push through.

"I have been through a harrowing experience, and it has forever altered my life, Sapphire. For the better. To say I see

TIANA LAVEEN

the error of my ways is an understatement. I am the error, and admitting my wrongs and trying to make them right is the new way. I just—" She shrugged. "I just hope there is some way that I can make it up to you. I can't even explain to you how embarrassed I am! How, for three days in a row, I tried to come up here, but chickened out. I'm on an internal tour, and I've been having deeply intimate concerts of self-examination, and I couldn't shake you loose. You left me changed, too."

"You must have to stay here again soon and want to make sure I don't mess with your food or something."

"No, no! I have no scheduled surgeries or anything like that. I'm here because I owe you an apology, woman to woman, face-to-face. I've been a class A bitch to many, but some instances stand out more than most. You were one of them. I unleashed my own insecurities and demons out on you. I am in the wrong, not you. It was one of the worst experiences I ever initiated. I am...I am deeply ashamed."

Tears streamed down her face and she wiped them off. The nurse visibly swallowed, and her scowl slowly dissipated. Silence reigned for a moment, then, at last, the nurse brought the flowers to her nose. She smiled.

"These are nice. Thank you for bringing them."

"You're welcome. It's the least I could do."

"I...uh, I accept your apology. You asked what you could do to make it up." She nodded. "What you can do for me, Emily, is to educate yourself."

"I am trying, and I will continue."

"You do that, and you make sure you do the same to others like you, 'cause let me tell you something, Black people in this country are sick and tired of the shit they get from people like you." Her eyes grew dark and steely. "Every time a White person like you says things like you did to me, it needs to be nipped in the bud. It won't just change when Black people like me call you out on it. I could've cussed you out that day and it wouldn't have made a damn bit of difference. It's going to take other White people, just like you, to call your peers out on this mess. When you hear racist jokes at the office, say something. Quit letting it fly. It's not funny. You're just as guilty by not saying anything about it.

"When your best friend makes a stupid statement about Chinese people havin' slanted eyes, or Ethiopians starving and bein' pirates, say something. It holds more weight when it comes from a person they trust and looks like them. Your views still hold more water with your own people, and that's just a fact."

"I understand what you're saying. That's good advice. I promise I will do that from now on. I was the problem. I want to now be part of the solution."

The woman shrugged and sized her up, as if trying to figure her out.

"Look, what's done is done. I don't know what caused you to come up here like this. I have no idea if you're sincere or not because I don't actually know you, lady. What I *do* know is that your views of me never defined me, but they sure as hell defined *you*. I know I'm a good nurse and didn't need you or anyone else to tell me that. If I only saw myself through the lens of racist White people such as yourself, I woulda slit my damn wrist long ago!" Emily's heart panged.

It was a dull ache, causing cracks to her fortress. "Every day I wake up reminded that I'm Black, like it's a bad thing.

"My skin is too dark. My hair too nappy. I have the European standard of beauty shoved down my throat on a daily basis. This is my existence. You're considered better than me from birth, period. Not shit I can do about it. On top of that, I am a woman and unlike your stereotypes about people like me, I don't have a bunch of babies and baby daddies. I'm married and have one child." She thrust one finger in the air. "I teach her to treat people how she'd want to be treated. Golden rule. I work my ass off, sometimes double shifts. I've never gotten welfare in my life and I worked three crappy jobs to pay back my college loans so don't you ever, for as long as you live, twist your lips to speak on some shit you don't understand and know nothin' about to a total stranger. You don't know me. I work with facts and action 'cause words don't mean shit. Talk is cheap. Now, thank you for the flowers and thank you for the apology, too." She sniffed the bouquet one more time.

"You're welcome." Emily could barely look her in the eye, but this had needed to happen. It was the only way to break through. Not to Sapphire, but to herself. "I wanted to get you flowers that were nice. The color, the quality, it all meant a lot to me when selecting them. I wanted them to be the kind I would expect from someone who'd acted in the manner I had. It was the least I could do."

"The florist cuts the thorns, but the thorns are the best part. They're real. We all got thorns. Pretending we don't is crazy. The thorns remind us that we hurt others sometimes, even the beautiful amongst us, even when we don't mean to.

Just by coming close to the flower, you get pricked and you bleed. My blood is red like yours. I hope you realize that now."

Emily no longer bothered to wipe away her tears, but simply gave a nod of understanding.

"You changing your behavior and telling other White folks like you to get their shit together is the best thing you can do, the best apology you can offer me. Funny that people bring flowers to folks dying in hospitals. All it does is remind them their time is almost up." The nurse laughed mirthlessly. "These flowers will rot and die soon. They'll be worthless. The flowers are wilting as we stand here. Their lives would've been in vain if we don't remember how pretty they looked, how good they smelled, and the thorns they had, too. So yeah, they're beautiful but dying. Just like you were, huh? But you being an example and a teacher to your own is what can make you live forever."

And then, Sapphire Daniels turned and walked away.

Chapter Sixteen
The White Elephant in the Room

Several weeks later

THE RELIC OF a stove had a silver, dented teakettle on the left front eye. The oven was off, the teapot cold and empty.

Damn. They've had that stove since I was ten, I think. They don't make that shit like they used to.

Cameron looked around the kitchen, then watched his father pop big, green, juicy grapes into his mouth, one at a time, smacking his lips loudly.

"Always get the grapes with the seeds, Dad. The seedless ones have been genetically engineered. Fruit is supposed to have seeds." Pops smiled, but he could see in his eyes he didn't give a shit about his views or beliefs. "They say it can happen naturally—it's called parthenocarpy—but that's rare. It happens in a science lab," Cameron added for good measure, just in case he was wrong and Dad's lazy expression was due to tiredness, not a lack of interest.

Cameron tapped his fingertips along the kitchen counter, standing with his ankles crossed. The spacious Brooklyn brownstone was pretty quiet since Mama had gone to the store to pick up a few things. The two didn't say much, but that was nothing new.

The old-fashioned kitchen smelled of a billion seasonings Mama insisted on having, all jammed in an open glass cabinet. Cameron's father tossed the rest of the grapes in the refrigerator then took a swig from a beer bottle. Tall, dark, and lanky, his hair full of short silver and black kinky curls that were in need of cutting, Dad was nonetheless looking well put together and in great health.

"How'd that meeting go that you told me about?"

"Good. Real good."

"That's good that you did that, you know, let 'em have their conference there after they heard you speaking about needing to come there," his father stated before polishing off his drink and casting the empty bottle in the trash.

"I can't tell people to extend the olive branch and then when they try to, and I have resources to help them do it, tell them no, turn them away."

"I agree wholeheartedly."

"They wanted to at least discuss what was happening out here, you know? Our people are dyin', Pops, over some B.S. Something has to change. If I can't be part of the change," he said, pointing to himself, "then I may as well shut up. Talk is cheap. Some people just like to hear the sound of their own voice. They stand up behind pulpits or lead rallies but when it's time to put some backbone and money where their mouth is, they're nowhere to be found. That's one of my biggest pet peeves." His father nodded. "That's like people sayin', 'Get a job,' but those same people don't offer any suggestions on how to do it. They don't show someone how to write a resume, they don't give recommendations for transportation to even get to the interviews should they get a call, they don't assist or help obtain these people's G.E.D. or any higher education.

"They don't suggest or offer computer classes for training, shit like that. You can't expect someone to reach their goals if nobody out here will help them, or at the very least, provide a way for them to get from A to B. Besides," he said with a shrug, "we all had some help, somewhere along the way. None of us got this far without some sort of assistance."

"Lotta folks would've been scared to have those guys around them. Not you though." His father smiled proudly at him as he leaned back against the counter next to him. Cameron looked into his father's eyes and saw bits of himself in them. He looked like both of his parents, a perfect blend.

"Look, at the end of the day, we attach fear to things, people, and places that don't always deserve it, and the stuff we should be afraid of, we just walk in on, blindly. I'm guilty of that myself." Cameron scratched the side of his head.

"What's gotten into you?" Dad smirked.

"What do you mean?"

"In the last couple of conversations we've had, you've admitted to not being perfect. That's not like my son." They both burst out laughing at that.

"Yeah well, it's true. I looked at it more simply, too. These guys were paying customers, Dad. As long as they didn't bust up my place, I was cool with it. Any chance for rival gangs to come together and have a sit-down, I'm all for it." He threw up his hands. "The Crips, Bloods, Latin Kings were there. It was like five different gang leaders representing. It was a beautiful thing."

"How long were they there?"

"For about two or three hours. We kept the music playin', the appetizers comin', the vibe chill, everything was cool. Of course I had beefed up security and they got a little heated at times, but no one came to blows. It was a get-together. We're the leaders, ya know? Just like you taught me." His father nodded and smiled at his words. "If we as Black men don't like how shit is going down, then it's up to us to change it. We have to stop waiting for someone else to save us from ourselves. If someone offers you help, and you need it, take it. There's no shame in that, but don't expect everyone to solve your problems. That's the difference between a boy and a man."

"That's right. Cameron. Wow. I'm proud of you, son. You've always been so passionate about these things and as you know, your mother and I have been concerned about you for years. Very boisterous, getting into trouble because you didn't respect authority."

Cameron grimaced. "Huh? I got arrested for protesting and fighting an illegal maneuver by a police officer who was tryna put his hands on people, and grabbing women all hard, tryna get them out of the way when we all had the right to be down there protesting Meyerson's discrimination against hiring Blacks. In my lifetime, I've never disrespected teachers, a cop writing me a speeding ticket, or what have you. I'm not out here tryna start shit; I just try to end it. I don't know what you're talking about, not respecting authority. That never happened unless my rights were infringed upon or I was provoked. Yeah, I *have* changed. A lot has happened this year. I'm trying to own my shit now."

"That's not what I mean. By authority, I mean anything, or really, anyone you disagreed with who had seniority over you, you made it known. I wasn't upset that you and I have had different political and world views at times, Cameron," his father stated, his tone a bit softer. "I was upset that you weren't always rational when you felt anger inside, and that would cause trouble. Do you know how upset your mother was when you were arrested?

"I know it was a protest, and I know that you were aware of the possible consequences, but that's still your mother, and seein' you locked up like some animal in a cage upset her so badly, she could barely sleep until you were released." A wave of guilt rushed through Cameron at that admission. "All I'm saying is that you're brave, son, but sometimes bravery is actually foolishness in disguise. Anyway, back to the gang meeting. Yeah, a lotta people would've been scared to do that, to let those people close to you like that. I admire that sort of thing about you and it concerns me, all at once. Anyway, this has been a hard year for you. We worry about you sometimes. When and if you ever become a father, maybe then you'll understand." Dad rested his hand on his shoulder as they looked into each other's eyes. "How have you been holding up?"

"Just like I told you last week. I'm fine. I'm Gucci. It's all good."

Cameron made his way into his parents' living room, a hasty retreat. It was full of overstuffed cream furniture. On the walls hung thick, gold-framed paintings of exaggerated featured Black women wearing colorful robes, pouring water from buckets atop their heads, and babies wrapped snugly around their backs. Large mauve vases with plastic emerald-green plants dotted the area. Not much had changed since he'd lived there as a child. Mama kept the place sparkling clean, but she loved her trinkets. He plopped down on the couch and shoved his hand in his pocket. His father sat beside him, and they turned their attention to the rerun of *Roc* playing on the television.

"Cameron, you might think I'm out of line." Cameron braced himself for a conversation he wasn't in the mood to have. "But I was curious if you're dating again? I mean, it's been a half a year now, right? That's not a real long time, but I just want you to be happy. You're a young man and well, you always kept female company. You never went long without it. You told me you wanted to get married and settle down. I just don't want you to give up that dream if that's what you still want. I hope that—"

"I can see where tonight's discussions are going. You're afraid for me. You don't want me to get stuck, become bitter. See, I told Mama to let you know that Brooke's killer has run off, and yeah, when I called the other night, I was pissed, but I can't live in fear, Dad. I can't make choices based on that. I need to be able to grieve in my own way, too."

"I didn't say—"

"I know you don't want me upset anymore, Dad. I know you're worried that I'll fall into my old ways because in your eyes, I have no handler any longer. You and Mama think I'm wildin' out, and I guess in some ways I am, but I'm far from stupid, and I do learn from my past mistakes, all right? Brooke had me settled down a bit. She calmed me. I learned a hell of a lot from that woman. You and Mama appreciated that from her. Now you're both worried because I had been drinking a lot after she died and the grief was taking me places I shouldn't go to, be with people I shouldn't be with."

"If you think this is about control, Cameron, it's not."

"It is. But your motives are pure."

His father averted his gaze, listening, patient.

"You can't control what I do, who I see, or how I mourn. I'm your only child, your only son. We don't even talk about Carmen's death—it happened so long ago, but it affected you and Mama to the point that you two focused on me so hard, afraid you'd lose me too, I guess." Dad's eyes shone with moisture. "This has been an ongoing issue, you and Mama being this way, and it hasn't helped either of you. I've been out of your house since the age of nineteen, never asked you both for a damn thing after that."

"I know that, Cameron. I am not bringing this up to get into an argument. It's to—"

"I know that. I'm just saying."

"Your sister dying did affect your mother and me, Cameron. But how could it not?" He tossed up his hands. "Yeah, that happened thirty-three years ago, but not a day goes by that I don't think about my daughter, and my son, too. I know you don't remember her much; she was your older sister and you were just a baby, but when I look at you, I see her, too. We love you, Cameron. And showing concern is nothing to apologize for. I'm not sorry about that."

"And I'm not mad about it."

They were quiet for a spell.

"So, are you seeing anyone?"

"I see we're back at square one. Doesn't Mama usually ask this sort of thing? This is weird, man." Cameron chuckled, and so did his father.

"I guess so since I never really asked you about this stuff before, but I'm curious. Considering the circumstances and all."

"I just, uh." He ran his hand across his forehead. "I didn't really expect to talk about this right now."

"Cameron, you know I'm not the kinda guy to get into your business." Cameron winced at his dad's words, in total disbelief at what he'd just heard. He folded his arms. "All right, all right!" Pops snickered, his dark eyes turning to slits. "I do on occasion, okay, but *not* because I wanna try and push you into the arms of someone new. Not because I want you preoccupied, even though, yes, Brooke did have a great influence over you. I just…I just want you to be happy."

"Yeah, I'm seein' someone."

Dad's eyes grew wide. "Really? Who?"

"She's—"

They both turned when Mama's keys turned in the front door. Moments later, the lovely woman stood in the foyer area. The swaying trees showed through the open door, and the sidewalk behind her was covered in brown, mustard-yellow, and auburn leaves. Closing the door, she tossed down her baggy, brown leather purse and wiggled out of her sneakers. She looked cozy in jeans and a white turtleneck sweater. Heading to the kitchen, she noisily set the white plastic bag she'd been carrying down.

He heard the refrigerator door open and close a few times, the rattling of the plastic bag, and the flicking of a switch, probably turning off the light. She stepped back into the foyer area, her long, black, wavy hair, framed with strands of silver at the temples, swinging about. She hadn't yet noticed him sitting there. Finally, she cast her sights in his direction and grinned from ear to ear.

"Cameron! Baby, so good to see you. How long have you been here?" She squealed as he got to his feet and she raced over to him with open arms before he got a chance to make a beeline to her. She embraced him tight.

"Not long."

He could smell her all too familiar signature perfume, Issey Miyake's L'EAU D'ISSEY.

"Are you hungry, baby?" She grabbed both of his arms and looked him up and down as if several years had passed since they'd seen each other. Mama was so dramatic. All he could do was laugh.

"No, Mama, I'm fine. I had a chicken sandwich and mac and cheese before I came here. Got it from Kings Table over there in BedStuy."

"How was it?" Her tiny nose wrinkled as if she were concerned. "I heard they are under new management and things have changed, and not for the better. I haven't been there in at least a couple of years."

Mama slowly removed her sweater. Cameron reached around and helped her take it off. "Thank you, baby."

She walked to the hallway closet and hung it up before returning to him.

"It was okay." He shrugged. "Their prices are higher now than what I recall. Anyway, I'm full. Thanks, though."

"Cameron and I were just sitting here talking," He

turned in the direction of his father, who was now sitting with his feet propped up on the table and a smug expression on his face. "It turns out, Camila, he's started dating someone."

Cameron rolled his eyes and sucked his teeth as he made his way back to the couch. He hadn't been saved by the bell, after all.

"Oh, really?" Mama sat in the love seat across from them, looking peachy and pleased. He reached for a magazine on the coffee table that he didn't give a damn about, and casually flipped through it.

"Yes," was all he offered.

"Well?" Mama waved her hands. "What are you waiting for? Tell us about her."

Cameron flipped the pages of the *Reader's Digest*, pausing on a photo of some gluten-free cookies. They looked dry and crumbly.

"Her name is Emily." He took notice of the look Dad shot Mama.

"Emily? That sounds like a White girl's name." Dad chuckled. "I had no idea Black people were naming their daughters Emily."

"That's good though," Mama interjected, wiggling her finger about. "It'll help her with jobs, I'm sure. You know they discriminate if you have an ethnic-sounding name."

Dad nodded in agreement.

"That's true. Back in 1982, there was a Black girl named Amy that I went to school with and she—"

"She's not Black." Cameron flipped to another page, then another.

"Oh," his parents said at the same time. Mama offered a nervous laugh as she leaned forward, clasping her hands together.

"I bet she's like that girl Jazmín you dated a long time ago. She was really pretty, a nice young lady. Jazmín was Dominican, honey." She looked at his father with a tight smile on her face as she attempted to refresh the man's memory. "Is Emily Dominican?"

"No."

"Puerto Rican?"

"Nope." He flipped more pages.

"Cuban? Japanese? Mexican? Hawaiian? Colombian?"

"She's White."

It seemed all the air in the room was sucked into an invisible vacuum. Cameron tossed the magazine back onto the table and buried his head in his hands for a moment, gearing up to speak his piece. When he finally looked at his parents, their eyes were practically bulging out of their skulls, and you could've heard a pin drop.

"Did you say White?" Mama questioned, her head cocked to the side.

"Look, I know, with my personal views, you're in shock." He pointed to himself. "And I can't blame you for that. I've been obviously quite outspoken on topics like race relations in this country and this must come as a surprise."

"A surprise? A surprise?" Mama veered back in her chair. "Is that what you're calling this? You are the same little boy who walked up to my friend, Cathy, a Swedish woman I adored, and still do, and told her that she was benefiting from White privilege and that she owed me and your father reparations."

Dad burst out laughing and shook his head.

"I remember that." Pops chuckled. "You had her over here for dinner and Cameron embarrassed us so bad."

"Cameron, you were only six or seven years old. I had no idea where you'd even heard such a thing. You are the same child who said that interracial dating happens when the Black person hates themselves and the White person is just curious or wants to make their racist family angry. You are the same person who told me that if the world was ending, and there was only you and one White woman left on the planet, then that would be the end of civilization because you would never make a baby with a White woman. You also said that—"

"All right, all right." He gestured wildly with his hands, feeling a bit embarrassed as his old opinions and judgements were thrust in his face. "Yes, *all* of that happened, but I said that stuff years ago, Mama. Back then, I likened myself to a real-life Huey P. Newton. Anyway, I didn't go searching for this woman and she didn't go searching for me. Well, I take that back. Actually, she kinda did, but not directly. It's hard to explain."

"Try me." Mama crossed her legs, rocking one back and forth. "I've got all night."

"Anyway." Cameron rolled his eyes. "This just kinda happened, all right? It wasn't planned. We've been seeing each other for a few months now. We met, we connected. Simple as that."

"How do you feel about this young lady, Cameron?" his father asked, sitting straight like some judge peering down at

TIANA LAVEEN

him from behind a bench.

"I care about her. I care about her a lot." He sighed as he looked listlessly at the television for a spell.

"Well…uh, yes, I'm stunned." Mama readjusted herself in her seat and shook her head.

"Do you have a problem with her being White?"

"Not really. I don't have the same racial and religious outlooks and philosophies as you, Cameron. My thoughts are far more conservative in some regards, and in others, more lenient. I think we are all God's children. I'm just still stunned that my son, the Black militant, is dating a White woman, but if that's what you want, that's fine."

"It's not that that's what I want or seek, it's that I'm accepting who she is because I enjoy her as a person. I don't think about her race anymore. That's not even an issue at this point, I've moved past that."

"So, you see her whiteness as problematic, something you don't like but she can't help it, so you've just accepted it?"

"No. That's not what I mean." He shook his head.

Now both parents were on him like hot gravy on mashed potatoes. The revolution would not be televised, but the damn inquisition would be broadcasted from every radio tower in the entire city of New York, it seemed.

"Even when I was with Brooke, Mama, I didn't see White people as the enemy anymore. You may not have noticed because I wasn't around here all the time. I was busy with starting the club and everything, but I was no longer calling them White Devils and blaming them for everything. I was growing older, and I was even working with more and more people who were not Black, and I saw good in some of those people. It took me getting out of my usual circle of friends, my environment, to even be open to the discussion. Brooke would take me places for her concerts, and that, too, aided in me seeing that people are just people. Some people are assholes, some people are not. Period." He shrugged.

His father picked up the remote control and put the television on mute.

"Brooke and I would have passionate debates about this all the time. She knew a lot that I didn't, and vice versa. We were teachers to one another, and I realized that some of the people who were treating her the best were not Black; they were White. It went both ways. I had to get real and be honest with myself about that, ya know?"

"I understand," Mama said softly.

"Brooke had friends of just about every ethnicity you could think of. Yeah, she was definitely Afrocentric, but she never excluded anyone. She could love anybody, as long as they were a good person." His voice cracked as the memory of her came rushing, blowing up his resolve. He lowered his head and shut away the tears before they had a chance to fall. He felt his father pat his back, giving comfort. "Yes, I still believe in White privilege and supremacy. I still believe that oppression and racism are systematically imposed on people of color in this country and that without it, the economy would crumble. It's all intertwined. I still believe we have to fight and protest these injustices. I still believe that when someone has all the power, they are not going to give that power up willingly, ethics and morals be damned." He took a deep breath. "I didn't want this. God knows I didn't, but it was almost like I was set up, like the universe was testing me. She's an amazing person. Emily is special. I think you'd both like her, actually."

"What does she do for a living?" his father asked.

"She's the head financial analyst for the Windsor Financial Group in Manhattan, has several degrees, real sharp woman."

"Wow. Windsor? That's impressive." Mama ran her hand along her calf, massaging it.

"Yeah, she's a Windsor, too, actually. Her full name is Emily Windsor. Her family, her father's side, started that company."

"Whoa." Dad's brow arched. "She's loaded then."

Cameron shrugged. "She's comfortable."

"Well, how did you two meet?" Mama asked. "You have me awfully curious now."

He hesitated for a long spell, his heart pumping hard within him.

"I'm not convinced you or Dad are prepared to hear that story, but it looks like you're about to hear it anyway." Ten minutes later, after he rolled out the details, one by one, bit by bit, his mother was hyperventilating and Pops had left the room to get some water for them, or so he'd said. When he returned, his complexion looked ashen as he handed them both a glass.

"Thank you." Cameron took a sip. "I guess I was thirsty after all." Setting the glass down, he stretched his legs and looked at his parents, seeing disbelief on their faces.

"Who knew that, uh, her race would be the least of the surprises," Mama said after taking a deep breath. "Cameron,

I know you don't want to hear this, but I think this is your way of trying to hold on to Brooke. That's not fair to this woman, or to you."

"I thought the same at first, but it's not like that, Mama. With the way I know her now, I'd be interested in her regardless of whether she had Brooke's heart pumping inside of her or not. Yeah, that is what probably made me call her, to get close to Brooke, but I had no idea what was in store." He'd made sure to not breathe a word of how Emily had taken on various aspects of Brooke's personality, talents, and traits. That was a rabbit hole he wasn't willing to jump in and travel with them, at least not yet. He did wish he had someone to confide in, however—someone he could trust to not think he'd lost his mind.

"Are you happy?" Dad asked, sadness in his eyes.

"Yeah. I'm real happy with her, Dad."

Dad nodded, then picked up the remote control and turned the volume back up.

"Then that's all that matters," Mama said with a huff. She got to her feet, though he knew she was awfully concerned and not buying it. That was just his mother's nature. She never kept drilling at him, but her worry always showed on her face. Cameron clasped his hands together, feeling strange and uncertain with what the future held.

Two down, a hundred more people to go.

Chapter Seventeen
Asking for a Friend

YAWNING, EMILY CROSSED her ankles and slid her arm behind the fluffy, white pillow. The bedsheets were Egyptian cotton, recently purchased from an online vendor who created one-of-a-kind bedroom accessories and linens. The television was on, broadcasting some reality show. Blinking, she checked it out. Oh yes, a rerun of that *Little Women: Atlanta* show. She'd never seen it before, but a colleague at work had remarked one day that it was an absolute riot. It was seven in the evening and it had been a long day.

She couldn't wait for Cameron to stop by later on. He'd been busy. He had a meeting with another vendor and touched bases with a caterer regarding an event he was hosting next month. He also had to fire one of his waitresses after she'd disrespected the patrons.

When he'd offered to take her to dinner and a movie after he was done with work, she'd let him know she wasn't in the mood to go out, as she felt like death warmed over. So he suggested just chilling for the night with Brooklyn-style pizza delivery, cheesy romantic movies of her choice, and affection galore.

She'd replied that she hoped for sex, though she'd warned she likely wouldn't have the energy to do more than lie back and receive, like a limp jellyfish. He chuckled, and had even offered to give her a massage. She could stay in her gown all damn night—no complaints. How could she say no to such a thing? That had definitely been an offer she couldn't refuse.

"Ouch!"

She stretched her leg and winced, then crossed her ankles again. Every muscle and tendon within her was screaming, feeling knotted, tight like a rope and in need of relief. She'd been back in the hospital earlier that day and felt like a piece of steak by the time they'd turned her loose. The doctor and nurses had beaten, poked, prodded, and moved her about with little to no regard. Not her usual doctor, but some brute who'd decided she wasn't flesh and bone and could be tossed around like a plastic bottle. She'd run on a treadmill with monitors and a host of wires attached to her, then endured an endless battery of tests to ensure all was well. Thus far, she had only minimal complications and she hoped, with crossed fingers, to be able to schedule cosmetic surgery to deal with the scar that started in the middle of her collarbone and drifted down to right above her navel. She hated it, though she had to admit Cameron's kind words regarding the crucial disfigurement definitely made her feel a bit better. She looked lazily over to the other side of the bed and took note of the stack of international newspapers she'd been collecting over the past couple of weeks.

Her argument with Cameron a while back still haunted her, and she wasn't certain that some of his words she'd ever be able to get out of her head. She didn't let him know how irritated she'd been at some of his declarations, the jabs, the way he cut her where it hurt, but he seemed to know all the same, and that made her feel that much more powerless when she was face-to-face with him. Everything she said to him, he had an answer for. She didn't always have to agree with his reaction or response, but she could not take away from him that his line of logic was often succinct and worth listening to. At the end of the day, this was part of her journey—a time-consuming, cruel, painful expedition, nevertheless. She was only upset for one reason and one reason alone—she'd met her match.

He'd been right. Cameron could go toe-to-toe with her, and he never backed down. It didn't matter if they were playing an arcade game, making love, or deep in a heated argument regarding racism. He was competitive, observant, slightly arrogant, and intelligent—a deadly combination. She liked being in charge, having no one coming against her and risking a verbal beatdown they'd live to regret, and boy did she enjoy delivering a well-timed punishment. However, just as she was an alpha female, Cameron was an alpha male in every sense of the word. On spiritual steroids. There was an untouchable wisdom about him, and she loved that. Her lips curled as she realized that, in some ways, he reminded her of her father.

Dad. Better call him.

She reached for the phone and dialed her father's cell phone. Perhaps this would be a good time to return his call from earlier in the day and tell him she was seeing someone.

I'll gauge the conversation and figure out the answer to that as we go along.

"Hello, Emily. How are you, honey?"

As soon as he answered, she heard what sounded like faint music playing and muted conversation in the back.

"Well, I'm great actually, just a bit tired, winded."

"You had your hospital visit, correct? I called earlier to check up on you, but my call went to voicemail." She heard a bit of clanking and moving about in the background, as if he were at a dinner party.

"Yes, and everything went fine overall but Dad, it sounds like you're busy. Is this a good time? I can call back. Where are you, anyway?"

"I'm at a business dinner with Schultz."

"Oh yeah, that's right." She smiled, forgetting that her father was taking one of his dearest associates to dinner to discuss stock options and such. "Tell Mr. Schultz I said hello. I'll call you back later tonight or tomorrow, okay?"

"I will tell him, but no need to call me back. In fact, he ran into a friend and is having a discussion with them outside. I have a minute. We're just waiting on our salads."

"You're at Le Bernardin, right?"

He chuckled. "Of course." It was one of her father's favorite restaurants. "So, what can I do for you, sweetheart?"

"Dad, remember when I brought up a while ago not remembering a friend that I had as a child? I couldn't recall her name, but I liked her."

"Yes, I vaguely remember you bringing that up."

"Well, it's still on my mind." Emily picked up one of the newspapers written in Russian and flipped it face down. She grabbed another and could see it was written in French.

I don't know French. Maybe Cameron will teach me.

"Well, if it's still on your mind then I suppose you can try to ask some of your classmates, see if they recall."

"She wasn't a former classmate."

"Oh. Who was she then?"

Emily took a deep breath and rested her head against the headboard. "The Black lady who used to come over and pick up Mom's gowns to take to the laundromat, remember her? She had a daughter."

Dad drew quiet, as if he were tracing his mind for stored memories.

"Oh yes, I remember her. Her name was Stella, correct? Maybe Sally or Sarah. Something like that. She worked for that laundromat and would often bring her daughter along for her errands. How old were you then?"

"Probably fourteen. Do you remember her daughter's name?"

"I can't say that I do. Your mother would sometimes invite Stella or whatever her name was, inside and they'd talk for quite a while. You and that girl would go to your room or to the game area and eat and talk, right?"

"Yeah. I liked talking to her. We would have good discussions. I wish I could remember her name." She beat the side of the bed with her fist as she surged with frustration.

"Well, sometimes we just have an experience for a short time, and it serves its purpose."

"What in the world is that supposed to mean in this context, Dad? All I'm saying is that I am having a problem remembering her name and it irritates me that I can't recall it."

"You've always been good with names so I am just saying, dear, that maybe she wasn't as significant as you think." She could almost see her dad shrugging his broad shoulders. "Sometimes, when we're having a hard time, we overthink things." Emily slumped back against her bed, growing irritated at him, though he may have been right. "Oh honey, Schultz is back."

"Enjoy your dinner. I'll talk to you tomorrow." She abruptly disconnected the call. Grabbing the heap of foreign newspapers in her arms, she slid off the bed and walked briskly into her living room, tossing them onto her coffee table to sort through later. After fixing herself a glass of sparkling water with a spritz of lime juice, she decided to turn on her record player and listen to some tunes.

I need to relax and get myself together. I'm all worked up now.

Flipping through her ever-growing collection of albums that she kept in an ivory ottoman, she selected "Off the Wall" by Michael Jackson. It had been given to her by an associate at work once he discovered that she was into the whole music thing now. In fact, he'd heard her singing in her office with the door slightly ajar. She had no idea anyone else was in that early and felt a bit embarrassed. Word soon spread that she was some sort of undiscovered songstress, though she'd played it off and ensured such a thing never happened again.

Turning it up to full volume she began to prance about, snapping her fingers, her long blonde hair going every which way as she swayed and sashayed about. After a few minutes of high energy bopping around, she caught her reflection in one of her vast floor-to-ceiling windows that overlooked the city.

She stepped closer, staring at herself as the twinkling city lights sparkled and glowed from near and far like some exploding diamond. Winding several strands of her hair around her finger, she stood there for the longest, tugging and pulling at her mane. A sudden hatred of the tresses that she'd worked so hard to groom overcame her. This had been going on for a few days, a fight she was losing.

No more than ten minutes later, she'd thrown on a baggy sky-blue striped sweater, yoga leggings, her oversized coat, and grabbed her car keys. She hadn't driven in such a long time, usually relying on an Uber or private driver from her father's on-call arsenal, but she was in a hurry and besides, what she needed wasn't more than five blocks away. She'd walk it if her body weren't so beaten down and exhausted. Glancing at herself once more in the mirror by her front door, she shook her head.

Time to take care of this once and for all.

She left her apartment on a mission she hoped wouldn't be impossible.

Chapter Eighteen
Throw a Monkey Wrench

"WHAT DO YOU mean? I did call earlier today, baby," Cameron explained as he approached her dwelling. A man selling hotdogs from a cart tried to wave him over, but he kept moving, not in the mood to be the unlucky guy to get his leftover twenty-four-hour street meats then suffer the diarrhea-like consequences.

"Oh, I must've not heard my phone. Sorry."

"It's cool, not a problem."

"Um, are you close?"

"Yeah, about two minutes away." He looked up at the sky, then his watch, and kept moving. "I parked about a block away. Didn't feel like dealing with your garage tonight. Last time, they gave me a ticket."

"I told you to fight that."

"Wouldn't have mattered." He shrugged. "I wasn't a resident and the visitor parking was clearly marked. I just noticed it too late. Anyway, lesson learned. Hopefully, that's the only inconvenience tonight because baby, I missed you." He grinned as he heard her laugh on the other end.

"I missed you too. Sorry I wasn't in the mood to do anything else but brood in my house. I'm a party pooper."

"Nah, you're a woman who had a serious surgery and you need downtime sometimes. It's not a problem and I've been wanting some pizza anyway. I haven't had any in a while, especially since I try to eat cleaner during the week. We can order whatever you want though. You told the doorman I was comin', right? He always acts like he doesn't remember me and tries to be funny. I'm telling you right now, Em, with the day I've had, he better not even think about—"

"No worries. Dennis knows who you are and yes, I told him that you were coming. He is just a little more protective, I guess you could say, of the women he knows live here alone." He rolled his eyes at that, but didn't say anything else. The guy was an asshole. Period. "I just got back from the drugstore, actually."

"Condoms? I have some with me. You know I only stick to a couple different brands. Some of them don't fit me well or leave a sticky film so I have to be selective. You don't want me busting through and you end up with a baby registry at Saks nine months later, do you?" he teased.

"No," she said with a chuckle. "I just picked up some beauty products."

"All right, cool. I see your building, baby. I'm about to come in."

"Great, I'll buzz you in when you get off the elevator."

Cameron ended the call and slid his phone into his pocket. He was happy to hear that Emily's physical therapy was now over and that her examinations at the hospital went well. He entered the posh building with a revolving golden door and immediately rested his eyes on Dennis, an older

White man who seemed to enjoy treating him like some chump. The guy stood with his arms crossed, white gloves on his hands, and a captain's hat on his head.

Look at this clown. Fuckin' ridiculous. He is mad corny.

"And who are you here to see?" Cameron grimaced and rolled his eyes before tossing his hands in the air.

"The same woman I saw two days ago, man. And last week, and the week before that, and the week before that, too. The same lady that's in apartment 7C. The big corner penthouse."

"What's her name?"

Cameron pulled out his phone, looking all serious and official. "I'm tired, okay? I don't have time to stand here playin' with you."

"I asked a simple question."

"Emily Windsor," he said after a brief hesitation.

The guy looked through his phone and shook his head. "I don't see you on the list."

"She already told me that she let you know I was coming. I just spoke to her. Call her then."

"What's your name?"

The man who's gonna fuck you up if you don't get the fuck outta my way. That's what the fuck my name is.

"Cameron."

"What I can do is have you wait here in the lobby area and I can—"

"I'm not sitting down in this lobby." Cameron pointed over to the rose gold and burgundy furniture that surrounded a glass table with an assortment of magazines. "I'm *supposed* to be here. Just call her so I can get out of here,

---

man."

"You're supposed to be here?" The man rocked back on his heels, a big sneaky smile on his face. "Oh, you purchased property here? I had no idea." He chuckled.

"I don't know what your problem is, but I am sick of this shit. I knew you were going to pull something even before I stepped foot in here tonight."

"Becoming belligerent won't help you."

"You haven't *seen* belligerent yet." Cameron cracked his knuckles.

"Is that a threat?"

"Every time I come over here, you give me the same exact crap. I never see you give anyone else a hard time but of course, no one else looks like me, right?" Cameron smirked.

"This is about safety. If I let everyone in here, I'd be fired and there would probably have been some robberies and homicides due to my lack of due diligence. I need your ID."

Cameron didn't take his eyes off the bastard as he reached into his pocket, removed his wallet, and took out his driver's license. He slammed it in the man's palm. The son of a bitch looked back and forth between him and the card, checking him out from various angles. Then, he went behind a small counter and began to type into a computer.

"What tha hell are you doin', man? This isn't a criminal investigation and you're not the FBI. I've been here *many* times already, and you know it. Are you trying to be funny?" Cameron approached the desk and rested his arms on the counter, his temper swelling within him. The guy ignored him and kept right on typing. Just then, Cameron's cell phone rang. He snatched it up and answered.

"Hey, I thought you said you were close. Everything okay?"

"No, everything is *not* okay. Ya boy Dennis here, the fuckin' menace, is giving me a hard time." The older man glanced up at him. "Guess he doesn't approve of me coming to see you. I'm sick of this shit." Cameron punched the counter with a tight fist.

"Cameron, calm down. I'm coming right now." Emily quickly disconnected the call.

"Was that Ms. Windsor?" the guy asked, acting oblivious.

"Are you like, on something?" Cameron huffed. "You know damn well that was her. She's coming down because you are harassing me and holding me up."

"I'm not doing any such thing. I am checking your information in the database," the man replied dryly. "I do that with everyone."

"Your supervisor is going to hear about this. Mark my words." Cameron shook his finger in the man's direction. "I saw how you looked at me the other day when I left her place the last time, too. This is a pattern of behavior."

"I don't know what you're talking about."

"I had come that evening, took her out, and we returned together. I watched you look at me help her in and out my car. You looked pissed, like it was some personal offense against you. When we returned to her place that night I didn't leave until the morning and I guess you filled in the blanks and felt some type of way about that. What? You're mad because she doesn't look at you like she looks at *me*?" Cameron sneered. "I swear to God you better be glad I've calmed down over the years. There was a day in time when I would've been in jail and you in the hospital over some shit like this."

"This is the calm version of you?" the guy said in an unsettling, high-pitched squeal. "You're acting like some crazy monkey, ya know that? Control yourself before I call the police."

"Crazy monkey? You wannabe cop, underdeveloped, inbred lookin' mothafucka." Cameron lunged toward the bastard, who stepped back. "I will reach across this desk and—"

"Cameron, Cameron." Emily seemed to appear out of thin air, wearing strange little hair clips in her hair, an oversized sweatshirt, and skintight leggings. Her bare feet beat against the glossy marble floor as she raced toward him like a lightning bolt. Grabbing him by the arm, she stepped in front of him like a block of bulletproof glass.

"Dennis, what seems to be the problem?" she asked sternly, resting her arms on the counter.

"And give me my damn license back, mongoose-faced bastard, since you wanna venture into the animal kingdom. Aren't you supposed to be over at the theater playing the hyena in *The Lion King* tonight?"

"Cameron, please," she turned toward him, "I'm handling this." She returned her attention to Dennis, who looked flushed and shaken. What did the bastard think he'd do? Just keep standing there and take it?

"Ms. Windsor," the man stated in an exasperated tone, as if he'd somehow been violated. "So many people come in and out of here every day. There's no way that I can recall everyone's face." He waved his hand as his eyes hooded. "Mr. Davis here apparently has taken offense to my asking pertinent questions so I can ensure that he is who he says he is, and that you are in fact expecting him." His voice was soft and pathetic, as if he hadn't just been showing out a few seconds ago.

"But I told you that I was expecting him, Dennis. I told you that my boyfriend was on his way, and even put his name on the guest list." She pointed to a clipboard with printed out papers. Cameron assumed his name was added on it. He had no reason to believe otherwise.

"I still have to check all of the information, Ms. Windsor. Someone could have pretended to be him. Those things happen, too."

"I don't really understand that, but what stands out the most to me right now is that I've never had any of these issues with my other guests coming to see me. You've let them through with no problem—ex-boyfriends, my female friends, my personal trainer when he used to stop by. My father never had problems coming in, either, and sometimes he'd walk right past you and you'd only smile and wave. This is in fact the first time, Dennis, that I have ever run into this problem with you."

"Well then, let me reassure you, Ms. Windsor, that this was nothin' personal." The man raised his hands and let them flop back down to his sides. The jerk was now avoiding eye contact, as if Cameron wasn't standing there at all.

"Actually, it doesn't. You see, this is the second time Cameron has complained to me about you doing this."

"But it's the fourth time that it's happened, Emily. And

I'm sick of it," Cameron said loud enough for the other man to hear him. Dennis shot him a surreptitious glance then looked back at Emily.

"I promise ya it's just procedure, Ms. Windsor."

"I'm going to be frank with you. I think it's because my boyfriend is Black." The man had the audacity to look surprised, and his beady eyes widened ever so slightly. "Dennis, I'm not going to debate this with you. Don't give Cameron a hard time when he comes here. I don't appreciate it and I will have you reported if this happens again." Her voice rattled as she yelled, as if exploding at the realization that the ugly truth was now right in her face. Cameron drew closer to her and wrapped one arm around her waist.

"Give me my damn license." He swallowed the expletive he wished to add at the end. Dennis motioned to place it in his palm, but he snatched it from the bastard's grasp. Cameron put it back in his wallet and took his baby's hand. "I'm telling you, you've messed with the wrong man this time. I make shit happen. I'm not the porch monkey that you may take me for, son, sittin' around, letting shit slide. This isn't the end of this."

They walked toward the elevators. Dennis didn't utter a word. Cameron looked behind him and watched him busy himself at the computer as if nothing had happened.

"Well, that was awesome." Emily grimaced then laughed dismally, shaking her head. "Good grief."

"I don't need you to call anyone. I meant what I said to him. I'm taking care of this. I hope his friends give him a going away party tonight because I'm going to have his job. I know *exactly* who to call. We can't let stuff like this go, Em.

You have to fight fire with fire. Now you've seen what I go through all the time. The shit you just witnessed? That happens often." She looked rather sullen at that moment. "Hey, why is your hair in clips?" he asked as they got on the elevator, still holding hands.

"I was parting it to dye it. You came a bit earlier than I expected so I had to put it on halt."

"I thought you always got your hair done at that fancy salon on Madison Avenue?" He pushed the number 7 and the doors closed.

"I do, but for some reason, I got a wild hair up my ass, pardon the pun." She giggled. "And wanted to dye it dark brown."

He pulled her in his embrace. "Why do you want to dye it dark brown all of a sudden?"

"I don't know." She shrugged. "I just think it suits me better now."

"But why would you do that?"

"What do you mean? I just wanted a new look. Women like to change it up all the time, Cameron. Besides, maybe it'll help me look less washed out."

"You're fine the way you are."

"You don't even like blondes. You said so yourself." She huffed as she pulled away from him and crossed her arms.

"Is that what this is about? Never mind, I'll get to the truth another way. Have you ever dyed your hair another color before?"

"No. Just various shades of blonde. I've been platinum blonde, I've been honey blonde, but always blonde."

"Okay, I get it now. You don't have to change yourself

for me, Emily." He shot her a disapproving glance as they reached her floor. They stepped out, Emily seeming a bit vexed from his words.

"I'm not."

"You are."

"Why can't you just believe what I told you? Women like to change it up a bit. Can't I change my hair color without there being some big conspiracy or self-loathing driving it?"

"I don't know. You tell *me*."

They soon entered her apartment and the place smelled fresh and clean as usual. Wiggling out of his shoes, he set them by the front door and marched behind her as she entered her master bedroom suite. He followed her into her bathroom, almost slamming into the back of her.

"What are you doing?" Her brows bunched. "Why are you so close?" She turned to face him and pressed her palm against his chest. He peered at her countertop, taking notice of two plastic bottles filled with dark chocolate-brown hair dye, a black rat tooth comb, a hair dying brush, plastic gloves, and some little tube filled with ointment.

"Don't do this." He snatched her to him and crushed her lips in a kiss. He finally talked himself into releasing her, and they looked into each other's eyes. "Come here. I wanna tell you something."

Taking her by the hand, he led her to her bed. They sat down, the television light glowing on both of their faces.

"I have reason to believe that you feel maybe I'd be more attracted to you if you had darker hair, and were less, I guess you could say, European looking." He struggled to find the right words as he saw the hurt in her eyes. "I…uh…had a sexual relationship with a White girl in high school once." The woman's jaw dropped open and then she burst out laughing. "I'm serious. It was lowkey. I didn't want anyone to know. It was just sex, you know? Well, she felt stronger toward me than I did toward her. Soon, she told me she loved me."

"What did she look like?"

"Her name was Lana. She had a medium-ish shade of brown hair and light brown eyes. She was nice, popular. But I never wanted her to tell anyone about us. One day, she came to school and her hair was dyed jet-black and cut in a hairstyle like the group from back in the day, Salt-N-Pepa. She had dark brown contact lenses and dressed more like the Black girls at our school all of a sudden." Emily sat a bit taller and crossed her arms over her chest, but he didn't miss her deep swallow. "She did that in hopes that it would make me want her, be with her in a relationship, but it didn't work. Look, Emily, you already have me, okay? There's nothing for you to prove."

She lowered her gaze.

"But see, here's the thing, Emily. This hair thing symbolizes more than just something about me, about us. This is about you, and personal acceptance. You told me last night when we were on the phone that you were ashamed of yourself. You said you've been studying and reading, and that though we still don't agree on everything, things are starting to click in your head. You can now understand my perspective a lot more, and you even apologized. You told me that you can't truly love me and not try to understand where I'm coming from. And now that you do, guilt has taken over."

"It has. I feel like I've awakened from a dream, like I was in some fog."

"Yeah, not being realistic and not at least trying to empathize with another person's pain then suddenly seeing that someone you care for has been deeply affected by the very principles you held dear can do that to you." She nodded. "You even admitted that you've fallen into a depression. I don't want that to happen to you. I was depressed enough for the both of us. When Brooke died, I didn't think I'd ever be okay after that. And you know what, baby? I was half right. I am not the same, but I *am* okay. I only became okay after I actually accepted what happened—not just in my mind, but in my heart—and truly understood that I would not be making her proud if I didn't get out of that funk.

"I know you may not think that on a conscious level, but subconsciously, I think all sorts of things are going on inside your head right now. You're still trying to find yourself, the *new* you. You've taken on some of the characteristics of my deceased girlfriend, and yeah, I've noticed it. It was out of your control; you didn't choose it. You've got an important part of a proud Black woman inside you and that heart beats within a proud White woman. There's no way that this isn't clashing with your own physical identity, the way you see yourself now. There's a power struggle between the two of you it seems. I've been reading about heart transplant surgeries for a while now, Em. You are right. You're not the only one who has talked about this sort of thing happening."

"So what do you think is happening? I'm curious to hear

your opinion."

"Here's my guess. In Brooke's quest to elevate you, you sometimes feel attacked and then you start second-guessing yourself. You are the exact opposite of what she looked like in so many ways, but I doubt Brooke cares about that. You both have the same body type and shape, I'd say, but that's about where the similarities stop. Your outward appearance means nothing at this point. It's what is goin' on inside that counts. You both were adamant about your beliefs, and you were loyal to those you loved. Those are excellent qualities. Do you realize how brilliant and incredible you are, baby? If you don't, I'm right here to remind you."

He tilted her chin upward and kissed her. She kissed him back, a sad smile on her face.

"Thank you."

"Focus on dying the inside of yourself, the old you. Paint over that shit with bold, bright colors. God made you blonde, and that's fine. No, I don't have any problem with women changin' their hair color, as long as it's not because they hate themselves. For fashion, to cover some premature gray or a changeup? Cool, but what kind of man would I be to let you do somethin' like that for all the wrong reasons? I love you and that's just not me."

"Maybe you're right, Cameron," she uttered, her eyes misting. She looked down at her bare feet. "I've been feeling strange again. It comes in waves. I looked at myself and hated my hair, every strand of it. I hated my skin, my body, all of it. It made me feel so powerless." Tears welled in her eyes then trailed down her cheeks. He leaned into her and held her tight.

"I know it's not my heart making me feel this way. It's not Brooke. It's remorse. I...I read about the Central Park Five and was sickened." She shook her head. "Someone else had to confess, come forward, for these young men to regain their freedom. And from my research, and trust me," she huffed, "I did a lot, the whole mess was steeped in racism and injustice. So many times I have judged people based on the way they looked, their accents, their clothing. And now look at me."

She pulled away and looked up, sadness reigning in her beautiful blue eyes. "You warned me. You told me I was going to get broken down, and that's exactly what happened."

"I need you to take one day at a time, Em. Stop trying to rush this process."

"I'm not rushing the process. I'm rushing the pain. It hurts."

He nodded in understanding. Bringing her close once more, he rested his forehead against hers. Through her tears, she began to move her fingers along his black button-down shirt until his chest was exposed and the clothing tossed haphazardly onto the floor. Moments later, he was pressed down flat onto the bed and gripping a fistful of sheet as she took him into her mouth, licking and sucking his hard nature, making his toes curl with lusty ecstasy.

He hissed and moaned when he came almost without warning, his ejaculation erupting into her mouth. She swallowed him whole, taking in every drop before licking her lower lip, absorbing the last of him. Spent, he tried to catch his breath.

She slowly slid away from him, got up, and entered her bathroom, closing the door softly behind her. After a few minutes, he switched on the television, selecting the news channel, and removed his socks, the only articles of clothing left on his body. He heard the water of the shower come on and drifted into a daydream as he teetered between a need to doze, hunger, and horniness.

When she came out, her blonde hair was wet and she had a black towel wrapped around her body. Emily snuggled up close to him under the sheets, and he immediately pulled her close, kissed her cheek, and wrapped his arm around her. Together they watched the movie *Black Swan*, simply enjoying each other.

"What do you do when you can't remember something important?" she questioned out of the blue.

"Mmmm, like forgetting where I put something?"

She ran her fingertips along his chest hair.

"No, well, kinda. I can't remember the name of a friend of mine. See, she was the daughter of this Black woman who used to take care of some of my mother's errands and she and I became friends. When some of my so-called popular friends from school came over and saw us together one day, they said stuff about her after she left my house. I stopped talking to her after that. She soon stopped calling me and asking about me. I guess she got the message. She and I would have good conversations up until that point and I really liked her. I've always regretted that, I believe, but only recently have slowed down long enough to acknowledge it, ya know? To admit to myself that I give a damn." He brought her hand to his lips and kissed it. "I just wish I could remember her name. Damn it. I want to try and look her up."

"What do you think her name started with? The letter?"

"Um, I think it was something like Sa…a Suh sound at the beginning. Her mother's name sounded similar to hers. Yeah, I'm pretty sure it was an "S," but that's not a good enough lead. I can't ask my mother for obvious reasons."

"Do you remember what borough she lived in?"

"I think Queens. Well, she was born in Queens but then moved to Brooklyn, I think. The cleaner's shop she worked for though was in Manhattan."

"What about the name of the place?" She shook her head. "Okay, maybe your father remembers where he hired her from, or an agency perhaps, and they can help you."

"That's a good idea. I'll call him back tomorrow and ask." She gave him a peck on the lips then looked back at the television. "Are you hungry, Cameron?" she asked behind a yawn.

"Yeah." He ran his hand up and down her arm. "We can order that pizza after the movie is over."

"I didn't think we were really paying attention to the movie though." She giggled.

"Not the movie on the TV. The porno movie we're about to make."

She slapped his arm playfully, and it didn't take long before he was sheathing himself with a freshly opened condom. Raising her long, gorgeous legs high, he placed them around his shoulders and entered her slow and easy. She moaned so helplessly as she gyrated her hips to his thrusts. They both watched him disappear inside of her, pull out, then back in.

The flickering of the television tossed shadows and light about the vast room, adding to the vibe. He went impossibly deeper, feeling her, and each second of bliss evolved into a minute, and then another. Stroking her silken bud, he pressed against her form with each plunge until he felt her familiar vibration against his body. She was coming undone, cooing and whispering his name with need.

He reached for her ankle and kissed it while delivering slow, perfectly timed strokes at first, then he hastened the pace. Gripping her thighs hard, he grunted as he erupted, releasing into the condom, her warm, tight walls squeezing his dick. What a welcomed erotic hug born of soft, sweet dreams. A sense of euphoria and a faint feeling rushed to his dome all at once. Collapsing upon her, he breathed hard and heavy, not wanting to move a single muscle. He would just lie there and rest until he was ready for round two. He closed his eyes, growing soft inside of her, but then blinked and came alive when she moved to reach for her phone.

"Hi, I want to order a vegetable pizza," she said in an overly cheery voice. "Extra onions and peppers, please. Size? Extra-large, just like my man."

He laughed at her then planted a kiss on her sweet lips.

Chapter Nineteen
What's the Tea?

"**S**HIT, I FORGOT to get that yogurt Emily wanted. I'd said I'd get her some next time I came in here." Cameron begrudgingly doubled back to the dairy aisle, his blue plastic basket in hand at the Gala Fresh Farms grocery store on Saint Mark's Avenue in Brooklyn. He bent down to check out the assortment of yogurts until he spotted a section of the Greek variety. Emily was going to spend the evening with him, and he'd even talked her into coming down to the club beforehand. His plan was to get her on that stage.

Every fiber of his being begged to display her voice for all to hear. He was certain he'd be met with the utmost resistance. Emily didn't like singing in front of others and had made that perfectly clear, but she just didn't know what she was missing out on yet. Emily would blow like a seasoned professional in her shower or while they prepared dinner together some evenings. He enjoyed every second of it, but she didn't do it as frequently as he'd have liked. He didn't wish to try and turn her into a star—that wasn't Emily's style—but she had a gift now, and he wanted her to show it off, even if only every blue moon.

Here it is. Chobani.

He snatched up the pineapple, coffee, and black cherry flavors and placed them inside his basket before getting a few packs of vegetable straws, his favorite snack.

"Cameron." He turned in the direction of the voice and his lips kinked up in a smile. He hurried over to the lady, who held onto a shopping cart handle with heavily ringed fingers.

"Mama." He wrapped his arms around her and squeezed. Brooke's mother was looking a bit thinner than he recalled, and perhaps he was just seeing things, but her dark eyes seemed dull, the brightness gone, as if a window shade had been pulled halfway down upon them. "Great seeing you. How've you been?"

"I've been hanging in there, Cam," she said. Her lips bowed in an all-too-familiar comforting smile as she placed a hand on her burnt-orange purse that sat in front of her in the cart. "How have you been, honey?"

"I'm hangin' in there, too."

"Last time we spoke I had to tell you that my baby's killer was still on the run." She shook her head as if in disbelief. "I was callin' you in a panic, over and over again. I just needed to talk to you—"

"Excuse me, sorry. Let me get out of your way here." Cameron scooted out of the path as someone tried to squeeze past them, their cart full of cat litter bags, orange juice, and dog food. "Sorry for interrupting you."

She smiled sadly at him, lines framing her eyes. "Seems like we switched places. I started out being okay, then everything went downhill. Things got dark." She ran the tip of her fingernail along her right palm, her gaze drifting briefly to her hand before meeting eyes with him once again. "You, on the other hand, appear at peace."

"Mama, I didn't take it well, either. You had to be strong for all of us. We relied on your strength, used it like medicine for the weak. We left you in a terrible position." He sighed.

"I wanted to be in that position. Being the one people leaned on was therapeutic for me."

He slid his hands into his pockets. "I was depressed, enraged, missing someone so badly that it hurt just to—" He focused on a pyramid display of graham crackers until the moisture in his eyes dissipated. "It hurt at times to even breathe. I felt like the police dropped the ball and fumbled." He shrugged. "This guy could do this to someone else. Take someone he didn't know out of this world with so little regard, all over a dispute with someone else. And he probably doesn't even remember why he was so upset in the first place. They gotta get him off the streets."

"I hope they do, sooner rather than later. Someone like that is definitely dangerous. I pray every day, Cameron. Every day. Maybe eventually God will answer my prayers. My fear is, maybe He already has, but it's the answer I don't want."

"I'm trying to keep a level head about it. I'm still upset and think about what happened every day, but I have to try and stay optimistic. You taught me that." A strange silence swam between them for a few moments. "You said I look at peace. I'm not."

"I hope you find peace then, Cameron. You look pretty

good." She grinned. "You *look* at peace. So maybe, despite it all, you've found it, in your own little way."

Flashes of Emily came into his mind, and his heart filled with love. "I wish serenity for you. I know you're nowhere near that place, but I hope that changes soon. You know, I think about you a lot. I've called many times, but it's hard to talk about sometimes." He cleared his throat. He missed her, the woman who was supposed to become his mother-in-law, but never did. Never would.

"You can always call me, Cameron." She reached forward and traced his chin with her fingertips. "We'll always be family. I don't care where you may move to, who you might meet and fall in love with." Her eyes twinkled in an all-knowing way, and chills ran down his spine. "You'll always be my son."

His eyes glossed over as he took her into his arms once more, squeezing her tight. When he pulled away from her, she had tears in her eyes.

"I realized I needed to be more like you. Stop being reactionary and stand tall, Mama. I can never fill your shoes, but even though you're hurting and don't feel so tough right now, you have a tranquility about you that I've always dreamed of having. You handle these sorts of things better than most. I'm convinced of this."

"I talk a good game, baby." She chuckled. "But let's get down to the truth. I had to go see a grief counselor. It proved too much to handle after a while, so I did what I needed to do."

"Nothin' wrong with that, Mama. More of us need to see counselors, therapists, ya know?"

"Definitely. It's like a stigma in the Black community to admit that we need some help. Things had gotten so bad that I was havin' bad dreams, too." He nodded in understanding. Lord knew he'd had his fair share of them as well. "Brooke was everything to me, Cameron. After losing her father, who was the love of my life—a brilliant, hardworking man—and then her brother, my amazing son, she was the final blow. The third strike to my heart. The one that almost took me out of here." She tapped her chest and blinked away the tears. He grasped her hands and squeezed them.

"I don't think most people could have endured what you have, at least not been able to go through life and still be okay. You're an inspiration to all of us."

"Cameron, I asked God." She sighed and paused, clearly needing a moment. "I asked God why He didn't just take me first, because there are times when I'd rather be dead than wake up another day knowin' my whole family is gone. My daughter and I were just so close."

"I know."

"This is a special kind of pain. It rips out your heart and soul at the exact same time and leaves a black, gaping hole." Her eyes narrowed. "You cover it with a well-placed smile, a big boom of laughter, or some pleasurable activity like taking a stroll down the street." Her eyes misted and gleamed, as if she were teetering on the edge of grief-given insanity. "But it never fully closes. It never goes away. I hope neither you nor anyone else I love *ever* has to experience the death of a child. It's not supposed to be that way; that's not the right order. One night, for about five seconds, I seriously considered ending it all. But I'm the strong one, right?" She smiled mirthlessly, shuffled a bit in her purse, then removed a gold pendant shaped like a microphone. "I keep this with me."

"What is it?"

"It was Brooke's since she was a teenager. She loved it. She used to wear it on her jacket." She ran her hand across the shiny gold piece, a proud smile on her face as it caught her reflection. "She'd lost it a long time ago and I found it soon after she passed, jammed in a floorboard of her old bedroom. Was in there tidying up. I had converted that room to a sewing and reading room, but still kept bits of her in there."

"I keep a little of her with me, too." Cameron pointed to a small diamond stud earring in his right ear. "It was hers." She nodded and smiled a bit wider, showing her teeth.

"Looks like we're both rather sentimental, hmmm? You know," she rolled the jewelry between her thumb and forefinger, "I wish sometimes I could talk to her one last time, Cameron. Just one more time." His heart thumped in his chest. "At least she did good, ya know? Not only in life, but in death. Someone got to live their life because of her." She shrugged. "So her death wasn't in vain. Speaking of that, a long time ago you asked me to find out who got her heart. You wanted me to get the lady's name. You ever follow up? I had thought about it but figured she might be a little unnerved about that."

"I, uh, yeah." He swallowed, feeling suddenly hot. "I did in fact follow up. Hey..." He looked at the time on his phone. "Let's sit down and chat for a little while longer somewhere else, if you have a little time to spare. There are some things I think we should probably talk about."

She looked rightfully confused, her brows bunched.

"Sure, baby, we can talk, but I got perishables and things. I guess I can put 'em back for a while."

"No, that won't be necessary. Let's get the rest of our groceries, finish shopping, and then I can drive you home. Is that cool?"

"That works for me." She smiled. "I took the train so I appreciate it."

"Great. Finish up what you're doing and I'll meet you in the front of the store in about, say, fifteen minutes. Is that enough time?" He took out his cell phone and noted the time.

"Yes, that's perfect."

"All right, great." In no time at all, the two had purchased their items and he was putting their groceries in his trunk and helping the middle-aged woman into his car. When he turned the engine on, rap music blasted out of the speakers and he immediately turned it off. "Sorry about that." He chuckled nervously.

"You're all right." She giggled. "I might not be able to hear out of my left ear for a week, but I'm okay."

He laughed at that. Soon, he was navigating traffic with no music in the car, no other distractions, only two souls that had been brought together by one who'd gone on to the great beyond.

"I don't even know where to start, Mama, but, the name of the woman who has Brooke's heart is Emily Windsor. Well, you are the one who told me that, but yeah, Emily is White, as you know. She's in finance, a really interesting person."

"How do you know that she's interesting?" He gripped the steering wheel tighter. "I take it then that not only did you speak to her after I gave you the information all that time ago, but you've talked to her extensively?" She crossed her hands over her purse that rested on her lap, her brow arched.

"Yes, you could say that, but it didn't happen exactly that way." He sighed. "I actually never looked her up, never called her. She, uh, she found *me*. How do I begin? How do I say this?"

"You've known me far too long to beat around the bush. Just tell me whatever it is, Cameron."

"Okay, Mama. Look." He tossed up his hand and huffed. "I can't make this come out any less confusing or crazy. I need you to please try to keep an open mind, okay?"

"Okay."

"Emily came to my place, told me who she was, and I freaked out. Fast-forward, I got in contact with her and wanted to talk. When we did, she confessed to me that she has, well, been experiencing some changes in her personality since she had the heart transplant."

She stared straight ahead, then crossed her legs and turned to look at him. "Such as?"

"Well, many things. For one—and this is a big thing, actually—she wasn't a good singer before the transplant. Now she sounds like a cross between Lisa Stansfield and Helen Terry." She said nothing. "I've heard her sing, okay?" he went on. "Her voice is astounding. You'd think she'd been singing her entire life."

"Okay, what's something else she says has changed?"

"Well, she admitted she wasn't exactly open-minded and progressive. She used to have a conservative viewpoint when it comes to injustice and democracy, so to speak." He looked in his rearview mirror and quickly switched lanes.

"Why are you playing games with me, Cam?" She gave a hoarse chuckle. Her years of smoking cigarettes, though she'd stopped over ten years ago, still clung to the tone of her voice, giving her a slight rasp. "Just say it. The woman has some racist views."

He nodded and smiled stiffly.

"Yup. So, now? Not so much. Here are some more examples that blew me away. She also doesn't eat meat anymore. Her favorite food was literally steak before the surgery. Now, if she smells it, it sometimes makes her nauseated. She likes to wear all sorts of clothing, though her sense of style hasn't changed per se, just expanded. She said she never liked homemade jewelry. Now she owns a small collection of it and loves it. She buys soy candles, loves dogs now too, and before she wasn't an animal person at all. Oh, and get this, Opium loves her. He raced up to her like she was Brooke. Now, these new likes and dislikes, who does that sound like?" He shot her a quick glance then turned back toward the road.

"Are you trying to imply that she is becoming like Brooke? That somehow my daughter's heart being implanted inside of this woman is now creating a whole new person, to some extent?"

He offered no reply. His intention and meaning were clear. He reckoned it was up to her to decide the validity of his words at that point.

"Well, recycling Brooke I suppose would be a better description." She chuckled and shook her head. "I don't believe that."

"All right." He swallowed down any other explanations he could offer, certain he was now at a crossroads with her. Unable to discuss the matter with his friends or family, quite frankly, Mama was his last hope. That hope was snuffed out like a candle flame.

"Now sure, Cameron, this woman had a life-changing procedure, but I don't believe that because she has Brooke's heart, she suddenly went from a racist, animal hatin', couldn't-hold-a-note-in-a-bucket, stuck-up princess to a music-loving, international lover, kumbaya, we're all God's children, songstress diva who loves a good thrift store sale and Bed Bath & Beyond."

For a time, the sounds of the city were the only noise he could hear.

"You're messing with me, aren't you? Do you believe this is really true?" He approached a red light and looked at her. He could see, at that moment, a glimmer of hope. She *wanted* to believe.

"It's true. I wouldn't kid you about something like this. I know it sounds wild and I was suspicious, too, Mama, but she told me some things, okay? Things only Brooke would've known." She pulled out a tissue from her purse and blew her nose. "I wasn't even going to tell you about this, at least not right now, but with us running into each other the way we did today and after what you were sayin', it was like I was being *told* to tell you this."

Mama was unreadable as she reveled in her silence, mull-ing things over. "At times, it's like I'm not in control of this narrative. It's like it's destiny, and I can either fall in line or miss out on something magnificent. I don't believe in fairy tales, Mama, but this is genuine. It's legit. This is actually happening. I have something else to tell you, too, and uh, I hope you're not angry with me after I do."

He reached out and took her hand. The skin was slightly loose, incredibly soft, and covered in raised veins.

"I already know." She took a deep breath. "You've been seeing this lady romantically," she stated dryly, not looking at him. His heart beat faster and wilder.

"How'd you know?"

"Your eyes lit up when you started talking about her. You used to look like that when you were talkin' about Brooke." Out of the corner of his eye, he could see her blinking back tears. Pulling away, she placed her hand up to her mouth and began to slowly rock back and forth.

"I'm sorry if I've hurt you."

"You haven't hurt me." A tear streamed down her face. "I would like to meet her."

"All right. I can arrange that. Do you want to meet her because you believe me now?"

She shrugged, her full lips puckered out as if she were annoyed. She readjusted herself in her seat. "Not really. Well hell, I don't know," she said gruffly. "Here's the thing, Cameron, something I learned a long time ago. Perception is reality for us. It doesn't matter what you tell me, or what I tell you; if we don't understand the core concept, it'll never be true to us. If we don't believe in the basic principles, then it can't resonate within us." She pointed to her chest. "I'm not going to sit here and tell you what to believe, though, and how you should feel. My daughter was into metaphysics, I believe they call it." She rolled her eyes. "Brooke wanted to talk about crystals all the time. She wore some, tried to get me to sage the house when I complained to her about things comin' up missin' or strange noises."

She waved her hand and choked out a choppy laugh. All he could do was offer a watery smile. "Regardless of all that, what I do know, Cameron, is that you tried to find my baby again in this woman, at least initially."

"Actually, I—"

"Shhh." She shook her head and placed her long finger to her lips. A thin silver band was wrapped around it, catching the light in just the right way. "Did I say you owed me an explanation? Is this relationship of yours a crime? Did I say it's a bad thing?"

He swallowed and turned away, gripping the steering wheel like a lifeline.

"No. You said none of those things."

"All right, then. I think that however a person heals, as long as they're not harmin' nobody, is their own business, Cameron. Some people get over a loss by keepin' busy. Some develop unhealthy addictions. Some fall in love again. Of course you'd eventually start dating sooner or later. You're young. I never expected you to mourn Brooke forever."

"But I still miss her, despite having moved on."

"I think honestly that's mostly because her killer is still enjoying his freedom. Makes it kinda hard to fully commit to the future knowin' he's out there living his best life, you know?" She took a peek out the side window. "We can't step into what's in front of us if what's in back of us isn't clearly defined. You ask yourself, 'Where have I come from?' If you don't know, you may accidentally take steps backward, thinkin' it's a new course or path when you've already done that a million times over. It's like reading chapter five and you haven't even seen chapter two and three. Then, to add insult to injury, you get tested on the chapters you hadn't even seen. That's what this feels like to me."

"It does." He nodded. "That's a good analogy. I wanted to talk to you about this for the longest."

"Well, why didn't you?"

"I was worried about how you'd respond. To *both* aspects."

"Don't be. Is it awkward for me thinking about it, like, in full detail? Somewhat." She shrugged. "Do I believe this woman is your pacifier? Maybe, but again, even if she is, that's none of my business."

"You find it weird that I'm dating the lady with my deceased girlfriend's heart, don't you? You can tell me the truth." He smiled.

"Do you?"

He took a deep breath and reflected on the question he'd so easily posed to her.

"Honestly? I used to believe that. Now? Not really."

"Cameron, I'm not saying that you don't care about this woman either. I am just saying that had she not been who she is and received what she got from Brooke, you two wouldn't be together. Like, had you and Brooke just broken up, organically, went your separate ways, and you ran into this woman, I just highly doubt you'd be with her now."

"I can't deny that, but this did in fact happen organically, too. Brooke's heart being inside of her is, well, you can't get any more organic than that."

She smiled at his play on words.

"Well, I am not who you have to convince. That's between you and God. You explained enough about her already to let me know that this had to have been a struggle for you at first, especially knowing you as well as I do. But you were hoping for a certain outcome, probably crossing your fingers that your prayers would be answered, and apparently, you got it. Doesn't matter how it started though anyway, right?" She smiled sadly at him, shaking her head. "It only matters how you live it day by day."

Soon, he pulled up in front of her apartment building.

The red maple saplings, cherry blossom trees, and American elms that lined the street in their full splendor in the spring and summer now consisted of half bare, dark, sprawling branches, their fallen leaves strewn all along the cold concrete. The sun set in the sky behind a thick veil of red brick walls, amethyst shadows, and fading golden light. Cameron cut the car off and helped the lady get her few bags into her brownstone.

The place still felt like home away from home. As always, it was clean as a whistle, floors so spic and span you could eat off them. The air in the place smelled like clary sage, Pine-Sol, and peppermint with a hint of thyme and basil.

"What you been cookin' in here, Mama?" he asked with a grin as he set her bags on the kitchen counter.

"I had made some mint tea earlier, a whole decanter of it."

"That sounds good."

"You want some before you head home?" she offered as she opened the stainless-steel refrigerator door and showcased a glass pitcher of tea garnished with a few mint leaves and thinly sliced lemons floating atop the golden liquid. "Come on. Your milk won't spoil. It'll only be five minutes. Besides, I miss your company and your beautiful smile."

Chapter Twenty
Airing Out Dirty Laundry

T HE SLICK STREETS and sidewalks were like shimmery white and silver skating rinks. Emily tightened her grip on her yellow leather purse as she made her way from the Uber to Queens Center, an indoor mall. Flicking off snowflakes from the lapel of her red fur jacket, she entered the shopping center and was greeted with the bouquet of hot, sweet cinnamon buns and buttery pretzels. Her thigh-high, black boots clicked along the glossy floors as she moseyed on over to the shopping mall map detailing the layout of the place.

After speaking to her father, whose memory failed him regarding her teenage pal of yesteryear, she took it upon herself to hunt her old nameless comrade down via other means. In her mind, where there was a will, there was a way, and she never backed down from a challenge, especially one that caused her so much excitement and distress at the same exact time. So last night, while Cameron lay in her bed fast asleep, she sat at her desk and got busy.

The guy was out like a light, snoring. He'd been so exhausted. Yet, his simple presence as she went through the motions, making calls and looking up information, gave her both a sense of comfort and fueled her to keep going. She made various social media posts on networks she'd not ventured into in what felt like forever, but she knew it was her best bet in regard to tracking the young lady down. These messages, some sounding rather unintentionally cryptic, went out in droves. She responded to all replies, but came upon dead end after dead end.

Days passed with no answers or resolution in sight. She was coming to accept the fact that this might be it. She just might have to let this crusade go.

As soon as frustration hit an all-time high and she considered throwing in the towel, finally, someone in her old circle of friends recalled the woman's mother, too. Apparently, she'd provided the same service to them as well for a short duration, and though she had no information about her whereabouts, she believed that her daughter was a manager at an AT&T store. She'd run into her just a year or so earlier when she'd gone to sort out her teenage son's cell phone issues.

Her old friend might have gone on to bigger and better things, but Emily decided it was at least worth a shot, if not to get her hopes too high. She immediately called the place of business and lo and behold, she got a name.

Sasha Tabar.

That was it. Her name was in fact Sasha, but the employee on the line stated that Sasha wasn't in; it was her day off. After inquiring when she'd return, Emily made plans to pay her a visit. Now here she was seeking out what she'd needed for so long, to gain closure, or perhaps, to say hello and rekindle an old friendship that hadn't lasted very long, but had hit her in a profound and meaningful way. With eyes narrowed as she let her finger roam about the map in search of the store, she finally spotted it.

There it is. AT&T is on the lower level. Making quick work of getting there, she ignored a luggage display showcasing leather wares. Mall shopping wasn't her thing, but she loved a good deal on some attractive gear. Besides, in her mind she was planning a vacation for the following spring, feeling in desperate need to get out of New York for a spell to clear her mind and regroup after one of the most troubling, exhausting, and profound years of her life. She and Cameron were already in discussions regarding their tropical getaway. It would be epic.

I'll double back over there later and check it out.

As soon as she entered the place, she took note of a long line near the entrance for customer service and several glossy posters on the walls featuring smiling models pretending to be patrons who were happily spending their cash on the latest gadgets. There were a host of brochures and bulletins placed in strategic areas, which gave it a bit of a travel agency vibe.

"Excuse me. Sorry." She negotiated her way through the crowd, ignoring the smattering of expletives thrown her way as she cut the line. "I'm not here to order service or pay a statement. I'm here to speak to Ms. Sasha Tabar." Placing her hand flat upon the counter, she addressed a young Hispanic woman whose thick, black eyeliner made her look like a cat.

"Is she expecting you?" the lady asked without making much eye contact, her eyes glued to her computer screen as she helped a patron standing nearby. Said patron was now glaring at her.

"Not really, but I need to speak with her. It's important."

The young woman gave her a glance, then nodded. "Mr. Fresno, I'll be right back to finish helping you. I don't see your last payment though. You might want to call your wife about this." The man standing before the register was gripping a stack of wrinkled papers and looked rather frazzled.

"I don't need to call my wife. She's the one who told me that ya billed us twice. Jesus H. Christ," he yelled as the woman walked away, leaving them there.

Emily tossed him a half-baked grin, the most she could muster. The guy didn't smile back. His bushy salt-and-pepper eyebrows dipped, framing deep grooves at the top of the bridge of his nose as his rather short forehead wrinkled up like a mastiff's. He crossed his thin arms over his small chest, resting them over his protruding belly. It had to be only thirty-five degrees outside, and yet this guy was standing there in a flimsy white T-shirt and baggy, worn jeans.

After a while, Emily turned in the direction of two feminine voices speaking in the distance. The young Hispanic lady she'd originally spoken to came out from a back area, a big smile on her face with someone trouncing behind her.

A heavy-set African American woman with huge breasts shoved in a long-sleeved pink sweater and long luscious black curls that draped over her shoulders and back approached with a big, pearly white smile.

"Hi, I'm Sasha. I understand you wanted to speak with me. How can I help you?"

She looks different, but it's her. I remember those eyes, that voice, that smile.

"Yes, I'd like to speak to you about something that happened a long time ago." Emily removed her black fur-trimmed gloves and set them aside, trying to steady her shaking hands. Emotions flooded her so fast, she thought she'd drown. "My name is Emily Windsor and you and I used to be associates, I suppose you can say." She laughed nervously. "No, that's not accurate. We were friends, actually. Teenagers who spent quite a bit of time together."

"Oh, really? I don't remember you."

Emily's heart sank like a brick thrown in the Hudson River. She looked about the place, seeing far too many eyes on her and people eavesdropping.

"Do you mind if we step over here?" She pointed to a few feet away.

"No, not at all," the woman said in a cheery tone.

They made their way over to a more private area next to a messy desk with a couple of chairs facing it.

"You don't recognize me at all? I'm told all the time that I look pretty much the same."

She shook her head.

"Your name isn't familiar to me, either. Did you go by something else?"

"Uh, no. My parents lived in Midtown Manhattan, Fifth Street. My father still owns the property and resides there, but owns other properties as well. See, your mother used to collect my mother's expensive garment pieces—her furs, silk blouses, things like that. You were always with her and you and I struck up a conversation. Before long we were calling one another on the telephone and you'd come to visit. You even spent the night a couple of times."

"Hmm." Sasha placed her finger to her lower lip and her eyes narrowed as if she were giving it deep thought. "It doesn't ring a bell. Sorry. That was a long time ago if you say we were teenagers." She smiled sadly and shrugged. "Is there something else I can help you with? Are you interested in an internet and television package?" Sasha reached for a brochure off a wall display.

"Huh? Uh…No…" Emily shook her head, feeling out of sorts, disconnected, shocked, let down, and perhaps humiliated, too. "Okay, just so I can ensure I'm not totally out of my mind, going crazy," she said. "Your mother did in fact work at a dry cleaners, right?"

"Yeah." She stood straight and crossed her arms. "She did for many years. There were a lot of people we came across, though. My mother had probably over fifty clients at any given time. Her schedule was very tight, especially when she picked up more hours."

"Well, uh, maybe your mother remembers me and my family? My mother's name was Juliet. Juliet Madeline Windsor. If you want, I'd be willing to take you both out to dinner sometime soon so we could catch up." Emily was hanging on by a tattered thread. She tried to hide the desperation in her heart, her voice, her soul, but she was certain she failed. This wasn't what she'd imagined. Not the reunion she'd envisioned at all.

"Well, my mother actually moved to Florida. Been there for twelve years, so I can't just go and see her whenever I want. But I can ask her when I talk to her today or tomorrow. Thank you for the dinner offer, though. Do you want to leave your name and number for me?" She quickly snatched a piece of paper with the company logo and an ink pen off the desk. Emily swallowed and clutched her bag. She displayed no hint of remembrance. Not a clue that she had any idea who the hell she was. It was almost as if she'd dreamed all of this up—but she couldn't have. It was real. Wasn't it?

"We talked about swimming at Coney Island, Sasha. See, for the longest I couldn't remember your name but I do recall all of these details, see? You told me about some boy; his name escapes me now, too, but you adored him, had the hugest crush on him. You said he wore an orange scarf all the time and you had tried to take it so you could smell him. Your favorite food was cheeseburgers loaded with pickles and onions and I thought that was really strange but funny. Our chef used to make it for you too, and you had a big collection of nail polishes. I even purchased some for you for your birthday. Your birthday is in July." Emily had no idea how she'd recalled all that just then. "I'd gotten you some nice ones from Europe. They had glitter in them."

"This is strange to me because I don't remember *any* of that. Wow. I mean, I do recall the boy with the orange scarf." She chuckled. "His name was Ronald Rodriquez."

"Yes. That was his name." Emily clapped her hands enthusiastically, hoping that this would unlock more hidden memories.

"We actually dated for a short while in high school and yeah, I did like nail polish a lot. But you? I don't remember you." She shrugged.

"But you've got to. Your favorite color was burgundy, Sasha. You told me you were a terrible dancer as a little girl, but amazing at gymnastics. You had gotten many trophies in competitions. And we talked all the time on the phone. How could you not remember?" Her voice trailed as they looked into each other's eyes, but they were miles apart. "You listened to my problems, the stuff I told you about my mother that I hadn't talked to anyone else about, private things, and then one day it all stopped. It vanished. I quit speaking to you because of dumb shit. I'm so stupid."

She hit her head with her palm and spun around as hot tears burned her eyes.

"Hey, don't do that. It's all right," Sasha said, trying to soothe her.

"I'm sorry." Emily's voice cracked. *I'm falling apart. I'm losing it.* "Sorry for wasting your time. I was going to come up here, ready to apologize for being such a little bitch to you due to peer pressure, but it looks like I'm saying sorry for something else altogether. I feel like a fool. I'll let you get back to work. Sorry for wasting your time."

Without waiting for a response, she flew as fast as she could out of there, mortification swimming inside her like a goldfish in a bowl. She felt hot all over with the overwhelming sense of self-loathing and regret, and her eyes burned from her running mascara. Making her way into a nearby public restroom, she quickly freshened up at a sink partially clogged with paper towels, not willing to make much eye contact with herself. She simply couldn't muster it.

How embarrassing. I really bungled that up. I looked like a lunatic to that lady. It's a surprise she didn't call the cops. She snatched a paper towel and dabbed at her face. After washing her hands, she made her way out of the restroom and reached in her purse to call Cameron, praying he'd answer so she could fall apart and have the pity party of a lifetime.

As she rounded the corner to do just that, she saw Sasha standing not too far away, looking in various directions, as if searching for something lost.

Emily stopped dead in her tracks like a deer caught in headlights until finally, their eyes locked. Sasha drew closer until she could smell the woman's light, airy perfume, see every beauty mark on her face, and take in the deep concern on her face. Worry, perhaps pain, taking the place of her stunning smile.

"I remember you."

Emily's lips curled in a smile and she breathed a sigh of relief. "I'm so glad. It came to you, huh? I've thought about you on and off over the years and—"

"I didn't want a scene at my place of business. I'm a professional and didn't want my employees to see anything they didn't need to, but yeah, I know exactly who you are." Sasha's eyes grew dark, and Emily sank inside of herself. Here was the part where she'd be cursed out, told what a horrible human being she was. How she'd left her high and dry.

"I'm sorry, Sasha."

"Sorry for what? This isn't about *you*. I could tell with the way you were rambling on, you have no clue."

"Clue about what?"

"Your sick ass father harassed my mother, Emily."

"What?"

"You heard me. That man kept making sexual advances all the damn time. It was nonstop, like some sort of obsession. My mom refused to keep going over there after a while, especially after your mother stopped paying her and started talking to her all crazy."

"My mother knew?"

"Yeah, she knew. She walked in on your father tryna kiss my mother. She was blamin' her instead of her nasty ass husband, but leave it to you to think I stopped coming around because of you or anything *you* did. You were always a little self-absorbed, but no, that wasn't it. We stopped comin' because of him."

Emily's heart began to beat slower and slower and s l o w e r...

"I...I had no idea."

"And my mother wasn't the only one, either, all right? She found out your father got around quite a bit. He was a big-time cheater." Sasha sneered, then sucked her teeth.

"I can't believe this. All of this time, I thought it was because of me, because I'd driven you away after caring too much what other people thought."

"I already knew your stuck-up ass friends didn't like me. I didn't hold it against you. I liked you anyway, thought you were nice and generous, strange and awkward like I used to be. We had a lot in common, regardless of the fact that you were White and rich and I was Black and poor. You were smart, and I liked that, too, but your father ruined everything. The final straw was after my mother was gone from y'all house, that still wasn't enough. Your mother blackballed her."

"Blackballed? I don't understand."

"That bitch told people that my mother stole clothing from her, never turned it in, and my mother ended up getting fired from a job she'd had for five years. See, before that, when she was younger, she had gotten into a little trouble for stealing some food in a store, so she had a record. My mother had gotten on her feet, finally had a job that was payin' the bills and keeping our family afloat. That all came crashing down, all 'cause your father was doing what he was doing, thinking he could have anything he wanted. My mother worked hard. She'd forged great friendships and built a reputation for being dependable and trustworthy and your mother made sure it all came crashing down." Sasha's voice rose and people began to glance their way. "Even after she wasn't working for your mother anymore, your father still didn't let up."

"What did he do?" Emily leaned against the wall, her mind throbbing, her ears buzzing as anxiety and pure anger burst from her core.

"He would send my mother flowers, gifts, nasty letters about the stuff he wanted to do to her, all kinds of crazy shit, and told her she was stupid for not taking him up on his offer when she'd made it clear that she wasn't interested and never would be and to leave her the hell alone. I guess nobody can say 'no' to Mr. Windsor, huh?" She smirked. "So yeah, I remember you, Emily, but I sure as hell wish I didn't. Funny how you can remember all that shit about finger nail polish, but couldn't even remember my damn name. Maybe you blocked it out. Maybe something inside of you knew the damn truth, too." Sasha turned away and marched off, her broad shoulders swaying with each determined step.

"Sasha, I didn't know. Please, you have to believe me."

She stopped and turned. "But if you had known, Emily, would it really have made a difference?"

"Awww, baby. Don't do this to me," Cameron pleaded.

"I apologize, honey. I have to take care of something, though."

"But I told her that you were coming by tonight, Emily. Mama was looking forward to it."

"Cameron, it's not like I'm meeting your parents. This is Brooke's mother."

"That's not fair and right now, it's beside the point. I want you to meet my parents, too. It'll happen soon."

"I know you do; that's not what I'm talking about. I'm not saying it's not important, okay? It is, but something has come up. I promise to—"

"You can't just cancel like this."

Emily sat in the Lincoln town car outside her father's residence, a tight grip on her phone.

"I'm sorry, Cameron. You know it's not like me to break plans." After the whole sordid Sasha debacle, the last thing on her mind was going on with her plans for tonight. At this moment she had bigger fish to fry, particularly one big shark she ought to nickname "Father Fin."

"Well, where is the fire? Why do you have to reschedule?" he said with a huff, clearly irritated. "You could at least

WHAT THE HEART WANTS

tell me what's going on and stop talking in code. I hate when you do that."

"I will tell you as soon as I'm finished. Baby, I have to go. Call you as soon as I can."

She disconnected the call before Cameron could reply, stepped out of the car, and made her way inside the building. Several minutes later, she was sitting on a cream couch in a high-ceilinged room, the wall-to-ceiling bookcases filled with hardbound books and the fireplace roaring. Father came in wearing a tailored black suit, his expensive shoes catching the light just right as he walked. He closed the double doors behind him. A smile on his face, he went around a liquor cabinet and approached her. Emily smiled, staring at the jumping flames as he bent down and kissed her forehead.

"So, you said you wished to see me this evening. First and foremost, how are you?" He returned to the liquor cabinet, pulled out a glass, and poured something the color of wheat inside it.

"Never better."

"I know you have to watch your alcohol intake, but would you like something else? Perhaps some tea?"

"No. I think things will be hot enough as it is."

Curiosity shone on his face, but he kept on busying himself with preparing his beverage.

She crossed her long legs and rubbed a hand over the smooth material of her black pants. Her form-fitting silky black turtleneck was adorned with a silver seashell pearl necklace, a gift from her mother. Running her fingers along the length of it, she observed her father through hooded eyes as he took the first sip of his liquor, looking much like a dignitary, then toast on the love seat across from her. In between them was a refurbished antique wooden table made with impeccable craftsmanship in 1890. It was one of his favorite pieces in the entire house.

On it sat a carved marble chess board and matching pieces, a one-of-a-kind set from an Italian sculptor known for his attention to detail. The thing had to be worth thousands of dollars—perhaps even the board alone. Emily leaned over and picked up the white marble king. She studied it from various angles. Running the cool piece of marble against her skin, the smoothness of it felt rather therapeutic, even the knobs and knots at the tip of the crown, but nothing could extinguish the fire that burned within.

"So, what is it you wished to speak to me about?" he asked.

"Remember when I asked you about my old friend? Her mother?" He nodded. "You told me you didn't recall their names."

"I don't," he said matter-of-factly, not flinching as he matched her posture.

"Well, let me refresh your memory." She looked for any tell-tale signs of distress, perhaps discomfort, but he showed none. "Her name is Sasha. Her mother's name is Samantha." She rotated the chess piece back and forth, back and forth. Faster and faster it twirled as she sandwiched it between her hands. "Samantha's family originally came from Jamaica, but she was born here, a U.S. citizen."

"All right. I take it you read up on her? Did you find her?"

"I'll be getting to that in just a bit. Anyway, Samantha

took care of her ailing father for years, and her own family, too. Her husband had gotten sick when Sasha and her brothers were quite young. Samantha's mother had passed away quite some time before that. It had been rather rough for her. In need of obtaining more work, she applied for a job at a laundromat, doing pickups to make it easier for clients. At first it was a part-time gig, but then, demand increased. People enjoyed this sort of service and would pay for the convenience. For Samantha and her family, this worked out great."

"Can you please tell me the point of this tale, Emily?" he asked dryly.

"Oh, Dad, the point is about to be crystal clear in just a moment. Be patient. Isn't that always what you used to tell me?" She winked at her dad and grinned, but he didn't seem amused. "Samantha met some amazing people along the way." Dad took another sip of his drink, his face unreadable.

"But one person she met, well, things didn't go too well with that. Now, don't get me wrong, things started out amazing with this person." Emily laughed mirthlessly. "Samantha was given huge tips by this customer. She was given gifts, too, and the couple was so, so, so polite to her—just Mr. and Mrs. Manners times one thousand. They even had an awkward daughter who was desperate to be noticed, needed attention, and wow, by golly, their prayers were answered. Samantha just so happened to have a daughter around the same age." She threw up her hands, still holding on to the white king between her thumb and forefinger. "And they hit it off amazingly."

Dad cleared his throat and looked away as if uninterested, but she wasn't discouraged. She kept right on.

"Well, this amazing couple with the awkward kid didn't have a care in the world when compared to many others. They were enjoying life. Family vacations, luxury cars, fancy clothing, the best schools, amazing clients. Whatever the husband wanted, the husband could get. Money could solve all the problems one had. Isn't that right, Dad?" He took another sip of his drink and glared at her, not a word coming out of his mouth. "Well, the daughter did in fact recall her father having a roving eye, but never knew of him actually cheating on her mother. She figured," Emily shrugged, "that's just the way men are. Dad treated her great though, and her mother never wanted for anything.

"But Dad did. Dad wanted Samantha. But much to his dismay, Samantha didn't have a price tag. Things ended badly. *Very* badly. So much so that when this guy's daughter asked him repeatedly whether he remembered her old friend, his memory was suddenly erased, as if he were in the *Men in Black* movie and Will Smith had waved that little do-hickey, that wand with the light, in his face. That girl, now a woman, realized that her father is full of shit."

She tossed the white king down onto the floor and heard it roll someplace away from her. Grabbing the white queen, she shook the thing as angry tears welled in her eyes.

"He let her jump through a bunch of hoops when all he had to do was tell the truth. What about me? What about Mom?"

"You have it all wrong, Emily. Samantha was the one hitting on me, okay?" he stated matter-of-factly. "She was asked to not return to our home because of it. It was rather inappropriate. She needed money and offered herself to me. I refused. That woman was very troubled."

"She sounded perfectly sane to me. I spoke to her on the phone today!" Emily yelled, gripping the chess piece with all her might until it hurt. A piercing pain radiated throughout her fingers, but she didn't let up; she squeezed all the tighter. "After all these years, that woman remembered Every. Dark. Hideous. Horrible. Detail. She told me *every*thing you did. Everything you said. The way you made her feel."

"And you're going to believe her word over mine? A woman who had a criminal record, I might add?"

"Oh, you suddenly remember now, don't you? As if I had a doubt. I finally found Sasha and after a pretty emotional discussion, some of it steeped in blame, misunderstandings, and accusations, we both comforted one another and calmer heads prevailed. I went into her office with her and she called her mother. That woman knew things about you that she shouldn't have. I am too disgusted to repeat them, but trust me, you did *exactly* what she said you did and probably then some."

"She was a thief," Dad roared, then slammed his glass on the table, forcing the liquor to slosh about. "She stole clothing from your mother, and jewelry, too. Your mother trusted her and she took advantage. We paid that woman plenty of money. There was no excuse."

"Then why did you lie when I asked you about her? You said you didn't recall her name because you had something to hide. I don't care about the misdemeanor she had gotten in trouble for. That doesn't make her story false. That's like saying a drug addict can't be physically assaulted. Or a thief

TIANA LAVEEN

can't be murdered. She was neither of those things. She didn't steal from Mom, I don't believe that. Still, even if she'd made mistakes in her past, this doesn't mean she couldn't be a victim of someone abusing his power. I am so sickened by you."

Dad swallowed. "You're believing a false narrative, basically fake news. I never flirted with that woman, or hit on her. Now am I going to sit here and tell you that I was one hundred percent faithful to your mother? No, I wasn't, but I never tried to sleep with Samantha! I never did anything of the sort. Now maybe she took my kindness as flirtation." He shrugged. "It's certainly possible, but I'll tell you this, Emily, your mother and I had a rather difficult marriage at times. It wasn't easy. Instead of working it out amongst each other, we both sometimes ran to others. Your mother wasn't innocent, either, I'll have you know. These were things we were not going to discuss with a child, private matters between the two of us. But let me make something perfectly clear. I loved your mother and I would have never done such a thing."

"Lies." She shook her head. "She told me about your business trips, the schedules you kept, and the way you tried to get her to come with you on some of them. She knew about your property in the Hamptons. You'd described the bedroom in great detail to her. She'd never been there. How would she have known? I remember those trips. There is no way she would have known about them had you not told her, and how in the hell are you sitting here lying to my face, over and over again? My God! What kind of a monster are you? How could you?"

"I've done nothing wrong."

"How could you do that to Mom? How could you do that to that lady? To our family? I thought you were a man of honor."

"Emily, you are losing your mind. This is preposterous. That woman wasn't even my type. None of this is—"

"You must think I'm an idiot. She was very attractive, Dad. I remember her, and even if she wasn't, that has little to do with it. You think homely women don't get sexually harassed? Give me a break."

Emily gently placed the white queen down. She reached for the black king and brought it up close to her heaving chest. "I'm leaving and going to go see my boyfriend tonight. He's Black. See, unlike you, I'm going to stand in my truth and claim it. I'm not going to hide behind my title, my money, my prestige." Dad grimaced and shook his head, as if she were some lost cause. "Mom had a lot of flaws, but she tried to be as authentic as possible. She became so enraged at what you'd done, she acted out and got Samantha fired. That was a horrible thing to do, but Mom was probably so desperate to keep you that she was hellbent on getting what she saw as the competition out of the way."

"Your mother was no angel."

"You're right. She wasn't. Not in the least. I know she liked Samantha, though, and I know Mom was lonely. And I know she sometimes drank too much while you were out and about, doing Lord knows what. And I also know she only started saying horrible things about Black people after I no longer saw Sasha coming to the house. That's no excuse, but it makes *perfect* sense now. Her hatred was based on a broken heart. She believed you when you told her that it was Samantha hitting on you, not the other way around, so she made up a lie as revenge. She believed your bullshit when she confronted you about it, but deep down, I bet she didn't really buy your story. Yet, she was too afraid to really give it much thought because she wanted me to have what she didn't have—an unbroken home."

Emily placed the black king down gingerly, ensuring it was perfectly positioned. She snatched her purse up from the couch and slid the strap over her shoulder. "I must be going now. I have a dinner date this evening and I'm running late."

"With your boyfriend that you've not told me about. I don't care that he's Black, Emily. You must've, though, since you didn't tell me before now, so if that was said to cause a shock, it doesn't. I honestly am not concerned about things like that." He placed his lips to the rim of the glass, but didn't drink.

"Nope. His skin color has nothing to do with why I didn't tell you. The story is far more complex than that. At this point, you're not worthy of hearing it."

"I take it you won't be at work tomorrow?" He sighed languidly as he reached for his glass and took another leisurely sip.

"Oh, I'll definitely be there. I have far too many meetings. However, you and I have nothing further to say; that is, of course, unless you're ready to come clean and finally tell the truth." Father simply sat there. Emotionless. "I didn't think so. That would've required courage and concern for others. Something you clearly lack."

Chapter Twenty-One
The Memory of You

FEATHERY SNOWFLAKES DRIFTED along the street like cotton filled with bubbles, kicking up from the ground and branches with the help of a burst of cool wind. The snow was no longer falling from the sky, but Old Man Winter had coughed up enough of the stuff to last New York several lifetimes. The area appeared deserted, lacking proof that civilization was still breathing, living to see another day. It was such an eerie image for the eye to behold, as if Brooklyn were suddenly some urban ghost town, existing as a mere frozen memory in the late hours of a starry night.

Parked cars on either side of the street were caked with hard snow from the previous snowfall, but the sidewalks looked freshly salted. Rows of brownstones stood tall and proud, some with ornate emerald and gold Christmas wreaths hanging on the doors, while others boasted antique bronze doorknobs and intricate ironwork detailing on the gates around the front steps. In a few homes, Kwanzaa ruby and black candles peeked from the windowsills, while others showcased ocean-blue menorah candles.

Cameron looped his arm around Emily's as they made their way up the walkway to Mrs. Coleman's home. When they arrived on her doorstep, the lights within her abode flickered from behind semi-sheer white curtains. As they waited to gain entrance, Cameron snuck a glance at Emily. She oozed elegance in her long black coat, turtleneck, and fine leather boots. Her wheat-colored tresses were pulled tight, away from her chiseled yet feminine face, into a lengthy ponytail that trailed down her back and hit right above her ass.

It wasn't long before the front door slowly opened, and there his second mama stood, dressed in a light gray shawl, black slacks, and fluffy white slippers.

"Heeeey." She greeted them with a warm smile, her bright eyes filled with light. "Come on in. Get outta the cold."

Cameron and Emily entered the dwelling, and as soon as the door closed and locked behind them, he drew her into a big, warm hug. She chuckled at his hesitation to release her, and she hugged him back with the same vigor. He imagined his need for her may have exceeded her need for him in recent days, which made him so glad to receive her affection.

"Mama, this is Emily Windsor." Cameron stepped aside and unzipped his black leather bomber coat while Emily extended her freshly manicured hand. Her gold and diamond bangles clanked as she moved. As Mama eyed her, head cocked to the side, her smile slowly drifted away.

"Please don't mind me. I don't mean to stare." An unnerving silence reigned amongst them. "This whole thing just intrigues me, I suppose you could say."

Emily nodded and offered a tilted smile, as if understanding, as if almost expecting such a reaction.

"I don't blame you. I imagine it's a bit out of the ordinary."

Mama hurriedly nodded and took their coats to break the tension. Before long, everyone was gathered around the long mahogany dining room table, each with an ice-cold glass of RC Cola and a slice of homemade lemon meringue pie in front of them. That dining room he'd been in a hundred dozen times. Christmases, family birthday parties, quiet get-togethers…

The walls were a pale yellow framed by a simple, attractive crown molding. Large oil paintings featuring Africans and African Americans hung on the walls in poses that celebrated music and dance. One in particular showcased an old woman with a thick white scarf wrapped around her kinky salt-and-pepper hair, sitting at a sewing machine, a look of determination and angst spread across her midnight-complexioned face as she worked the foot pedal barefooted. She held a piece of blood-red fabric under the pivoting needle of the machine, completely absorbed in her task. He used to be mesmerized by that image. It looked so realistic, as if one could reach out and touch her, feel the hem of the gown she was creating.

"I'm sorry for initially canceling, Mrs. Coleman, then saying I was coming again last minute." Emily sported a forlorn expression as she spoke. "I'm a reliable person. Cameron can surely attest to that." She tossed him a glance paired with a quick, cutesy smile, but it was short lived. "You see…" Emily's lips crimped in a frown and her complexion deepened. "Today did not go as planned. In fact, that would be quite an understatement. We're not promised perfect days, now are we? Anyway, I apologize once again. It wasn't my intention to cancel and then toe the line this way, wishy-washy and causing confusion."

Earl Hines and his Orchestra's "Sweet Georgia Brown" played on an old, scratchy record player.

"I understand that things happen. Is everything all right, though?" Mama sat at the head of the table, running her palms against some white lace doilies, over and over, as if they needed a good ironing. She normally used them as placemats.

"Honestly?" Emily's brow rose. "No, but with time it will be. On another note, I want to tell you that it's an honor to meet you."

"Why? I'm in no one's history books." The older woman shrugged, sporting a bit of a smirk. "I'm not famous or infamous, even. I've done nothing for you." She squinted, regarding Emily in a discerning way, as if trying to figure her out—like a human puzzle bearing fresh and old scars connected to a life she herself had brought into the world.

"I beg to differ. Without you, there would've been no Brooke. Without Brooke," Emily placed her hand over her chest, "there'd be no heart, a second chance at life."

A slight smile crept along Mama's face and Cameron nodded in agreement.

"I suppose since you put it that way, you're right." Mama took a stingy taste of her soda, going through the motions, then placed the glass back down. "RC Cola and pie isn't exactly the tastiness of meals. In fact, the thought of it would probably sound kinda nasty to most folks." She giggled, drawing them into the banter. "But see, when my

Brooke was a little girl, Emily, she loved them together. Would always ask me to make a lemon meringue pie and let her have a glass of cola. She said the bubbles in the soda would make the meringue tingle in her mouth, like that Pop Rocks candy the kids used to have. She said 7-Up didn't do as good of a job as the RC Cola or Coke, so that's what I used to give her."

Cameron nodded. "I remember that candy."

"You may not believe this, but I made the pie on a whim this morning, not even thinking about this visit. For some reason I decided I wanted to make it. I make all sorts of pies. I'm not a great cook, but I make great cakes and pies. So I looked in my refrigerator and pantry and sure enough, I had all that I needed to make it. Once you two came over, I grabbed the soda and poured it in the glasses too, not thinkin' much of it. That's strange, isn't it?" She tapped her finger to her lower lip. "And now, here we are."

"Maybe it's not so strange after all, Mrs. Coleman. Maybe Brooke knew I was coming by."

The quiet took over then, blanketing the room like a thick fabric that floated from the sky and covered all of them. The three just sat there for a spell, casting glances at one another.

"So I understand from Cameron that you two are an item," Mama stated, breaking the silence. She dipped her fork into the fluffy, sweet and sour dessert.

"Yes." Emily lifted her chin and leaned over, patting his hand while sporting a proud grin. "I love Cameron very much. I know it seems, well, strange. That word is being used a lot lately." She laughed nervously. "But I can assure you that—"

"Rule number one." Mama lifted her finger in the air as she paused to swallow the dollop of pie she'd just shoved into her mouth. "You have no one to answer to regarding your love affair with Cameron but yourself and God. Rule two, my questions and curiosity about *you* are mainly about my daughter, Brooke. Cameron and I had an interesting conversation a while back, and it was me who asked to meet you, not him tryna gain approval or shove you down my throat. He told me some things had been going on, and he was truthful with at least his interpretation of the situation. I can't say what's fact or fiction regarding that sort of thing, but what I can say is that sometimes pain brings people together.

"I don't understand why some people struggle with that, ya know? Comin' from a hurt place, we try to heal. Our minds and hearts do what our bodies do. When there's an injury to, say, our arm, our body makes that wound sore. The nerve endings start screaming to let us know that hey, you've been hurt. So we look and we see it. We pause, we say, 'Hey, I'll be damned. I'm bleeding.' Then, the body goes into repair mode, and before long, we've got a scab. We might even have a scar, depending on how deep the cut is— something that won't ever fully go away, just remind us of what happened, but proves that we made it, we got over. Sometimes we try to heal by doing things we shouldn't, though, just to make the pain go away. To make the angry voices in our heads shut up.

"Other times, we cling to people in the same boat, or those who have overcome and made it to shore. Now, I don't know what you and Cameron are doing, how this came to be, but what I do know is that you both were hurting and trying to heal, probably in more ways than one based on what he's shared with me about you." Emily nodded. "Now, yes, this visit is happening to appease my curiosity, my need to heal. It's for me to find some closure, but I want to also ensure that you are feeling all right, young lady, in good health."

"I am. I'm healing well and I have a cosmetic surgery scheduled to address the scar, actually. It will probably require at least a couple of surgeries, but I'm glad I'll be able to do that soon."

"Well see, although I understand that a young lady such as yourself would care about such things—being physically appealing—I was more concerned about your physical and emotional well-being. We all have scars and sometimes no amount of cosmetic pulling and tugging is going to change anything, 'cause see, they're on the inside." Mama slapped her chest hard, her eyes full of passion. Emily's, on the other hand, misted with emotion. Cameron noticed it before she blinked the tears to oblivion. "And another thing, though I see Cameron as my son and always will, his business is his business. Don't you let nobody guilt you into explainin' yourself about this relationship, you hear me?" Mama's voice turned serious as she waved her finger in Emily's direction.

"Yes."

"It doesn't matter what I think, what your friends think, what your favorite cousin or the milkman thinks, young woman. This is between the two of you and everyone else is on the sidelines. It ain't our show. We can have our opinions, and I certainly have mine, but this isn't any of my concern. The minute you go explainin' everything, people will take that as an invitation to get in and *remain* in your business."

"Understood." Emily sighed, maybe in relief. "I do have a question for you though?"

"Yes?"

"I'm just curious. What *is* your opinion about Cameron and me being together?"

Mama looked between the two of them.

"I suspect some codependency. It's a curious thing, but not irrational to me. Under the right circumstances, despite some parts of the wheel being bent or strangely designed, it makes sense. Cameron was very much in love with my daughter. He was grieving. He is curious about who you are; he was from day one but didn't pursue finding out until you showed up on his doorstep. Things happened—like how Opium reacted to you. You said things that piqued his curiosity. I think initially he wasn't trying to fall in love, but it happened. I can't say completely why, and he probably can't either, but that's the funny thing with love." She winked as she brought her glass to her mouth with both hands and took a swallow. "It doesn't ask for our permission, and it does what it pleases. See, that's how love will do you. Brooke told me that Cameron wasn't even her type at first, Emily." He laughed and nodded, knowing full well what she was talking about.

"Brooke liked what we call square guys, all right? That wasn't Cam. He was wearin' baggy pants, gold jewelry, and a baseball cap and in her words, he looked like some thug. But then he wore her down and she fell for him hard. She found out looks were deceiving and Cameron wasn't a thug at all. He was one of the most passionate, outspoken, intelligent, funny, and amazing men she'd ever met. So, it's not any surprise to me that you got hooked on his magic. Destiny, love, a life-saving heart surgery will do things like that. Our heart changes our mind. The heart always gets its way, baby. When the heart stops pumping, the whole damn operation shuts down. You can lose a kidney and keep on steppin'. A finger, a toe, an eyeball even. But you lose your heart? It just stops working…well, you know all too well what happens after that, don't you?

"The heart wants what the heart wants. Like makin' a pretty White girl that looks like some damn model—you look just like you've stepped out of a fancy Parisian magazine—fall in love with a man like Cameron. That pretty White girl didn't like Black folk though, and still, she fell head over heels for a Black man who is proud of himself and where he comes from. And still, he had the patience and foresight to allow her to spread her wings as she travels this thing we call life. That's what happens when our chest opens up. Everything we didn't know we needed has a chance to fly in. Today ain't no bad day for you. I don't care what happened. It's a *good* day because you're still alive."

Emily burst out in tears.

Suddenly, Mama got up from her seat and hurried to gather Emily into her arms, giving her a firm squeeze.

"Now you listen to me. I believe you're a good woman, Emily. You're trying to find your way, and you're doing a good job at it. You just heed my advice and keep people out of your business, just like I said. I do appreciate the fact, though, that you felt compelled to explain it to me in the first place, but baby, you owe me nothing. My daughter is gone." The older woman shrugged, sadness in her eyes. "Ain't no coming back from that. Cameron has to go on with his life, and you have to go on with yours." She placed a kiss on Emily's cheek then reclaimed her seat.

Emily pulled herself together, blinked back her tears, and stared into her lap. "Thank you for your kindness and understanding, Mrs. Coleman. I've never encountered anyone like you before."

"As my husband used to say, and not always during the best of conversations, I'm one of a kind." They all laughed at that.

"It's been a long journey to get to this point," Cameron said. "For both of us. I'm not explaining our relationship, Mama. Just saying that neither of us took this step lightly."

Mama nodded in understanding and covered one hand with the other on the table.

"I bet you've learned a lot about yourself, haven't you, Emily? That maybe you're stronger than you thought you were."

"In some ways, but I..." Emily swallowed, hesitating. "I also learned some things about myself that were not so, shall we say, nice? It's rather depressing when you can only stand yourself in small doses. This isn't a woe is me type of situation; I'm not that sort of woman. It's more of an awareness, if you will."

Although Cameron wanted to interject and take up for his woman, he felt compelled to keep quiet. Something was happening in that room, and he did not need to disturb it.

"Give me some examples of what you mean." Mama fell back against her chair, concern in her eyes.

"Well, you already hit on one, but I'll expound. I went through my storage, for example. I have a closet I use strictly for things that I don't want just lying about." Mama nodded. "Odds and ends. I'm a bit of a clean freak, but there are items I don't want to part with, either. So, I took a look inside of there not too long ago and was stunned. I don't know why I was shocked." Emily shrugged. "But I was. I found books I'd been interested in a long time ago, some of which I didn't even recall purchasing or borrowing. Books that encouraged alienation from people who weren't exactly like me."

She took a deep breath, then continued.

"Another example is that I discovered how selfish and afraid I could be. How my strength was a screen to cover and protect something on the other side that was an emotional hoarding paradise. Found out that a friend of mine, that I'd ditched, her family was practically destroyed because of mine." Emily's voice vibrated with emotion as she clasped her hands together. "I kept my emotions away from others. I am known for keeping my cool, you know? For making an amazing poker face. I pride myself on it. I hate being so emotional right now. I was never like that before." Emily tapped her fingertips against the glass. "That is one change that I *don't* appreciate."

"Now that Brooke is your copilot, so to speak," Mama laughed, "tell me somethin' that's changed that you love."

"I love that I can sing now. I prefer to do it in private,

but I enjoy it so much." The two women smiled at one another. "Cameron has tried to get me to sing publicly several times, but I don't want to."

"I'm going to keep trying, too. She's amazing. I don't want it to go to waste."

"Let me tell you, if all this crazy stuff Cameron told me is true, about you taking on some of my daughter's attributes, trust me, it won't go to waste. See, Brooke was an extrovert. She also loved to read; she owned a lot of books. She read everything that wasn't nailed down. Cameron and I ended up having to donate so many of them. She could be emotional at times too, and she was confident in her talents. A bit of a showoff, but in a good way." Mama grinned. "Do you mind singing a verse or two for me? It's just the three of us here. You don't have to, but if you want to, I'd like to hear a little somethin'."

"Oh? You want me to sing?" Emily ran her finger along her chest where the scar was. "Well, I suppose a little bit wouldn't hurt." Her cheeks turned several shades darker. "What would you like to hear?"

"How about you surprise me?"

Emily nodded, cast Cameron a glance, then got to her feet. He could see she was nervous, running her hands together as if rubbing in some invisible lotion. Emily took a few moments to mull it over, took a sip of cola, then closed her eyes and began to croon Minnie Riperton's "Les Fleurs."

Cameron's chest felt like bursting when tears started to pour from Mama's eyes. The older woman rocked slowly back and forth, smiling as Emily belted out the entire song in her dynamic voice. Her singing was like hot honey poured over the coldest ice. It boomed with soul and handled the delicate layers of the song perfectly, filling the room with the colors of vibrant banana yellow and deep tangerine. Each expertly delivered note held onto layers of warmth, certain to thaw the hard snow, the ice, the hatred made of hard bone. It could break apart a rib cage of anger, melt it right off the coldest man's body, and go straight to his beating heart, turning him into a new soul.

"Beautiful." Mama clapped enthusiastically when Emily returned to her seat. Tears streamed down both of their faces, though Emily bore a smile. "Brooke loved Minnie Riperton. That was one of her favorite songs."

"I didn't tell her that." Cameron reached over and grasped Emily's hand, squeezing as he smiled at her.

"I believe you. That right there was from the heart," Mama said, looking elated.

Time passed, and there was abundant laughter, second slices of pie, hot coffee, and sweet cocoa with tiny marshmallows. They talked and talked, sharing stories of yesteryear. Mama eventually pulled out an old photo album and showed them pictures of Brooke. They looked at faded pictures of her as a baby with her brother in the first pages, then of her growing up, until several months before her death. Before they knew it, it was late into the night, though it felt like only a few minutes had passed since they'd arrived.

"Mama, I don't want to leave, but I have to get Emily home. She has an important meeting in the morning."

"Oh my goodness, of course. Look at the time." She seemed truly shocked as she glanced at an old clock in the dining room that showed 1:32 a.m. on the display. "I've had such a nice time meeting and speaking with you, Emily." They all got up from their seats.

"Me too, Mrs. Coleman. Do you mind if we kept in touch?"

"Of course not. I'd love that. Cameron, make sure you give her my number." Mama followed her out of the dining room to the small closet where their coats hung. Cameron reached for the older woman and enveloped her in a big hug once again, this one just as long and needy as the first. Emily followed suit and a three-person embrace ensued, but then, just as suddenly, she pulled away. Mama let loose of Cameron and Emily held on to the woman's arms as she looked into her eyes.

"What? What's wrong?" Mama asked, her lips hanging open, apprehension in her gaze. Tears streamed down Emily's face, as if her eyes were pipes on a sink that had burst wide open.

"Brooke wants you to know that last night, when you were on your knees, on the floor of your bedroom saying your prayers, she appreciated what you said about her, her father, and her brother. She wants you to know that they're all together. She said it helped her when you said you needed her to know you're okay. You said that she doesn't have to keep looking after you, that she can go on, stop worrying. Well, she heard you. She knows you can smell her Egyptian musk perfume and feel her energy. She loves you. She's had a bit of a hard time keeping away from this house, but now, maybe she can."

"Lord." Mama began to shake like a leaf. Bringing her hands to her mouth, she broke into a heart-wrenching sob.

Cameron held her and rocked her, keeping her head close to his chest.

"I don't know how I do this, Mrs. Coleman. It just comes to me all of a sudden. No warning or easy way to explain it. I just know these things as she delivers the information. I wouldn't call me psychic, because it's unpredictable and not frequent, and it only has to do with Brooke, but I can feel her emotions all the time." Cameron released Mama, but Emily slid right in his place and put Mama's hand on her chest, in the middle. "She told me you've been wanting to do this but thought it might be rude to ask. Go on, feel your daughter's heartbeat."

As they stood there quietly, Emily and Mama cried while Cameron fought the urge to do the same.

"That's my baby's heart. That's Brooke." She fell apart then, crying like a newborn.

"See, people think the heart is on the left side of our chest. Actually, it's in the center and leans over a little to the left. You feel that? What a strong heart she has. She'll always be physically alive, Mrs. Coleman, through me. I promise to take your advice and to always show gratitude for the gift your daughter gave me. And I'm so grateful to be alive. Through a weak heart, I died, but through Brooke, I've been born again."

Chapter Twenty-Two
Something From the Heart

Several weeks later

OF ALL THE *self-deprecating things I could do, this had to have been the worst.*

The sun was setting, but Emily had no plans of leaving her office just yet. A chill took over the room despite the heat she'd turned up an hour prior. Something about feeling a little bit uncomfortable helped her work more efficiently at times. She looked out the window she'd opened for this purpose and rested her chin in her palm. Hints of spring were trying to burst through the crevices of concrete, outside and within her mind. New notions formed into abstract shapes and absurd art, tiny sprigs of foliage and new considerations she'd concocted. Simply put, life was going on.

There basically was no stopping it.

Her phone lit up when a text message came in.

Cameron: *Calling you in a bit. Busy? You said you had a big meeting. Did it go okay?*

She quickly typed: *Went very well. Always busy, but will make time for you.*

Emily slid the phone to the side and stared back out the

window.

It's a nice evening. Maybe I'll take Opium for a walk when I get to Cam's house tonight. He won't be in until later. I could start dinner, too.

She had a copy of his key, and he had one to her place as well. Not surprisingly, a new doorman now worked at her building, too. Cameron must have called someone because he'd told her he'd be following up with the situation, but he'd never given her details as he didn't want her to get involved. Being a man of his word, in less than a week from the day of the incident between the two men, Dennis was gone.

The cell phone rang, shaking her out of her thoughts.

"Hi, baby," she said. "Nice to hear from you."

"I was talking to Jeff about the new television monitors in the bar, so I couldn't call you earlier today. Glad the meeting went well. What's up?"

"Nothing much, sweetie."

"Cool, cool. Well, I didn't want anything. Just seein' how you're doing. Oh, shit. I almost forgot. My mother asked me to ask you if you wanted to go to a concert? She has two tickets for Candy Dulfer for next Thursday night. She and my dad can't go and neither can I. You know I'll be in New Jersey that week for the promo, but maybe you and a friend can go and—"

"Hell yes, I want them." Emily guffawed. "Do you know how hard it is to get those tickets? How much do I owe her?"

"Baby, stop. You know she's gifting them to you, especially after you did all that work for my parents' portfolio free of charge."

"Well, that's awfully sweet of her."

Cameron got into the details of his day. She reflected for a moment about how things had changed over the course of time. She'd finally met Cameron's parents—delightful people who offered pleasant conversation. Both were well-spoken and appeared rather reserved, and yet she sensed a bit of a vigilante spirit in Cameron's father. The man had shared stories of his college days, allowing her to understand that the apple never fell too far from the tree.

Yeah, but the tree I come from is dying and brittle. Am I rotten fruit?

She swallowed as she rolled it over in her mind, still listening to her boyfriend.

"And then that was pretty much it. I'll see you later, all right? Are you still sliding through?"

"Yes, I'll be over. Do you have food at the house so I can make some spaghetti?"

"No turkey, no beef, no nothin', right?" He sighed, sounding defeated. All she could do was chuckle.

"I tell you what, I'll make you some with turkey meatballs, but mine will be meatless. You're disgusting." She cackled.

"You love me anyway." She could hear the smile in his words. "You don't complain when I eat the kitty." Her face warmed with a blush. "All right, bet. Yeah, everything should be there that you need. I have a bag of salad in the crisper, too. I'll pick up some garlic bread on the way home."

"Sounds like a plan. I love you and I'll see you later."

"Love you too, baby."

Emily disconnected the call and turned back to what she

was doing before she'd fallen headfirst into a daydream.

One after another, she deleted various files from her computer.

I should have done this last week. He's hopeless. I have integrity. I am not going to praise someone I no longer respect.

Her father was to be presented with a very prestigious award later that month and she'd made several drafts of a speech that had been in the works for over a year. This was no small feat, nothing to ignore. She'd been asked to deliver a speech at the special ceremony and dinner, which she'd graciously accepted, but now, things were different. Much different.

They'd barely spoken since she'd confronted him about his sordid, despicable past, and his behavior in regard to Ms. Samantha Tabar, which he still hadn't admitted to. But now, things were down to the wire. She'd be expected to stand before a room filled with hundreds of people, many of them in her family's elite circle of financial giants from the city of New York.

I won't be attending this ceremony. No ifs, ands, or buts about it. I'd rather be slathered in butter and forced to run naked in a forest full of starving bears.

After she completed ridding herself of all relevant documents, she opened up her email account to draft a fake narrative to the chairman about why she suddenly could not present her father's award.

Perhaps a sudden business trip would be the excuse? Either way, they'd have to get someone else.

As she began to type the professionally written lie, there was a soft tap on her door, followed by a much harder one.

Seeing as her office walls were clear and she didn't have the partition blinds pulled, she recognized her visitor—a man who'd afforded her half of her DNA, the one in the trash basket on her computer.

"Come in." She turned back toward her computer to continue her task, not willing to be deterred.

"Hello, Emily." Her door slowly opened then closed.

"I'm surprised to see you here." She looked back at him.

"Why's that?" He drew closer, unbuttoning his suit jacket. The towering man stood there impeccable as always, with not a hair out of place on his head.

"I was told that you were in the Bay Area, wouldn't be back until tomorrow."

She kept on typing as he spoke, trying with all of her might to find an excuse to be rid of the unwelcomed guest as soon as possible.

"The final convention was canceled, decided to come home a bit early." He pointed to the chair before her desk. "May I sit down?"

"It's your company. You can do as you wish, but I don't want to discuss anything with you that is not business related." Soon, she heard the blinds being pulled closed, and moments later, her father was sitting before her with his dark burgundy suit jacket flopping open, revealing a crisp, cream shirt and a black and maroon tie. Her heart raced.

"Great work on the White report. You did a fine job."

"What a fitting choice of words. White. Like White privilege? Taking advantage of someone with less money and status as you is amazing?"

"I thought you didn't wish to discuss anything that

wasn't business related?" She hated the smirk on his face. "Hmmm, I'm the scum of the earth to you now? After all of these years of watching over you, encouraging you, raising you, being with you every step of the way during and after your operation, you throw me to the wolves at the first sign of a problem. I suppose you're prone to nosebleeds up there on that high horse, huh?" He gave a stilted chuckle and crossed his legs. He ran his hand along his ankle, tugging gently at his sock.

She ignored the piranha in her presence and continued to type her email.

"Emily, we can't carry on like this. We need to talk, okay?"

"I'm busy."

"So am I, and yet I'm here anyway."

"I only wish to discuss nonbusiness related matters with you if they are truthful, including an honest confession. I am no longer going to be captive to your delusions, the lies you tell yourself to sleep at night and any other sordid coping mechanisms you may utilize in order to see yourself as anything other than what you are."

"Harsh." He smiled, showing his teeth. "Well, I suppose I deserve that. Okay, let's talk on *your* terms." He tossed up his hands.

"Why the change of heart?"

"Some things have to take priority. Like family."

After a slight hesitation, she gently pushed her laptop away, sat back in her seat, and crossed her arms over her chest, regarding him through hooded eyes. Every bone in her body felt heavy, as if she were sinking in her skin. A hatred had been born within her, one built on the twisted back of a dashed dream. An almost angelic image of her father had come crashing down; he never existed, and now, she was lost.

"Well? Talk."

After a few moments of silence, he leaned forward, his forehead wrinkled as he looked off into the corner of the room, avoiding eye contact.

"Unfortunately, my dear, you are almost exactly like me." He smiled sadly as he turned back in her direction. "You look very much like your mother, but personality wise? I'm written all over you, Emily. Stubborn. Goal driven. Logical. Dogmatic. Punitive. Pragmatic." He glanced at his Rolex.

"Oh, am I keeping you from going someplace you need to be?" she jabbed. "Perhaps in Hell."

"No." He didn't react to the viciousness of her tone, his face sullen. "Just making sure that I stay on task here. Don't want to waste your time."

"Good. The sooner you are gone, the better."

"Very well. First of all, I wish to apologize for the precarious position I put you in regarding your childhood friend, Sasha. If I had known that you were as hellbent on finding her as you obviously were, I would have arranged to speak to you about this sooner. Let me start from the beginning, how this all came to be. As I've already admitted to, I was not faithful to your mother. Was she aware of it? Yes. It was a different time period. Men such as myself were not punished, if you will, for being unfaithful. As long as we took care of our families then it was overlooked, even more so in my father's generation. He did the same to my mother."

Emily opened her lower desk drawer, pulled a bottle of water, and took a swig. "Was your mother also unfaithful to me? Yes.

"But that still didn't make it right. A tit for tat game in which there are never any winners." He ran his thumb along his palm. "As I also already stated, instead of us seeking marital counseling, which honestly probably would've alleviated many of our issues, we made poor choices. Marital counseling was also looked at as taboo in my family, but that's another topic for another day." He shrugged. "We ran into the arms of others. Your mother and I, well, we had a peculiar relationship, Emily. She was with me before I had become a success, but she couldn't really handle the dynamics of my lifestyle. It was new to her—the demands of it, being a new wife. She didn't have good role models, either. Her family was dysfunctional."

"We're not doing this."

"Doing what?"

"I would prefer we not make this about my mother," she stated dryly. "Don't try to blame her for the fact you didn't have enough self-respect to not run around on her. And don't blame your father for also being a philanderer. Funny how you didn't mention that he was apparently a bad role model as well." She sucked her teeth and rolled her eyes. "You're speaking of a woman who can't talk. I cannot ask my mother if what you are saying about her is true or not. That's unfair. She can't defend herself from these accusations, and as you've already proven *several* times, you take no issue with lying to me, straight to my face, so why should I trust anything you say right now?"

"Because at this point, I have nothing to gain by lying." Their eyes locked on one another. "Look, Emily, it's like this. Your mother is not the main focus of what I am trying to talk to you about tonight; however, she plays a key role. I won't get into every single detail. I imagine some are unnecessary to disclose, and I know how much you loved your mother and how close you two were, but she is part of the story so I must include her."

She huffed in frustration, but decided to hear him out.

"Anyway, I am aware that you know a few of the traumas your mother suffered. She'd admitted this freely. As you also know, my family didn't wish for me to marry her. They saw her as troubled. My father, your grandfather, was well established, as was his own father, but it was imperative that we prove ourselves to him, not simply ride on his coattails. My two brothers and I did just that. We worked hard in school and at our jobs. When the time came, it was expected that I would marry someone with a similar background as my own—from an ethics or religious standpoint, similar socioeconomics, things like that. I saw your mother and some of that went out the window." He smiled and blinked several times.

"Mom was White. She was Christian and her family wasn't poor so from your perspective, since we never really delved into this much, what was the issue? Was it Mom's eccentricity? You said she was troubled, but she didn't seem troubled to me. What are you referring to?"

"Okay, let's take this bit by bit." He sat a bit straighter. "Her family wasn't poor, you're right. They were successful in their own right. Her father owned two very successful chocolatier shops, but her parents were divorced, as you know, and there was a drinking problem with both of them, which unfortunately, your mother had also taken on."

Emily glanced at her computer for a spell. Yes, Mom's drinking at one point in time had been an issue. It seemed to almost show up overnight and then, less than a few years later, the problem vanished, as if it had never been an issue at all.

"In any case," he sighed and placed his hands on his thighs, "your mother and I met by literally running into each other on the street. It was like something from a movie. I knocked her groceries out of her hand, then helped her pick everything up. We exchanged numbers and the rest was history. Let me be clear though," he said. "Your mother arrived to me with baggage, *emotional* baggage that is, but none of that could stop me from falling in love with her."

"Oh." Emily tilted her head up and grinned, a cold gesture. "How kind of you."

He grimaced and continued.

"Your mother was truly one of the most beautiful women I'd ever seen, Emily. As I got to know her, though, I discovered she was beautiful on the inside, too. She was kindhearted, whimsical, charming, and also quite witty. So, when you came to me months ago and mentioned the whole racism thing, wondering about me and your mother," he shrugged, "I never saw her that way. I know it sounds cliché, but she was nice to people from all walks of life. I never heard her speak disparagingly about people of other races."

"But she did use the word 'nigger' to describe Sasha's mother. I never knew why she was upset with her, but I heard Mom call her that all the same. She wasn't speaking to me, she was on the phone, but I heard her with my own ears, Dad. I now know the reason behind that, but I heard it nevertheless. Do you understand where I am going with this? You two must've had similar thoughts. A racist can't be married to a nonracist, Dad. A Satanist can't be married to a devoted Catholic. A staunch vegan who stops eating meat for spiritual beliefs can't be married to someone who inhales steak and pork chops by the mile."

"That wasn't it. I think as I get further into this, you'll understand. No, we did not share those beliefs, and even though she said that word, I still don't believe your mother was a racist."

"Neither do I, now that I know what you did." She seethed. "And trust me, I am not blaming my own bullshit in my life on you and Mom. However, it is telling that I heard those things being said and not one time did you tell her to stop it."

"You don't understand, Emily. I will get to all that in a minute. Can I please finish without your interruptions?" She hissed, crossed her legs, and began to pivot in her chair. "The problems arose in our marriage after the miscarriages. That was the beginning of the end. It had nothing to do with your mother's background, her parents, incompatibility, none of that. There was a deterioration in the marriage after several miscarriages. It changed her. Forever."

Emily arched a brow. "Miscarriages? Multiple? How many miscarriages? I only knew about one."

Dad sighed once again, briefly closing his eyes.

"Before your birth, your mother had suffered from at

least three miscarriages. After you were born, we tried to have another child, but it was impossible. There were at least three more miscarriages. She was mentally spent and I was emotionally tired of having to keep picking up the pieces."

"But Mom said—"

"It doesn't matter what your mother said because it wasn't the truth."

"Why so many? What was going on? Was she drinking?"

"No, not at that time. Her drinking came into play afterward, long afterward. She had trouble conceiving, Emily, because your mother used to…" He faltered. "She used to do things that caused scar tissue. She had contracted Chlamydia at one point and didn't realize it. It was not found in time before it wreaked havoc on her fallopian tubes. She had *not* contracted it from me. It predated me."

Emily glared at her father, not believing her ears.

"How dare you sit there and try to imply that my mother was sleeping around with no regard."

He shook his head. "I never said she was a bad person, Emily. She was, however, promiscuous due to looking for love in all the wrong places. She'd contracted an illness that was left untreated, so, it caused irreparable health issues."

"Are you serious right now? You're really trying to do this?"

"I never caused her pain over this. I hadn't been a choir boy myself, but she beat herself up over it all the time once she found out it had affected her ability to have children. You were a miracle to even be here. That's why we doted on you so much. Several doctors had told us she could never conceive due to the pelvic inflammatory disease, even after the infection was cleared. And then, well," he shrugged with a big smile, "*you* came. Funny, we weren't even trying at that point. We had decided to take a break from it all."

"Fine. Let's say I believe you and this isn't just a smear campaign you've launched to make yourself look better. What does *any* of this have to do with Samantha and Sasha?"

"Well, I'm getting to that." He held up his finger. "Contrary to what you may believe, Emily, your mother was socially awkward at times. She never really felt she belonged because of the way my family treated her. They ostracized and alienated her. After you were born, they were kinder, but again, the damage was done. It wasn't just that, either. Your mother had had a hard time as a child and uh, some thought patterns are just hard to undo, even with intensive therapy. She did receive some privately, I found out later." He clasped his hands together. "There was something your mother needed, something no one could give her. That's the reason she'd been so unrestrained, actually. She was looking for love in all the wrong places, as they say. As you know, as *everyone* knew, she was drop-dead gorgeous, so unfortunately, that made her receive attention from some male suitors who didn't always have her best interests at heart. Your mother's life changed completely after you were born. She was head over heels in love with you. You were the apple of her eye. However, adults need adult friends, too."

Emily took several sips of her water, not certain she wanted to hear the rest. She imagined things could go from bad to worse in a matter of minutes.

"Your mother wanted friends. I was gone a lot of the time at the office or traveling for business and she would get lonely. I would encourage her to join groups, clubs and what not, but it never seemed to work out. She didn't have many friends at all. Unfortunately, women were often jealous of her or afraid their husbands would take an interest in her. Just silly, ridiculous shit." Emily rarely heard her father swear, so the way he spoke surprised her. "So when she met Samantha, they really hit it off.

"Samantha was kindhearted, had a bit of a rough background as well, and before long, the two were going out places, getting their nails done, shopping and taking you two girls along. I had no idea about all of this until your mother told me about it one day out of the blue, but I was happy for her. I hadn't met Samantha yet, mind you—just heard of this Black woman with a little girl who you seemed to take a liking to as well.

"Fast-forward a few months, I happened to be home and met Samantha." Dad took a deep breath. "She was physically stunning."

"But before now you told me she wasn't your type. What a liar you are."

"We've already established that I lied to you about it. You've lied about things, too. Every human being on planet Earth has. Now let's move on," he stated tersely. "Anyway, that has always been a weakness of mine, Emily. I will admit it." He pointed to himself. "All human beings, including your father, have something that makes us a bit less than perfect, okay? I enjoyed the company of beautiful women. It made me feel important, wanted, powerful. I didn't particularly have a type, per se, but I knew beauty when I saw it. Anyway, let's backtrack for a second. Your mother was obsessed with this thought that because she never gave me a son to carry on the family name, I could never truly love her. I have no idea where she got that idea. I was happy to have you, didn't give a damn about you being a boy or not."

Emily believed his words to be true. Father had never made her feel as though she should've been a boy or that he wished to have a son. He treated her as if she were the best gift he'd ever received.

"But I did have this thing for beautiful women," he continued. "My mother used to make jokes about it when I was just a little boy, saying that I always looked at the pretty women and smiled wherever we went. Being a man of means, I was rarely turned away. Women liked how I approached them. I didn't have to lie often about my marital status. They wanted the jewelry, vacations, cars, furs, their rent paid." He tossed up his hands and laughed.

"And you were good-looking and had money. Goody goody for you."

"Well, I wouldn't say I was the most handsome man in the world, but I would venture to lean on the side of charming and was able to use my assets to my advantage. For instance, I'm tall, well built. I have a nice head of hair, even in my old age." He smiled at her but she didn't smile back. "I would try to accentuate those traits."

"Okay, are we finished talking about what a sexy, affluent Don Juan you were back in the 1990s? Because I'd like to know *why* you did *what* you did."

"Samantha, I discovered, was living from paycheck to paycheck in her little apartment. My tried and true ways to get a woman's attention didn't work on her. In fact, she literally became angered, making it clear my wife was her friend and customer and she'd never do such a thing. I was still quite young at the time, so bullheaded, and when it came to things like this—rejection—I was, well, stupid. There's just no other way to slice it. Rather than leave well enough alone, Samantha became some sort of a preoccupation for me."

"Why?"

"Because she was the only one who'd ever said no to me." A brief silence stretched between them. "That intrigued me. It upset me as well. As time went on, though, my motives changed." Emily looked at her father and, for some reason, it felt like the air was slowly leaving the room. "I was now jealous of the relationship your mother was having with Samantha. I was afraid." He hung his head. Seconds passed, but they felt like minutes. "I was afraid your mother would realize that there was life outside of me and leave me. See, the miscarriages beat up her self-esteem even more, but I realized that she was now even more dependent upon me. I had friends who were divorcing left and right. I didn't want my marriage to end and despite what you may think, I *loved* your mother."

When he looked at her once again, his eyes were full of tears. She tried to compose herself, remain calm.

"I stood up against my father for your mother, Emily. That was something us Windsor boys just didn't do. I loved her just that much and refused to be bullied or have the threat of being disowned hovering over my head. You said that your mother was afraid I would leave? No, honey, it was the other way around. I was scared out of my mind. She was tired of the cheating. She was tired of my overworking; she was just tired. We both were just exhausted. Her mood swings, the drinking, the sleeping pills, it was crazy.

"She had affairs to try and make me react, leave, do something. But I just turned a blind eye to them because I knew they were acts of revenge. She never loved those men she was with. She loved *me*." He pointed to his chest. "It was a cry for help. We were a mutual mess, Emily. Your parents were completely fucked-up." He laughed dismally. "Is that raw and truthful enough for ya?" Dad's East Coast accent was now dripping all over his words. Long gone was his class and elegance. He was passionate. Infuriated. Emotional. Angry. Hurt.

"It was all an act," Emily murmured over a forced breath.

"Yes. Ignore all the wonderful articles, the photos of us in magazines. Toss all that aside. The truth was quite different. We were miserable. Money didn't buy happiness. I wanted that relationship between Samantha and your mother busted up, over with, final because she was encouraging your mother to leave, to take you away from me if I didn't stop what I was doin'. She was giving me an ultimatum. See, Samantha was messing up everything. Or at least, that's how I saw it at the time.

"Your mother was getting braver. She was talking to me in a different way. She was dressing different. She'd slowed down the drinking, too. Samantha had some strange power over your mother. It was the oddest thing to me. As strange as it sounds, that was the final straw. That's when panic set in. I had lost my mind. I decided to switch gears. I told your mother that Samantha had been flirting with me to try and get her to get rid of her. At the time, it seemed the only way to save my marriage. I never knew your mother would go so far as to get the poor woman fired from her job. Emily, you have to believe me. I just figured she'd fire her from picking up the clothes and stop the friendship—not getting her blackballed. She told me that Samantha was stealing from her, too, but now I'm pretty sure that that never happened. It was just a way for your mother to rationalize it all…I think your mother believed she was telling the truth about that. Some jewelry and a couple coats did in fact come up missing, but I know in my heart it wasn't because of Samantha. I had no idea your mother had done those things."

"I can't believe this. So, you mean to tell me that though initially you were in fact trying to sleep with this woman, you stopped that course of action and then changed it up so that it was nothing more than a setup to see if she'd actually do it so that you could report it back to Mom?"

"Yes."

"You're sick. You're completely crazy. I didn't think this could get any worse, but I was wrong, so wrong." She shook her head vehemently.

"Emily, you've never been married. It's hard sometimes. It's a crazy ride. I had an image to uphold and I couldn't get a divorce. Too much was on the line. What you don't understand is—"

"How. Dare. You," she spat. "I have been on the phone with Sasha practically daily. We've been going out, trying to get to know one another, partly due to my own damn guilt, but also because I missed the hell out of her. You not only ruined Samantha's life and me and her daughter's friendship, you caused Sasha to have to stop taking gymnastic lessons because her mother could no longer afford it after Mom blackballed her. This is all your fault. Every bit of it."

"I did not know your mother was doing these things. That is the truth, Emily."

"Get out." Emily's voice trembled as she jumped up from her seat. "I will turn in my thirty-day resignation. I can't work here anymore, no, not for someone like you. Oh my God."

Like some tree suddenly growing from the root, her father stood tall, his chin held high, his expression stern.

"Stop reacting and just listen. If *this* is the reason why you abandon ship, that is a cowardly maneuver on your part. No one, including your own father, should force you out of a job that you love with loyal clients that rely upon you. I always taught you to first have all the facts before making any life-altering decisions."

"Don't talk to me about what you taught me. You taught me a lot of shit that this conversation doesn't demonstrate at all." She grabbed her purse and tucked it under her arm. "If you won't leave, I will."

"Do you have all the facts, Emily?" he questioned calmly as he crossed his arms over his chest. She paused and glared at him. "Right before I walked in here, I was able to talk to Ms. Samantha Tabar in Tampa, Florida. I have been trying to reach her for several days. I had a lot of time to think while I was away, and ended up hiring someone to track her down."

"Why didn't you just ask me for her number? You've already admitted guilt."

"I didn't want to ask you or Sasha for the information. I wanted to do it all myself, show the initiative. I firstly apologized to her and let her know that though I was very much an adult at the time, I had no idea that my horrible actions had created such a domino effect. I then told her that no amount of money or apologies would alleviate the shame, ridicule, hardship, and anger that my actions had caused her family. But I was determined to try because of my little girl." His voice cracked. "My little girl made it quite clear what had happened and what I'd done.

"I played a childish, desperate game and it hurt you. It hurt Sasha, it hurt your mother. It hurt Samantha and the rest of their family. I then proceeded to send her a very generous check, though she'd asked me not to. I found out she'd been trying to purchase a house in Tampa, but her credit wasn't the best. I hooked her up with one of my Floridian buddies as well, to help get her credit repaired, but in the interim, she has enough cash, from me, to buy a very nice home of her choosing."

Emily's heart rate began to slow to a more normal pace. She could breathe again.

"I also apologized profusely, let her know that my wife—my dear, beautiful, complicated, loving wife—had made a mistake. She was hurt and if she were still alive, she'd apologize, too. Samantha was sad to hear that she was dead, even after all that had happened." Tears flowed from his eyes, and for a tough moment, he didn't speak. "I had to tell her about the accident, how your mother inadvertently took too many sleeping pills one afternoon, just days from your birthday that she'd been planning, then never woke up. I explained that I'd been too much of a chicken to ever admit to my wife that it was *me* who'd backstabbed her, not her one and only friend, Samantha Tabar. I asked that she not tell Sasha of the amends I attempted to make until I at least spoke to you first. She agreed to that and told me that she had forgiven me a long time ago, though it had proved difficult, because Jesus forbids her to do anything less than that. She thanked me for my efforts, but I know there's nothing I can do to fully repair the heartache I caused. I'm not an atrocious person, Emily. I just did an atrocious thing."

They looked at one another, neither moving, as if frozen in time.

"If you wish to still leave the company, fine Emily, but at least now you have all the specifics and can make an informed decision. Yes, I am guilty, but I am not that same man from way back then. He's been dead a long time now, but regardless, I am still your father. Your mother's death subdued me, humbled me. Maturity and watching you struggle with your health all put things into a brand-new perspective. You were born with a weak heart. Sometimes I blamed myself for that." Emily dropped her gaze. "Here I was, a new father, holding this precious baby girl. You were a miracle, then your mother and I are told that you've got some heart trouble, and it could take you out of here. That was sobering.

"Once your mother passed away, it all had to stop. I no longer could just live for me. I had to live for my daughter, make better choices. I stopped working over seventy hours a week and spent time with my little girl. The best part of me."

He placed his fingers over his eyes and, she imagined, died a bit inside as he sobbed. "I pushed aside some of my resentment toward my father and enjoyed him for the last few years before he too passed on. I built better relationships with my brothers. I began to go out to the Hudson and ride that boat, the one I named after you." She smiled sadly and nodded. "Remember? I'd take you out there with me sometimes."

"I remember." Emily's eyes watered. "It was a big white boat with the letters 'E.M.I.L.Y.' spelled across the sail in blue. You used to point to it and say, 'Who loves ya, kid?'" She giggled and cried as the memory resurfaced like a lost jewel in the sea.

"I *still* love ya, honey. I'll always love you, Emily. I came from a family that was a 'do as I say, not as I do' tribe, okay? The advice I've given you has been right on the money. How I lived my own life, well," he said dismally, "that was a different story. I never wanted to fall from your grace. You'd put me on a pedestal and I loved it there. But hey, I'm not perfect." He threw up his hands and shook his head. "I would do *any*thing in this world for you, Sugarsnap."

She hadn't heard that nickname he'd given her in so long.

"You're what happened when your mother and I still knew how to show love for each other. When it was us against the world. Your father isn't who you hoped for, huh?" he said softly, his complexion flushed. "I am good with money, but not with showing love all the time. If love were dollars, everyone I care about would be rich. I'm sorry, Emily. You deserve better. Your mother deserved better. You can't buy a strong heart, you can't buy love, and you can't buy integrity and honor."

Tears streamed down his cheeks as he made his way out, closing the door behind him.

Emily stood there shaking. In disbelief. After a while, she placed her purse back down upon her desk and slumped in her seat. She brought the laptop closer and began to retrieve the documents from the trash can icon. Then she hit "delete" on her drafted email to the chairman.

It was time to write something for her father. Something from the heart.

Chapter Twenty-Three
Founding Father

EMILY APPROACHED THE podium after about thirty minutes into the ceremony. Cameron looked on, listening to his sweetheart with open ears.

"Good evening, everyone. I would like to thank the speakers and presenters before me, as well as Chairman Owen Yahrish. An introduction regarding my father's background was already made, so I won't bore you with repetition. My name is Emily Windsor, daughter of Charles and Juliet Windsor.

"Tonight, we celebrate the charitable contributions of those unsung heroes in the financial industry from the states of New York, New Jersey, and Pennsylvania. These people give not only their funds, but their time—an invaluable resource. My father, Charles Windsor, is being presented with the 'In Times of Love' award."

She paused for a moment.

Come on baby, you're doing just fine.

"For those of you who know my father, you are aware that his love language is money. What that means is, many people show love in various ways. My father has always been affectionate, but financial generosity to those in need has always been his forte.

"A big deal was made about this event, and a lot of planning went into it. It's a way to say 'thank you' to the people in our industry for giving back. My father was never vocal about what he was doing. He once told me that when someone gives from the heart, they shouldn't have to tell everyone about it. They should just do so in private because it's the right thing to do, and ego and desire for praise should have no part in this. Contrary to what some may think, Charles Windsor understands what it means to earn every dime. He valued hard work and the power of money from an early age."

She smiled wide.

"Yes, my grandfather established the Windsor Financial Group, located in Rockefeller Center, and we're accepting new clients, just so ya know…shameless plug." This caused ripples of laughter in reaction. "But back to the reason why we're here. My grandfather made his three sons earn their keep. He made them prove to him that they were worthy to be a part of his company that he'd built from the ground up.

"The thing is, though, we can never build without the help of others. Yet they are often invisible to us. We dismiss them. The garbage collectors, the construction workers, electricians, painters, house cleaning teams, furniture makers and designers, receptionists, hair stylists, drivers, mechanics, personal assistants, window cleaners, food delivery truck drivers and catering businesses. The list goes on and on. These people help us achieve our dreams and, without them, saying our vocational journey and even domestic lives would be difficult would be an understatement. I wonder how many times we pause, step outside of ourselves, and actually thank these people? Do we even know their names?" Her voice rattled. She took a deep breath.

Cameron felt such pride. His baby wasn't just talking to the people in that audience. She was talking about herself, too.

"The other day, I asked that very question to my father. I went to his house as I was writing this speech, ladies and gentlemen, because I needed the answer. I sat down in front of that man after having gone through a few storms with him. We haven't always seen eye to eye, and this posed challenges for our relationship. So that day, he told me…

"'Emily, I know everyone. Andre McKenzie is the garbage collector who goes around in the back of the building on Thursday mornings and picks up all the big cans.' My father admitted that he and Andre would occasionally stand back there together and complain about Starbucks coffee while stuffing donuts in their mouths, jabbering on about if they build one more damn coffee shop here, they may as well name this place 'Starbucks City.' The slogan? 'Smell the rich aroma of your money burning.'" The room burst with laughter. "For those of you who are confused, my father apparently believes Starbucks is overpriced." She shrugged. "I will continue to stop there every morning, despite his threat to place a spending tracker on my phone for Starbucks alone."

She waited for the audience to settle after another bout of giggles.

"He told me that the company that does our interior trash collection, dusts our desks and chairs, vacuums our floors and spruces up the place is a well-vetted maid service called 'Maid in the Shade.' The owner's name is Teresa Berry. He knows her husband and children's names, too. My father then went on to tell me all the staff in the IT department. He told me who the contact name was for our security system.

"He told me who his own trusted plumber was, including personal details about the man. This conversation went on and on until it was crystal clear that my father was definitely hands-on and he understood that it took a village, not just his own determination and skill, to make his life run as smoothly as it does. He realized the importance of seeing the faces, remembering the names, the human beings behind the machine, if you will. He didn't build Windsor, nor did his father, all by himself, you see?

"One must not just take a silver spoon. Your curiosity should be piqued to find out where the silver came from to create that utensil. Who designed it? What factories created it? What resources were used? Who decided upon the pricing and why? We can't just be takers. We must be givers.

"Since my father often donates anonymously, he does not get the recognition many others do. However, due to his generous donation to Apple Kids Incorporated, Enigma Studies, and most notably, the Harper Housing Group, he is now the recipient of this award. The Harper Housing Group, which named him as their main benefactor, had him go and assist with cutting the ribbon for their new building in Brooklyn. The hidden donator who scarfed down donuts in secret and hissed at Starbucks as he was driven past them on every corner had been outed."

The crowd woke up again, the merriment palpable.

"He begged me to not disclose the amount he'd given. I keep track of his donations. I've done my father's accounting for several years. He also begged the director of Harper Housing Group to at least not print the amount in their publication, and they agreed to that, but the information somehow leaked anyway. I'm sure you can google it all if your curiosity gets the best of you, but that money came from my father's own personal bank account, and let's just say that Harper Housing Group, which specializes in helping lower-income working citizens in the city of New York find adequate living quarters, was able to place 224 families—not individuals, but entire families—in housing so they could have a roof over their heads and a place to sleep at night."

The room erupted in applause.

"A warm bed. Safety, security, a night-light, a teddy bear. Isn't that what children want?" She spoke softly as the room drew quiet. "As a little girl, I never needed anything. I wanted some things, like most children, but all of my needs were met, so I never experienced not knowing where my next meal was coming from, never worried if Mom or Dad was getting laid off, wasn't concerned if Grandpa would have to skip his medicine that day because the money was short that month and he needed it to last a bit longer." Cameron's heart beat fast as he fell deeper in love. "Being as close as I was to my father, however, I would watch him and his passion for his work.

"A person like my dad *shows* you how he cares and feels about the world around him. And that's why I wanted to follow in his footsteps." She reached for her glass of water sitting on the podium and took a sip. "We're all given special gifts, talents. Some of us, if we're lucky, are given a second chance to prove ourselves to the world and our loved ones, and to our own conscience. I have a friend that I just reunited with. My father used his love language of choice to assist her and her mother because of some mistakes made in the past.

"I found out about more details concerning this because in his typical way, he hadn't told me everything he'd done to right a wrong." Emily appeared to be blinking away tears, her body full of emotion. "See, in math, mistakes can be found and corrected. You discover that, for instance, an invoice has an overcharge of $7.52. You can then make it right. In life, however, it's a bit more complicated. There's no delete button. No calculator, no big eraser to make it all go away." She paused, as if needing a moment. "The people being honored tonight, my father included, looked outside of themselves and reached out to lend a hand, to help others, just as others have done for them to help them reach their goals.

"When we can see ourselves in others who are traveling a different journey—that's when we evolve, when we turn that corner. A corner that leads to lovely music we'd never heard before, barking dogs we just wanted to run up to and play with, small market stands with people selling wooden jewelry and crystals. Things we never cared about before we had a soul transplant. A change of heart. Frank Sinatra said, 'If you can make it here, you can make it anywhere,' and he was right. New York City never sleeps. There is always work to do, fun to be had, tasks to cry about, and Starbucks coffee to purchase to make my father increasingly angry."

The room erupted in new waves of laughter and though Mr. Windsor was hard to see from where he sat, Cameron got a brief glimpse of her father bending forward, his body shaking in mirth.

"Every day is a challenge and a gamble if you wish to rise to the top. But sometimes, we have to slow down. We have to look into the eyes of the people around us. We have to hear their voices, converse with them, allow them to tell their stories. We have to hold back judgment, because if one or two things had been different in our own lives, we too might have needed a helping hand. I was born with a birth defect that affected my heart. Most people, outside my family or closest circle, didn't even know. I never discussed the issue. I had to receive a lifesaving heart transplant last year. It not only saved my life, but it changed my life. Made me appreciate the world around me in a whole new way.

"Being born into a family of means does not equate to understanding, appreciation, happiness, and love. Some of the wealthiest people in this country are miserable." An almost reverent sobriety filled the room. "Some of the happiest people in this country make minimum wage, but their determination and love for their family and friends make all the difference. My father, I must say, is humble. My father is human." Her voice quaked. She gripped the sides of the lectern. "Made of flesh and blood, a mere man. As a child, and even a young woman, I saw him as a knight on a horse. My father was a provider. A protector. My friend.

"He was the first man I ever loved." Her father stood from his seat and drew closer to her. "He taught me how to ride a bike, how to give a proper handshake, and how to punch someone in the nose should it be warranted." That drew a few chuckles. "Let me explain that." She held up one finger as she laughed. "It was important to him that I stick up for myself, you know? Have high self-esteem and defend myself when needed. He taught me that love doesn't always come out expressed the way we intend it to. Sometimes it's a bit sloppy around the edges, but it always feels good when it's handed to those in need.

"So, my father is a complicated soul, yet one of the best people you could ever know. I needed the lessons he taught me. This world needs his contributions and our clients need his insight. I do believe awards like this are needed," she said. "It's the world's way of acknowledging a good deed, even when said deed is done without cameras, contracts, and press reports. It's a way for us to remember that money can change the world, and it can be used for great things. Things that truly matter.

"A woman once told me, 'What's the point in being rich? You can't take it with you.' That, to me, simply means: Do the best with what you have while on Earth. Make certain that your children have something to build upon. Ensure that your affairs are in order for your spouse and take that vacation you so desperately want. Make smart decisions, but for God's sake, value and live your life! Life is so precious, so *very* precious, and I'm thankful to have mine. I came into this world fighting for it, and I almost lost it. But thanks to the gift of a woman I never met, a woman who loved the world and became the giver that I never fathomed existed, I am now her *new* song and her heart beats inside of me."

A tear fell from Cameron's eye, and his heart burst with feeling.

Lowering his gaze, he composed himself and looked back at her. At his love.

"I want to thank my mother, who's passed on, and my father, for giving me life. Money, contributions, and donations are amazing...but love? That heart beats all!"

The room erupted in applause as she bowed her head and waved, stepping away from the lectern. Her father walked swiftly up to her and took her into his arms. Placing a kiss upon her cheek, he squeezed her tight and they were smiling at one another, talking.

Cameron couldn't make out what was being said. But what did it matter? Their hearts and souls had already agreed to make amends, and the heart often ended up having the last and final word.

Chapter Twenty-Four
Young at Heart

E MILY TRAILED TWO steps behind Cameron. He led the way out of his home, his fingertips dancing against her own.

"Hold up. Someone left some trash out here." He released her once they exited the front door of the building and roamed around picking up random junk. A paper bag here, a bottle cap there.

She surveyed her surroundings. It was such a beautiful day. Opium lopped his heavy head against her thigh and she scratched the top of it, looking down at his cute, furry face. Cameron finished cleaning up and soon they stood on the sidewalk, side by side, looking up at his building.

This is where I stood for what felt like forever that first time. Brooke led me here. She wanted to go home...

As if reading her thoughts, Cameron grabbed her hand and squeezed it. Opium sat between them, distracted by a small bird fluttering from branch to branch on a nearby tree.

"So that's it, huh? Up for sale."

He'd not given her a warning. He'd simply made a decision and it was final.

"Yeah." Cameron sighed, a sad smile on his face. "It's

time to move on. I had moved on mentally. I had moved on emotionally. But I hadn't moved on physically. She's gone. You know that, right?" Emily nodded then leaned her head against his shoulder, stroking his arm. "I can no longer smell her around me. I can't feel her touch. She doesn't sing and dance in my dreams. She's satisfied that I'm okay. She left. And now, this is the final step."

"I'm going to miss it here." He cocked his head to the side and rested his beautiful eyes upon her. "It felt more like home to me than my own place."

"Did it?" He looked down at her. She could look up into those eyes for the rest of her life. They were so sexy, yet haunting. The deep, rich shade of brown against the snow white. Like dark coffee seeping into ivory carpet fibers as a heartbeat lost its light.

She reached up to caress his face as he sported a heartbreaking smile, the kind born of a pain that no one could describe because the English language hadn't come up with the words for it yet.

"Yeah, this was home for me. See, it's like the very first time you had me over. I can tell you this now, but it felt so familiar. I instinctively knew where everything was, Cameron. I knew where the yellow plates were in the kitchen, your favorite cologne. I knew where you kept your books of handwritten poems, the candles and the volume of prayers, too. Things like that kept happening, but…" She shrugged. "I didn't see a reason to keep telling you. I believe, though, you were curious at the time, you know, when we first met. Why wouldn't you be? But honey, you were still in so much emotional pain that it would've made it all worse. I would

TIANA LAVEEN

share a little with you, just enough to let you know I was for real and this wasn't some cruel joke, but some things, well...some things I knew to keep to myself."

Much to her surprise, he nodded in understanding then kissed the top of her head.

"I've got enough money saved up to move now or wait. I'll play it by ear, I suppose." He jammed his hands in his pockets.

"It'll sell fast, Cam."

"I know. These buildings rarely have vacancies." He looked around the area. The sweet spring air perfumed their surroundings, making the sadness of the situation a bit easier to digest. To take in.

"So, what's the plan?" She crossed her arms over her chest, then her ankles and chewed on her inner jaw. "Moving to a different borough? Staying close? Relocation closer to work?"

"You know me, I have plans, that's for sure." His teeth gleamed as bright as his eyes as he kept his gaze on her, running the tip of his tongue along his lower lip in a seductive, panty-wetting sort of way. Her lips curled in a smile, though confusion reigned.

What was the guy up to now?

"Why are you looking at me like that?" She grinned wide, wondering what puerile or sexually charged joke would roll out from between his lips. She could still feel him inside her from their romp an hour prior. Her pussy throbbed in fond memory. He slowly reached for her hand and rubbed the pad of his thumb along her knuckles. He turned his gaze to the hand, then began to softly massage it while drawing her closer to rest his lips against the crook of her neck. Her eyes fluttered when he kissed her collarbone, then slipped from her grip, taking a few steps back.

Glancing at the building that he and Brooke had shared, built a life together in, Cameron seemed to be thinking of something vital, something important he needed to sort out for the final time in his own mind. Emily remained quiet, simply watching, giving him the space he needed. He faced her once again and this time, his eyes were glistening with moisture.

"Oh, Cameron. Don't be upset, please. Look, if you're doing this for me, don't, okay? You want to stay here, that's fine. It's obviously breaking your heart to leave. I never felt in competition with Brooke, anyway." She averted her gaze for a moment and grimaced. "Well, that's not exactly true. When we were first together I did."

And there was that one time, a long time ago, when we made love and he called out her name while he climaxed.

She'd said nothing at the time, wasn't even sure he knew he'd done it. On the inside she'd cried, but he'd never done that again. She knew to never hold it over his head for she'd met him at a time when he was still falling apart.

"So Cameron, you know this isn't necessary, okay? Stay if—"

"Baby, baby, baby." He smiled as he took both of her wrists into his hands and squeezed. "I'm not sad. Not in the least. I'm happy. *You* make me happy, baby." He leaned in, lifted her chin, and pressed his soft lips against hers. She shuddered from his touch. He took a deep breath and they stared into each other's eyes—dazing, gazing, falling deeper in love. Suddenly, he released her and dropped down on one knee. She thought she was shivering before, but now? She was shaking like a leaf.

No...no way. He's not going to do what I think he is about to do.

Her eyes must've been huge. The muscles strained in them as she placed her hand against her mouth, watching Cameron dig about in his jeans pocket, sneaking glances at her as he did. A gasp escaped her mouth when he pulled out a small black velvet box, then popped open the lid. Resting in the palm of his hand was a glowing diamond ring. It was exquisite. Impeccable.

"I had this ring specially made for you, Em. I figure I'd say that now, you know, just to make sure you don't turn me down....a security blanket in the form of a guilt trip," he teased, his eyes filling with mirth and tears.

"It's beautiful." She jumped up and down on her tippy toes, thankful she'd decided upon a pair of black ballerina flats that day to go with her leggings versus the four-inch heels she'd been eyeing in the back of her closet.

"So, you know what comes next." He glanced at the ring proudly then looked up at her. "Emily Windsor, would you go to McDonalds with me?"

"Cameron!"

He burst out laughing and swiped at his eye with the pad of his thumb.

"Okay, okay. Will you marry me, baby? Will you be my forever and a day?"

"Yes!" she squealed.

Opium sat there looking at them as if they were both

nuts before turning away to sniff something along the ground. Cameron stood, slid the ring onto her finger, and before he could do or say anything else, she framed his face with both palms and brought him in for an urgent kiss. Suddenly, she heard muffled cheering, as if a television was on and the window open in some nearby apartment. "What's that?"

Cameron pulled away from her, her lipstick smeared all over his mouth, and reached down to the ground. She hadn't even noticed. He'd had his phone propped up in that bag he'd used to put the "trash" in. When he brought his phone up close, a video call was on. There, all piled at a restaurant table together, were her father and Cameron's parents.

"Congratulations," they all said with big smiles on their faces as they pushed each other a bit trying to get into the frame.

"Oh, Dad, you're gooood." Everyone burst out laughing. "I just saw you this morning and you acted totally normal."

Her father nodded and grinned from ear to ear, his complexion deepening.

"It was hard, Emily, but I'm glad I pulled it off. Congrats, you guys. We had the phone on mute on our end so you wouldn't hear us until it was time."

"Emily, I want to see the ring," one of her friends yelled, bopping up and down with glee. Emily shoved her hand closer to the phone as Cameron held it up. "It's gorgeous."

"It really is," Cameron's mother said, the woman looking beautiful as ever. "Congratulations, both of you."

"Thanks, Mama."

His mother blew them a kiss.

"Hey, hey, where are you guys?" she said over the noise and commotion.

"We're down here at the Bourke Street Bakery," Father explained.

"On Twenty-Eighth Street? You went without me?" She stomped her foot. "How could you? Is it good, Dad?"

"Uh, yes, but we can discuss that later. Do you really think this is the time for that? You just got engaged, for God's sake." Everyone burst out laughing at her antics and her cheeks warmed with embarrassment. She'd been wanting to try that spot for months. "This is where we agreed to meet is all, and it worked out well. Anyway, we were watching and listening from Laura's phone from the time you walked out of the building until right now. I'm really happy for you guys."

"Thanks, Dad. I'm still in shock. He took me totally by surprise." She flicked a stray tear away from her eye and rested her head on Cameron's strong, broad shoulder.

"Cameron, your parents, though I just met them, are some amazing people. Well, looks like from this point on there'll be lots of wedding planning."

"Yeah, looks that way." Emily grinned.

"Please make a budget, Emily, and don't bust my chops since you know that I promised ya that whenever you get married, I'd foot the bill. You've always enjoyed saving your money, but spending *mine*." Cameron's father chuckled and Emily winked at him. What could she say? He was right. "And don't try anything slick. I know all of your secrets. I am going to go over the invoices with a fine-toothed comb."

Emily and Cameron burst out laughing at her father's

antics. They spoke to their family and friends a bit longer, then disconnected the call. Enveloping him in her arms, she layered his face with kisses, never wanting to let go.

"So, not that anything needs to be decided right now, but eventually we'll need to go house hunting together, too. Get a place of our own. We've got a lot to take care of, but we can pace ourselves. I figure women take like two or three years to plan for their wedding, right? But here's an option: We can move in together before that, but only if you want."

She kissed the tip of his nose.

"That sounds like a good idea. The length of time needed for planning a wedding depends on the venue, what caterers you want, things like that," she explained as he nodded in understanding. "What about the apartment you were looking to rent?"

"I just thought about us moving in today, actually. I mean, if we move in together, we could save some money. It's kind of a long commute from my job to your place, but I think it may still be worth it. I can rent a place. It really is up to you. It's just temporary, either way. We'll pick out something nice together eventually. Something we both love."

"No doubt. I can't believe this is happening!" she screamed with elation. "I love you, Cameron. Damn, you're sneaky. I had no idea you were up to something, especially not planning a wedding proposal."

He squeezed her tight and spun her around.

"This, to me, was a great place to propose. It was where I saw you for the very first time. On top of that, according to you, it was when you were beginning to wake up...to transform. Your heart led you here. Your heart led you to *me*." His smile slowly faded as he held her close, a serious expression on his face. "When I say the words 'I love you,' they mean something, Emily. I don't tell just anyone that. I need you to know and understand that I love you, baby. I love you like nothin' else in this world. I love you with everything within me, my total heart and soul."

Three Years Later

APPLAUSE BROKE OUT as Emily stepped down from the dancing lights of the blue-lit stage in her husband's crowded club. It was one thing to be in the audience, but quite another to perform. Her heart practically burst out of her chest from the intense adrenaline rush. Her nerves were a total wreck. Refusing to make eye contact with anyone in the audience, she quickly made her way through the crowd, a tight smile on her face. The sleeve of her navy-blue gown slipped off her shoulder as she made a mad dash in Cameron's direction. He chuckled at her reaction.

Dressed in a black button-down shirt and pants, he looked sexy as ever, but she still wished to smack the smug expression off his face. When she finally made it to him, he placed his bottle of beer down and planted a kiss on her lips.

"See? It wasn't that bad."

"Shut up."

He snorted, clearly amused. "Baby, don't be that way. Did you hear the crowd? You rocked this shit. It took me four years to get your ass up there, but I finally did it."

"I hope you enjoyed it, and I hope you taped it," she hissed. "Because I'm not doing it again. I was so nervous I thought I was going to pee on myself."

"You do public speaking all the time. You've been on television. How is this any different?"

"It's way different. When I'm talking about money and investments, I'm confident. Singing, I am apprehensive and self-conscious. It's not my God-given talent. I've essentially borrowed it, received it from some strange strike of lightning."

He seemed unsure as to how to respond at first, then he said, "Forget all of that. You need to come again next week. They're buyin' drinks. That means more money for us." She twisted her lips. "All right, all right." He smiled, throwing up his hands. "But at least you tried. That's all I wanted. You sounded beautiful tonight, and what a perfect song to choose. 'Through the Fire' by Chaka Khan."

"Thank you. You know I've been on a Chaka Khan binge lately."

He wrapped his arms around her waist.

"I love seeing you discover these artists, the ones I grew up hearing." He pressed his lips against hers once more. "You look a little sleepy. Baby, let me close out in the back and then I'll take you home, okay?"

"Sounds good." She winced as she pulled out a chair from the bar and took a seat.

"Are you okay? What's up? Need some water?" Cameron placed his hand on her shoulder, looking downright frightened. She smiled at him.

"I'm fine. It's just that there is so much pressure on my

bladder now. The baby dropped. A drink of water would be good."

"You've got it." He gave her another quick peck and raced away yelling, "Yo, Derek! Get Emily some water, please. Back in five minutes, baby."

She sipped on the water they brought her and tapped her foot to the music of a live jazz band that played in the club that night. Boy, did they sound good. The music vibrated through her, and she imagined her unborn son could feel every single note, like a heartbeat going wild.

As she ran her hand softly along her protruding stomach, emotional pleasure flooded her soul. Smiling, she glanced up at the television above the bar, the noise so loud she couldn't make out the words, but at one point a commercial came on for a heart medication. Her smile slowly faded.

What a ride.

I thought I was invincible, that my weak heart wouldn't catch up with me. It did. I almost died. She blinked back tears. *I was dying—not just physically, but spiritually. Ignorance is a sort of death, too, especially when you're getting worse. I went through shock, anger, sadness about the discovery of who I really was as a person. It still haunts me to this day, but we have to forgive ourselves, right? That's what Mrs. Coleman always reminds me to do.*

I love her. What a wonderful woman. Brooke was so lucky to have her as a mother. I go to her home and have pie and cola at least a few times a year, and we just sit there and laugh, cry, and talk. She really made my day a few months ago with the good news, though. They finally caught that bastard who killed Brooke. He got thirty years, no chance of parole. Justice was served, in more ways than one.

Emily ran her hand along her stomach once again, feeling love and joy. *You know what, son? Mrs. Coleman can't wait to meet you, honey. Somehow, we know that some of Brooke will be with you too, because well, she's a part of me and always will be. Even though she's gone, she left a gift inside me, something you're feeling up close, baby.*

Emily glanced at the drink menu. There was now a drink named after Brooke. It had been her idea—a vegan strawberry smoothie, vodka optional. It was red like a beating heart and went down smooth. *Brooke, life is funny, isn't it?* Emily shook her head and looked around the place.

Dad needs to come down here more often. Now that he's got more time, he definitely should. It's good that he's somewhat retired, with me running more of the show. While I'm on my maternity leave, he will step in for a bit to pick up the slack, but I told him to not get used to it. I'll be back.

She giggled as she reflected.

I can't believe he's engaged. I never thought he'd get married again. I'm so happy for him, though. Gina is a really nice lady. They started as friends, then their connection grew…just like mine and Cameron's. Speaking of friends, mine have been amazing. Sasha was not only in my wedding party, but she's one of my best friends now. She's such an amazing person and she's taught me so much. We have a ton of fun together, too. I just can't believe how much has changed. How much I'VE changed.

"Are you ready, baby?"

Her handsome man stood before her, his coat on and hers draped over his arm.

"Yes, I'm ready." He helped her out of her seat then assisted her with getting on her coat. They exited the club and the cool night air hit her in just the right way, awakening her senses. Her hair blew back from her face as the crunch of autumn leaves crushed beneath her heels. Looping her arm around his, she listened to Cameron talk to her about all the things he needed to take care of that following week. He helped her into the car, then took off down the street. Empire of the Sun's "Walking On a Dream" played on the radio during the first part of the drive. She listened to the song and reached for her man's hand to squeeze it. To feel his closeness.

"Are you sure you're okay, baby? You look a little pale."

"I always look pale," she joked, causing him to smirk.

"You know what I mean, silly."

"Yeah, no, I'm fine, just a little tired." She caressed her stomach and leaned back in the seat. "I can't believe in less than two months he's going to be here."

"Cameron Brooklyn Davis. Sounds like a jazz musician's name, doesn't it?" He shot her a glance out of the corner of his eye as he traveled farther down the busy street.

"Sounds more like a Wall Street data analyst name to me. In fact, I will make certain of it." She winked at Cameron then burst out laughing.

He shook his head, his eyes dancing.

"That sounds good, too. Real good." He squeezed her hand. "The great thing is that he can be *both*." He brought her hand to his mouth and kissed it.

They continued on their trek back to Manhattan. She couldn't wait to get to their lavish apartment, with an office for her and a poetry studio for him, and let herself sink into the thick sheets on their bed. Perhaps the hubby would give her one of his amazing foot massages as she drifted off to sleep after drinking a soothing cup of honey and lemon tea. She watched the world go by as the music played on low in the car, the leaves slowly blowing against the ground and the colors of life flowing together, creating the oxygen for the world to breathe. It was late on a Saturday night, but the traffic was bumper to bumper and the city was alive with blinking, bright lights and people milling about, enjoying their time away from their grinds. But of course, from where she came, there was always a hustle, a dollar to be made, a scheme to hatch and cash in on. She grinned as she felt the baby kick.

I love feeling you. So alive, so resilient. I was told by two doctors to not get pregnant with you due to the heart transplant, but I did. I was told the pregnancy would be rough because of blood flow. But you, my son, have been nothing but kind to me. All I need is for you to grow big and strong. I was told that I wouldn't live past age thirty and that getting a donor would be difficult, and yet, I'm still here. I was told many things that weren't true. Sometimes the truth hurts more than the lie; sometimes it's the other way around. But you can't depend on a lie. It'll always let you down.

Her eyes watered with tears of joy as she thanked God, thanked Brooke, thanked Cameron, thanked everyone who'd played a role in her being able to sit there, in that car, listening to music, feeling her baby within her, and experiencing life through new eyes for the first time.

Not everything is cut and dry, black and white. Like dark coffee flowing through the white fibers of a rug, leaving a stain upon one's entire existence.

Money isn't the root of all evil, but choosing ignorance over knowledge is.

She closed her eyes and fell into a soft daydream. Her man kept holding her hand, their baby moved about, vehicles honked, the music in the car continued to play, and life went on.

One single heartbeat at a time…

The End

If you enjoyed *What the Heart Wants*, make sure to let others know by leaving a review!

Join Tule Publishing's newsletter for more great reads and weekly deals!

About the Author

USA Today bestselling author Tiana Laveen writes strong, resilient heroines and the alpha heroes that fall for them in unlikely happy-ever-afters. An author of over 50 novels to date, Tiana creates characters from all walks of life that leap straight from the pages into your heart.

Married with two children, she enjoys a fulfilling life that includes writing books, drawing, and spending quality time with loved ones.

Thank you for reading

What the Heart Wants

If you enjoyed this book, you can find more from all our great authors at TulePublishing.com, or from your favorite online retailer.

TULE
PUBLISHING

Made in the USA
Middletown, DE
21 February 2023

25280560R00231